D0648147

The
INFINITE

Other *Leisure* books by Douglas Clegg

Naomi
Mischief
You Come When I Call You
The Nightmare Chronicles
The Halloween Man

DOUGLAS CLEGG

The INFINITE

Leisure Books ®

First edition September 2001

Published by

Dorchester Publishing Co., Inc.
276 Fifth Avenue
New York, NY 10001

ISBN: 0-8439-4927-9

The name "Leisure Books" and the stylized "L" with design are trademarks of Dorchester Publishing Co., Inc.

Printed in the United States of America

1 2 3 4 5 6 7 8 9 10

For Richard, Ann, and Kelly Laymon—
but particularly for Dick, who, along with his fiction,
will never be forgotten

Thanks to my editor, Don D'Auria, for being one of the few who understands both writers and horror fiction. Major thanks go to Katherine Ramsland, who provided me a fascinating glimpse into real ghosthunting with an early draft of her nonfiction book, *Ghost.* More thanks to Lisa Rasmussen, Alicia Condon, Brooke Borneman, Tim DeYoung, Kim McNeill, Thea, Kevin, and the whole Dorchester publishing group—I can't thank you enough. Thanks to Maria Liu for fashion and lifestyle information, to Kelly Laymon and Richard Laymon for special firearms duty, to Andy LeCount for baseball talk, and Matt Schwartz for other stuff. As always Raul Silva made it all work. Additional thanks to you readers who have kept up with Harrow and its metamorphosis over the past century, from *Nightmare House* through *Mischief,* and now, *The Infinite.* Hauntings will never go out of style.

Be sure to drop by the website at www.douglasclegg.com.
Or write to dclegg@douglasclegg.com.

PROLOGUE

Histories and Nightmares

1

The walls, half torn and partially burned, grow dark with night—above you, the twilight sky spits rain. You see before you what looks like a boy who has been burned from head to toe, his blistering skin still steaming, and the stench of some dead thing nearby—

The deafening hum of locusts in the trees—

The hunt has begun.

His eyes watch you as if you were the one who set him afire—

The hunt is coming for you.

And then he reaches out, and you know that when he touches you, you will be his. His body bursts into a brilliant green fire, a fire like a fast, verdant forest in summer, a fire like life itself as it burns, as his fingers graze your throat.

Someone whispers, "Mercy."

A sound like whiffling through the air. Something heavy swings across the sky. The piercing of flesh with metal, and then the word "Mercy" becomes the green burning dream itself.

What is your greatest fear?

It lives here.
What is your greatest love?
It lies in wait for you.
Why is there blood on your hands?

2

In 1926, there were some murders at a house called Harrow, and then, after its inaugural moments of infamy, it was forgotten; strange sightings at the estate; fires that came and went out, nearly by themselves; rumors of someone seen at a window to a room that had no exit or entrance; a cult of some sort that had once convened at the property in a previous century; a scandal that had come out of a family there; a brief flurry of interest by spiritualists early in the twentieth century; other claims, as well, although the house, for all intents and purposes, lay fallow for many years, sleeping perhaps; time, the cloud of memory, covered the house as it transformed in later years into a school; and then it was reborn as merely a private home again, just this past year

You can still see it, if you go there, if you seek it out.

3

The Hudson Valley is a twisting highway of a river. Along its banks, villages and towns have grown over the past few centuries, but still the charm of the old within them outweighs the changes that the twentieth and now the twenty-first centuries demand of them.

Much of the Hudson Valley within two hours of New York City has been dulled in some indefinable way by the neighboring tyrannosaur of Manhattan—the small island has reached beyond its boundaries and turned once idyllic villages into commuter towns, like ghosts of another time, another century. Prisons along the river, like Sing-Sing, are well-known, and towns with names like Peekskill and Fishkill and Ossining and Sleepy Hollow and Poughkeepsie and Watch Point and Rhinecliff and Beacon—all names that somehow evoke curiosity, that seem to have stories behind them that might lead to the uncovering of some long-buried mystery, even while the towns themselves often look like many other commuter towns outside the large cities of the United States of America. West Point stands guard along its western banks, a sentry; but the wilderness still exists as the river goes farther north; even the villages here seem to be a surprise, as if they have been hidden too long within the woods and rocks along the shore.

But within these towns, some large, there are histories that at times seem more gothic than their outward surface would suggest. Sleepy Hollow is no stranger to this, with the story and legend penned by Washington Irving; Bannerman's Island with its crumbling castle that once housed munitions and now stands as a reminder of the hidden past (do you see it from your car as you turn the corner up the road? Can you just glimpse the top of its battlements?). Farther up, there is the hidden treasure of Wyndcliffe, the old mansion once owned by Edith Wharton's aunt, a dilapidated manor if there ever was one; and even the current glory of the great Vanderbilt Mansion in Hyde Park as it shines in the last of the sunlight—even this seems mysterious; once upon a time, some enormous and uncontained life flourished with wealth and style out along the river. The Hudson River Valley artists attest to this with the beauty of their canvases, with the gentle slopes of the forested hills, and the curves of the river set against a purple mist of dawn or twilight. This is a place of curiosity and beauty, and were you to drive it, or take the train from New York, even at the beginning of this new century, you would gasp with the beauty, with the roughness of the land and the elegance of the old houses, with the placid aspect to each town, with the sunny feeling that everything was somehow all right here, and yet . . .

The yets of life are what make you slow down. The fawn grazes in the front lawn of the Italianate manse on the side road where you're lost, yet you hear rustling among the leaves and ferns in the woods, as if the fawn is not alone. The town is both beautiful and empty as you enter it, with antique shops full of all the things you've never wanted. The people seem open and happy, but you know this is not the fullness of human life, for happiness and openness are masks, and you drive farther, along choppy roads, feeling the fresh river breeze as you go, until you finally admit that you are somewhat lost. And you find, when you ask one of these fulfilled inhabitants of the beautiful village, that you're in Watch Point, which is barely a blemish on any map. It has been called a valley of ashes that runs beside a muddy river; it has been called a picturesque and untouched village of muted beauty at a rocky bend in the Hudson; it is really neither. Watch Point is a town like any other small hamlet on the off-roads of America, a river town, a town that depends on the distance that its residents are willing to travel to earn a living; a town with an indistinct character that is somehow old, its woods are both new and ancient. And there, as you twist and turn the roads, slowing down for the sound of a gurgling stream or the birdsong that seems as if it were created by a pure spirit of goodwill, you see the towers of another mansion rise above the staggered trees—but this seems beyond your sense of "mansion." It must be a lost city—it must be the Chichen Itza, the Machu Picchu, the Teotihuacan of the Hudson Valley, for it looms and grows as the road winds; its walls are long and high; and there is a gate that was locked in the past, but it is now open, and you long to enter and see the magnificence of this place.

It's like something from a dream, but not the dream that wakes you gently.

This is Harrow, and it has been Harrow for more than a hundred years, and it will be Harrow long after your glimpse of it has come and gone. There are those who have said that it could not be burned down, though some have tried.

4

Originally, there were seventy rooms in Harrow, but more were added when the school was built around the main structure of the manse. The school buildings were utilitarian and somewhat boring, blocklike structures, efficiently created. The bedrooms of the old house became administrative offices and classrooms; the conservatory became the school library, its beautiful structure reduced to stone and architectural absurdity; and the romantic aspect to the look of Harrow was covered over in what became known as Harrow Academy.

But the house would be back one day.

A fire broke out a while back in one of the towers; the stones of the house withstood the attack. Even the arched window at the front survived, with its luminous blues and greens and yellows, and its scene of some saint's martyrdom remain. Still, the fire spread elsewhere, and yes, you could say it was supernatural, the way the flames flared into a green-yellow aura from a distance. You could also say that perhaps the fire knew what to burn, for half the house and property remained untouched and the other half seemed to have caught the worst of the fire. Perhaps it jumped in an October wind from one tower roof to another; perhaps it spread through the more conventional means, for it was said that one of the boys who had caught fire went running through the house, spreading the flames as he went.

After the fire, a feeling of religious life, of some creator-God, of dedicated worshippers, seemed to hang vaguely about the house—its solemn demeanor, the chapel-like curve of the library dome, the cathedral of its towers and parapets. Some God of War and Power had been worshipped here, and its designer felt some great kinship with Jupiter—the house runs at an odd angle in its north-south configuration, almost as if it were built along some bending stream beneath the ground, a lightning-bolt shape, almost (were you to view it from the air).

Harrow remained untouched in some way. It was like a charcoal sketch where the burns had occurred; one of its towers had been damaged beyond repair, but the house stood, a large manor with a mix of Gothic and Georgian and Victorian, its form suggesting an ill-conceived castle designed by one who has no sense of proportion or beauty. The burning of the tower and parts of the school beyond the house served to make Harrow seem defiant to human life. There have been those who have found Harrow to be disturbing to the eye, and there are those who believe it is a large and embarrassing mess that deserves a wrecking ball as much as it deserved the recent fire. Others think of it—when they see it—as a glorious beauty, a wonder from an age when craftsmanship and love of art for its own sake flourished.

Its architecture is not hideous—but its beauty is a bit of an acquired taste. The school had cleaned up much of its disturbing nature, with buttresses and additions and joints to the body of the house; but now, after the fire, and after the wreckage of much of the newer wing of the school, Harrow is there, again, bowed but not defeated.

There are a few houses like this, along the Hudson River as you go farther north, beyond Rhinecliff, New York—shells of houses, mansions, nearly castles really, that no one has touched for months, or perhaps years. They were built well before the turn of the previous century, and they've found no life in the twenty-first century as it is born. This one, Harrow, has an overall feel of the Gothic revival—its arched gable rooftops that seem like stern soldiers all in a row on four sides. That is the part of the structure that most clearly resembles a house—the rooftops are sharp and regular and range across the long, wide building. But the towers—what a mess they make of the look of the place, with their Romanesque turrets; and at some point in the house's early growth, a neoClassic look of carved stone pediments and even a dome, topped by a cupola, which sits upon the library roof, had been added; faces of lions and griffins were carved along the arched stone doorways; and, uncovered in the fire, words graven into the stone of the cupola that read STET FORTUNA DOMUS, which roughly can be translated as *May the house's fortune stand.* Another phrase, left over from the school itself, also remains, this above the doorway into the house itself:

Journey With Us Into Enlightenment And Wait For What Will Come.

The arches of stone in the back were brought over from Europe, it was said, by the eccentric millionaire who built Harrow in the first place. In old pictures of the house, the abbey behind it was more solid, more a separate building, but now all that is left of it are a series of arches blackened by the recent fire. The house has always looked haunted, even to the boys who had, for many years, called this the Old Building of their school. It has always seemed a curious and vulgar presence on its gentle hillside, with its sparse woods and beautiful view of the sparkling Hudson River. After the fire, other parts of the house, never quite seen before, were revealed, which led to the brief news story that Justin Gravesend, who had planned and built the monstrosity, was somewhat like the Winchester widow in California who had built nonsensical room upon room until her death. For, behind walls, where it was thought to be an empty and slender chamber, there were rooms filled with objects, covered with layers of dust and spiderwebs; and in the boiler room, someone claimed that there was what looked like an Egyptian tomb behind the wall that had just fallen.

Much of this was damaged by the fire, and then, when other systems of the house had failed, there had been some flooding in its lower chambers when a heavy rainfall hit two or three days after the fire had been put out

This particular house was large and rambling; half of it had burned to the ground, half of it remained standing and in good condition. There were no takers after the initial flurry of enthusiasm, and winter came and went. The school that had occupied the house and its grounds for many years relocated to Kingston and was renamed for a saint, as if to bless its new incarnation. Few traces of the school itself remained, as if the fire that had begun one October night had spread only to the newer additions. As if the fire knew that it could not destroy the old house at all, but could merely chop away at what had been added to cover it up. The caretaker of the house had closed it up and put up warning signs, so that the local wild boys wouldn't root around in the blackened stone.

Enough of the house remained; an empty monument to some bygone era; a home waiting for its family to return from a long journey. Still, this is pure fancy, a feeling or a vibe in a passing stranger or a newcomer who sees Harrow for the first time.

The power of the house, no doubt, is within the human mind, for in fact it is merely a structure of stone and timber, as vulnerable to the elements and time as any other house.

It is not evil, despite claims; neither does it lie in wait like a dragon for the uninvited guest, though this is just what a woman named Ivy Martin said, on a visit after the burning.

5

Mr. Trask Finds Something

It was 1962 when Mr. Trask, then only known as Gus, came to the town of Watch Point with his ambition to make a decent wage and stay out of trouble. He spent most of his time working at washing storefronts and hauling his bucket up to the school on the hill, working after hours two days a week there when the two daytime janitors had gone off shift.

He was the only one who saw a student named Jack hang himself, although he told no one that he'd seen the act, for fear that he'd be somehow blamed. He had thought to try and stop the boy, but it really was too late. By the time Mr. Trask got near enough to notice that the boy was not just playing with the rope, but was, in fact, tying it about his neck, well, the boy was already a goner. Mr. Trask had gone for help, but the truth was, he probably could've stopped the boy, had he been faster, his guilt told him, or smarter, or even just wiser, for he felt that in some small way, he was responsible for the boy's death, even though he had never really noticed the boy before seeing him hanging by the rope.

Years passed before the day of the big fire up at the school, but Mr. Trask was there two days later—after the fire department and the police had made sure it was safe for the cleaning crews. Mr. Trask helped clean up the wreckage and refuse. It was an icy day, that one, and he remembered seeing the blackened timber and the scorched walls and thinking, on one level, *what a pity*, and on an entirely different level, *it's about time this place came down.* Although it hadn't really come down at all. He would tell his son, later, that it was as if the house had just shaken off what the school had put on its shoulder, "just like it took off a big coat."

Huge Dumpsters were carted in all the way from Poughkeepsie, and people were finding all kinds of things there, some of them very old, some of them fairly new. The library had burned a bit, and some of the newer buildings, but the old place itself remained and looked quite satisfied with itself, Mr. Trask thought. There was a great deal of sadness, too, for some of the parents of the schoolboys who had died were there, initially; and the television cameras, briefly; and the nosy noodles who poked around in the aftermaths of such tragedies to find out if there was more to the "secret initiation ritual" that became an inferno.

A girl had survived; Mr. Trask would never forget her face, poor thing. Half of her shoulder and neck burned, her arms all bubbling with sores. She was from St. Catherine's, a girl's school less than an hour away, up visiting the night of the fire and somehow caught up in it. He saw her picture in the local paper and her face on TV. He thought of her, while he wandered the piles of damaged wood and furniture from the school. He thought of how awful it must've been to go through what she went through.

It was while digging through the mess that he found one item—well, a shard of a bowl, more than anything. But it struck him as something special, this bit of pottery did. The big house, as old as it was, had kept some things to itself for many years, and now, Mr. Trask had himself a bit of a bowl with a bit of an unusual design to it. He just thought he would take it home and put it up on what his son called his doohickey shelf, with all the other foundlings of a lifetime spent picking through trash barrels. It was his son who managed to steal it—and a signed First Edition of Mark Twain's *Huckleberry Finn*—and put it up for auction on the Internet at eBay.

The Twain was snapped up fairly quickly, and for a decent price, but the bit of bowl—which Mr. Trask's son had assumed was of Native American origin, although he could not be sure—sat there for a couple of weeks before someone wrote to him asking about it.

"Dear Sir," the email began. "I understand that this item has come into your hands in the town of Watch Point, New York. I'd like to find out a bit more about it, as the markings that I'm seeing on the rim of the bowl are quite interesting. At first I thought it was Coptic, but I sense that it may be Roman. Might I ask what it would take to borrow it from you, for research purposes? I could pay you a 'lender's fee' of sorts, which we could negotiate. Please call me or email me at your earliest convenience. Sincerely, Jack Fleetwood"

Then, Fleetwood's address and phone number were beneath this, as well as something called the PSI Vista Foundation.

Mr. Trask's son had to show his father the note, because his son didn't want to completely deceive his father, and the son was beginning to worry that the bit of bowl was worth more than either of them knew. Mr. Trask overcame his embarrassment and quickly contacted Fleetwood and inquired what kind of amount he was thinking of.

When Mr. Trask heard the amount of the lender's fee, he felt his heart race, and after he hung up the phone, he turned to his son and said, "Well, I'm glad you did it. That'll keep the heat on this winter."

When the bowl arrived, or the bit of it that Mr. Trask had found, in an overly careful wrapping from Watch Point, New York, Fleetwood's daughter asked, "Why would you pay a thousand dollars to borrow this for a few months?"

"This," her father said solemnly, "may be part of what I've been looking for all my life. It's from Harrow."

"That school. Everybody's talking about it," his daughter said, with no small amount of morbid excitement in her voice. "Seven kids dead and some bizarro fraternity doing crazy things."

"There won't be much of a school left. Gravesend, you were a naughty old man," her father said, and lifted the pottery up to the light. "Faded; all this craftsmanship. It must've passed from hand to hand and been kept hidden by secret dealers and collectors for centuries."

"It's ugly," his daughter said.

"No," Fleetwood said. "It's beautiful."

6

Ivy Dreams

Her heart beat like a jackhammer; her body felt soaked in the sweat of fear; she tasted the sourness at the back of her throat; dread grew.

The dread is all around, someone said, an annoying voice, like a mosquito at her ear.

Stainless-steel knives hung in the air, shining in the last of the sunlight. She thought she saw a cup there, too, and it reminded her of one of the Tarot cards, but she didn't know which one. The beast was after her, and all she could think of was how to get away from it. She heard its snarls and growls from the underbrush. *It's in the trees. It's coming for you. It's almost here. It's almost here.*

The muddy landscape twisted with thorny vines. Something bit her on the arm, some wild animal. There was no pain, just an annoying tug as teeth went into her skin. When she turned to look at the skin along her forearm, she saw human teethmarks in three perfect rows up to her elbow. *It's the Ace of Cups;* she felt it was true, even though she had no idea what it meant. The bite on her arm was shaped like a cup.

Remember: it's a dream, Ivy told herself. *This is not real. Dreams you can handle. Lucid dreaming. You can do it. Live through this one.*

What she had thought were gleaming knives above her were only fireflies dipping in and out among the hedge and the thorny bushes. Something calmed around her, as if the unseen beast had settled nearby.

Still, she knew there was something terrible here.

The dread.

Cold twilight. Something was on fire somewhere. She moved through a brambly wilderness, afraid of getting bitten again.

The words in her head: *fight or flight. Fight or flight.* Her heart beat abnormally fast, so fast that it reminded her of holding a sparrow when she'd been a child, and feeling the fear in the bird as she felt the warmth of its feathery body cupped in her hand and its tiny heart beating so rapidly that it seemed to be a constant vibration rather than a steady rhythm. *The heartbeast,* she thought, not realizing she'd meant *heartbeat.*

Who was she? What kind of dream was this? She was there, as if she had just entered some alien consciousness.

Someone else's body, not her own. Who was it? Young. She felt young. A noise from above startled her—she glanced up. Above her head, the stars of twilight, through a thin veneer of just-darkened sky, as if a single stain had spread from heaven.

Who am I in? Whose hands are these? She looked at her small, curled hands and could not remember.

The bird flew from the dust.

The trident swung from the shadows.

The glass broke on the floor.

The heart beat against the cage.

The shadows of the wings of moths hovered around some light within a darkness.

And then she saw the house.

A certain slant of twilight moved through the trees, across the darkened stone, grazing the towers, torn as if by the fire of a dragon.

She did not feel alone as she approached the place. She felt someone. A presence.

She was not alone, and she knew this place.

The house was there, the looming shadows of its towers, the stone wall around it, covered with brambles and blooming roses, the thorns so thick it would take a machete to chop through them all. Yet, she passed through the brambles and wall and was propelled forward by some hidden drive within her.

She moved toward the house, as if an undertow drew her beneath the waves of consciousness. Or . . . she thought . . . *as if it's breathing me in.*

The door was open and the entryway was scorched black; there were candles lit around the foyer.

She traveled slowly through its nearly barren rooms, aware that she was dreaming. The floor was distressed wood—perhaps it was cherry? She was not entirely sure. There was no furniture to speak of, except for a long shelf with a few books set upon it. She saw a mirror above the shelf. Going to it, she looked for her reflection but saw nothing but the room and the furniture in it—for in the mirror image, there was furniture, there was a long sofa with a Persian carpet on the floor, and several large Amphora vases placed at the corners of the room. This mirror reflection was a place that no longer existed, and for the barest moment, she wondered if she was, herself, the dream, and the house, the only reality.

She felt the iciness in the air and she sensed the wild animal, the dangerous creature that lurked—

And then the white bird flew up from the center of the room. She saw the words written across the torn paper of the far wall:

Mercy, a child had written, the messy handwriting could be none other than a child's—in red crayon—over and over again, a hundred or more times: *Mercy Mercy Mercy Mercy.*

And then she felt the hand at the back of her neck, touching her, letting her know that she existed in this realm, and someone she once loved whispered, "I am the infinite." The noise was everywhere, an unending cry as if it were meant to shatter the world.

And she knew, in the dream, that it knew. That the house knew. She was coming. She was going to be there. She was not going to let it go.

She was the beast. She was the dread.

When she heard the baby crying upstairs, she felt a terrible ache within her own body. She felt a tingling along her breasts. She wanted to go hold the child and quiet it, and she no longer was in the strange house. She was somewhere familiar, and she stared up at the ceiling in her bedroom. It was morning. The ache was there—from the last of the dream. The sound of the child crying.

It was an emptiness that was like a cold dawn.

But this was one of many dreams. Most of them she forgot by the time the sun hit her bedroom window.

Most of them did not involve blood.

But some did.

And she knew, in her heart, that someone had experienced this. Someone, somewhere, had seen the knives in the air and had written the word *Mercy* across a filthy wall.

Someone had felt the bite of human teeth upon her arm and hand, and the remembrance of this, of this feeling, this dream, left

Ivy Martin shuddering when she thought of it, for it had seemed so real.

The bite, and the crying of the baby.

"This time, I am not mad. I have seen—I have seen—I have seen!—and I can doubt no longer—I have seen it!"

—from "The Horla" by Guy deMaupassant

"Bluebeard turned to his wife and said, `I must go away on business in the far counties, and while I am away, I shall entrust you with the keys to my secret chambers, on the condition that there is one place that you never enter, and that is the last room of the chamber, with the smallest of the keys.' And the young lady, as much in obedience as in fear of her husband, replied, 'As you command,' but from the moment she held the keys in her fingers, she knew she must go and see what manner of treasure her husband kept away from her in his locked room."

—from a retelling of the classic fairy tale "Bluebeard"

BOOK ONE

Lifetimes

Part One

Invitation to Harrow

CHAPTER ONE

1

His biggest mistake had been picking up the hitchhiker in the rain.

Mark Carpenter was not the kind of man to ordinarily pick up hitchhikers at all. He generally passed them by, and felt that the world would somehow care for them and they'd reach their destination. But he had always harbored a fear about hitchhikers, as well. He had seen a "Twilight Zone" episode once, in which a woman had picked up a hitchhiker only to find out that the hitchhiker was Mr. Death himself. He had heard more realistic stories about people picking up hitchers who went on to rob them . . . or worse. He had fears, and had not been a fool in his life, even living in a small town. If he didn't know the person directly, he didn't pick that person up. What if the hitchhiker had a gun? A knife? What if the hitcher was an escapee from a prison or some kind of mental institution? He knew he was a bit crazy to think all these things, but it was what one thought when one saw a hitchhiker in the road on such a terrible night.

Of course, this one was a bit different, which may be why he had let down his guard.

She was a pretty girl, from what he could see of her. She had a face that he would call heart-shaped, and maybe she had small eyes, but something about her whole demeanor gave off vibes. The needy kind, but not the clingy kind; that's what he would've said. She needed help. She was in need—that much was apparent. She needed him, and that made her prettier to him, in a way. It was his weakness—pretty girls. Pretty young women. Lost. Needy. She was like a breath of young love—that's what he thought, although it was the part of him that he kept buried most times.

She was young love, this girl, in need of a ride home.

Mark Carpenter felt bad for her. He'd been to visit his father in Kingston and had only come back in the middle of the night, in a storm no less, because he could not stand to sleep in the same house with that man and decided that enough was enough. He had not been in a good mood since leaving his father's house. After crossing over the bridge to the east side of the river, he'd taken an old familiar route back to his home in Watch Point. It had been nearly midnight when he'd somehow gotten lost—he blamed the storm and all the roiling thoughts about his father and some sense of failure he'd always had as a son—but then found his way back by way of the old route (they even called it the Old Road).

He was nearly in town again when the hitchhiker ran into the road. Or was standing there. He couldn't remember, later.

All right, for just a second, he could admit, he thought of something more than just helping someone. She was pretty. Maybe even sexy. Some part of his brain ran a fantasy, but he shut it down fast when he guessed her age. She was a bit young, although, in the rain, and from a distance, she had looked older. She had, he told himself, looked nineteen when he first saw her. In the headlights.

She was no more than sixteen. Maybe fourteen. It was hard to tell with girls these days, he'd say later. The way they grew up fast. Her mascara ran down her face, and the top of her blouse was ripped back.

She held the flap of torn garment up, for modesty.

Something bad had happened. He was sure.

On these muddy roads, this time of night—in a nearly freezing gale of a storm—she seemed to be a silver tear on the windshield as he pulled his Toyota Camry to the shoulder of the road.

The trees whipped the air in a frenzy. He hesitated getting out of the car.

She ran over to the passenger side, her form a blur in the downpour. He leaned over and unlocked the door for her.

The first thing he said to her when she slid in beside him was, "Not a fit night for man nor beast," in his best W. C. Fields. He wondered if he'd said it wrong, because it didn't sound funny or reassuring at all.

She was in tatters, from her stringy hair to the clothes on her back, but he tried not to look at her too much. He didn't want her to feel threatened by him. She seemed so scared already.

"You all right?" he asked. Rain beat down hard on the windshield. A field of some sort lay beyond the trees—he saw it in flashes of lightning.

"Something's after me," she said, desperation in her voice.

"Someone hurt you?" Still, he didn't feel comfortable looking directly at her.

All right, he could admit it to himself: He didn't want to be thought of as one of those men who pick up girls on the road. It didn't seem right. He had never picked up a hitchhiker before, but she had been standing there in the road, essentially in the middle of nowhere, close enough to the nearby town but far enough away—particularly in the storm—that it seemed wrong to leave her.

He didn't like the whole situation, and considering that his wife already suspected that he chased women, this wouldn't look good. Not that his wife would find out. He just didn't need to make this known.

"Where you going?"

"Anywhere. Just drive," she said. Her voice was ragged, like her blouse. He noticed—out of the corner of his eye—that there were smudges on her face. Dirt?

"Who hurt you?"

"No one. No one hurt me. Just drive. Please."

"All right. All right," he said. He pressed his foot on the accelerator, driving back onto the road.

"Can I tell you something?" she asked, that desperation strong in her voice. That need. "Can I trust you?"

It reminded him a bit of his daughter, this girl, and it bothered him that she might be in some unfortunate circumstance. Had someone hurt her? Had someone bothered her? He tried to push other, darker thoughts out of his head. "Yeah. Sure," he said.

"I mean, something really important. Something that hurts to tell."

"Yeah. Yes."

"The rain's nearly stopping."

"Is it?" he said, and wished he'd remained silent. Without realizing it, he'd slowed down.

"Keep driving. Please."

His hands tensed on the steering wheel. "You live in the village?"

"If I tell you this, you have to promise. Promise not to tell. Anyone."

"I'm Mark, by the way."

"Promise me you can keep this secret."

"All right," he said. He would've thought she was nuts, but there was such an ache in her voice that he believed her. He was a trusting sort. But he believed her, and knew that something was wrong. Something bad had happened to this child, and he wanted to help her.

"Do you know the house outside town?"

"Which one?"

"The one that used to be a school."

"Oh. Of course. The fire. Those kids."

"I had a bet with my friends, and we went out to stay in it. Just for one night. Last night."

"That's dangerous. It's condemned."

"Are you going to listen?"

"Sorry."

"We went to stay in it. Three of us. We drank a little, and I was there with Nick. My boyfriend." She began whimpering like a puppy; she was sobbing. He glanced over at her, but the car slid in the road, and he had to return his gaze to the front.

The windshield wipers slashed at the rain.

"We stayed up late and wandered around. It was half ruins, but there's plenty still there. There's room after room. And everything was okay. Everything was okay."

"Did someone hurt you?" he blurted.

She ignored him. "Everything was okay. And then, sometime at night, I started feeling cold. Not just cold, but really cold. Like something was touching me with ice. I looked over for Nick, but he wasn't there. We had candles everywhere, and Joey—he was the other one who came along—was sitting in a corner of the room, shivering. When I asked him where Nick was, he said nothing. I felt ice all over my neck and down my back, and I got up. I nearly knocked a candle over, but I caught it in time. I was all wrapped up in a blanket. Joey kept shivering and wouldn't say anything. It was like he was somewhere else. And then I went looking for Nick, and I went out into the moonlight. This was last night. It was a full moon. A clear night. Nick was standing there, looking up at the moon, only he wouldn't look at me when I called to him. I kept saying, 'Nick, Nicky, why'd you go?' but he wouldn't look at me. And then I touched him, only I couldn't. Something was wrong. It was like my hand went through him."

Mark smirked. "Like he was a ghost," he said, and then wished he hadn't.

"But this is the secret," she said, not missing a beat. "This is the secret."

"All right, all right, calm down. I'm listening."

He remembered it later—the hesitation. The beating of the rain, and the rhythm of the windshield wipers. The lightning that lit up the road, briefly.

Finally, she whispered, "I am the ghost."

Mike pressed his foot on the brakes. Enough of this tomfoolery. This was some kind of prank, some kind of Spring Break joke. "All right, all right," he said.

But he was alone in the Toyota Camry.

When he told the police in Watch Point about it, the first cop he spoke with laughed, and the second said, "That's Nicky Verona, he and Joey Willis. Bad kids. Really bad kids." He wanted to add: but only bad in the small-time way, the shoplifting, the lies, the loitering, the drinking-outside-the-convenience-stores kind of bad. The bad kids of a village the size of Watch Point.

Ne'er-do-wells.

It probably would've ended there, but the second cop, named Elliot Brooks, decided to call the Verona household to see if Nicky was around. He was not. Had not been back since the night before. This wasn't unusual, Mrs. Verona said. Nicky was wild. Then Brooks called the Willises. He found out that Nicky and Joey went off on some camping trip for their first weekend of Spring Break.

Brooks decided to check out Harrow, the property on the edge of town, the site of a terrible fire the previous year, a fire that had destroyed some of the property. A tragedy on the grounds had closed down the school that had operated there for decades.

The body of the girl was found, in a small room with a leaky roof, surrounded by snuffed candles. Joey Willis still shivered in the corner, staring at the body, but Nicky Verona had already taken off for points unknown.

The girl, identified as a local teenager named Quincy Allen, a resident of nearby Hyde Park, had been missing for several days from her family's home (supposedly at a week-long get-together at a friend's in Albany). Strangely enough, she'd had a heart attack, and someone on the scene noted that given her eyes and the position of her hands, it appeared as if she'd been frightened to death, if this were at all possible.

The only thing Joey Willis had said that made any sense to the local police was: "I told Nicky it was wrong to do it. I told him it was crazy to do it. But it wasn't him, was it? It was that place. They surrounded us. They made it happen."

Mark Carpenter, who had picked up the hitchhiker, still did not believe any of this ghost business. He began drinking at night, and told his wife that he could not have imagined all of it. "She was there! I saw her. She sat next to me!"

2

This was the tale that Ivy Martin heard at a party in Manhattan, when someone knew that she had a connection to the house.

3

Those words, "She was there! I saw her. She sat next to me!" were the punch line to this story that made its rounds among people who had an interest in such legends. Ivy could practically still smell the annoying cigar smoke of the teller of the tale, and the awful scent of overly ginned breath. It was Fleetwood who stood by, looking—to Ivy, anyway—like Mr. Death with blue eyes and dark hair, waiting to grab another soul. She shot him a glance, then—*you brought me here to hear this story, didn't you?* And Fleetwood had smiled, nodding, as if he could read her mind. Which he could not, she was sure, because a few choice words were included in her thoughts at the moment as well, and none of them complimentary toward Jack Fleetwood.

Jack had been annoying her with stories of Harrow ever since they'd met, ever since she'd mentioned her interest in psychic phenomena and her connection to the place itself.

He had told her first about what he thought of Harrow, and the phrases that lingered with her were *murderous intent, diseased land, haunting ground,* and *spirit portal.*

It was just before Easter, and her friend Jack Fleetwood was having his gathering, which he called Spring Fever, at his brownstone, with the strange people Jack often attracted in his role running PSI Vista Foundation, which Ivy had become more involved with over the past few months. The storyteller was drunk when he told the tale, and he wasn't specifically telling it to Ivy, but once she heard the name of the house, she wanted to hear the entire story. She could pull this moment out later—something that Fleetwood would term *synchronicity*—but which she considered serendipity more than anything. She was at a Foundation where stories of ghosts and the paranormal were the norm. She had used the Foundation's library to get hold of a copy of a book from the early twentieth century called *The Infinite Ones* by Isis Claviger, a moderately successful medium of the time. Claviger had written about a house in the Hudson Valley, which, as it turned out, was the house in the story that the drunken man in the tweedy jacket spilled across the guests near him. Then Fleetwood had asked her questions about the house, and she had come to his party.

It felt arranged, but Ivy had begun to accept this kind of thing. The invisible thread, she thought of it—it connected people of like minds. It was always there, and she had found herself caught up in it in the recent past as well.

An unbroken chain, that's what it was, Ivy told herself. It was what tied her to Stephen.

Stephen Hook had been the young man she'd loved, several years previously, and he was dead, but he, too, had a connection to this house.

Don't think of his face, don't bring him back in memory, please don't; she often lay in bed at night thinking these things. But her memories of him always returned, and more often than not she woke in the morning, her face still wet from tears cried in the night.

Stephen and Harrow. Jim and Harrow. Jim was Stephen's younger brother, and he, too, was dead. Mr. Death was everywhere. *Everywhere that I go,* she thought. *And it's all about that place.*

The house was called Harrow, and Ivy had already been thinking of the property long before she'd heard the story of the hitchhiker and of this man named Mark Carpenter. She knew that some kind of legend would spring from the house again. She knew that a place like that could not contain its mystery for very long—unless she was mistaken about it.

Unless it was not the place she believed it to be (for she had read the history of it, brought to her attention by Fleetwood and his Foundation, brought to her attention because of her connection to the house. Harrow was a name she wished she had never heard. Harrow would somehow be her undoing, she was certain. And yet, she could not stop thinking about it).

What this someone-at-the-party didn't know was that she had been dreaming of the house since October of the previous year.

Ivy Martin was a tall drink of water—as her father used to say, much to her annoyance—at five feet nine inches, a blonde with a passion for the mysterious and a knack for making coin no matter which way she turned. She felt she resembled a stork or a scrawny pony, but she knew that she was considered fashionable and stylish by Manhattan standards. Her sense of her own unattractiveness had been emphasized in her hometown, where she was more often than not called *scrawny* and *tow-head.* It was only as she got older that these became *thin* and *blond.* She never knew where her drive had come from—her mother told her that she got it from God or the Devil, but it was a burning desire to not be poor or uneducated or without security. She had read Ayn Rand at fifteen, and had determined that, like the heroes of the novels *The Fountainhead* and *Atlas Shrugged,* she would go on and become her own hero in life even if her mother and father could not be heroes themselves.

She determined that she would become more than she was meant to be; and not being the ice goddess some of her boyfriends had claimed in her youth, she did what she could to temper this ambition with compassion and an understanding of how the heart needed tending as much as the fire she felt within. She excelled at academics but was mostly uninvolved in the more social activities of school—she worked baby-sitting until she was sixteen, at which point she began an unglamorous job at KMart that helped pay bills her father seemed unwilling to pay. Even with her minimum-wage income, she scraped together some savings and began investing in the stock market just based on an intuition. She had been raised poor, and had a small talent early on for business and finances; by the time she'd reached eighteen, graduating in the number-two slot in her high school class, she had already begun investing in the stock market and, more by accident than design, had happened to buy a little stock called Microsoft, a then-little-known company, before she turned nineteen—and within a few years the shares she bought had leaped and split and grown into a small fortune.

If stocks and investments were her area of luck, love had not been. After her parents' deaths, the only man she had ever loved had died—and even so, she had felt her love for him was wrong. They had been too young—but she had been the older of the two and should've known better. And then her unborn child had died, within her body, the same night. Other deaths seemed to surround her to the point that she thought it best not to involve anyone too intimately in her life. She had set that part of her life aside to run some small businesses and follow her sense of the seriousness of life. Her money grew further, and she had more than she figured she would ever need. Now, nearly thirty years old, she felt the jigsaw puzzle mystery of her own existence might be coming together; and certainly the story of the hitchhiking ghost girl was one of the pieces.

It was one of those stories that seemed almost an urban legend, although, in this case, it was very much a suburban legend: *a friend of my sister knows this guy named Mark Carpenter, and he was from this town called Watch Point in the Hudson Valley, and one night, in the rain, he was driving down a lonesome road when he saw a hitchhiker in the middle of the road.* She heard the story at one party, and then someone called her and told her about some ghost story in the Hudson Valley; and she knew that somehow fate was pointing her this way. When a third peson told the story of the hitchhiker and Harrow, she knew she could no longer ignore it.

It always ended with Mark Carpenter's verbal eruption of the truth of the story.

That "Mark Carpenter" chose to drive a Toyota Camry could add to the factual way the legend would sound: it was a specific car, and the driver had a name: Mark Carpenter. Even the girl: Quincy Allen. Quincy was an unusual name (although, Ivy knew, no more unusual than "Ivy"), but for the small villages and burgs along the Hudson Valley, up beyond Cold Spring, it wasn't that out of place. It sounded right.

Ivy had then called the police department at Watch Point and, indeed, there was an Officer Elliot Brooks. He seemed a young man with a deep, sonorous voice, who told her that he did not wish to discuss the death of Quincy Allen. So Ivy knew that the legend had some truth. She knew that it connected to Harrow. She researched it further and, after making some inquiries, discovered that Harrow could be had for a fairly modest price, in the condition it was in—less than half a million, although who ever bought it had to commit to renovating and repairing it within a year's time.

4

One night she had a dream, and all she could remember from it was a white bird and the word *Mercy;* a giant spear of some kind—a three-pronged spear—covered in blood swept the air; and a voice that whispered, "Your flesh is my release," and then she saw him. But before she saw him, her eyes had begun filling with tears, as if she knew he was going to be there.

Stephen.

As if he had never died. Beautiful, young, in love with her, and fighting everything within himself to keep from touching her in the dream. His sandy brown hair was swept across his forehead, and his nose was wrinkled slightly, the way it used to when he laughed too much, and he had that grin. It could win her over in an instant. He was alive, and there with her, and he wanted to hold her—she could see it in his intense gaze—and she ached to be held by him.

She woke up, sweat soaking into the white sheets, her skin tingling like pinpricks along her spine.

She knew what to do.

She had been dreaming of Harrow for several months, ever since she'd seen the news about the fire at the school. Ever since she'd had the connection to it that she wished she could shake.

The rest fell into place. She made the calls. She argued with people. She checked with her financial planner. She decided to sell some stock.

She went on a trip up to Harrow.

Like the legend of Mark Carpenter and Quincy Allen, it was another rainy night, but spring was like that in New York.

5

Coincidence abounds.

That was Ivy Martin's first thought when she saw the street called Mercy, and then when she noticed that she wanted to stop in a town called Red Fork to ask directions, and in doing so, found herself sitting down—in the rain—at a small diner called the White Heron. Although there had been no heron in her dream, there had been a white bird, and that was enough. A white bird and even the word *Mercy.*

She noticed the sign, too, just inside the White Heron Diner, just felt marker on white poster board: FORTUNE SMILES. TIME FLIES. LOVE GROWS. CUSTOMERS TIP.

Coincidence abounds, she thought. How often does this happen, this déjà vu from dream to reality, from the subconscious flow of images in a completely illogical dream to the hard world of life with its benches and diner booths and signs? She didn't know, but she felt this all added up in some significant way.

There had been a sign, too, in the recesses of her memory—the dream within a dream, the writing on the wall that said something about *Fortune,* only she couldn't quite remember what it was.

"I had a dream like this," she said to the middle-aged woman who waited tables. The woman had a small name tag pinned to her lapel: NANCY. She had her hair done up, with a small pink waitress cap tied around it. She was small and stocky and smelled of crullers. She wore white lipstick and pink fingernail polish, and she looked as if she'd stepped out of 1964.

"I was in it?" the waitress asked. Her voice was a husky baritone, probably from thirty years or more of chain-smoking while screaming out orders.

"No. Nobody was in it. Just things," she said, and then she grinned slightly. "Dreams are crazy things."

"Everybody's got a dream," Nancy-the-waitress said. "And all of 'em's crazy. I dreamed I was gonna grow up and be Nancy Sinatra. That's why I'm called Nancy. You gotta try the egg cream. You try the egg cream, you're gonna climax." She said it brusquely, with humor, and it made Ivy smile. "It's that good, the chocolate egg cream."

"That sounds good. And the chicken salad." Ivy stretched her neck a bit to work out the stiffness from the tense drive.

"Chick salad, cream!" Nancy shouted to the old man behind the steel counter. He dropped his cigarette into his cup of coffee and snapped something back.

A couple two booths over were dropping quarters into the jukebox, and some crooner came on who Ivy could not identify. She leaned back into the booth, closing her eyes.

She saw him in the darkness of her mind.

"Fortune smiles," he said.

Opened her eyes again, to the diner.

Don't dream again. No point in it. You'll be there in another half hour.

She glanced out into the cloudy darkness, the rain obscuring the road. Now and then, a flash of lightning lit up Route 9, but there was really nothing to see out there.

"Mud slides on some of the side streets," Nancy said when she brought the tall glass of chocolate egg cream and the salad platter over. "Don't forget. You drink that down, you're gonna climax."

You're annoying me now, Ivy wanted to say. She used to say things out loud but had begun to censor herself over the past few months. It had gotten that bad. She'd begun to say what she thought, which, to her mind, was the end of sanity. Things slipped out at times that she regretted. She found herself thinking out loud and had to train herself to just keep her mouth shut. She no longer wanted to be polite when she didn't have to be. She no longer wanted to hold things back. She had begun telling people off—minor incidents, with the postman, or the pharmacist, or her accountant. Nothing too damaging, but she had stopped keeping it all in. But she had to change this. *You can't get along in the world and tell it off at the same time.*

Her imbalance between saying what she wanted and keeping it bottled up had begun since she had heard about the fire at the school.

6

Ivy knew she would go to the house as soon as she confirmed the legend of Mark Carpenter, Quincy Allen, and the ghost in the night. She had decided that she would go to the village, which was up the river another few miles from the White Heron Diner, and find out if what had been bothering her for so long might have a basis in fact.

Nights could be wicked in June along the Hudson River. It was one of those brisk, shivery river nights, the rain spitting and cursing with thunder and lightning. Even then, she wanted to keep driving. She wanted to find the village, and then the house. She had spent so much time thinking about it, even obsessing over it, ever since she'd heard about the fire and the deaths, and the boy she had met, briefly.

The boy she'd felt such a connection with. Now she had to see for herself what had happened to Harrow.

7

The history of the house had been difficult to uncover, but she had found most of the supporting documents to the murders that had occurred there in the early decades of the twentieth century, as well as other events, including her own personal connection to Harrow, as if it had been there all along.

Finally, Ivy Martin knew that she must buy the property. It was owned by the county and she had to pull some strings to get through to the right people, plus she had to arrive at the office with a certified check for nearly half a million dollars, which seemed dirt cheap for the acreage, although no one selling it to her felt it was worth half that.

She called Jack that afternoon. "I did it."

"It's hard to believe. All that cash," he said. Jack Underwood had an accent right off the Brooklyn Bridge. She liked hearing it. "You sure this is how you want to invest?"

"Well, it's for something, isn't it? I'm used to investing in what interests me. It always has worked out before."

"I suppose," he said. Then he added, "Of course. And it's important. I'm convinced of that. I'm just glad you're convinced."

"The Foundation can supply the rest. You have until November. If you can bring me proof by then, it's yours. Free and clear."

"You sure this is what you want?"

"What I want is to find out. That's what the Foundation is there for, correct?"

"Absolutely. And I've got three candidates for this."

"Will they come?" she asked, hope in her voice like a bird chirp.

"Ivy, these are the three that agreed. Two said no, but these three have all given their okays. I think two of them need the money."

"The third?"

"She's genuinely interested."

"You believe all of them are gifted?"

"Certifiably."

"That's good."

A pause on the line.

"But if you find out, then what?"

"That's for me to know," she told him, although she thought she should say: *There is no "then what."* He would think that was funny or quaint of her, but it felt true. She had no idea what this would bring her. Or why she wanted the property so badly. She switched off the cell phone.

Ivy Martin glanced out the window of her condo in Manhattan, to the Hudson River and the white and green lights on the far shore. She thought about the others, the three candidates for this rough experiment, about her own finances and how she just might have made the dumbest financial mistake of her life, and about her need to know. It felt as hot as the fire of the sun, that need. It felt as if it were the only goal she had left.

Her overwhelming need to find out what exactly was in the house that nestled among the hills of a town called Watch Point, New York.

Even that was a lie she could live with. And she felt as if the great lie within her had been planted—like a seed—the day her child died. The day her love died.

And she needed Harrow.

She could not afford to waste a moment; she could not hesitate. It was now, or perhaps never, and all she had to do, after all, was spend money.

CHAPTER TWO

1

The letter, with check and contract attached

I hope this letter finds you well.

As you know from the screenings, you are one of three guests we'd like to have with us during the month of October at Harrow. Each of you has been picked for your extraordinary abilities. Each of you has expressed a desire to come to Harrow and undergo this unusual experiment. Enclosed you will find a roundtrip airplane ticket to LaGuardia for the twentieth of October. Also enclosed find a certified check for five thousand dollars. This should cover your additional expenses, and is a bit of an advance against the ten thousand dollars promised you for your time in our study.

In addition, I'm sending under separate cover a portfolio on the history of Harrow and the nature of its alleged hauntings. Although there are only news clippings covering something that occurred there in 1926, and then, last year, when Harrow was still a school, we've included additional notes on other allegations of poltergeist activity and sightings in and around Harrow.

You'll notice in the photographs of Harrow that part of the building burned down.

We've carefully reconstructed portions—using the original materials as much as possible—in order to maintain the integrity of the house. The remnants of what was the school have either been destroyed or dismantled in order to bring the house back to its original state. The Foundation has generously allowed us fairly unlimited resources for the study, and we've got surveillance and recording equipment.

On a less scientific note, you'll find every amenity here at Harrow, and the nearby village of Watch Point is both picturesque as it sits on the banks of the Hudson River and peaceful.

Should you have questions, there's an 800 number at the top of this page for you to call at any time for any reason. A release form and contract are enclosed. Please read them both carefully, and have your lawyer go over the ramifications with you. This should be a fascinating and fulfilling moment in all our histories, and it is my pleasure to welcome you to what we are officially calling the Harrow Exploration.

We have no doubt that, with your help, we will learn more about psychic phenomena than has ever before been documented. I will warn you that Harrow is not the house of legend. It is a lovely place, despite the damage done by the fire. It is not the "Devil's Playground" or the "Nightmare House" that the media called it after the fire. This is no Amityville Horror. Despite my colleague, Dr. Lingard, claiming that he has recognized manifestations of demons within the house, I am not of the mind that there are evil spirits at work. It is not some bad place. I want to dispel any preconceived notions you may have if you've read any of the press on Harrow. There were definite murders at the house in the past, but you and I both know that houses don't kill. What I have no doubt of is that Harrow worked on the minds of its inhabitants to create the psychological states that induced murder. Similarly, the house was also a place of creativity and imagination during its long existence, but no one wants to believe that the house could also influence these positive attributes. Yet, it has.

What exists in Harrow, it is my belief, is a verifiable phenomenon. Just as each of your talents is a verifiable phenomenon, and just as each of you has no doubt been misunderstood in your life, the property at Watch Point, New York, has some talent that has yet to be defined. With your help, with the underwriting of this project by Ms. Ivy Martin, and the additional support of the PSI Vista Foundation, the New York office of which I run, I believe we will discover the secret of just what can thrive and fuel a house such as this.

In previous telephone calls, e-mails, and letters, each of you has asked what my real interest in Harrow could be. Money? Fame? Well, a little of both, I will admit. A book deal? (I can hear our best-selling author, Mr. Crane, laughing even as I write this.) Perhaps a book deal would be nice, with one of those seven-figure advances that would definitely be put to use in further paranormal research. But the truth is: I think we'll get answers. All of us. I think we'll find out a little bit more about your abilities within the geography of a place known as a locus of psychic activity. Briefly, there are two documented cases of strong paranormal activity at the house. The first took place in 1926, when a gentleman named Esteban Gravesend came to claim his inheritance. We believe that Mr. Gravesend himself had some psychic link to the house that he did not understand, and thus, it could not be controlled within the psychic vacuum of the house. The second, last year, with the death of several schoolboys, but in particular, one young man named James Hook, who perhaps was a psychic key in the lock of Harrow.

Inadvertantly, he turned the house on, just as you or I might flip a switch. I can't be sure of the young man's involvement, but it would seem that he did not have the capability to control his own gift, and thus it grew out of control within the house.

Are you in danger, the three of you, at Harrow? Well, first: Nothing has been verified. The house is clouded in local legend at this point in time. Virtually, the hauntings surrounding it are gossip. But secondly, since each of you has exercised some knowledge and control of your talents, I believe that you will provide a safer environment within Harrow than would an unsuspecting person who has some unknown ability. It would be the person with the talent that has not yet been documented who would pose a threat to themselves and others, I maintain.

However, there are legal waivers to sign here, because I can't, in all honesty, suggest that you are in "no danger" at Harrow. And I will tell you that, yes, a girl died on the property when she camped there with two friends. However, it still is a question in the minds of the authorities whether she was murdered or simply had what appears to be a heart attack at an extremely young age.

I completely understand if you decide not to accept this check and invitation to spend these few days in October with me at Harrow. I do think that you will be cheating yourself out of the experience of a lifetime by not accepting this; and I believe you will also find out more about the extent and use of your already impressive talents if you decide to accept.

I look forward to seeing each of you again.

Sincerely,

Jack Fleetwood

New York Chapter President,
PSI Vista Foundation,
1123 Oatman Place,
New York, NY 10011

2

The manila envelopes were each addressed to Chet Dillinger, Cali Nytbird, and Frost Crane.

Part Two

Chet

Chapter Three

1

St. Christopher Township, Eastern Shore, Virginia

"The wolf's at the door," his mother always said, or at least that was all he could remember her ever saying to him. Sometimes he just heard howls in his brain when he thought of her. Howls, like a wolf, like an animal waiting at the other side of the door. Chet liked to imagine her standing on the front stoop of some thatched cottage out of a Brothers Grimm tale, holding her forest-twig broom or carrying kindling in for the fire, and saying it to him, "The wolf's at the door."

It made him feel safe and magical, even later, when he was living with the Dillinger family and nothing was safe or magical there. With the Dillingers, it was always about surviving until sunset through their squabbles and the way there always seemed to be dog piddle and cat scratches all over the furniture; the Dillingers fought, too, with fists and plates and shoes and anything they could get their hands on. But his mother—in his mind, she was something of a goddess. He could only remember her once, from a dream, and he couldn't remember—years later—what she looked like. "The wolf's at the door," she had said in his sleep. She didn't occupy flesh, as far as he knew. She had crossed over into the territory of legend.

The truth was, she was a kind of legend, but not the kind you'd want as a mother, not if you were born on the wrong side of the tracks in a town like St. Chris during years when all that trickled down were dribs and drabs of rain and, occasionally, a run of good luck that might last 'til Sunday.

Everybody in St. Chris knew his mother, in that way that only small towns know women like that. St. Chris was at the lowest peak of the Chesapeake Bay, an ornery part of Virginia that was neither fish nor fowl—and the stink of chicken farms and oyster trawlers mixed in the air on a hot August day, waiting for the sea breeze to blow it off to kingdom come. A sandy stretch of nothing, that's what it had been called more than once, with some fishing and some sea spray and a flat marshy land. The strip mall that had been built in 1968 had not changed in all those years. Three trash dumps had attained some minor fame in the mid-1970s, when an environmentalist group had come out to protest what had become the mountains of waste. The locals, however, paid no mind to the trash heaps that steamed in the long summers; they were considered an in-bred lot that had, with their one hundred and seventy-five residents, exactly four family names between them.

Chet's mother had been a Goodfellow, and he should've been named Chet Goodfellow by all rights, but when one becomes orphaned, the names change fast. There was even some question from the rather snotty Goodfellow clan that his mother had not really been one of them, for none of them claimed to have any relation to her. She was what they called a shady character (in the days when she was young and still fresh to the boredom of St. Chris and its stink of fish and oyster); she was known as often for sales of illegal substances as she was for her tendency to be too readily available to the summer beach crowd and the general male population of St. Chris. Sometimes she got hot, and sometimes she poured herself across the dry land; at least that was what was said about her. She had the beauty of a woman who has nothing but flesh, and lots of it, and her curves molded to her clothes instead of the other way around. She had a voice like a ship's whistle, but she had a face that was vague and just pretty enough to give her the edge over the other women of town.

She had been reviled in silence—even the church-going folk said nothing worse than, "What do you expect with women like that?" but would not go deeper into her reputation.

Her favorite picture was called "The Peaceable Kingdom," the one with animals of all shapes and sizes, and she had a large print of this she'd bought at a garage sale over in Hillary for five dollars. She kept the print over her bed, a bed that was equally legendary with the lonely husbands of town, who often found their way onto its wrinkled cotton sheets with small flowers on them, found their way into her arms for a night or an hour, or as much as they could spare. She was lonely, too, and not quite as slatternly a woman as the silence would have suggested—her name was Roselle, and everyone old enough to have known her daddy knew just why she had turned out like she had.

When she was pregnant with Chet, she didn't let up on her smoking and drinking and the wildness of her ways. Even the landlady, Mrs. Poole, chided her for her wantonness with the words,

"You're gonna kill your child before he's got a chance to breathe." To which his mother would reply, "If the kid can survive me, he can survive anything. And shut your pie hole."

But Chet came out with all his toes and fingers intact, and a slight overlap of skin across his face. The labor was fast and easy, and Chet's mother was mostly unconscious for the few hours it took to deliver him into the world.

"What the hell's that?" his mother asked, her words slurring from the bite of whiskey. "That crap on his face? Is he some kind of freak?"

"A caul," the nurse said. "It means he's special."

The next thing Roselle knew, she was holding the baby in her arms and he was all bloody. She felt a warmth course through her that had less to do with the maternal instinct—of which she had none—than the feeling of her body burning up from some fever. "Somebody should love this baby," she said. "Ain't gonna be me. Somebody should."

He still hadn't been named, but he was a Chester if there ever was one, that's what the doctor said, and where there's a Chester, there's a Chet, and seeing as how the doc was a big fan of Chet Baker—the doctor kept the old LPs in his bedroom to listen to the sweet sound of trumpet before he went to bed—so Chet was named by the whiskey-soaked doctor who had delivered him into the world, screaming and coughing and looking like he was going to be the ugliest baby in all creation.

As the doctor had another glass of the fine brown burning liquid, he practically christened the newborn with the Jack Daniels.

In fact, everything about Chet's world was whiskey-soaked, right down to his diaper.

2

His first memories were just patches of visions: He saw the woman who was skinny and long as a straw with a head as small as a green apple, and she smiled at him a lot and sometimes picked him up. He thought of her, years later, as Green Apple Lady. She had eyes that were like little holes, and teeth that were barely more than yellow corn. He thought she was God (once he knew what God was), and he remembered God cooing to him and telling him all kinds of sweet things, and bringing him a big tit, drawn from beneath the buttons of her shirt. On some instinctive level, he knew this was not his natural mother, although he would never be able to know why he knew this. He saw the flying things over his head. He didn't know what they were, but they seemed to be clowns and birds, all tied together with strings. Only later did he know to call this a *mobile.*

He remembered learning that the top of the place where the Green Apple Lady cooked him his slushies, as he liked to call breakfast, was very, very hot. When he was old enough to speak, he tried to say, "Burn," the way the Green Apple Lady did, only nothing came from his lips like it did for the Lunkheads (so Chet had named them in his mind, although never aloud). The Lunkheads all lived in the house at the end of the lane with Chet and the Green Apple Lady, and Chet never thought of them as his brother and sisters because they pinched him and rolled him around the floor when he was too young to fight back or to even know that what they were doing was not the way the world was supposed to work.

He began coughing with the Green Apple Lady, and maybe that's why she didn't keep him. It might've been the cats. The

Green Apple Lady had nearly twelve cats, and although, as a very young child, Chet adored the scurvy little creatures with their breath fresh from sampling the recent catch down at the docks and their haughty but affectionate airs, he found that he coughed more when around them. He never knew why for sure, but the coughing became constant (asthma, he'd hear the word a year or so later), and the Green Apple Lady and the Lunkheads didn't want him around. He learned later that he had never been officially adopted by the Green Apple Lady and her Lunkheads, but only borrowed, according to the doctor who had delivered him; it was from this same doctor that he learned that his mother had taken off for parts unknown. "New York or somewhere," the doctor had told him on one of his yearly visits for some horribly painful shot.

As he grew up, the Green Apple Lady and the Lunkheads faded away. The cats did, too, which troubled him, since he had become smitten with their antics and personalities; yet they were no longer part of his life. He probably didn't know about how the Lunkheads—two girls and a very fart-filled boy—had left him in a shopping cart at the Gas 'N' Go off the main highway just when he'd turned four, or why he had ended up with the Dillinger family in Rustic Acres, but it was all a blur once the fights began.

And it was one of the early fights that brought out something inside Chet that he could never quite put back in.

Chapter Four

1

Rustic Acres was the name given to the trailer park that was situated between the bay and the sea, so perfectly set in a flat land of farms and emptiness that it seemed as if St. Chris were a hundred miles away, even though it was only a twenty-minute drive to town.

Some pine trees added scant scenery around the trailers, which were uniformly pale green. The Dillingers owned the park, which, to Chet's mind, meant they owned the known world, although, apparently, it also meant that there was never any money for new shoes or trousers when the first day of school came 'round. It also meant (according to the Big Woman) that Chet would have to be cautious with his coughing lest the medical bills run up too high.

The Big Woman tried to get him to become a Christian Scientist just to avoid the whole medical bill situation, but since the Big Woman herself was of another church (the St. Chris Jesus & Bible Church), she didn't push him too far into the hands of Mary Baker Eddy. Jesus apparently shared space in the trailer, for the Big Woman was always telling him that Jesus was sitting there in the corner with him whenever he'd been bad (and he was bad a lot, for he grew to know the corner and the invisible Jesus quite well as time went on).

They lived in what could kindly be called a cottage just at the edge of the highway, at the front of all the trailers. The joke about Rustic Acres, as it was said in St. Chris, was that it existed at all.

Chet prayed that as he got older, these memories would fade: of the metal mailbox stuffed with the Big Woman's contest prizes and coupon books; of the snarling, snapping dog that Chet had loved at first until the Big Boys had gone after it enough with rocks and sticks that the dog was permanently trying to bite anyone within four feet of its tethered world; the smell of rain that came off the bay that Chet dreaded because it meant a storm, and a storm meant days on end inside Rustic Acres with a family he had come to think of as his punishment for being so ordinary.

Mrs. Dillinger became known to Chet as the Big Woman, just as her husband was called the Big Man. The Big Man was a fisherman, some guessed; others believed he worked on one of the local farms; some even believed that Mrs. Dillinger had murdered him and buried him under one of the trailers of Rustic Acres, for, after all, he hadn't been seen in nearly a year. All Chet knew was that he'd never seen the Big Man since he first arrived.

Chet became a Dillinger almost immediately. The Big Woman was a God-fearing woman who hustled Chet down to the St. Chris Jesus & Bible Church, a congregation of twelve souls stuffed into a one-room apartment near the strip mall. On Sunday, Preacher raised Chet up by the armpits and plunged him into the bathtub, all the while casting out Satan and baptizing him to be born again. Preacher was a good soul—Chet could tell right away—despite his wanting to go on and on about the Fires of Hell and the Death Everlasting.

Preacher was a fatherly kind of man and had a face like a chubby angel but with gray hair and a mustache and a twinkle in his eye whenever Oreos or Lorna Doones were mentioned. Sometimes he'd tell Chet Bible stories and share cookies with him, down along the shore in late summer, and ask him to tell the Bible stories back to him, which Chet did with some alarming imitations of Preacher, too.

Chet began to read the Bible as often as he could from there on, because he realized that since he had been born into this religion anew, he should probably understand just what sort of people he'd be praying to. His favorite parts of the Good Book tended to be about guys being thrown into lion's dens, and a really dirty story (so he thought) called Song of Songs, but he read a lot of it, and then pondered on as much of it as he could bear. His mother, of course, had been a godless woman—a fallen woman, Preacher told him—but her sin did not need to fall on him, as well. Preacher had his good side and would tell Chet that he met his mother twice—once at the Krogers, when they were both shopping for breakfast cereal. His mother, Preacher told him, was attractive and fine in many ways, although she was not a churchgoer and she had not accepted Jesus as her savior. The second time Preacher met Chet's mother was one night down at the docks, when Preacher went down to think about how Our Lord had walked on the water. He had seen Chet's mother, Roselle Goodfellow, out in the waves "naked as the day she was born, laughing and dancing, and I'd be one to say she had the Devil in her, only she looked beautiful and happy and she was with some friends, and I will never damn someone to hell for being happy in God's ocean," Preacher had told Chet with a wink of his eye.

Chet knew, though, that he had a lot to make up for. He could accept Jesus as his savior and get on with life. That was how Chet saw it as he turned five. He was smart enough to understand that a little bit of Christian fervor would get him through some awful nights in the Dillinger home.

The Dillinger boys were, in many ways, his own personal devils.

Let's call them by their nicknames, though, because, since arriving in the Dillinger household at the age of four, Chet wasn't sure they had any other names. There was Stash and Cuff and Boo, all of them slovenly and large and tow-headed. Stash was the oldest and biggest. He was nearly fourteen, and he had a haircut that was perfectly round on the sides because his mother put a big bowl on his head and used it as a guideline to trim his white locks. Stash was actually nicer than either Cuff or Boo, and he seemed to always be happy or dreamy to Chet—when he wasn't mean mad as a bull—and how was Chet to know this was the influence of weed? Stash smoked it whenever he could, out back in the woods, and had started Cuff on it, too. Cuff was eleven, and the meanest of the bunch. Chet once watched him cut the head off a chicken and laugh when the body kept running around in the dirt. Cuff then turned to Chet and warned him that if he didn't "keep it in your pants and do what you're told," that he, too, would get his head cut off. Chet didn't like thinking about his headless body running around for a minute after his head rolled off. Boo was pretty mean, too, but was only two years older than Chet, and this gave Chet a great fondness for Boo, despite Boo's temperament. And then there was the baby, which, as far as Chet knew, had no name. He didn't even think it was for sure Mrs. Dillinger's baby because it looked different from all the other Dillingers.

And then there was Mrs. Dillinger, which is what Chet was supposed to call her except when the social worker came 'round, and then he was supposed to call her *Mama.* Once, when the social worker dropped in unexpectedly, the mud was all over the linoleum in the living room, and bowls of food were still out from two nights previous, and Chet heard the social worker cry out that the baby was lying in its own filth.

And Chet forgot to call the Big Woman *Mama,* and he knew that was why she was so sad after the social worker left. The Big Woman pointed at him with her stubby finger with the chewed-up fingernail that almost wasn't there anymore, and said, "You are not doing this right, Shit." She called him "Shit" instead of "Chet" sometimes, although when he asked her about it, she told him something was wrong with his hearing; and the boys would chuckle and nod. Because the social worker was going to come back the next day, Chet had to help the Big Boys clean the place up.

"I don't like this weather," the Big Woman said. "This weather makes me sad. Don't it make you sad?" She drew Chet up on her lap. He heard the baby crying in the TV room but decided it was smartest not to say anything. "It makes me sad to see the rain. And winter's coming. I can feel it. I get this hurting in my bones. It's a lot of pain." She squeezed him a little too tight, but Chet knew that this was an okay squeeze. She treated him the way he treated his teddy bear when the Big Woman was feeling good. "You know? I love children. I love little children. They are the joy of life," she whispered, nuzzling his ear, kissing him gently. "I'm sorry you got a cough, Chet. Some say that children who cough are gonna be angels and that's a good sign. So you're my little coughing angel, Chetty Chet Chet." After she'd fallen asleep in the Barcolounger, Chet slipped from her lap and went to the kitchen to warm up the bottle for the baby, who was still crying.

When he arrived in the bedroom that he shared with the baby, he saw why it had been crying.

Cuff had it in the air and was swinging it around.

2

"No!" Chet cried out and ran over to try to rescue the baby from Cuff's twisting arm, but out of nowhere, a big beefy arm swung down and whapped him under the chin, so that he was thrown off-balance. Chet fell into a pile of dirty clothes in the corner of the room; he started his coughing, but ignored it. He thought he heard a dog barking out along the dusty road beyond the window. He tried to stand up—the baby was still in the air, and Cuff swung it back and forth near the tall lamp with the torn shade. "Please," Chet said, finally managing to overcome his wobbly feet. He lunged for Cuff and the baby, hoping that he'd catch the baby before Cuff could drop it.

And then, the baby flew out of Cuff's hands. It seemed to go in slow motion, like the baby was floating underwater and not in the air. Chet felt something surge through him—like an electric shock—and he was sure that every hair on his body stood on end. The dogs out on the road had begun howling and he remembered that the wolf was always at the door, always howling—

And the baby floated in midair, only it wasn't in slow motion, and by all the rights of the laws of gravity and nature and God, that baby should've hit the far wall, hard, its head smashing. Instead, the baby just floated, and Cuff stared, not at the baby, but at Chet himself, who stood there, his mouth open, a howl coming from within him, a keening wail that was unlike anything human.

This only lasted a few seconds, and in that time, Chet got to the baby and grabbed it where it floated, and brought it down to his own bed as if it were a balloon that had gotten loose. The baby screamed louder than he'd ever heard him, and Chet was relieved, but had no idea that he was the reason the baby had not died that day.

Cuff, rather than thank his lucky stars for this brief miracle, began to wail, and went running to the Big Woman to come quick because Chetty was some kind of baby-killer and was about to hurt the runt of the litter.

Chet didn't mind. He was glowing from the feeling of the baby in his arms, pressed against his own small chest. He had never been much of a crier, but tears poured from his eyes as he held the baby, and he didn't want to let it go when the Big Woman came in and made a grab for it. Finally, he let her have the baby, but only because he was afraid she'd hurt it if she kept tugging it from his arms. She slapped him some before taking him down to where the dogs lived beneath the trailer, and making him think about the evil Godless thing he had done.

Chet didn't know if it was him, or if it was a miracle from God, or if the baby had just suddenly learned how to float. He didn't care. He slept that afternoon in the damp chill with the trailer dogs and found that he didn't even mind that the Big Woman kept him out there until three o'clock in the morning. She walked back and forth and renounced him as a spawn of hell and begged him to repent and to accept the Lord as his Savior. Being a good boy who liked God, Chet renounced anything he was asked. He fell asleep saying the 23rd Psalm, remembering each part of it with his ten fingers, although he kept forgetting the line about the Valley of the Shadow of Death.

He knew then that the wolf was truly at the door.

3

Chet felt the wolf sometimes, too.
Not outside, but inside.
Within his own flesh.

Chapter Five

1

Sometimes when the Big Woman punished Chet, she made him sleep with the dogs outside, or in the Stow-It hamper, even when he was seven or eight, smushed down with the dirty laundry and covered with the smell of mildew and pee. He remained there, wanting to get out but sure that the Big Woman waited on the other side, ready to push him back down into the filth. During those times, he would feel the wolf stirring inside him.

The wolf made him think ugly, awful thoughts. In the darkness of whatever punishment had been handed him, he imagined the wolf coming through into his mouth and hands and ripping at the Big Woman's meaty neck, tearing it open. He could smell the blood within the bread of her flesh, and he wanted to tear at it and gnaw at her bones right down to the marrow. Then the wolf would spring for Cuff and slice him up with its claws, from his steamy belly right up to his chinny-chin-chin, and the wolf would gobble down the boy's heart while it was still beating. The visions within him were hellish and horrible, and Chet longed to think prettier thoughts, but sometimes he could not. Those were nasty times for him, and there was no God that could save him when the wolf tried to break free of its tether. It took everything he had to keep it at bay, and even then, the howls within his mind were terrible.

He prayed and prayed when this vision would come to him, for he knew the wolf was bad and he didn't want to let the wolf out.

He felt a curious strength seep into him as he imagined taking Cuff and Boo and tossing them up and down in the air, just as they did the baby; or scratching their eyes out until there was nothing but blackened holes there; or putting them in boiling water and drinking them down like soup once their flesh had separated from their bones.

He hated these visions. These sensations. He didn't know where the wolf in him came from, but he knew it was there.

And he knew, at a very tender age, that he must do everything in his power to keep the wolf at the door and not let it through.

2

Chet Dillinger—he had to take on the name of what had become an accursed family for him, yet he never stopped thinking of himself as an orphan—grew to a height of six feet by the time he was fourteen years old. He stood like a marker of some greatness against the small huskiness of the other Dillinger boys, who never seemed to grow beyond their twelfth year. Still, they remained formidable with the speed of their lunges, and what had developed into muscle-bound bodies for teenage boys. The Big Boys had become the bullies of the area, and Chet found himself more often than not apologizing to his classmates when one of his older foster brothers stole lunch money or ended an otherwise normal discussion with a swing of the fist.

But there was more to Chet than the Dillingers.

He had discovered baseball in sixth grade, mainly because it was the first year the school gave him a glove and a bat. While most of the kids were afraid of the baseball hitting them, Chet had been handling the rocks thrown at him by the Big Boys over the past few years; a softball heading his way seemed minor. The bat felt good in his hands, and he felt a wild kind of anger come out when he swung it. The ball heading toward him felt like it was something else—not a ball, but some *thing* that he didn't want in his life. So, when he swung the bat, he did it hard and with meaning. The ball needed to be far from him. He didn't want it around as he ran base by base, often making a homer.

He liked hearing the crack of the bat. One of the old women at church gave him his first pair of cleats when he was in eighth grade—they didn't fit perfectly, but he wore them constantly, to the point that they stank and turned gray, and eventually holes began sprouting along the edges of the shoes.

By ninth grade, he was back to wearing sneakers but knew that he'd somehow get cleats again. He wore his baseball cap everywhere but to church; he even organized a charity game at church and got the preacher to play a little baseball, too. Even his asthma didn't kick up in the dust of the baseball diamond, or as he ran around the bases.

The summers were his favorite baseball season; he delivered the local newspaper to earn some money, and in the summer this went into overdrive when he mowed lawns and even did some work down at the docks, where the fishing boats came in. But every day, after work, he gathered a few of the guys and one or two of the girls together and got a game going.

Baseball became the thing (besides doing some work at church) that got him away from the Dillingers and Rustic Acres—at least in his mind. It had begun as a sandlot game, although the sandlots in St. Chris tended to be either swampy or so sandy it was hard to run around the bases. The smell in the air was either fish or truck fumes, but it all seemed like heaven to that kid as he slammed the bat against the ball and felt, in that moment, that life could be good. That it had possibilities.

By the time he was in ninth grade, Chet knew everything there was to know about the Baltimore Orioles, his favorite team. He was up on every game of the American League Eastern Division and knew the stats on the New York Yankees, the Boston Red Sox, and even the Toronto Blue Jays. His idol was Cal Ripkin, Jr., the starting third baseman and designated hitter for the Orioles. Chet could not get enough of Ripkin. He knew that Ripkin was from a town not more than a couple of hours from St. Chris—Aberdeen, Maryland. Ripkin had a long career in baseball, since he'd been playing with the Orioles since the early 1980s. Chet knew every record that Cal Ripkin, Jr., had ever held; and Chet read every magazine or newspaper at the local library that had even a mention of Ripkin.

Chet found that he himself had a small talent with the baseball bat—he could thwack a modest homer out of the makeshift diamond, and sometimes the ball would be lost for days from his hit. He imagined himself completely surrounded by a major league team; and one of the coaches at high school told him that if he practiced enough, he might make it to the minor leagues when he got older. "You've got some charm with that bat," the coach had said, patting him on the shoulder. "Year or two from now, I bet you're going to make varsity."

He found that, with practice, he could outrun most of his classmates, too. This helped with the few obvious bullies in school, and it never hurt to be considered a bit of an athlete when it came to girls. On the baseball diamond at school, the kids began calling him "Charmin' Chet," mostly as a joke, and mainly because he always had a Charm's Pop lollipop in his mouth while he pitched. But the truth was, the words just went together, "Charmin' Chet," and, with the exception of the Dillinger family, most of the kids and a few of the teachers liked having Chet around. His asthma came up sometimes when he ran bases, in great gusts of coughs and hacks, but he didn't care—he let his lungs expand and expel and his nose run and just went with it. Sometimes he paid for this later on, and had to lie in bed at night practically nursing his inhaler ("That thing costs us a small fortune," the Big Woman would say. "You need to get better and get over this weakness of yours.")

The Dillingers were outside his charm. Things went on in the house that seemed darker to him than a long night without stars or moon. The Big Woman was getting sad all the time, and let her hair go all messy and matted; she wore sweatpants and too-small white T-shirts; she didn't wash much, either. The Big Boys played their usual pranks on him and each other.

The baby had died when it had arrived at its fourth year, having expired, Chet believed, from not wanting to grow up a Dillinger. Chet himself had tried to exhaust himself to death in what the Big Woman called Good Works. Saturdays, he worked cleaning the church he attended every Sunday, and after school, if he didn't scare up an informal baseball game among his compadres, he often worked on some of the other trailers in the park. The people who lived there were nice and liked him, and would often let him stay for dinner if the Big Woman didn't mind. They never mentioned the death of the baby, and Chet didn't like to think about it too much. Chet often thought of the poor creature, whose name had never been clear beyond "Baby." The child had never had much of a chance in a house of such darkness as the Dillinger home.

Chet continued to dream of his mother, and of her words ("The wolf's at the door"), but she had taken on the quality of a story told to him innumerable times so he was never sure if he had ever really met her or even suckled from her breast beyond the first ten minutes of his life, and he decided one day that he had to run away from the Dillinger clan and get out on his own.

So, one night, he stole an extra pair of shoes from the largest Dillinger boy's stash, grabbed two of his favorite T-shirts, slipped on a pair of ill-fitting jeans, and took off for parts unknown from a particular Chesapeake awfulness called St. Chris and the realm of darkness within it known as Rustic Acres.

3

The night he left—sneaking like a thief (as the Big Woman no doubt characterized his departure later on)—he sat down and pulled up a spiral notebook and tore a page out of it.

He had begun to fancy himself a bit of a writer, because it was the one area in school—aside from baseball—in which he excelled. He had fallen in love with the stories of Ray Bradbury and of Jack London, and he'd even begun to read a novel called *Moby Dick* that would take him more than a year to finish, but he held the story within, close to his heart. So, when he wrote his farewell note, he decided to make it his first literary achievement. His going away note, he felt sure, would become mythic in Rustic Acres, if not in all of St. Chris.

He wrote:

Dearest Dillingers,

I really truly have enjoyed these years living in your house and carrying your name even though it is not really mine. I will miss the tantrums. I will miss the nightly fights over the remote control. I will think a lot about how Cuff used to fart in the middle of dinner and then make out that one of his brothers had done it. And how the rain came through the bathroom because no one would fix it. And how the dog went crazy from all the nastiness, because even a hound could not stay sane with the bones from your house. I will remember knowing that the milk was always sour and the eggs always stank. I will miss church, but not for the reasons you may think (especially since you believe in all your heart that I am somehow the spawn of the devil). I will miss church because it was the one place where I didn't have to believe that the whole world was about you and Rustic Acres. You put clothes on my back and food in my stomach, and I will be forever grateful.

Yeah, I know I'm a bastard and my mother was some kind of whore and my father was probably the Devil himself. I deserve much worse than what you gave me during these years. And I know that there were times when I felt that we were all real close and could somehow get along and get through things. Those times were like the hurricanes out on the shore. They came sometimes.

They threatened to come. They didn't always arrive like clockwork. You can't depend on a hurricane, I guess.

So now I'm out of your lives. If you come looking for me, you won't find me because I won't come back to this. I won't ever be someone's servant again unless it's a servant of God or someone so special they're worth serving. I doubt any of you will shed a tear over this. I don't blame you. I am completely a bastard and should be disowned. No doubt you will continue to live in Rustic Acres and say harsh things about me, and you may be on the mark with those things.

I will be fine. Don't worry about me, although I know you won't. I will probably miss the baby most of all, but I'm willing to bet he's in a better place than Rustic Acres, that's for sure.

Sincerely,
Chet

P.S. If you come looking for me, I will make you sorry. I mean it. I thank you for every good thing you've done for me. But not for the bad stuff.

4

This last part, his postscript, seemed to him particularly nasty, but he felt he had to write it. The Big Woman had begun to get moodier over the past two years, and she'd slapped him a few times in a way that made him worry about what else she might do. She definitely scared him by the time he was ready to get out of that place. He was more scared because of the wolf that was somewhere lurking inside him than he was of her slaps, but just the same, he didn't want to stick around and find out what would come of it all.

He left a second note for the preacher at church, and his wife. All he said was:

Thanks for your kindness. I'm leaving. I'm going to find her, someday. Keep saying prayers for me because I definitely need them even if I am a sinner. If I could, I'd spend my whole life sitting on the dock with you and telling Bible stories and eating Oreos, but I know that childhood is in the past now. I have to be a man. If I could've had any parents, I would've wanted them to be you both, even though I am not a very good Christian and I probably will come to a no-good end full of Hellfire and without hope of Deliverance. I have too much wolf in me and not enough lamb.
Chet Goodfellow

Although Dillinger was his adopted name, he signed it with his mother's name, and he knew Preacher would understand.

Chet left behind the legends of his mother's harlotry and addictions, and the vague notion that to have a mother, one must also have a father. But as all the men in St. Chris seemed to look so alike—one to the other—Chet would be hard-pressed to know where his dimples had come from, where his brown hair had arrived from on his head, and from whence his sharp nose—unless all the men in town had taken turns with his mother, which the Big Woman had always told him was exactly what had happened.

The night he escaped his bonds, he took off first for the shoreline and found a trucker on the highway willing to give him a lift as far north as Baltimore. He spent the night trying to entertain the trucker with tales of St. Chris, all of which were true, none of which the trucker—a man with a long face named Daw, whose breath was afire with whiskey—seemed to believe. His first night in Baltimore was bleak; he managed to find a church with an open window. He slept on the pews and tried not to think that God might be angry with him for behaving so badly to the Dillingers (who had, as the Big Woman had always told him, put the clothes on his back and the food on his table). When he awoke, a woman dressed in black came to him and told him that he needed to go home.

He took her order to heart and went in search of his mother, for she was not dead, nor had she vanished. She lived somewhere to the north, in the Yankee land, and he intended to find her. Before he got much farther than Baltimore, he was captured again, and somewhere between Baltimore and Philadelphia he ended up in what they called a group home, which seemed as hellish as the Dillinger place, and if it weren't for the fact he'd been sent to a therapist, he would never have known about his real talent.

Chapter Six

1

"Some people call this telekinesis," the therapist said, as if it were like any other malaise.

"What's that?"

"It's moving things. With your mind."

"It doesn't happen much."

"When you're angry, I'd guess. When you really want it to happen," the woman said. She was pretty and small and had eyes that were so round and beautiful that he thought he was talking to God. So he knew then that God was a black woman with round eyes and a narrow forehead. He wanted to tell her about how he was sure he saw God in people, but he also knew that this was information best kept to himself.

"You think I'm making it up," Chet said. He felt that she could look right through him. "But you know, don't you?" He wanted to add: because you look like God to me. But that sounded crazy, and even thinking it, he knew it was crazy, and probably a result of having been brought up too much in a church. Still, no one in the little church near Rustic Acres would have ever thought that God would be one of the disciples of Freud and Jung.

"I think you believe you have this power," the therapist said.

"I really do. First time I noticed it was with the baby. Then, once, when I was twelve, I made a cherry bomb explode in Cuff Dillinger's hand."

"When we play with fireworks, sometimes they blow up. It wasn't you. But you take the blame, don't you?"

"No," he said. Chet thought about what she was saying and shook his head. "No, I really did it. I imagined the fire in the bomb and I let it go. And the baby really floated. Just for a couple of seconds, but he really did. My stepbrothers saw it, too."

"There are people who have claimed this kind of ability. But I doubt it has ever existed," the woman said. Her eyes were pure darkness, and he liked looking into them when she spoke. She must be knowledgeable, he knew, because she had all kinds of diplomas on the wall and because she was a therapist for a lot of the boys. Especially the ones who got in trouble—as he had—for throwing his bed against the wall.

"You lifted the bed how?" she asked.

"I didn't lift the bed. Not really."

"Now we're getting somewhere."

"I was so angry at . . . one of the counselors . . . I just looked around for something to throw. There wasn't anything in my room to throw. I mean, nothing. Not even a pencil. Maybe a lamp, but I didn't want to break anything. So I looked at the bed and then it just happened." He didn't want to tell her the rest, about the wolf. The wolf was inside him and was trying to get out. He had fought it as much as he could, but something gave—it was like a wilderness had just opened up inside him. But he couldn't tell the therapist all that. She would've thought he was completely insane.

"You picked up the bed and—"

"No," he said. "I was across the room. I stood there. Something's getting stronger about what's inside me. It really flew across the room." Then he sighed. "It broke the lamp anyway. I wouldn't have broke that lamp."

The therapist he had begun to think of as God also sighed. She watched him for a minute without saying anything. Then, "You told me last time about your mother."

He nodded. "Her name is Roselle. She lives in New York City. I think."

"Do you know her last name?"

"It was Goodfellow. But I think she changed it."

"Why do you think the Dillingers don't want you back?"

He let out a laugh. "They're chicken. Cuff almost lost two fingers when the cherry bomb exploded, and maybe you don't believe me, but he knows how it happened. The Big Woman—Mrs. Dillinger—hates me, but she's scared of me, too. They think I'm from the Devil."

"Do you want to talk about your anger?" the therapist asked.

"Anger?"

"Well, your anger at your foster mother. You know in fairy tales, the stepmothers were often considered terrifying and deceitful. If your foster mother was like that, it would be perfectly normal for you to be angry at her."

"I'm not angry at them. Not really. I feel bad for them."

"Why?"

"I got out. They're stuck. They're still in it."

"And you're not angry at all?"

"Maybe because of the baby. I don't know anything for sure, but the Big Woman was never going to let that baby grow up right."

"Do you think she killed it?"

"No."

Chet was silent for a while and closed his eyes, not wanting to see the faces that came at him through memory. The faces of the Dillingers, but most especially the baby.

He opened his eyes and stared at a point on the wall beyond the therapist. There was a crayon drawing of a house and some flowers that a little kid must've drawn. "I think I killed the baby."

"You think you did?"

"Not directly. But I think there were things I could've done to save it. And maybe some part of me felt it was safer dead. Instead of alive. I know that sounds horrible. But I don't think death is so awful. Sometimes life can be pretty awful. Sometimes I wish it was me who had died instead of the baby, and then it would be alive and might've gotten out of there. And been okay."

"Do you think someone actually killed the baby?"

Chet sighed. "No, not in the way most people would think. I think they killed its spirit. Once you kill someone's spirit, it's no surprise when the rest goes, too, don't you think?"

"Perhaps. Chet, let's focus back on you."

"Okay."

"What is it you want?"

"Me?"

"Yes: Chet. What is it Chet wants?"

"To find my mother," he said. And then he didn't say another word the entire session.

2

Within a year of life at the group home, Chet met Jack Fleetwood, who had heard of him through a loose grapevine of therapists and doctors and quacks, all of whom heard about the second incident that

Chet had experienced, despite the supposed confidentiality of their professions. None of them felt it was all that secret, that there was a teenager somewhere who claimed to have had some kind of telekinetic experience. It had been almost a joke, until it reached Fleetwood's ears, and he was a man who kept up with people who idly spoke of this kind of thing. It was nothing phenomenal, just that Chet, then seventeen, had fallen in love with a girl from Park Pleasant, a nice apartment complex nearby, and had, at the age of sixteen, lost his virginity to the eighteen-year-old vixen, only to find that when he was in the throes of his first physical passion, something horrible occurred.

Later, he described it to Jack Fleetwood, who was a paranormal researcher at the time up at a place with a funny name (PSI-something) in New York City.

3

Chet, on tape

"I don't like talking about it. I really don't. And I don't like the fact that the whole damn neighborhood turned out. It's not funny. It's embarrassing. It was bad. We . . . did what we did, you know . . . and it was December and cold as hell . . . it must've been forty below. It was frosty and the grounds around the apartments were covered with snow, crunchy snow, solid snow.

"And then, you know, right when, right when it happened between us, they came.

"They all came.

"They just appeared like from nowhere. I have no idea how it happened, but they came and I didn't notice them at first. I mean,

I thought I was in a dream. I thought I was dreaming. I thought maybe I'd gone crazy. I thought maybe, since this was my first time, and probably my only time now, I thought maybe someone raised them nearby and had accidentally let them loose. There were hundreds of them. All different kinds. Monarchs. Viceroys. Butterflies I'd never seen before.

"They were at the windows beating against them. Flocking. It was almost scary. Corrine noticed them first. Then I looked up. I thought it was a gag. Or a dream. But I go running to the window, buck naked, and I just barely open it to see why all these butterflies are there, and that was probably the stupidest thing I could've done, because they all came in and covered me, they practically covered my face and I was afraid of smothering to death, but it wasn't like that.

"It was like they were holding me or something, and then there were more. It was out of nowhere, but I knew it was from me, I knew it was like the baby floating and the bed flying and the cherry bomb exploding. There was something about me that did it, only now other people could see what a freak I was.

"And they were all down there, the whole neighborhood, people out in the parking lot, pointing and taking pictures of this swirl of color all floating around. And Corrine looks at me and starts screaming like I'm a monster.

"And then it was in the papers and it was all over the place, and I guess that's how you heard about it. They went away after a little while. They just went off into the woods. I guess they all died. I guess they all weren't supposed to be out yet. They froze. It felt good at first, you know, when they were all over me, like they were going to fly me up or like they were nesting against me, all those blue and yellow and red wings fluttering around.

"I freaked and I got out of control and I thought I'd kill myself by jumping out the window, but that was when they let go. That was when they left me alone. Corrine was still screaming, and the cops showed up, and her parents showed up, and then all kinds of crap happened.

"All I want to know is how do I get rid of this so I don't have to be a freak anymore. So people won't stare. So I can just get out on my own and be left alone."

4

By the time Chet was nineteen he'd given up on finding his mother and was working in a gas station in Dover, Delaware. He'd married a girl from Wilmington briefly at eighteen, but it had ended after three months when she'd left him for a guy who worked construction outside Philadelphia. He knew he wasn't the most exciting of husbands, because he didn't really like to party like the other guys he knew, and his wife had been a little wild, although he understood her, and he missed her after she left. Then he found out she had managed to get some kind of legal annulment without him. He had no regrets about this, and took it as a normal course of life.

The wolf, his mother had said in his dream of her, was at the door, after all.

His obsession with baseball continued, and he kept hoping he might get good enough for the minor leagues, although he had no idea how one went about this. Because of his group home situation before he turned eighteen, he hadn't really been that involved in the sport his last two years in high school, and he had a sinking feeling that he would never attain that one dream, to play baseball for life. His asthma had begun returning, particularly when he was out on one of the nearby baseball diamonds behind the local school. Perhaps it was the dust, perhaps it was his own exhaustion at what life required, but he found himself coughing and having to go get himself a new inhaler every few months. His doctor told him to rest and take it easy; to stay inside his air-conditioned apartment in the summer; but Chet had to be out in the hot, humid days of August, pumping gas, and found that the coughing seemed to keep pace with his new addiction: cigarettes.

Were someone to point out to the young man that cigarettes and asthma didn't mix, he'd probably look at that person and grin. "Yeah, but it's the fastest way to check out." Chet would not even know he was saying something that might indicate a passive approach to suicide. He didn't really know he was unhappy.

Then, one day, the letter and contract and what seemed like more money then he'd make in a year pumping gas arrived in the mail from Jack Fleetwood. He'd briefly met the man he had called Dr. Fleetwood through one of the group-home psychologists two years before. Dr. Fleetwood had asked him a few questions, none of which Chet could recall, and then asked Chet if he would mind being hypnotized. Chet nodded his assent, although he thought it was a little funny to be doing this kind of therapy, and then the next thing he knew, he was saying good-bye to Fleetwood. He figured that would be the last time he'd ever hear of or from the man. That is, until the phone calls in early summer, and then this, the check. The letter. The contract.

Chet tried reading through the legal spiderweb of words in the contract but could not make them out much despite his love of reading. There were a lot of paragraphs and sub-paragraphs and sentences that went on for nearly a page at a time. It all looked fairly plumb; he could not see the wrong of it, although the ten thousand dollars seemed excessive for a few days in a mansion somewhere up in New York State.

But something about the invitation; the money; the sense of a new and fresh adventure, where he could crawl out of the past and into someplace where his specialness might be noticed—his charm—this brought another feeling with it.

The wolf, sniffing at the door within him.

Sniffing and raising a paw, and beginning to scratch.

PART THREE

Cali

Chapter Seven

1

Dear Dr. Fleetwood,

Thanks for contacting me. I'm glad you're a fan of the show. I've never really been much for ghosts or ghost hunting, but I am intrigued. And of course the money is generous. The one thing I have to inquire about now is whether or not there is any possible danger involved. Not from ghosts, but from whomever else you're hiring for the last week of October. How much is each one of us screened? I know psi talents well enough to know that they don't always go with well-adjusted people, as you probably know from my own background.

If you are not aware of my background, I'll tell you here: I was arrested and subsequently incarcerated at the age of fifteen regarding suspicion of murder. If you don't know the full story, I'll send you articles, but I will at least reassure you: all charges were dropped. There was nothing connecting me to the crime involved other than my premonition about it. But because of this brief experience with the law, I had several years of psychotherapy. Both my parents and I wanted to make sure that this was genuinely a talent and not a sign of mental illness or possible psy-

chopathology on my part. As you know, I studied with Dr. Jane Orien in Carmel in her paranormal studies program, and I've worked on various criminal homicide cases with regards to psychometry.

What I've learned through these studies and experience is that there are people who have talents in these areas who have mental disturbances as well as psi ability. And yes, this has always been an issue when I meet others like this.

So, this rambling e-mail is being sent to you just to ask: does everybody who is coming check out?

Sincerely,

Cali Nytbird

P.S.—to answer your question, Cali is my real name—full name, Calista. My last name is not Nytbird, but because of both my radio show and the work I do with the NYPD, I try to protect my family from possible reprisal with a pseudonym. Suffice it to say, my last name is very pedestrian and, I think, quite lovely, but I've found the pseudonym protects as well as influences, and yes, I did legally change it.

2

Dear Cali,

I have followed your radio show for a few years, and I attended the lecture you gave on the relationship between homicide and psychic imprints. I have spent many years keeping up with those who have had psychic disturbance or enhancement in their lives, and yes, I think the others who are coming check out, both mentally and physically. Frost Crane, the best-selling author, has agreed to be a guest at Harrow; and a young man named Chet Dillinger, who I met very briefly when he had an early paranormal experience, has also agreed to come. I had invited a few others, prior to sending the check and contract, but for various reasons, they were not interested, or, I felt, they would be an uncomfortable mix with the three of you. Besides the four of us, my daughter will accompany me, and the new owner of Harrow, Ivy Martin, who is, in many ways, the primary inspiration for this venture, as well as the financial angel of the entire undertaking.

I can assure you that, if nothing else, you will enjoy the week at Harrow because of the company assembled.

I also know about your past, from what you've said on the radio, and about your twin brother, Ned, who shared your ability. I understand the darkness that sometimes accompanies these wonderful talents, and like any kind of human creativity or intuition, it is a difficult and often unsatisfying way of life for those who are endowed with an ability.

But I think you can put your fears aside in this case, and just come and enjoy the study of Harrow and any phenomena we uncover there.

Thank you for the note, and I look forward to seeing you. This will be fun, and it will be fascinating, I have no doubt.

Yours,
Jack Fleetwood
President
PSI Vista

3

Dear Dr. Fleetwood,

Unfortunately, because of my work, my life is far too much in the public eye—at least, more than I think it should be. Yes, the history of my brother's mental illness is very well documented, and I do feel that his own paranormal ability pushed him over the edge. My grandmother maintained that this was a hereditary condition, so that my brother's violence and his self-mutilation went hand in hand with the visions he sometimes witnessed. I have met both charlatans and genuine psi subjects since my studies began and since beginning this radio show. What I've learned in all this is that: Sometimes a kook is just a kook.

Sincerely,
Cali Nytbird

4

Dear Cali,

First, let's get rid of this Dr. Fleetwood nonsense. I have a doctorate in paranormal studies, and I'm not fit for medical practice. Jack is fine. Regarding the kook factor: agreed. I have met many kooks in my day, as well as genuine talents. The three who are participating in the Harrow study are genuine. I would stake my reputation on it.

Now, since you live near Manhattan, why haven't we ever seen you at the Foundation? We're not far from the Christopher Street PATH station in our little brownstone, and if I could ever intrigue you with our extensive library, please drop by. You don't need an appointment. Otherwise, I look forward to meeting you at Harrow.

I'm not completely hooked on this whole e-mail thing. But if you need to talk more on the phone, just give me a call.

Yours,

Jack Fleetwood

5

Dear Jack,

I am always the last to know. I am going to trust your judgment, and I look forward to meeting you at Harrow next week. My life is hectic at the moment. I seem to be consulting too often with the NYPD, which, as you can imagine, is full of skeptics. But I will definitely take the last days in October off for your ghost-hunting endeavor.

With only slight trepidation,

Cali Nytbird

Chapter Eight

1

Cali Nytbird hesitated when her cell phone began to ring. She was in midsentence, practically shouting across the table—there were so many people yapping in the Starbucks coffeehouse, she wasn't sure she'd hear anyone on the phone. She had just downed enough caffeine to kill a horse, and still she felt exhausted when she thought about who was calling her.

All right, she could admit it to herself: *exhausted and jumpy.*

Only three people had her cell phone number; one of them sat across from her. One of them was her mother, who lived across the country and never called this time of day. The third person who had this number, Detweiler, a police detective who had pissed her off lately, no doubt was calling. *At long last. Too little, too late.* He'd probably be calling about an investigation; he never talked personal business on the phone. She didn't want to answer it, but it was part of a job she'd taken on just a year before. A dirty job, to some extent. A job that made her feel as if she was filthy herself. But a job she felt obligated to do, mainly because she wanted to help track down murderers—and if her gift helped with that, it was God's will, just like her mother used to tell her. Cali had her own doubts about cosmic will, from God or otherwise, but she did feel she had a duty to the world, in her own small way.

She glanced across the table at her sister, Bev, who looked as if she was going to spit her coffee across the table at her. Bev was the sensible and smart one in the family pecking order. Cali was the wild, impetuous one, at least according to her mother: the adventuress. Bev, Mrs. Sensible, with her perfectly groomed coif and her suburban ways and even that little jacket she wore—right out of the Paramus Park Mall. Bev had been married to the same guy for nine years. Cali refused to get married. She loved Bev like they were best friends instead of sisters, but Bev was never going to understand the crossing wires of Cali's romantic life with her business life. *Even I don't pretend to understand it.*

Bev leaned into the table and mouthed: *Is it him?*

Cali opened the phone, nodding, and said into the speaker, "I'm in the middle of my life. Where is it?"

"Thanks. Upper West Side. Off Seventy-second and Central Park West. Near that trattoria you like." His voice was razor thin, like he'd been up for three nights shouting. His Brooklyn accent still came through, and despite her annoyance at his call, she felt a brief sigh, almost within her soul.

"Trattoria Sambuca. Love that place." Cali raised her eyebrows to Bev, who was shaking her head. Bev sipped her espresso and glanced back down at the copy of *Vanity Fair* she'd been leafing through. But Cali knew that Bev would hear every single word and probably dissect it for her late that very same night on the phone after Bev's husband had gone to bed.

"Where are you?" he asked.

"Starbucks. In Chelsea. The one on Eighth and Sixteenth."

"Cappucino?"

"Chai. Bev's here. We went shopping," she said flatly.

"You went shopping in the real world?"

"Can't buy everything online. Yet."

"Amazing," he said. "Wait, let me guess: You're carrying that shoulder bag you got at Paige Novick—the turquoise one with that kind of mesh thingy on it. The one I think looks sort of like an old bowling bag. And you're wearing your Kate Spades, even though you should be wearing boots or something with the way the weather keeps changing. And your jacket. It's . . ."

"This the fashion police?"

"I just know you, I guess. Maybe I'm a little psychic, too."

Cali wanted to scream, but she counted to five silently. Then she said, "It's been two weeks. Now this."

From across the round table, Bev whispered, "Yeah, give it to him."

"Two weeks of grunt work and in bed at two A.M. every night, up at eight the next morning." He paused. "Sorry. I kept meaning to call."

Cali covered the mouthpiece. She laughed, shaking her head. "He's claiming he's a workaholic now."

"Maybe he is," Bev said. Then she grinned. "Not a bad quality sometimes." Bev's grin was like the sun coming out—it made Cali feel a little less cold toward Det.

Just a little less.

Cali whispered into the phone, "This is the last time, Det. My fee goes up for this."

"Homicides don't come cheap," he said.

"How long?"

"Not sure. Six, seven hours."

"Male or female?"

"Perp probably male. Victim, female."

"As usual," she sighed. "Give me twenty minutes. And give me something to read, okay? I don't want to walk into a snakepit of cops and not get to work."

He didn't respond.

She got a feeling. "What's going on? Something you want to tell me before I hike uptown?"

Another pause on the line.

"Joss is here, too."

Cali sucked in some air, shaking her head. Her mind went blank for a second. That name: Joss. *Colin Joss.* The moron cop who had managed to get under her skin and stay there like some kind of tick. "Get rid of him before I get there."

"Can't do that, Cal."

"Do what you can. Bye."

She hung up her cell phone. Closed it; slipped it into her jacket's inner pocket. The hum of the coffeehouse came back to her, as if she'd blocked it completely while she'd listened to him on the phone.

"Don't tell me," Bev said. "You have to run."

"I am, he said, the woman of his dreams, he's madly in love with me, he can't resist me. He says. He even knows what I'm wearing, practically. I thought he was obsessed with me. I thought he was too into me. Then"—she snapped her fingers—"two weeks, no calls. Suddenly there's a murder, and he manages to take two minutes to call."

"I warned you about cops," Bev said. "You have a bad history with cops."

"And you have a bad history of telling me what to do," Cali added, laughing.

"Big sisters are like that," Bev said. "If you had listened to me when—"

"I know, when Gary Atkins proposed, back in New Hope, I'd have three children by now and be teaching school instead of living in this big, ugly city and doing fortune-telling on the radio and running after cops and going to look at where people die."

"I never said that," Bev said, more seriously.

"Okay, okay, you never said it. *Exactly.*"

"But I've been thinking of it."

"Spend the night at my place?" Cali asked. She wanted to beg actually, because she was afraid that she and Det would work, and then she and Det would get all hot and heavy again, and that was the last thing Cali wanted.

"I've got to get back home."

"You could call Mike and just be there for me tonight?"

"Can't, Cali," Bev said. "Not tonight. I have an early day tomorrow. And I'm not going to be used as your excuse for avoiding him." Then she leaned over the table and whispered, "You packin'?" in an ironic tone.

"Always. In here," Cali said, holding her purse up. "My new boyfriend."

Bev withdrew, leaning back in her chair. She didn't like guns, she had told Cali often enough. Cali had grown tired of hearing it all, but it didn't matter whether Bev said a word. It was written on her face. Cali called the gun "my new boyfriend" as a joke, but it scared her, too, sometimes. Det had suggested she carry it with her, ever since the death threats. .380-caliber Sig Sauer P230, a supposedly comfortable semiautomatic that made her feel like she was carrying around a bomb. But still, it was a NYPD-approved bomb that might protect her life from the nuts who tended to go after women who helped investigate murders. Cali had taken to it fast.

"Okay," Cali said, trying to forget the gun in her purse. "You going to call me tonight?"

"Oh, yes, I want the whole story," Bev said, the sparkle returning to her eyes. "Now, get going."

2

Traffic was terrible. The cab was a snail in a river of molasses. It took Cali Nytbird thirty-five minutes to get to the crime scene.

The building, called the Mohegan Hotel, was large, but more a fortress than a hotel, which it had been in the twenties and thirties. The stonework facade had lions and griffins cavorting and fighting, all wrapped up in Celtic-like carvings; some scaffolding wrapped around the building where parts of the stone had been crumbling. It was both cheap and ritzy, and Cali guessed, just by the wrought-iron gateway and the leaded-glass front door to the security area, that no one lived here for less than six thousand a month. The guard took her name, and she was about to ask where the elevator was when Det appeared (out of thin air, as usual, acting as if he had been stood up by his date). He grabbed her arm, and she tugged it free.

"Traffic?" was the first word out of Det's mouth. (*Remember this,* she thought, for later. *Savor it. Torture him with it.*)

"As bad as ever at six P.M. on a Tuesday with a cabbie who likes to take every street that has trucks double-parked on it," she said. "Bev says hello."

"You look amazing. Even stunning," Det said, just like it was a date. (All right, she admitted, it was the way they had dates, damn it. He called her in on a breaking assignment, and then they ended up going out for a drink or going for a walk or something. It never ended like business, and this was against everything she had always believed in, but for one thing, she wasn't meeting guys outside of her two jobs, and for another, she just had this thing for Det Detweiler.) Det glanced at her shoes. "I was right. Wasn't I right? Kate Spade. And that"—he pointed to her shoulder bag—"see? I remember these details, it's what I'm good at. Nice jacket, though. You've been shopping. I would guess, that's a what?" He reached out to touch her shoulder, but she drew back.

"It's a denim jacket. That's all. Salvation Army store." She held out her hand. "Got anything for me?"

Detweiler grinned. He had a nice smile—nothing to write home about, not a dazzling one, but the kind that just started the meltdown on her heart. Just a little. He was solid and a bit husky, and he had nostrils that seemed too big and blond hair that flopped around where it wasn't thin in patches, and sometimes he even drank too much beer when they were out together, but that smile always got her.

She admired him; she found something very . . . together . . . about him. It was the mystery of romance, she figured.

He reached into his pocket. "Sixth floor, overlooking the park. Beauty place. Real nice. Good place to die, you ask me." Then he began whistling, which sometimes annoyed her, but now it felt comforting, and when she recognized the tune— "Uptown Girl," the Billy Joel tune—she hummed along as they got on the elevator together.

She felt less like humming along when she saw the woman's body in the apartment, nineteen knife wounds in her back.

Chapter Nine

1

"All right," Cali Nytbird said, her eyes still closed. She held the scrap of paper in her left hand and what looked like a thin ring in her right. She blocked them all out, and within seconds of closing her eyes imagined herself in absolute darkness that alternated with a brilliant purple-and-yellow light. It was the place she called the Getaway, and it was where she went when she needed to focus on what she had in her hands. It would guide her to whatever imprint the object had.

In this case, a piece of paper, which was less imprinted than she had wanted, but Det would not let her touch any of the other evidence because his department had lost a high-profile case a few months earlier purely because there was some suspicion that too many people had been around the crime scene. So, a piece of paper that the killer or victim had held—that was all she had to go on.

For a moment she savored the cool loneliness of the Getaway.

Until, of course, someone said something.

"Vibes," one of the cops chuckled. He must've been standing less than a foot away from her, which was unusual. Det generally made sure she had her space among them. He was getting lax.

Cali ignored him. While the comment could have come from any of a number of cops or even one of the other investigators, she knew exactly who had said it. It would be Colin Joss, from the Third Precinct. He was a prick, and had always made comments behind her back, some of them racist, which hadn't surprised her. She was used to it. If they didn't believe what she was doing, they either pulled race—she'd been called "Voodoo mama" more than once, even though she had been raised in the Church and had never had kids, as she shot back to this one—or they hinted that she herself was a criminal in some undefined way. When Joss was nice he called her Radio Lady; when he was less than nice he'd ask her if she brought her "goofer dust." She had wanted to pull out the pepper spray she carried and give him a nice shot of it. She never did, but she fantasized. Sometimes the nastiness from Joss was less subtle, and words were said that she didn't even like to think. Words that barely touched her but still she had their effect.

She tried to forget everything. *Get Joss out of my head. Get him out.*

What came into her head instead was the moment when she was seven years old, when she had gone to the Getaway for the first time, when her grandfather had died, and she held his gold watch in her hand, and in just a few minutes had experienced the last moments of his life. His left arm felt as if it were splintering, and he grasped it with his right arm, and he kept saying words over and over again that made no sense to her. She was terrified by the aloneness of the experience, by the dark room it put her in, and by having to be there as she watched him die, alone, in a nursing home bed when he was supposed to be recovering from heart surgery.

Then she was in the Getaway in her mind again. She was alone there, and no light came up.

After several minutes of trying she opened her eyes again. The room was anything but the gray feeling she had in her head (her moods, as far as she was concerned, had colors, and the mood now, for her, was charcoal gray, like a dark mist). The floor was a black shiny marble, although Cali assumed it was fake, because it looked too good and, in its own way, too cheap against the more expensive-looking white rugs that looked as if animals had been killed just so someone could walk across the floor without getting his bare feet cold. The cops stood there. Detective Detweiler sat in the chair, looking up at her. At least he believed in her.

"Nothing."

Someone swore in the back of the room, and Cali's eyes flashed. "Look, I get a bunch of cops breathing down my neck." She looked directly over at Colin Joss. He would've been handsome if his entire aura weren't hideous.

Detweiler held his hands up defensively. "Okay, okay."

Joss snorted. "What the hell is she going on about? We have work to do. This is a waste of time."

Cali remained silent and tried to keep her anger in check. It was her temper that had gotten the better of her once before and had created distrust. She glanced at Colin Joss. He was handsome and pale and blond, and on some level she knew he wanted to caress her. The thought disgusted her, but it was better than the other thought that crept into her mind when she looked at him. He also wanted to kill her. To smother her. To stop her altogether.

She pulled back.

It was just a room—they called it the hot room of the crime scene—and there were six cops on hand, all getting their shoeprints all over everything, but Det had not been able to stop that. He needed her. He trusted her.

Trust, she thought. Closing her eyes again.

But there was nothing.

This was why she'd been called in: she was psychic, had been since the day she was born, according to her grandmother, and her specialty was psychometry, which meant she could hold an object associated with, in this case, the murder of a young woman and, if the situation was right, find out something about the murderer or victim that might help in the investigation. The scene was fresh—the murder had only occurred three hours earlier. The forensics expert had come through and collected, and the photographer had snapped, and the body had finally been moved. That was when Det had called her up to the apartment at Seventy-second and Central Park West.

Behind her closed eyes, Cali could not get Colin Joss out of her mind. It bothered her that one prick in the police force could cause her so much grief. *Psychic grief,* she smiled to herself. *Psychotic grief,* she played with the phrase in her head. The first time they'd met, on a fairly routine homicide that the department still hadn't been able to solve after three months, Joss had asked, "What are you?" and she had told him that she was a psychic who seemed to have a knack for what was called telemetry.

But he had persisted, "No, I mean, what are you? Your name: it sounds fake. But then, you're the radio lady, right? You make up all that bullshit about people's problems and you make up a name to go with it. You ain't black, you ain't white, you ain't Chinese, but you're a mutt or something, right?" To which she'd replied with a slap; Joss had taken it, but she knew it would not end with a slap with a guy like that. Usually Det kept Colin Joss away when she was around.

She had said to him then, "My name is Calista Nytbird, and yes, I changed the spelling of my last name slightly. So what? My mother was Chinese and Scottish, my father was African-American and Cherokee. I guess we're just everything that makes up America, and you're just some guy whose grandfather came over from England fifty years ago." It wasn't the most mature—or even smart—reply in the world, but she hadn't given a damn. Still, it started a minor war between them that wasn't going to end any time soon.

God, I hate knowing he's here in this room. I feel like he's just going to interfere with any work I do here.

She decided to go ahead and tell Det to clear the place. She opened her eyes and was about to say something when she realized that she was still in the hot room, only the murder was happening, right now, in front of her.

Her inner vision began, and she got the feeling again, of a kind of fear that was nearly exciting—and this scared her more than the look of hunger in the killer's eyes.

2

The man glanced back, as if he could see Cali *(but he can't. I know he can't. He's just feeling something. He's just hearing a sound in the hall).* He had a thick mane of dark hair, and his skin was bright red from his fury. In his left hand was the broken glass, and in his free hand, the woman. She was slim, blond, frail—her white blouse was torn, and she was trying to push a table against the closet door.

Cali looked up at the door. It was narrow.

A tiny closet.

Why would this woman do that when a man was about to slash her with broken glass? The smell of whiskey and cologne mingled in the air, and Cali noticed that the room was actually chilly. Cali glanced around the room and saw that the air conditioner was turned on high. She smelled something else—what was it? Something like . . . peppermints. It was odd—the scent of fury in the air, the knowledge of an impending murder, and the smell of peppermints.

The man played out his role (Cali tried not to think of it as murder when she went into these states, because it would make her crawl under a table or weep for days; she just thought of it as a replay of a movie in her mind, and it kept her safe). The woman shrieked briefly, and then she was quiet. Cali felt her heart racing but tried not to look directly as the man kept stabbing the woman, more curious about the closet door and the table.

She walked across the room, to the table, stepping around the man, who was now on the floor, on his knees, hunched over the woman's body.

What's behind there? What would she be trying to hide from him in her last moments of life?

Then Cali felt some kind of shuddering feeling go through her flesh. It was as if human fingers were tickling her beneath the skin.

There was something awful coming.

Something she didn't want to have to see.

Inside that little closet was something terrible. Something she didn't want to be inside this room to see. To know.

But the man made her face it.

He rose from the woman and, wiping his hand over his bloodied mouth, staggered to the table. He pulled it back and grabbed the doorknob to the closet.

It was locked.

He went back to the woman's body and went through her pockets but found nothing.

"You bitch!" he shouted.

He stared straight at Cali, who stood before the closet door. "You goddamn bitch, you made me do this! You came here and you knew I would have to do this, and now you just wait there for me and play this game!"

Cali had never experienced this before. He was yelling at her? He could see her? He could sense her?

The thought occurred to her: Perhaps he was psychic as well.

But no, his eyes looked through her. He was yelling at someone else. Someone she couldn't see. Was he tormented?

Then she felt it.

Like icy fingers tickling her spine.

Something else was there. Someone else—a presence was in that room. More than just the man and the dead woman and Cali.

Something . . .

She turned and looked at the closet door.

Whatever . . . whoever . . . it was. Inside that closet. That small closet.

And then she was wrenched from the sense memory of the murder.

3

Cali Nytbird opened her eyes.

That awful feeling again. Whenever it happened. Whenever she had to come back to reality from a vision. It was like getting socked in the solar plexus, getting the wind knocked out of her. Every single time. It was never pleasant, but she had learned, over the years since her ability had manifested itself, to swallow the nausea and the sense of displacement.

It always took her a moment or two to remember to breathe. She glanced at Detweiler, who still watched her. He was good with her this way. He wasn't like the other detectives and cops. He had some empathy for her situation.

Basically, he believed.

"You see it?"

She nodded. "I'll describe him to Marie, but he's going to be hard to find. He killed her yesterday. Not today."

"Impossible," Detweiler said, and then grinned. "All right, all right. The air conditioner, right?"

"It was freezing in here when he killed her. He turned it up so high, it might as well have been February in the middle of Central Park. It kept her fresh." Cali hated even describing the victim as *fresh*. But it was true. She was surprised Detweiler hadn't figured this out.

"So he's been back at least once to turn off the air conditioning."

Cali shrugged. "I guess so. I don't know that. Someone turned it off." Then she pointed at the closet door. She glanced over at one of the cops. "What's in there?"

The cop smirked. (*They all despise me,* she thought.) "Just what you'd think would be in a closet."

"That's no answer," Detweiler said, giving the cop a dismissive look.

"Sir, it has some coat hangers and shoes."

"Locked or unlocked?" Cali asked.

"Unlocked now," the cop said, his voice a monotone. He would ignore her and just do his job. "We forced it."

"Mind if I look?" Cali asked.

"Be my guest," Detweiler said.

Cali went over and curled her fingers around the glass doorknob. A light shock. She drew her hand back, and then touched it again. A brief vision flared within her mind:

A little boy of eleven or so stood before her in a darkened room. He wore a light coat and jeans and sneakers and a T-shirt with some words on it. What did the T-shirt say? She could see it well. His hair was strawberry blond, and his face was freckled. He had dark circles under her eyes.

Cali knew that the boy was already dead. This was something other than a living being. She had heard about entities, although she had never believed much in them. They were hitchhikers to some extent. They latched on and didn't let go.

She let go of the doorknob. Without turning around, she said, "A little boy. The name I'm getting is Sam. Maybe Tim. He was about ten or eleven years old. That's about all I know."

And then Cali felt something else. Something forbidding. Something dark.

Do not open this door, she told herself. *Do not.*

She had never felt this before. She had gone into three investigations and had been frightened at times by the visions, but she had never felt this. It was taboo—that was the sense she had. She must not open the door.

She turned back to face Detweiler. She looked up at the faces of the cops. They seemed blank to her. Erased. Something was clouding over in her mind. Something was scratching at her thoughts.

"I . . . I can't open it."

"Cali?" Detweiler asked.

"It's unlocked," one of the cops said.

"No," Cali said, glancing at the rookie who'd made the comment. Then back at Det. She didn't want him to see her like this. She was afraid she'd start crying in front of them, and she fought against the tears, because to the cops it would look like weakness and what they'd called "femaleness," instead of what it was: rage and sadness. *Hang tough, Cali. Don't let them see you break down over this. It's a vision. It's an image. Like a movie. It's not happening right now. It happened a while ago.* "You don't understand. I . . . can't . . . open . . . it. Something . . . something's stopping me."

And then she felt a gentle touch on her hand.

A child's voice whispered, *Poor old lady, she swallowed a fly.* Something grabbing on to her. Holding on. Embracing. Just around her waist. She opened her mouth to scream, but immediately it felt as if a hand had been clapped over her mouth, silencing her.

Chapter Ten

1

Later, she and Det were having dinner at Big Chef, in Jersey City, a few blocks from her apartment. She had taken him up on his offer to drive her home, and his shyness apparently was eroding, because as soon as they'd passed through the Holland Tunnel he'd asked if she was feeling well enough for dinner, and as soon as she'd said yes, he asked her where the best Chinese restaurant was "out in the Joisey wilderness." She glanced over at him: He was a Papa Bear, and she liked the feeling of being near him. He was too old for her (that would be what Bev would tell her), even though it was only a ten-year difference. He was too mean for her—he could bark orders to his men far too easily, and sometimes he could be cold toward her, as well. The past two weeks of his no-call streak was good enough for that.

But there was something so compelling about his presence, she could put those other things on hold.

He had this way of cocking his head to the side when he was listening to her that she found endearing, though not exactly reassuring this particular night. His head was going to the side a bit too much, as if he had no way in hell of understanding what she was trying to say.

She let him finish his egg roll before continuing. "All right, here's what it was like. It was like being taken hostage. By something in that apartment."

"The killer?"

"No. In fact," she said, taking a discreet sip of the sweet and sour soup, "I would guess even he's scared." She paused, savoring the taste of the soup. "This soup is good. It's different from the other restaurants around here. Want some?"

"No, thanks." Det waved away the spoon she offered. "Wait. He's scared of who?"

"The kid. I'm pretty sure it's him, although I didn't see him beyond my initial vision. Maybe our killer killed this boy. Or maybe not. I wish I could be more precise . . . but it's not like that. I want to be careful not to add anything other than what I actually felt."

"Wait. Gloria Franco didn't have any kids."

"Yes, she did."

"No," Det said, reaching across the table.

If he touches my hand in condescending sympathy, I'm going to throw soup at him, she thought.

Very lightly, Det touched the ends of her fingers. "She really didn't. She lived alone. There are no records of her having a kid."

"So say the neighbors."

"So says the city of New York."

"And it's wrong," Cali said, bringing her hands into her lap. "She had a baby. Maybe she didn't acknowledge the boy. Maybe someone else raised him."

Det nodded. "Okay. So someone else raised it. Or something."

"A little boy, Det. Not an *it.* A boy. And thanks for the vote of confidence."

"Hey, I got all the confidence in the world in you. You know that."

"All right, so here's my guess: He was raised in that apartment. Gloria Franco raised him, and he lived in that closet. Sam. Or Tim."

"That little . . . it's practically a crawlspace."

"I'm sure it's happened at least once in human history," Cali said. This was one of her favorite phrases to volley back at Det whenever he became incredulous.

"Okay."

"So this kid is raised practically in secret."

"Tell me why."

Cali shrugged. "Who knows? Mama's crazy. Something's wrong with the whole picture we have, right? Gloria is murdered. Nothing is taken from the apartment. It's a fancy—if tacky—apartment, and some of that junk in there would bring in some solid cash. Including all that jewelry she had. As far as we know, it's a motiveless crime."

"There's always a motive. Even if it's not apparent. We catch the killer, we know the motive."

"Maybe. But I have to tell you, I think something else went on in that room that day of the murder."

"And what's that?"

Cali held her breath a second before saying it.

Then, "An entity was there. The boy."

"His ghost?" Det cracked a smile.

"No," Cali said. "An entity. A being that looked like the boy. Something else. Something I . . . well, I don't understand. I just have heard that they exist like this. That they don't let go of something. Or someone."

2

They made love that night with an intensity that nearly drove her mad. Cali was not one to take lovemaking lightly, and she had only slept with him twice since they'd been working together (fooling herself that it might be love, but she knew it might just be loneliness and lack of planning), but there was an energy she and Det seemed to be creating, in working together. She couldn't control it, and her heat for him erupted in his sedan that night.

She had told him to pull over, which he did, bewildered though he'd been. She'd wrapped her arms around his waist and leaned into him for what should've been a chaste kiss—but it felt like lightning going through her when their lips touched, and she wasn't sure what was happening or why she felt the steam in her thighs and the thirst in her throat for his love, but she did, and she let it go. She straddled him in the car, neither one drawing their clothing off, but the kisses burned and she felt an animal run loose within her; she saw his eagerness in his eyes and in his returned passion; and her mind seemed to have closed down. Somehow they made it to her apartment, and she raced up the stairs with Det following behind, huffing and puffing a bit because he wasn't used to running up three flights of a brownstone after a woman. They made it as far as the kitchen table, and she drew him against her, whispering obscenities in his ears, words that she had never dared say aloud—

And somewhere in there, somewhere between raising her hips

over his face, between the grunting and groaning and vile whispers, she knew that it was not Cali doing this, it was Gloria Franco, the dead woman. This was her passion, her passion with the man she loved, the man who would kill her. Cali could not control it. Det matched her every move, and turned as she turned, and held tight to her when she bucked backwards against his erection; and the wildness continued like the beat of a heart racing toward attack.

Cali felt drugged and was nearly watching herself ride Det's body, even the pain she felt, the sharp pains along her wrists and ankles, as if someone was holding her down; even those caused a pleasurable sensation. She closed her eyes for a moment, and when she opened them, the other man—not Det—was inside her, and she looked at her porcelain white arms and her small breasts and the way her hips undulated against him. She turned to him (Cali did, but knew she was Gloria; she had somehow gotten infected with Gloria's memory in that room of death) and the dark-haired man with the blue piercing eyes reached up and covered her mouth with his large hand, and then the first stab of death came into her.

3

This was not the first time she had felt this strange form of possession by the dead. It had happened early in her career as a psychic, when she held a scarf that had belonged to an elderly man who had gone missing; his essence came into her briefly, and she walked to the end of a pier in Chelsea and was able to show the police the precise spot where he had stood and leaped joyfully to his death. It had taken all she had not to jump in the river at that point, but the dead man had so much bliss upon ending his life—and his pain—that it was fairly easy to resist the pull.

But Gloria Franco was another story. She was an animal of a woman. She was, Cali surmised, ruled by how she felt, by her desires, her hungers.

And she knew something else about Gloria Franco now.

She knew that Gloria Franco had set up her own murder.

4

Det still gasped, practically collapsing on the kitchen floor tiles. "Baby, that was . . . you were a lust monster or something."

"Shocking," Cali said, feeling suddenly exhausted and reserved. She coughed; felt embarrassed; felt relieved that whatever had been driving her through this sexual frenzy had evaporated like mist. "That's all we can call it."

She glanced around the kitchen—her shoes were near the door, her hose hung near the edge of the sink; his gray jacket had been flung down on the small rug next to the kitchen table and his tie and shirt were all crumpled in a corner.

"I've never seen you like that," Det said, sitting up, drawing his slacks back on.

Cali closed her eyes. "That's because it wasn't me. It was something else. Maybe Gloria Franco." That should've been a joke, but as soon as she said it, it didn't sound hilarious at all. It sounded as if it was true.

"Jesus," Det said, shaking his head.

5

"That was probably the hottest sex I've ever had," Cali said with some regret, ten minutes later. She had gotten an Amstel Light out of her refrigerator for him. It wasn't his favorite, but it was all she had in the way of beer. "And I was barely there to enjoy it." She had slipped into her flannel bathrobe, pulled tight at the waist, and wished she could just cuddle up with him for a while, but she was afraid that something else might come out within her again. She didn't want to ever feel that way again.

"How'd it happen?" Det asked. He had tried to hug her, or hold her, but she drew away from him each time.

Cali shrugged. "I guess being at the murder scene. Knowing the little boy was in that closet. Knowing more about Gloria than anyone knew . . . She was an adrenaline junkie, Det. Gloria wasn't into sex, she was into annihilation."

"Don't worry about that now. Oh, baby, I'm so sorry. If I had known, I would never . . ." Det said. He reached for her. "If I thought for a second it wasn't you . . ."

Cali pulled away. "It felt like . . ."

Det looked at her, his face shiny with sweat. "Rape?" He cringed a bit when he said it. He took a long swig from the beer bottle.

"No." Cali shook her head. "Not like that. It felt good, don't get me wrong. It just . . . well, it was like someone else was there. Watching me. Feeling what I was feeling. Pushing me on in some way that didn't feel like me. But not like rape."

"Jesus," Det said, wiping his hand across his face. "I wish I had known."

"How could you have?" Cali said. "As far as you knew, that was all me." Then she looked directly into his eyes. "Do you love me?"

"You know I do."

"I feel dirty now," she said, hugging herself as if she was freezing. "I'd like you to go home now. I feel dirty, and that probably seems dumb, but it just is. Sorry."

"You sure?"

She nodded.

6

"I hate to leave you alone after this. I feel . . . somehow . . . responsible," he said weakly. He was just out the door of her apartment when he turned around. His eyes were so solemn, she wanted to overcome her resistance and just give him a big hug before he left, but she felt cold inside. Cold and yet still very needy. "I feel . . ."

"How could you be responsible, Det? It was beyond anything I've ever felt. Part of me wonders—I mean, right now, I wonder if maybe I didn't imagine it. Maybe it was me. Maybe it was. But whatever that was, it really wasn't your doing."

"I know, but . . ."

"I'll be fine," Cali said. "I'm exhausted."

"Friday?"

"I'm going up to that house."

"Oh, yeah. The experiment."

"Yep."

"You going to do a broadcast from up there?"

"No. They won't let me bring anyone. No recording equipment. Nothing."

"Not even me?"

"No way." Cali laughed softly.

"How long?"

"Less than a week. Oodles of bucks for a long weekend."

"Not a bad deal. You think there'll be ghosts up there?"

Cali paused, trying to block the feeling of having sensed the little boy at the apartment in the Mohegan Hotel. "Not like I believe in ghosts."

"Okay, whatever. Residue. That's what you call it, right? Entity and residue."

"Mmm-mmm. Psychic residue. Like a tape recording. Just like when I hold things."

"You know," Det said, a brief hesitation in his voice. "You know, sometimes all this stuff you do frightens me a little. For your sake. I want . . . I want you to be happy, Cal."

"Yeah, I know. Me, too."

"Sometimes," he began, but she knew what he would probably say next. Either it was going to be, "Sometimes I don't know whether to believe you really can do this or if we're all just fooling ourselves." Or something along those lines. He'd almost said it before.

"Don't," she said. "I'll see you Monday, and by then you'll probably have Franco's killer." He hadn't heard her; she shut the door gently; listened for his footsteps as he went down the stairs; she latched the door and turned the dead bolt.

Even locked away in her one-bedroom apartment, Cali didn't know how she would keep out the dead woman or that little boy.

Chapter Eleven

1

A drink would help.

Beer was not really her drug of choice. She got a bottle of Sterling Vineyard's merlot from the cabinet under the microwave and managed to uncork it without stabbing her thumb more than twice. The first sip was delicious, and she closed her eyes, just savoring it. It had a warm but crisp flavor, fruity and mild. The second sip made her thirsty, and she drank the rest too fast. A second glass of wine went down smooth, but her nerves remained frazzled. "Don't get completely drunk just because you're scared," she said aloud, as if her own voice would make her feel less alone.

She was almost happy when the phone rang as she was flipping through the cable channels, finding nothing to watch on the nearly seventy channels available to her.

"Okay, the dirt," her sister said before Cali could get a breath out of her mouth.

"Oh, Bev. It's been too much of a night."

"Come on, I want to know. Did you slap him or did you kiss him?"

"What do you think?"

"I think you should pull out that little gun you own and point it right at him and tell him to get out of your life. But that's only what I think."

"And . . . that's your solution," Cali said, having to smile despite herself. The wine brought a whole new buzz, and now Bev was getting goofy.

"Tell me about the murder."

"You know I can't. Not yet."

"Damn. How about a hint?"

"All right. It involves the kind of people we hate."

"You mean rich people with inheritances?"

"Yep."

"So it was a money murder?"

"Bev. No. It was a murder. That's all."

"A woman killed her boyfriend who treated her like shit half the time?"

Cali looked at her telephone, as if she had no idea what crazy person was talking on the other end. Then she hung it up. The warm sisterly feeling was gone. Cali didn't want to talk about the homicide. She didn't really want to talk about anything. She just wanted someone to talk to. Someone who would just listen.

She went to feed her cat, and afterward she opened up her notebook computer on the couch to check her email. Sitting in her inbox: twelve notes she hadn't opened in a few days, just because she hadn't wanted to write back to anyone. She looked through them, deleting as she went. And suddenly a ding sound went off, and a pop-up window arrived on her laptop's screen. It was Bev, sending an Instant Message to her.

Sorry for digging! Bev wrote.

Hi, Sneaky, Cali wrote back.

Hang up the phone on me, will you? So what's the deal?

The deal is, I don't want to talk about any of this. How are the girls?

Getting competitive for my bathroom, that's how they are. And Jimmy's not keeping up with math, and Mike blames the teacher. You know who I blame.

Jimmy's not going to be a math whiz, I guess.

You guess good. He can still do better than a C. So you okay?

Of course.

You didn't sound all that okay on the phone.

If I tell you something, Cali wrote. Then stopped herself.

Bev wrote back: *If you tell me something, I will keep it a secret. I promise. Remember the promises I've always kept?*

True.

You love him?

I don't know.

He hurt you?

No. Not hurt. It's something else. Something I haven't really talked about with you. Or him. Yet.

Several seconds went by before she wrote anything further.

Then Cali typed in: *I think it's getting worse.*

Worse?

Like when I was eight and I couldn't stop it. Like in church when I started that fit.

Oh, Cali.

It's taking me over again. I had a blackout, only not quite a blackout. Something else took over. It wasn't good. It was pretty awful. But it happened after. It happened when I was in his car. After dinner. And then up here. Someone took me over and used me for something, Bev. I don't know what. I can't really explain it.

But it was like those fits, only I didn't start attacking anyone. It wasn't like that. It was . . .

Oh my God.

It was sexual. It was awful. I feel really dirty. I feel really disgusting.

I'll get in the car and drive up tonight. You shouldn't be alone. Not after that.

No, I'm fine. I have Gelfling.

A cat is not going to make you feel secure.

Yes, he is. He'll sleep next to my face and I'll have cat dreams all night and feel completely secure. Seriously. I'm fine now. Just shaken.

Not stirred.

Absolutely, Cali typed. *'Night, Sis.*

'Night, noodle-nose. Call me tomorrow.

Will do. And thanks, Cali typed. She was about to write "Nighty-night" when a new Instant Message appeared on her screen.

2

It's me, the message read, but the sender's identification was some screwy set of symbols that were unreadable.

Me who?

Me the one who lives inside you now. POOR OLD LADY SHE SWALLOWED A FLY I DON'T KNOW WHY SHE SWALLOWED A FLY PERHAPS SHE'LL DIE.

3

Cali stared at the words on the screen. She quickly went to her Buddy List on the screen and blocked all Instant Messages. Telling herself it was just the usual Internet nut, she checked for shoes at Bluefly.com. She didn't find the shoes she wanted but ended up buying an Amy Chan purse she'd been lusting after for nearly a month and then went to look at books at Barnesandnoble.com and bought a few mysteries, including two of her favorites, Carolyn Hart's latest cozy mystery, and a book called *Houses With Spirit: Investigations into the Paranormal* by Jack Fleetwood and the PSI Vista Foundation. She had met Fleetwood twice, at conferences in Manhattan, and he had been urging her to join him and a few others for some investigation up the Hudson Valley. Which she had decided was the right thing to do. Get out of town in a few days. Get away from all this.

Get away from the Getaway.

Maybe I need to read up on it before I commit to anything.

Then she got offline and shut down her laptop. She checked the latch and dead bolt on her front door and checked all the windows. All locked. Outside her bedroom window, a siren was howling. She glanced out at Wayne Street and saw the usual drunks hanging out on the corner, near the bar that seemed to be open at all hours; then across Grove to the brief line of shops there.

One o'clock and all is well.

Then she went to get her gun, putting it on her bedside table just in case she got scared.

Just in case someone was thinking of bothering her.

She slept that night with Gelfling, her cat, snuggled under her arm, but even in the comfort and warmth, it took another three hours to fall asleep.

In her dream: a little boy's voice whispered, *poor old lady, she swallowed a fly. I don't know why she swallowed a fly. Perhaps she'll die.*

PART FOUR

Frost

Chapter Twelve

1

Someone took a pitchfork and rammed it into the freshly turned earth.

For some reason the words came to Frost Crane in, not a dream or a vision, but a voice.

The voice was his own, and he said the words aloud, and he said more, but it felt like he was spilling, as if he had opened his lips and the pins and toads of someone else's mind were pouring from within him:

Pitchfork threatens. Fire burns. Birds fly. Glass breaks. Nail holds. Bird wings. Step closer. Wild birds. Red sun. Shall not, shall not, shall not.

And then he began chanting something, some kind of prayer or hunting call, a series of words within a rhythm that he could not understand.

That was the beginning for him, and it struck him rather late in life, this talent.

Unlike his love for gambling, in this game it always came up aces.

2

From Frost's Journal

"We dream through our lives.

"Lulled by television and movies and books, these fictions of heavens we allow others to give us while they sell Coke and Tide and Mercury Sables, while they take our own dreams away, and these beautiful celebrities who we believe are fully awake while we dream, living the lives we know we can't awaken to.

"Then one day, when we wake to what our lives have become, we long for the dream again. We find other dreams. We search for dreams. We pay for dreams. Words like freedom and illusion mix together until we think we're all individuals sitting down on a Monday night to watch the latest TV drama or on a Thursday afternoon, a television judge presiding over the lives we can't possibly live, when in fact, millions of us are there; or in the theaters, as we watch Tom Cruise make love, or Arnold Schwarzenegger make war, or Katharine Hepburn knowing there is no difference between the two. Our dreams live our lives.

"We take the dreams available, because we have lost what brought us to the dreaming in the first place.

"The voices came to me and they said things I don't understand. And now others are trying to make something out of them to say that I can prophesy things. This is crazy. I know it. All I'm saying is we all know these things, what will happen in the near-future, maybe a few minutes from now, because I'm convinced that time bends somehow within our consciousness, so that we can sniff out the near-future (not the future, because I did not predict the train crash outside New Haven except ten minutes before it happened, and I only happened to be on television in Hartford then by the slightest coincidence, so if I hadn't let it out of my mouth then, maybe I wouldn't have made the 'CBS Evening News,' and maybe I wouldn't have undergone these damn tests and this damn study and maybe I'd be living a normal life again.)

"I don't believe in the normal or the ordinary. I think that's Death. I think the ordinary human life is like the shit of existence, and it lives under my feet, and I refuse to step back into it, to become mired into that cosmic crap known as the human heart or the human condition, because in fact, as we all know, it sucks. Can you watch your father lose himself to Alzheimer's (as I have and as many of you have), watch a man who is balanced and steady and sharp, a man who took care of his family, damn it, and did good most of his life, a man with conscience and care, a man who loved his son and whose son loved him, who now has no idea whose face belongs to who and is unsure as to whether he ever had an existence before ten minutes ago? Or a woman who once you looked up to as "mother," who guided and prodded you and created a sense of the wealth of the world and the sights to be seen and the love to be nurtured, who has become bitter and cold, and then breaks parts of her body just to feel the pain of life rather than the numbness of the everlasting pills? Is that where ordinary life leads?

"I have felt it myself, in the world I lived in before the moment of my liberation. The moment before I got the smell of it, the voices that came into me and took me out of this human excrement called 'ordinary life,' where the weak thrive and the strong are crushed and people who call themselves good and Christian and kind are out there stomping on people, stomping on them, while I have to watch it in silence (before the voices, mind you, before I HEARD WHAT I HEARD) and just be ordinary and typical and shut my mouth up with my own fist to keep from saying what I'm really thinking.

"Well, you can tell where this is going now, this ramble, this brutal spit in the eye of the world that I find reprehensible and lacking. My mother, dying by her own mind, into an ordinary sunset, and my father, his mind in some other dimension as he treats me with the kindness of one who can't remember, and my wife—my ex-wife—suing me for this, suing me for that, well, she can have the ordinary house and the ordinary doom.

"I will tell you a secret, Dear Diary.

"I will show you my soul.

"My soul is a good one. Despite my nastiness in this little leatherbound book. My soul is a good one, and for 98 percent of all life I intend to do good and be kind and generous, but there is 2 percent of me that is completely monstrous. Now, think about this: Most humans are monstrous at one time or another of their lives. I don't mean they all murder, though I would guess a lot have murder in their hearts. But most humans have done bad things; some, more than others. Some, inadvertently. Hell, you'd have to be one of those Hindu monks who can't even kill mosquitoes for fear of harming karma and the universe, if you lived your life without doing something bad. So, let's say I live until I'm seventy-five. That's pretty much what I'm planning. So out of seventy-five years, I do good, say, sixty-eight of those years. This is not a bad life, right? And let's say, seven of those years, I do some bad stuff. Nothing major. Not like pushing a button to send off a nuclear warhead or something. Bad in a way that maybe only I know it's bad, and maybe whoever was the immediate recipient knows it's bad. Okay, so I do bad stuff for seven years total of a life of seventy-five years.

"Does that make me bad?

"Monstrous.

"Give you another what-have-you: say a guy is twenty, and robs a store. In robbing the store he shoots—and kills—the cashier. The guy gets caught, and by twenty-one he's serving a life sentence. Now, twenty years later, he's out. Some people call this fair, some call it wrong, but think about it: if the guy lives 'til ninety, the murder of the cashier was not his life. It was a little monstrous moment, am I right? It was a mistake which seemed right—for him—at the time.

"Another thing I've learned in my whole 'fabric of reality shredding.' Maybe life is predetermined, and you can't go against your fate.

"Of course, I wouldn't tell this to anyone, but I have to write it here, because I am beginning to suspect this is true. After all, the voices tell me about things that are going to happen. I believe I'm effecting reality by speaking about them. But maybe it's all written down somewhere, and we just step in the dogshit of existence.

"You with me on this?

"Maybe the guy who shot the cashier was acting a part, and his real life was about prison, and his real life was about getting over the monstrosity of his youth.

"Just one little thing I'd thought I'd share: I awoke one day with blood on my fingertips.

"I have no idea whose blood it was. Maybe it's mine. Maybe it's not.

"I wallow in the extraordinary. These voices I claim for my

own personal revelation, and every one of you in the world could have this, as well, if you'd open yourself to it. Just open your mind to what can come from it, let your body be a doorway to a higher consciousness, you fools, and know that to be like this is to be cursed above the ordinary and to be exalted beyond the pulp of flesh and blood."

3

Frost Crane awoke from the dream that had been his marriage of eleven years, the dream of what his job had been, of what his future had been, and was plunged into a brief reality. The reality came back, at times, like a burp of cosmic proportions, and while he tried to make this burp happen often, it only came to him now and again. But when it did arrive, it illuminated the landscape of life for him.

The phenomenon began with curses.

Frost knew the moment he said them that he'd regret the string of obscenities just loosed from his clenched soul. They'd just drawn up and thrown themselves out at Maria, and she had taken it like a good soldier with a minimum of china destruction and only one major obscenity back at him.

"You loser," she said, and crossed the small kitchen to the sink, the plate she'd been carrying dropped to the floor, smashed with cranberry sauce and marshmallow-fucked yams and wishbone—yes, Thanksgiving, he thought as he watched her, this had to happen during Thanksgiving dinner with her mother and father in their dining room, with a baby in the crib, with his brother and his brother's boyfriend probably trying to decide when exactly they should leave, and with the two pumpkin pies Maria had fixed still cooling on top of the Hotpoint stove.

"I just can't do it anymore," he said.

"Now?" she asked. "Now? Right now? You couldn't have done this yesterday. You couldn't have done this the day after tomorrow, after they'd left? It had to be today. Five o'clock. Before the pumpkin pie?"

His hands felt heavy with nothing to hold. "I feel dead."

"You feel dead," she said. "Well, that's news. Just hold it in. Just now. Hold it in. Forget about feeling dead. For one hour. For one hour in eleven years, you go to that dining room with me and you forget about how you feel."

"You're right," he said. "I am a fucking loser."

Her voice dropped to a whisper. "Someone else?"

"No. I told you. It's uncontrollable."

"This need?"

"Yes."

She laughed, turning to him again. Her face was slick with tears and perspiration, and her light brown hair clung to her neck. "Please tell me this is a prank. Some kind of joke? Please don't tell me this is about getting me back for the time with the percolator."

"No. It's not. I'm sorry."

"Christ," she said. "Why don't you go for a long walk? Through the garage. You don't need to go back in there. I'll tell them the truth. I'll tell them. I'll make it work."

"It doesn't work," he said.

And then the voice came through him again. A wind, is what it felt like. An inspiration.

An obscenity.

4

His walk was a long one, after all.

He had begun believing that what he'd felt was insanity. He didn't feel any different when he went into the garage, around the mess of their bicycles, the Maytag, the boxes of books he'd never unpacked four years before when they'd moved in, and then, when he pressed the button, the garage door swung open—twilight there among the sticks of trees. It was arctic cold—and all he had on was a red sweater his mother had given him the year before as a Christmas gift. His mother, still the farmer's wife. The farmer was dead—Frost's father, who was equal parts laborer and warm papa to a brood of children, of which Frost was the middle child. His mother, hair pulled back, wrinkles like lines of corn, ever the farmer's wife. *The bales! she would say when he and his brothers were out working. Pitch the hay. Pitch it, boys, you Frost, your back, use your back, you're strong, pitch, supper'll be good!* Now he was removed from it all, the sweater a reminder of his mother's industry: The wool was from their sheep. The wool was her love, and it held him in the world he'd stepped into after leaving the farm to his older brothers: He was a suburban farmer now, but it was time to pitch the hay and harvest and shuck and make the new crops grow, the crops of suburban quiet, the harvest of discontent. The suburban homes along the stretch of blankness called Willowbranch Drive were undisturbed by the chill—the straggles of trees at the edge of the curbs, the abandoned tricycle at the edge of a quarter-acre lawn, the glimpses of other families at their windows with wineglasses, with pies, with all the things that each had and believed that only they owned it.

His shoes hurt—they were the two–hundred–dollar pair Maria

had bought for him in the city, and he never had liked them. They were too formal. If he had his way, he would've changed into an old pair of sneakers. Into a ragged pair of jeans, the ones he could still fit into from college, the ones that made him feel young. At thirty, he was feeling old and ragged himself, but in khakis and hurting shoes and an Eddie Bauer shirt and a sweater—and it was all cast aside in his mind because he felt the presence within him, the Other, perhaps his own insanity.

He walked down Willowbranch, up Orchard, along Pepper Lane, into Belleview, until he came to the hills, the place where the suburban blight had not yet touched, and he went up into them to find the origin of the presence that had drawn words out of his mouth as he had sat with his brother and his brother's lover, and his mother- and father-in-law, and his wife at the dining room table and told them, in a booming voice, "The madman is among us, the murderer, he comes as a wolf in sheep's clothing, he is ravenous and here already only you sleepers refuse to wake," and then the profanities, and then he had run from the table to the kitchen, which was when his wife dropped the first china plate. But this was only his beginning with the gift that had appeared from nowhere, the mind within his mind awakening.

He became known for his predictions, for his ability to speak with the dear departed; that was the showbiz side of his life. He wrote a book called *Touching Tomorrow,* which sold in a half-assed sort of way, but it got him on Oprah, and by the time his second book came out, this one titled *The Spirit Realm: The Afterlife and How To Communicate with Our Loved Ones,* it was on the *New York Times* bestseller list for fourteen weeks, rising to a solid spot at number three. For anyone else, all of this would have been wonderful, but Frost's ex-wife managed to get all the money that taxes and the lawyers and an unscrupulous business manager hadn't managed to get; to say nothing of a rather leaky contract from Frost's publisher.

And also, his gambling. He gambled in Connecticut at Foxwoods, he gambled at Atlantic City, he gambled in Reno and Las Vegas, and he even gambled online.

He was sure the voices would help him win, but it didn't always happen that way. Sometimes, if he was playing the one-armed bandit, he'd plug the quarters in and come up with a good thousand-dollar win on an investment of maybe three or four hundred dollars; but he didn't stop there. He'd plug the thousand back in and then end up losing a few hundred more. It was like farming—sometimes the crop was good, sometimes it was wasted, but he was a farmer after all, and putting the coins in the machine was just like pitching hay with the pitchfork; it seemed useless at times, but it rewarded him at other times.

Sometimes it was a thousand more dollars; sometimes it was a bad crop.

The voices never came to him when he gambled. The fabric of reality never ripped apart in the casinos.

Was he poor? No doubt he felt poor, but his bills were often covered, and he lived modestly and chintzily, biting pennies as if he could draw blood from them, and then using those pennies to turn into quarters for the slot machines.

5

And it should've been enough, he knew. To wake up from the dream of his life, to the truth.

But, of course, the voices didn't just tell him good, sweet things. The voices told him about the shadows, as well. They asked for favors. They wanted a servant.

He found he could not resist the voices inside him.

And one dawn, he found himself standing over the dead body of a young woman.

He remembered her from a dream. He remembered her with her long, elegant fingernails with beautiful, small, and perfect designs upon them. Her face, so fresh and sorrowful, as if she'd just lost a great love of her life and now was reduced to being at a crossroads—a bus station, perhaps, with a light rain falling, and her life was nearly half over, she would think, but he knew that her life was nearly over.

The voices again, yes, he was sure they had brought him to this woman with one desire:

To take away her hurt.

And now, looking down at her, he wasn't sure how much of it he had dreamed and how much had been his own doing.

She was dead, but more than that, she was mutilated.

He pressed his hands against the sides of his scalp and massaged, hoping the blood would go to his brain and he could remember what had happened. He had a slight panic, not from fear of discovery but from the fear that he had no control. That the voices were the power, and he was merely the pawn. But something had bent in time and reality, he was sure. Something had curved in the light of day—he had not killed her, but somehow his encounter with her had turned liquid and her molecules had shifted and boiled and turned around, and he vaguely remembered that her flesh had become like Turkish taffy in his fingers, and he had pulled the sweet, flowing thickness from her and spun the sugary confection of her life around and around and around in his hands. He had not killed her, but he had somehow made her atoms change their orbits and melt against each other, and the voices had managed it all, had orchestrated it, but they had not been the power.

He had been the power.

Her clothes were torn, her face barely recognizable. He didn't know if he had done the damage to her. He only knew he stood over her as the sun's first light came up, and he was in the woods. His body covered with sweat. His sweatshirt stained with what he presumed was her blood. He thought he might have tried to save her, perhaps from something that had lured her into these woods—some psycho who had brought her here, a demon lover who had then murdered her. And Frost had come upon her.

Or did I kill her? How could I not remember that? How could the voices come into me and do that?

And she was still there. Lingering. He felt her presence amid the great forest.

She was dead, but not dead.

Her voice was within him now.

All right. This is how you collect the voices, he thought. *Not every time, but sometimes. You bring them into you.*

You taste their souls.

Chapter Thirteen

1

He buried her deep in the woods—and by midafternoon he jogged back to his Chevy Suburban and felt the forgiveness of the dead woman with the razor grin on her face. Her voice was gathering together with the others within him. It was a power surge.

Don't do this often, he made a mental note. *Don't do this, but when you do, you grow a little, don't you? You feel a little more about things. You are more connected.*

He felt her grace and was redeemed.

After another hour or so, during which he drank himself into a state of oblivion with a phenomenally foul malt liquor, he wasn't sure if he had really done what he remembered doing. Had he buried a woman at all, or had the fabric of reality shredded a bit and he had seen someone else doing this? He could not be sure, although, as he knew that he himself was a basically decent person, he would not normally be a party to murder. Or, if he had murdered a woman, he would not hide her body in some wooded area. He would no doubt go to the authorities, primarily because he didn't like messes. Perhaps it had been a movie in his head: Perhaps the voices had transported him in his mind to a murder victim, but he had not in fact been there at all. Perhaps even the bit of blood on his sweatshirt (which he sliced into thousands of bits with a box cutter and then put each bit in various trash bags so that no one would ever sew the sweatshirt back together) had been imagined and was part of the hallucination that the voices brought to him.

He decided that he must've imagined it all; it must've been a blank spot.

Later, he knew there were other blank spots in his life like this. Times he could not account for his behavior. There were tastes in the back of his throat just as he opened his eyes to find himself driving to some unknown location, not remembering why he was on the road at all.

And then, when the shit hit the fan, so to speak, it was because of a middle-aged woman named Cathy who had nearly been killed by a bus and he had told her—moments before—what to do if the bus came at her. He didn't know her from Adam, as they say, but that didn't matter. The voices came out of him and told her which way to jump should the bus arrive too soon, and she had stared at him like he was crazy (people often did). But, apparently, the three-fifteen bus had arrived a few minutes early, right around the next corner of Oak Run and Graymeadow Drive, and she had indeed jumped a little to the right rather than her instinct, which was to scream and get hit, and her life had been spared. Now, this should've been a minor thing—for even the voices had been vague—but when Cathy told the story of her brief run-in with death (and the beginning of her lawsuit against the city bus line), it grew into a more prominent prediction.

It made its rounds, as gossip often does, until it became a local legend.

Then, when the voices came out of him again (against his will, mind you, because Frost did not want the attention), they came out big and blaring, and this time it was about schoolchildren at some school he had never heard of—a fire, the voices, said, and Death, and this, oddly enough, brought Frost to Hartford, Connecticut, for a local television broadcast about prophecy and second sight, and that was when he met Jack Fleetwood, who wanted to study him at some place called PSI Vista. It was also within that live broadcast that Frost had let the voices predict the train crash outside New Haven, a few minutes before the crash occurred.

This made him famous, and his desire to get away from ordinary life intensified.

Of course, he needed money for this.

PSI Vista offered him ten thousand dollars to stay at their headquarters for three months. He had laughed at first at the offer because he knew that as a best-selling author he should be worth more, but within him, he knew that he wasn't, and that he would need a fast infusion of easy cash in order to get by until Christmas. Ten thousand smackeroos would be a nice amount to take to Foxwoods and play the slots and turn it into maybe a hundred thousand clams or more. Then he could take that money and turn his life around. These are the things he told himself.

The PSI Vista headquarters were nothing more than a crumbly brownstone on Jane Street, two blocks from the Hudson River, in Manhattan. It was the home of Jack Fleetwood and his daughter, Miranda, an annoying teenager who seemed to have read every book ever written—at least, she knew all the ones Frost had ever heard of. Frost occupied the top-floor bedroom for his stay. A staff of three others worked the first two floors during the weekdays, and sometimes interesting guests dropped in. There were lots of books and videos about ghosts and psychic phenomena, and Frost enjoyed spending time going through it all. It felt educational, although some of it sounded suspiciously like bullshit to him. Still, it was cozy and clinical at the same time, with the vast library at the basement and first-floor level, as well as the two bedrooms and an office on the second floor, and the large suite on the third.

The only therapy that Frost refused during his stay was hypnosis; however, he was happy to talk about anything he knew about his extraordinariness whenever asked.

2

Interview Six
Subject: Frost Crane

Q: So let's get back to the nature of your experience.

Subject: You mean, the sweats?

Q: Sure. The fever. The feeling you get just before it comes on.

Subject: I feel like I'm going to vomit, basically. And then I feel good. Not just good, but so good, it's like I took a drug and I don't ever want to not feel that way. The sweats are only in the beginning. The cold feeling, too. And then I start to feel warm and bright.

Q: Bright?

Subject: Yeah, bright. Like a thousand flashbulbs go off, you know how that happens? I mean, you know how sometimes if you use a flash on a camera and it goes off, it does more than just light everything up, it sort of scorches it with light? It makes it brighter than it's supposed to be, and then you look at the picture later, and it looks just like normal light, but when you were there, taking the picture, it's like that flash painted over everything with this brightness. Like an essence of brightness.

Q: Like it's hyper-daylight?

Subject: More like the light ripped off the skin of the world, and it's what's underneath everything. It's light, only most people don't get it. Most people are ordinary. But see, I get it. I get the brightness, and I get to see under things. But it's like a ton of flashbulbs all going off, and it's only a glimpse, and the feeling fades fast. I kind of feel cold again, when it's gone.

Q: And the voices come then?

Subject: Right. After the brightness is gone. Like whatever rips back that skin has gotten out. Or sort of like—I guess—when you open up a helium balloon. You ever do that? You open up a helium balloon and suck it in, and for maybe ten or so seconds you start talking like Mickey Mouse. That's what it's like. Brightness and Mickey Mouse. And a little bit of pitching hay.

Q: Pitching hay?

Subject: I grew up on a farm. My least favorite chore was making sure the animals got fed, and making sure the stables and barn were cleaned out. But I usually got stuck with it. I hated it. But sometimes, when I was digging the pitchfork into the horseshit or the hay, I'd just go on autopilot and time would pass. Sometimes for hours. I wouldn't even know that more than twenty minutes had passed, and sometimes whole days went by if I was just using the pitchfork. That's what this is like—it's like something that you start and that it just goes on without you even knowing it's happening.

Q: And the rage. Want to talk about that?

Subject: I wouldn't call it rage. Not exactly.

Q: What would you call it?

Subject: Maybe fury. Fury at having to get the silence. The darkness. To not be in that light with those voices anymore. It's like being alone after your best friend leaves you. It's like locusts in late summer. That's what my mother would've called it.

Q: Locusts? On the farm?

Subject: It was like that. She used to say "It's a locust summer," and that meant it was like when the locusts came down in a dry August and just devoured the crops, the time my father had gone away, and it was just my brothers and me and my mother, and she said "I feel so alone," and then when she was feeling alone again, she would call it a locust summer, because it's like everything is going wrong at once and the locusts are raining down and the noise is loud but you can't do anything about it.

Q: So . . . do you mean, when the voices leave . . .

Subject: I mean what I mean. It's like the noise of the world comes back, and what kept things clear in my head—the voices—they're gone.

Q: Do you understand everything the voices say?

Subject: No. Not hardly. Only sometimes. Like that whole train thing. I said it, but when I was saying it, the voices were saying other things to me. It's like what I say is confusing because what they say is so clear.

Q: They don't say things directly. Things you're going to see?

Subject: You still don't get it. I don't see things like that. I hear them.

Q: You heard the train accident?

Subject: No. Christ, you still don't get it. Okay, this is just too hard to explain unless you've been there. The voices are saying things to me that are creating images as soon as they say them. Just words. Just chants. And when I say them out loud, sometimes they become real.

Q: Do you mean to say you believe you caused the train accident in Connecticut?

Subject: I mean to say. What a phrase. It's so ordinary. This is not about ordinary. This is about different. This is about better. This is about special. And yes.

Q: Yes?

Subject: Yes, I caused the train accident because of what I said. The voices and the brightness give me the power so that my words create reality.

Q: You "create" reality?

Subject: I told you it's hard to explain if you're not in it. I mean I can make things change in life if I say what I connect with in the bright moment. When the voices are there. I can bend the way things work. For just a second.

Q: So the train, and the woman who almost got hit by the bus: by saying what you did, you caused those things?

Subject: I brought them into being. Yes. It was my will. My will does this. I am the one who opens the place within myself so that I can hear the voices. They would not exist without me. They are my choir.

3

After three months of living in the brownstone, doing all the tests, speaking at the lunches that brought in contributions to PSI Vista, Frost Crane had to go home again. He hated saying good-bye to Fleetwood's daughter, Miranda, who at sixteen was already becoming voluptuous and sensual without seeming cheap to him. He had been something of a star—a celebrity—at the Foundation, among its tweedy members and art-house curiosity-seekers. But that would all change—he was out the door with a few thousand in his pocket, and even that he soon lost after a bus ride down to Atlantic City to participate in one of his favorite pastimes.

This time, home wasn't a nice suburban house outside Boston. Maria now owned the house. She owned everything they'd ever had together, and then some. This time, home was a little studio apartment in Albany, New York, and a job he loathed in the state tax office, and he felt again like the little man with the little ordinary life, and he knew that he might as well be dead, because the voices weren't coming to him very often.

And then the phone call arrived from Jack Fleetwood and, a week later, the check and contract, and suddenly October was looking good to Frost Crane again as he thought of the adventure to come: a few days in some mansion and possibly the chance to escape the ordinary forever.

4

From Frost's Journal

"What's probably the craziest thing to do, is the very thing to do (aphorism # 210).

"Go where angels fear to tread (aphorism # 211).

"Someday I need to collect all these little platitudes and put them in a book. I think they'd be useful to people, particularly people like me.

"All right, I'll tell it to me straight: I got debts. Lotsa debts. My ex keeps getting more, and what she doesn't get, my damn and mostly useless Lawyer from Hell seems to get. And the IRS. I can't shake 'em. So I have to take this. I have to take this, and maybe I can make something out of it, so I won't just be wasting a week or two. I'll be making it work for me. (Isn't that how it's supposed to go? You make things work for you?)

"Well, it's almost October, and it's almost time to head up to Harrow, the house up on the Hudson. I've been to Poughkeepsie twice, but never to Watch Point. I hear there are some good antique stores there, so maybe I can buy some stuff for my little hovel. Ha ha ha. What a laugh.

"I put the initial 5K in the bank, but I have a feeling my ex'll be coming after that, so I may have to transfer it to a different bank. I hate the idea that she might come after my money, sometimes I feel like that's all she does. Reminds me of my mother, who only wanted money from me once I was old enough to make any, and I am so tired of supporting these women and watching them live like queens while I exist on barely enough to scrape a good meal together.

"Went to the store and bought some more mousetraps because I'm getting a little tired of my nightly visitors. I was playing with one of the mousetraps, and those little suckers come down hard (in this case, on my beknighted finger). I wonder what would happen if you put mousetraps all over someone's body and just snapped them all at once. I don't mean like five or six mousetraps, I mean maybe two hundred or more, and just had them on nipples and fingers and nose and toes and even genitals, how would it feel? Not like I'm going to try it in this lifetime, but it would be interesting, since sometimes pain feels good if it's all over and not limited to one specific place. I've killed maybe three of the mice with the traps this past month, and each time I feel a little sad for their sorry little lives, and the way they have to scrape around for their bits of peanut butter and cheese and cracker scraps, and then they go—through their own greed, mind you—to their deaths in the steely jaws of the God of Snapping Jaws, the mousetrap.

"I wonder if we're not all like that. Scraping by. Scraping and scraping. Getting our bits of food and crumbs from some other table, and then when our greed becomes too great, we have to go toward our miserable fates.

"All right, it's a pitiful way to look at existence, but now I know that there's no God. (Don't fool yourself; if there is a God, he's bad and mean, because who would set their creations down in this world? I ask you? It must be a God of Snapping Jaws, with the mentality of a cruel four-year-old, sending us to this shit-hole of human existence, not some kind of loving queerish God who thinks that love, love, love runs everything.) I ask you, now that I know there's no God, what's the point of any of it? I was thinking about the people on the train, the one that crashed, and I keep thinking: What were they thinking when the train started to lurch? Were they afraid? Actually, I doubt they had time for fear. That whole animal fight-or-flight mechanism must've kicked in, and they probably just reacted for the next twelve seconds, before they ran head on into the God of Snapping Jaws.

"I really like that idea. The God of Snapping Jaws would make sense. Perfect sense! And I can see Snapping Jaws (which is what I'll call him) just making the world work the way it does. I mean, you're born helpless into who knows what kind of family that molds you and spits you out, even though I will admit my folks were pretty damn good, and they taught me good things, and important things, but every family—you know this if you're sneaking in and reading my journal or if I ever publish this thing, which I very well may do—every family has their own form of damnation for their kids. And Snapping Jaws set it all up. So you're born into this miasma, and you grow up with these crazy ideals (doing good, helping people, taking care of business, and such), but of course, if Snapping Jaws runs the universe, than this is a big joke on you! Because the universe is not about doing good or helping people. I mean, Catherine de Medici knew it when she was looking down at the slaughter of the Huguenots. The rich people on the *Titanic* knew it, as they watched their lower-caste members in steerage drown. Anyone who has ever watched someone of lesser strength die has seen the Snapping Jaws universe at work. I'm not fond of ol' Snapping Jaws. He's a big, bad boogeyman, and his metal teeth come down hard and out of nowhere for the recipient. But if this is the way the world works, then it is just the way things are. It's like the way bugs will take over—the world is for them, for the mandibles and the snapping jaws, for the metal teeth and the exoskeletons among us.

"(Bugs are king, he sez. Roaches thrive, sez I. Every time I see a fly I think of *Lord of the Flies,* and I think of the boys on the island all fighting, and I think of Snapping Jaws, and I think of how the smallest of the world will be the greatest and how the greatest—these men and women who walk on two legs—will one day bow down and be covered with wriggly maggots after Snapping Jaws gets them in his trap.)

"My mother used to say the world was full of givers and takers, and I thought maybe I should be a giver because there were too many takers. But I know from my voices that there's no point in being a giver. No one cares. You can't save anyone on this planet, not with Snapping Jaws running the show.

"Why am I writing this today?

"Well, I think I have some kind of edge with Snapping Jaws. Between the money and the contract, and the invitation to this house. I think this is where the voices want me to go. I think this is the point in life when the universe opens up and shows you the way to your destiny. I don't think you can avoid what's meant for you. What Snapping Jaws puts in your path, you've got to take care of—it's there for you, not for anyone else.

"If you miss it, you'll end up in those metal jaws.

"All right, since I'd been thinking about this, I went out and did something good for someone else. I just needed to; it's part of my balance. I left a larger-than-usual tip with the waitress at the diner at breakfast, but that wasn't really it. What I did was, I saw this kid crossing traffic against the light. Traffic was all over the place, whizzing by him, and he was maybe nine or ten and obviously not too smart. (I often wonder if when kids do these insane things, if maybe they're not long for the world anyway; I mean, you can save them once, but twice? Three times? When does it stop before they just off themselves, and all you've done is delay the inevitable?) I went out and held my hands up to the cars, and this one, this truck, was bound and determined to speed up even though he probably didn't see the kid. So I grabbed the kid up and scrambled to the other side of the highway.

"No one will know that happened. No one needs to know. The universe knows. I rescued him, right then, from old Snapping Jaws. And that's good. Because Snapping Jaws doesn't believe anyone does that kind of stuff.

"And if you can come up against Snapping Jaws, then you can do anything.

"That's where the voices have helped. That's where I've learned. That's why I've been picked to go to this house.

"I'm here to defy the way the universe goes.

"I'm here to change the course of human history.

"The voices that have been within me, they're evolution.

"When I go to that house, I know it will be the beginning of the true millennium. No, I'm not so egotistical as to think that I'm some kind of Second Coming or anything. I'm talking about others, too. I can't be the only one given an ability like this, and if there's something more to life than Snapping Jaws, then that means there's a Will somewhere here that has let me in on one of the secrets. Others have to be in on it, too. That Foundation, it has other people coming to this house.

"I'll bet we're all meant to meet.

"I'll bet we're destined to be part of each other's lives, and maybe when we all get together, it'll be like the spark at the first flint that man ever held in his hand.

"It's evolution of the species, and I'm one small part of it, one small part, a spark in a great darkness.

So I sez to myself, sez I: over the river and through the woods to the haunted house I go.

Swift as a shadow, short as any dream;
Brief as the lightning in the collied night,
That in a spleen unfolds both heaven and earth,
And ere a man hath power to say, "Behold!"
The jaws of darkness do devour it up:
So quick bright things come to confusion.

—*A Midsummer Night's Dream* by William Shakespeare

Poor old lady, she swallowed a fly
I don't know why
She swallowed a fly;
Perhaps she'll die
—Mother Goose rhyme

BOOK TWO

Palace of Night

PART ONE

Arrivals

Chapter Fourteen

1

Cali had to take the PATH train from the Grove Street stop in Jersey City into the City in order to get her car. On the brief train ride, she sat beside an older woman with a large amount of gray hair, quite beautifully curved and twisted into a Danish on the side of her head. *Don't forget to eat something,* Cali made a mental note. *Maybe a Danish. Lots of coffee.*

She glanced about the rest of the train compartment and wondered what everyone did, all those people who didn't feel the "tell" of things. That's what her grandmother had called the ability. "It's the tell," Nana had said, her hair also beautifully gray and long, her eyes small but enlarged whenever she put on her thick glasses. "Your great-grandmother had the tell, and I have it, and you have it now. It's a special ability, but no one will understand it, and no one will believe you. Not in this world. But in the next, they'll understand it."

"Do I need it in the next world?" Cali asked. "In heaven?"

Her grandmother had smiled, nodding. "Of course. Things don't end with death, baby. All the problems you have here, they just keep going on and on until you work at them yourself. That's why death solves nothing for nobody. But in the next world, you're going to help some people out who need it the most. In this one," her grandmother sighed, "well, in this world, I don't think there's any help for anybody."

Her grandmother had died when she was twelve, and Cali probably missed that old lady more than anyone in the world. Mainly because Nana had understood. Nana knew things that Cali wished she could ask her about, too, but of course it was too late. Nana was off to whatever the next world was.

If there is a next world.

2

She got off the train at Christopher Street and went to grab a cup of coffee at a Starbucks on Greenwich Avenue, and gobbled down two Krispy Kreme jelly donuts as well, feeling like a bad kid sneaking into the cookie jar. With the sweetness in her mouth and the buzz of the strong coffee, she made it down to the garage where she kept her car.

Cali kept her Honda Civic at the city-owned lot that abutted the Hudson River, and it was always a hassle getting it out. Sometimes the battery was dead, because it had been sitting so long, but when she arrived and put the key in the ignition it started right up. A *good omen.* The car was from '95, but only had fifteen-thousand miles on it, owing to her lack of using it. She'd had it since she was fresh out of college. She had bought the car on an outrageous payment plan, which her first few jobs had barely covered; she had worked two jobs simultaneously to cover her car and her dinky little first apartment in Bayonne. She loved her Honda, and even the old smell of it made her feel good. And free. She had always felt trapped by public transportation, in the snaky underbelly of the PATH trains or the New York subway.

The car was like freedom.

Except in the city itself.

Traffic on the Westside Highway was bumper-to-bumper, but once she got beyond the city there was practically no one on the road. She went on up the Hudson and stopped for another cup of coffee at a deli in Sleepy Hollow, home of the Washington Irving story about the headless horseman.

Stopping in Sleepy Hollow had seemed appropriate if she was going to spend a couple of weeks in a haunted house. Part of her thought it would be a blast, and creepy, but in a good way. Part of her felt as if she were an idiotic subject in a big experiment. And part of her, she had to admit to herself, was happy to get away from Det for even a few days after the night when the lust monster had somehow gotten the better of her (or had it been Gloria Franco?) and away from the movie in her brain of Gloria Franco's murder, and the child-entity she had somehow seen near Gloria, the impression she had that the murder was part of a larger ritual.

It took another hour and a half out of Sleepy Hollow to make it to the turnoff to Watch Point. The leaves on the trees at the side of the highway had already begun turning to deep reds and flashy golds, and a comfortable chill set in as the afternoon wore on—the air was fresh and clean. Cali felt her head clear of all her troubles, all her thoughts.

She stopped at what seemed to be the only stoplight in all of Watch Point. The town was not untypical for the smaller villages along the Hudson River. Because of narrow old streets, and shopfronts that practically came up to the edge of the car, the town was laid out in a grid around a green common, and she had to make a series of annoying one-way-street turns to get on Packet Hill Street, which led out to the train station; and then she took a few more lefts, missed one major turn, and within minutes felt lost, and in the smallest burg in America.

A teenage girl was walking a border collie with a curly fan of a tail. Cali pulled over and rolled down her window. "I'm looking for Matheson Avenue."

The girl, a dark, stormy little thing with what might've been purple bangs that hid her eyes almost as well as her sunglasses did, scowled. Her lemon yellow sweatshirt hood was pulled over the rest of her scalp, although Cali could still see some purple hair sticking out. "It's closed off. At least the way you're going. There aren't any houses up there. Well, maybe one, but you don't want to go there."

"I'm looking for a place that used to be a school. Called Harrow," Cali said, somewhat exasperated by this stony reception from a local.

The girl raised her sunglasses slightly, squinting her eyes at Cali. "Harrow? That's where you're going?"

Cali nodded.

"It's on the other side of town," the girl said, then pursed her lips together. She slipped her sunglasses back down on her nose and shook her head solemnly.

"If you could just point me in the right direction?"

The girl pointed up the road. "Go left there, then take a sharp right. When you come to the fork, take the middle."

"Middle of the fork?"

"That's right. The middle," the girl said, dragging her pooch off a tree he'd been liberally spraying. Then she shouted, "You don't want to go there. It's a bad place. It's dangerous."

The middle of the fork. Cali drove forward, following the girl's directions, and in fact, she came to a three-pronged fork, with a middle, only it was really a second turn off the left fork. She took it and saw before her a sign for Matheson Avenue, which looked, as the girl had said, as if it should've been closed down. It was cracked and full of enormous craterish potholes, and what wasn't crater was mud and gravel, so that driving to the avenue involved going at five miles per hour as she negotiated the twists and turns. The street she next turned onto—another left—was called Jackson Street and had the distinction of being so tree-lined that it was as if she were entering a primeval forest. Within about a mile, that was exactly what it was—giant pines and thickly vined undergrowth turned with the narrow road up a low slope.

Breaking through the trees, she got a view of the house.

3

What she saw made her gasp. She had read briefly about Harrow, the boy's school that had once been a private home, but she had no idea quite how magnificent it would be. It was like an eclipse of the sun—it was that much of a block to the horizon. It held sway over the land around it.

Fleetwood's book had made it out to be more of a convoluted English manor house, with a few architectural eccentricities.

In fact, it was a dragon of a house.

Two large towers rose from the back of the house and made her think of a castle; the house beneath it was long and large, a villa of a house; she had been told that part of it had burned and, indeed, there were crumbling walls, and even from a distance she saw the scorched landscape around it.

A stone wall surrounded the manse, and signs were posted all around its periphery warning trespassers to keep out.

"Good God," she said, aloud. "If I were a ghost, this is where I'd go."

4

"You came up Jackson?" Jack Fleetwood said, taking her bags from the trunk. "That's the long way. If you had taken a right on Matheson and then a left on Tryon, you'd have cut ten minutes off. Watch Point is walking distance that way. It's a major hike from where you drove in."

"I got a good view of the place. It's something."

"It is," Jack said, and then walked toward the front door. Suddenly, out of nowhere, a dog began barking, and Cali nearly jumped out of her skin. She glanced to the left, and a black-and-white blur was coming toward her at lightning speed. She stood perfectly still, and for a moment thought of reaching for her shoulder bag and pulling out her gun, but the dog slowed and then sat down right in front of her.

He looked up at her face. As if he already knew her.

"That's Conan," a girl said, also from nowhere—but nowhere turned out to be down a narrow path to the left of the large circular driveway.

It was the girl with the purple bangs, and the border collie that looked up at her with both a solemn and soulful look was, indeed, a dog that could easily be thought of as Conan the Barbarian. Cali opened her mouth, not understanding, but then, she got it. *Fleetwood has a teenage daughter. This is her. Some joker.*

If dogs could grin, this one did, with a full set of shiny white teeth, and between those teeth, a squeaky ball, which the dog squeaked a few times to emphasize that he owned it.

The girl turned past them both and headed off in the direction of another house, on the other side of the drive. She whistled, and Conan turned his head slightly toward her. Then he looked up at Cali. She was sure he was saying: *I want to play ball, but I guess I better go.*

The dog turned and trotted off toward its mistress.

5

"This is Miranda," Jack Fleetwood said, and the sixteen-year-old girl with the purple-striped hair sank further down into the sofa. Now that she had her hooded sweatshirt off, Cali saw all the glorious purpleness and even a streak of pure white down the side of her hair. She was quite striking and sullen, even for a girl of sixteen. Her jeans were so baggy that two of her could've fit into them, and her T-shirt read BRITNEY BITES, and she looked as if she hadn't slept in days—but then, Cali had seen girls in Manhattan like this. It was all makeup—she had made raccoon circles around her eyes with mascara and eyeshadow, and her lips were a dark blood color. Her nose was pierced with one small ring, and her left ear was studded with four small garnets. She had slipped the nose ring on for tea—Cali figured to Fleetwood's daughter, this was probably "dressing up for company." Underneath it all, she was pretty, and Cali felt an honest vibe from her. The girl was annoyed at being there at all. The dog, Conan, was curled up next to her, his snout on her knee. But his eyes were on Cali.

Of course, I'm the intruder. He's protecting her and making sure I'm not going to be a threat.

"Hello, Miranda," Cali said. "I guess you could say we've already met."

"Mira."

"That's a beautiful name. And strange. Sort of like mine."

"Whatever," Mira said, drawing her knees up so that her Birkenstocks were scraping the sofa.

"Feet down," Jack said. "And dog down. That's an expensive couch."

He snapped his fingers, and Conan leaped down from the couch, immediately curling up again on the rug by the fireplace.

Mira shot her father a fierce glance, but then slipped her legs over the edge of the sofa and let them touch the floor. She had long legs for a teenager.

Cali nearly laughed, remembering herself at that age. Virtually the same: pissed off, defiant, not feeling very good about herself, not liking the fact that she was the tallest girl in her class, not enjoying feeling different . . . Mira no doubt felt like a loner, as Cali had. "You live in the village," she said.

Mira didn't look at her. "Not this village."

"Mira," Jack said.

"I mean Greenwich Village," Cali said.

"Yeah," Mira said. She dropped the sullenness and actually sounded polite.

"I grew up in Pennsylvania, but when I was sixteen we moved to the East Village. My father used to play jazz piano at a club called the Glowworm. Near Tompkins Park. You know it?" Cali asked, knowing that Mira probably only shopped in the East Village.

Mira glanced up for just a second. "Sure. I've been there. Good music. Expensive cover charge, you ask me."

"My dad was really into it. I used to go there with my sister, and we'd hang out in the back and listen to all the really cool blues players back then."

Mira shrugged. "Sounds interesting."

"I knew you liked the blues," Cali said. "Just by looking at you."

"You read my mind?" Mira asked. In her voice, Cali detected a slight fear.

Cali glanced at Jack Fleetwood. Had the father intimidated his daughter with these kinds of fears? Surrounded her with the whole idea of psychic or paranormal abilities, and somehow kept her in a box? She said, "No, I'm not much of a mind reader. I could tell by your style."

Mira chirped a smile, which disappeared as soon as it came.

All right, Cali thought. *We'll get along. We'll be friends now, Mira. I think we understand each other a little. I think your dad was probably a little bit like my dad.*

"What's your ability?" Mira asked.

"I read things," Cali said.

"Like . . . books," Mira said, softly sarcastic.

Jack Fleetwood jumped into the conversation. "Psychometry. She works in criminal investigations. She picks things up."

"I know what psychometry is," Mira said, not looking at her father, but keeping her gaze on Cali. "I'm around this crap twenty-four hours a day. I've heard you on the radio a couple of times. You do Tarot, too, right?"

"Sometimes. I don't think the Tarot is magic or anything. I just think it helps focus your mind sometimes. The images are cultural. It's just a way to focus on a problem and see a metaphor for the situation that might be helpful."

"I know some Tarot readers who think it's mystical," Mira said, as if it were the most obvious thing in the world. She shrugged. "Dad has all kinds of kooks at the Foundation."

"Not me," Cali said. "And I've only done that a little. On request. It's psychometry that's my specialty. You like all this paranormal stuff?"

"It's okay," Mira said. "Of course, I don't have any special talent."

"Everyone has some degree of—" her father said.

"Not me. I couldn't tell you what time it is right now, let alone anything about the future or the spirit world."

"You believe in ghosts?" Cali asked.

"Do you?"

Cali grinned. "Not really."

"Me neither," Mira said, erupting in laughter. "I think this is going to be one big waste of human potential." She glanced sidelong at her father: "Sorry, Dad."

Jack looked up at Cali, shaking his head, smiling. "I hear it all the time."

"So, you touch stuff and feel vibes?"

"Basically," Cali said.

"All your life?"

"Ever since I was a kid. First at seven, and then when I was maybe eleven, something else happened. It was nothing very dramatic. My parents were talking divorce, and my older sister was acting like I didn't exist because she was fourteen and hanging out with older boys. She didn't want a younger sister following her everywhere, I guess. I can't blame her. I was really needy as a kid, and a little bit of a constant liar. I made up stories just so people would think I was interesting. I even had imaginary friends, at eleven, and that seemed too old, even to me."

"I don't know. I could use some imaginary friends right about now," Mira said, practically under her breath.

"All kinds of things were going on in my body—the pubescent stuff every kid has to deal with—I thought my family was about to break apart, and then the only friend I had ran off. Our dog. His name was Custer, and he was an Irish setter mixed with golden retriever. All I had of him was his dog collar, because I'd taken it off that morning to give him a really messy bath. So all these things were going on in my head—it was all happening at once. I thought the world was falling apart, and because Custer had gotten loose and hadn't come back, I thought it was my fault, and no one would be able to identify him because I took his collar off with his tags and everything. So I practically blacked out from worrying. I lost consciousness for a couple of seconds and hit the planks on our front porch really hard, but I was holding on to his dog collar. And that's when I knew I was stuck with this ability."

"You saw your dog?"

"Not really. I saw everything about the dog. Pretty much any interactions with people. All these memories came back about when he was a puppy and I'd been holding him. I thought it was just me remembering. But when I came out of it, my mother told me later I sat up in bed (she'd brought me to bed and hadn't been able to get the collar out of my grip), I said 'Custer's downtown behind Lambert's Kitchen Store.' And that's where they found him, although nobody had believed me. My grandmother believed. She was into all kinds of old superstitious stuff. She told me what this ability was, and because I was a little obnoxious kid at that point, I believed her. Then I felt special. That was probably my downfall, because it didn't always work. It doesn't. It's not a hundred percent true, what I get from reading things. Sometimes I'm wrong. It's just that every now and then I'm right, and that's what I guess helps in the criminal stuff I'm brought in on."

"You a cop?"

"No. I do a late-night radio show three times a week, and then work sometimes with the NYPD on a few cases per year."

"Wow. You got a gun?"

"Always," Cali said. "You ever shoot a gun?"

"We don't keep guns," Jack Fleetwood said.

"I don't blame you. If I didn't have to, I wouldn't. But shooting a gun is not a bad skill to have," she said, directly to Mira. "There are times when guns are good."

"We live in a violent culture," Mira said, like she was reciting from a sociology class. "Guns only add to the problem."

"We live in a violent culture because we're violent people. Basically. People add to the problem," Cali said. "I don't love guns, Mira. But once you've been attacked, you can't go back to believing you're safe. I wish it weren't so, but it is. The gun can be destructive, or it can be a tool for safety. We don't need to promote or destroy firearms. We need to work on the human heart."

Mira's face brightened, as if she'd had a minor revelation. "True." She paused, almost dramatically. Then, in a much lower voice, she said, "So, tell me: You ever shoot somebody?"

Chapter Fifteen

1

Chet took the long way up.

It had begun drizzling rain when he rolled out of bed that morning, and he knew that he might just get fired from his job at the gas station purely because Larry Hooper didn't like his employees telling him when and how they would take time off from work. Chet didn't care; the check was in his bank account, swelling it beyond its norm to the point that the bank had called to verify that he had put the money into the right account. Since he was overdrawn now and then, Chet had not been surprised at the call. He could barely believe his luck, because it seemed like all the money in the world to him.

He dressed in his cleanest pair of Levis and made sure he wore his white shirt, because he knew that he couldn't show up at this mansion in New York looking like a hillbilly. He wore his best brown shoes, and stowed his sneakers and a few other things into his green knapsack. He dropped by the ATM and took out four hundred dollars, which he figured would cover him for the four days and then some—he didn't want to scrimp too much while he was at this place, because he knew that the money was mainly to cover any expenses he had. Still, he saved on cabfare and walked all the way to the bus depot.

It wasn't that the train wouldn't have been more convenient, but the bus was just so damn cheap, he had to use it. Sure, he could've used some more of the advance cash, but he didn't know how long that money would last, and he didn't want to end up being completely poor again if he could help it.

Besides, the bus made the trip last longer, and he got to know a really nice lady of about sixty or so who sat next to him for most of the trip. She was from Washington, D.C., and she was going up to New York to see her grandchildren.

When she asked him about his trip, he said, "Just going to see some friends." He felt a little paranoid about the whole idea of going to a house and watching to see if ghosts were there.

From the first view of New York City, he thought he'd see his mother somewhere on the street as the bus went up to the Port Authority, but there was no sign of her. Part of him wanted to go wander the city and at least try to find out her whereabouts. But the city was too vast—even riding through on the bus, he was amazed by how the buildings never ended, and there was no horizon once you got on the street.

He changed buses there, and then changed to another bus on up the road. All in all, an entire day had come and gone, and by the time he reached Watch Point, New York, deposited at the train station, he felt as if he'd been on the damn bus for days instead of hours.

The train station was desolate.

He was the only person to get off at Watch Point, and when the bus drove off he reached into his green bag and drew out an oversized sweatshirt with a big floppy hood. He pulled it over his head and shivered slightly. It was colder in Watch Point than even in New York City. The wind actually whistled around the bends of buildings.

It was dark, and the streetlamps played out a feeble but romantic light. It reminded him of a movie of a small village—it was so perfect. There were no taxicabs at the station, so he walked up the broad sidewalk, looking in the windows of the closed-up shops. There was a bookshop called the Whistle Stop Bookshop; in the window was a display for children's books, including one of his favorites from childhood, *From the Mixed-Up Files of Mrs. Basil E. Frankweiler.* It was a story about a brother and sister who run away from home, and they had done what Chet as a child had only dreamed of (until he was fourteen and did, in fact, run away). He grinned, seeing it displayed there. It was like an old friend.

Across the street was a fairly lively little Italian restaurant, and for a second he entertained the notion of grabbing a bite to eat there. He'd only had two bologna sandwiches all day, with some Mountain Dews on the side, and his stomach growled and gurgled just watching the people at the window tables eating pasta. *There'll be food at Harrow,* he told himself. *I'll be there soon.*

He walked past windows with women's clothing and an appliance store full of shining new stoves and washing machines near the front of the giant glass window; as he walked, he passed one or two people—a boy about his age who looked like he must be in college. He was better dressed than Chet, in a thick wool sweater and khakis; Chet felt like a slob from the wrong side of the tracks. His jeans had a few holes in them, and his sweatshirt was stained and smelled musty to him. *Some first impression you're going to make.*

A middle-aged couple passed by, and the wife nodded to him

with a sweet smile. He nodded back and continued up the slight hillside, until he saw the Exxon Station at the convergence of two sloping roads.

Inside the convenience store of the gas station, he poured himself a big cup of coffee, mixed liberally with cream and then coated in sugar. He needed the boost. Then, what he liked to think of as "an All-American gas station sandwich," which came in a small triangular plastic case. Inside, a sliced egg salad sandwich on the whitest and flimsiest bread imaginable, and still, it tasted okay. After he'd paid for it, and sat munching it out under the bright lights of the gas station, the guy who ran the pumps asked him where he was headed.

"Some house here. I need to call a cab."

"A house? I've lived here twenty years. I know most of these places. Whose is it?"

"I think her name is Martin. Something Martin."

"Oh, Jeez," the guy said. "That old rattrap. She bought it six months ago, and she hired everybody in town practically to work on it. And then some. She had a team of contractors come up from the city. She must've spent a small fortune on it. After the fire last year, it's not worth a dime, in my opinion. It's one of those old messes that are all along the river—Bannerman's Castle, Wyndcliffe—mansions that were once something but are now just rotting and too expensive to maintain even when they're not rotting."

"Yeah," Chet said, munching on the last of his sandwich. "I hear it's something."

"It's something," the guy said. "It was a school last year but got shut down when some kids died. Half the building got burned, and what wasn't burned, she tore down."

"Why'd she do that?"

"Not the house. The school buildings. The school sold to her in April, and as quick as you can say 'jackshit,' she took out a lot of that building. My brother Pete worked on it. He said that she was crazy. Two people got hurt bad in the construction. Or I should say, destruction," the attendant said. Then, "She throwing a party?"

"Kind of." Chet grinned, feeling pretty good now. All right, it was clear: the Martin lady was certifiable, and this was going to be some kind of lark in the park for a nice wad of cash. Life could be worse.

"Well, you want a lift, I can give you one in twenty minutes," the guy said, and then thrust his hand out. "Boz."

"Chet." Chet took his hand and gave it a good, hard shake. "I pump gas, too. Down near Baltimore."

"So, you want a lift?"

Chet nodded. "I was about to break down and get a cab."

"As it so happens," Boz said, "I am one of three cabbies in town. After my shift here. Usually no one needs one unless they're going to the depot, or some of the old ladies who want to get their hair done in Poughkeepsie but can't see the road."

"Quiet little burg," Chet said.

"Quiet and full of nutcases." Boz laughed, and then the bell rang at the full service pump, and he dashed over to it.

2

Boz drove a '69 Mustang that had once been bright yellow, but nearly thirty years after the car's creation was a mottled and scratched white with an occasional splotch of color. It had dents and bangs all over it, and the seats were torn as if by a wild animal. "I got it for three hundred bucks four years ago, and I been working on it since then," he said proudly. "This is how you get up to Harrow. It's a weird road."

"Weird?"

"I don't mean *weird* weird. I mean weird like it zigs and zags a little. See? Pothole!" Boz cried out, and then pressed his right hand on the windshield as the car practically bucked like a bronco on the bump. "One time I hit one of those and the windshield cracked."

"No kidding."

"All this gravel flew up. I've had to get a new windshield twice already. This road sucks." Then, brightening a bit, Boz nodded ahead. "Look beyond those trees and you can see just a little of it."

Chet looked forward and saw what looked like the top of some medieval castle, rising above a stand of trees in the distance. The sun was just going down behind it, and what he saw became shadowy in the sudden October night.

"Dracula's castle," Boz said. "That's what we used to call it. It used to be full of preppies, but they all burned up. Well, not all of 'em. Just some of 'em."

Chet didn't register anything from this—Fleetwood had told him of the tragedy of the year before when part of the place had burned.

"Sorry," Boz said sheepishly, detecting the brief silence. "A little graveyard humor. None of us from town ever really liked the school. Or the house, for that matter. A girl whose sister I used to know, she died there last spring. It was pretty mysterious. I wouldn't want to discourage anyone from going there, but it's weird, like this road. Pothole!" he shouted again in warning, and the Mustang lurched.

The Mustang made its way up the mostly gravel road to the formal entryway between too large stone posts. The property was hidden by a tall stone wall; and as the car rounded the bend, going past an empty guard booth, Chet felt as if perhaps he had made the wrong decision in taking Fleetwood's money. He caught a glimpse of what looked like a dismantled fountain, just a large hole at the center of the drive. To the right of this, a large white house; straight ahead, Harrow. Four cars were parked in a marked lot on the left-hand side of the drive, a Honda Civic, a BMW, a Jeep Grand Cherokee, and what looked like a fairly generic midsized rental car.

The doorway was open, and a man of medium height with thinning hair and a very pale face stood there in the front porch light, looking as if he were lost.

3

"Well, I guess this is it. Thanks," Chet said. "I appreciate it."

"No prob. Like I said, the woman is crazy. She's hot, though."

"Hot like pretty?"

"Hot like burning up," Boz said. "But she's a crazy bitch."

4

Chet ambled up to the porch, feeling as if it was his first day at school. He swung the knapsack around and tried to grin so that the guy on the porch wouldn't know how nervous he was. Crazy thoughts went through his head: what if this was some big joke?

What if this was one of those cults that pulled you in with promises and money and then kidnapped you? What if this was a house full of psycho lunatics?

A dog came bounding up from a muddy field just beyond the driveway—it was black and white and its fur was caked with twists of dirt and twigs and fallen leaves. It began barking playfully. It nearly jumped on him as Chet stepped up on the porch. Then the dog turned and ran off again, as if it had its own secret agenda.

The man with the thinning red hair kept a flat line of a smile as Chet approached him. He looked like he had once been happy in life but now had some tragic sense of life's little secrets. *He's one of us,* Chet thought, and it calmed him a bit. *He's got something like I do, and he knows how it keeps you separate from other people.*

When Chet got closer he offered his hand for shaking. "Hi. I'm Chet."

The man glanced at Chet's hand, and then back up to Chet's face. He didn't extend his own hand. "I'm Frost Crane, and that mangy animal was Conan. Why she can't just leave her mutt at home . . ." the man said, his voice like a mouse squeak crossed with a fart. "Frost Crane," he repeated in a more normal tone. This time he said it as if Chet was supposed to know who he was. Was he someone famous? Chet didn't watch as much TV as he probably should—he had never seen the guy before. Maybe he was a politician?

"You the owner?" Chet asked.

"No," Frost said. "I'm a guest."

"Me, too," Chet said. "Anyone here yet besides us?"

Then the door opened, and a man just shy of Chet's height, with jet-black hair and a thick mustache, held the door back. He was stocky and besweatered and had the kind of face that seemed warm and inviting—the way Chet had always imagined his father would be, if he had a father, and the way the preacher in St. Chris had seemed to him. "Hello," the man said, somewhat out of breath. "I've just been running some interference here." He nodded toward the other man. "Frost, good to see you. And Chet." He glanced over at him.

Chet didn't recognize him until he had stepped into the house and then realized it was Jack Fleetwood, the man who had asked him questions a year or so before. He thought of Fleetwood as much younger than this guy, who must've been forty or even older. "Dr. Fleetwood," Chet said, shaking his hand. "Good to see you, sir."

"Let's dispense with the doctor," Fleetwood said. His voice was amplified a bit by a slight echo in the entryway, which was icy cold to Chet. "I find these academic degrees make one think of a pediatrician or something. I trust you two had good trips."

Frost Crane shot a withering glance at Chet. "We came separately. I drove up."

"This is some place," Chet said, ignoring Crane's tone of voice. The ceiling was done in some kind of swirling plaster, and the walls were covered with an overly flowered Victorian wallpaper. The foyer opened on an enormous hall, with statues of soldiers that reminded Chet of history lessons about the Spanish conquistadors. Two paintings hung on a far wall—one, a portrait of an old man, and the other, what looked like a scene of some beautiful valley with low mountains rising beyond it.

"Isn't it grand?" Fleetwood said, ushering them in farther. "The wallpaper has been replaced to more closely resemble the house's original paper. Much of what was here—when the school burned—had to be destroyed. But come on, set your bags down here. We'll go to the rooms later—unless you're tired?"

"I'm a bit beat," Frost said, so quietly that it was hard to hear him. Then, a bit louder, "The cab that brought me here hit a doe. He was driving fast along the woods. It darted out, and he hit it."

Chet blinked. "Shit," he said.

"It made me a little nauseated," Frost said. "There was a lot of blood." He took a breath. "I've never been in a car that hit an animal like that. It was sickening."

"That's awful," Chet said.

Fleetwood shook his head. "People need to drive more carefully. There are a lot of deer up here, I'd guess."

"Bambi," Chet said soberly, and then cracked a smile. "Sorry. Just made me think of *Bambi,* the movie. You know."

Frost Crane's face turned sour. "I hate cartoons. I don't even mind hunting. It's a sport. But not with a car. Not like that. If you're going to hunt, you use a weapon, and a car should not be one. But that's just me."

"Would a cup of coffee help? Supper's going to be in less than an hour, and you're welcome to retire to your rooms right after, if you'd like," Fleetwood said, his voice on the edge of begging.

"I'm a bit beat," Frost repeated, and glanced at his watch. "I took the train. The train always tires me. I couldn't nap. And I couldn't enjoy myself because someone was sick. Coughing the whole trip. And then, the deer. Well. It hasn't been my kind of day." He made a funny noise—as if he was smacking his lips. He glanced up the large, box-cluttered staircase. "My room up there?"

Fleetwood nodded. "But could you at least come in for ten minutes? To meet the others?"

Frost was silent; he glanced at Chet, as if for some support. He turned toward the staircase. "Which one?"

"There are seven on the first landing. They're very rough. Pick the one you'd like," Fleetwood said, and then shrugged.

"I'd like to meet everybody," Chet said.

Frost Crane went up the staircase, stepping over some papers that were piled to the left-hand side. Chet set his knapsack down and followed Jack Fleetwood into the next room.

CHAPTER SIXTEEN

1

"This was the house's original anteroom, but the school turned it into an administrative office," Fleetwood said, taking Chet through the first room. It consisted of a large desk and several more boxes.

"What's all the stuff?"

"Equipment, gadgets. Nothing fancy, just for sound and pictures. We've got cameras in every room and along the halls. Video, all hooked up to some PCs in my bedroom. Just for monitoring."

"Even the bathrooms?" Chet laughed.

"No, we've left those for privacy," Fleetwood said. "But it's all in your contract."

"Yeah, I'm sure," Chet said. "You think you'll get ghosts on film?"

2

Frost Crane was generally pissed.

He'd had the worst day of his life—or so it had felt—and the voices hadn't come to him at all for days. It was like a dry spell, which was all the better for coming to Harrow.

He was sure that whatever was in the house would do something for it. He had arrived in a terrible mood at the front gate of Harrow, dropped there by the ruthless and deer-hating cabdriver who had no doubt overcharged him for the brief ride from the train station. He had managed to swallow the dreadful food on the train, but it only made him sick. He had spent half the train ride to Watch Point in the bathroom, either retching or dry heaving, and he had been feeling dizzy ever since. He wondered if he was dehydrated.

His first view of the house had not impressed him.

Yes, it was a large thing, this property, but it looked no different than some of the other prep schools he'd seen in the world, those that had taken over large manors and had destroyed whatever architectural beauty there had been. He was almost gleeful that the school had caught fire—served someone right for tampering with a grand old house. Frost was generally unimpressed with the outside of the house. It reminded him of a cross between an embassy building and a child's version of a medieval castle. Besides which, the rot was everywhere: The stone wall that surrounded the property was crumbling in spots; the front gate could not close completely. (He'd tried to close it when he went in, but there was no way the two sides would meet, nor was there a lock in sight. Frost didn't really like the idea of a house without locks, and he had heard that there were local kids who got up to trouble here; that's what the cabdriver had told him.) The weather was another story: It had seemed about twenty degrees colder in Watch Point than anywhere else in the world, and he had to wonder just how far north he was as he walked the potholed drive up to the front door.

And then, that kid, what was he, seventeen? Was Frost being

thrust in with a group of teenagers? This was going to be an absurd holiday.

But at least there was the money.

And maybe, Frost thought: *Maybe I can get a book out of it. Then I can really make some money.*

3

Frost Crane was a bit more impressed with the inside of the house. Fleetwood, of course, was there, with his overly congenial air masking his ambition, but Frost let that go. He was sleepy and tired and nausea had been overtaking him since he set foot inside the gate. He was sure he'd either throw up or his bowels would release and deliver something truly nasty into his John Henry briefs; he was happy when he made it up the stairs—"Messy place," he whispered under his breath—and first found the bathroom at the end of a brief, alleylike hallway off the main corridor. It was warmer upstairs than down, and he took a few seconds to notice the exquisite floors—surely oak or cherry, and although they were quite scuffed and somewhat sunken, the craftsmanship was beautiful. The bathroom was basic and unimpressive, and obviously had once been made for students, for there were six urinals and three stalls, and he immediately went into one and coughed up what little food he'd had on the train. After washing his face he was annoyed at the lack of towels (there were none in sight, so he wiped at his wet face with his hands); he experienced some dizziness and leaned into the sink and drank water directly from the faucet; and then went to the bathroom window to see what kind of view could be had.

He rolled the window open to reveal what seemed like another rooftop just beneath, and a courtyard with white stone arches that seemed like the bones of some cathedral. Large square lights had been placed in what might've been a garden; it lit up several large sculptures of classical figures as if it were daylight. Everything beyond those lights was complete blackness, and it wasn't quite six o'clock. The incoming chill made him close the window again.

Feeling less dizzy, he went back out into the hallway and picked up his suitcase and jacket. He found three rooms, each of which seemed suitable, though none of them particularly spectacular. They still had the look of offices, although some antique furniture stood in corners, out of place. He chose the room with the view of the back of the house and its arches and towers. It was a small room but had an enormous four-poster bed with dragons and gargoyles carved into the posts; the bed was neatly made, and a small portable telephone rested on the bedside table. There were two lamps—one tall standing one near the window, and a smaller one that sat on what might've been a child's desk, near the bed. Frost glanced at the large mirror near the wardrobe and offered himself a smile, although inside he had already begun to sense that something was wrong.

The voices will be back, he told himself. *They'll return.*

Surely they'll return.

Then he went to the bed and lay down across it. He was asleep within seconds. He awoke briefly a few minutes after settling down, when he thought he heard a noise, but the room was dark, and he thought nothing of it. He closed his eyes and drifted off again.

It felt like just minutes later that the lights came up in his bedroom, and he opened his eyes to see a teenaged girl with purple hair standing by his bedroom window. "Christ, it's hot up here," she said, turning to him. Her expression was neither happy nor sad, but a mixture of the two. "We've got drinks downstairs. Dinner's in twenty minutes."

"All right," Frost said groggily, recognizing Fleetwood's daughter, Mira. Her hair had been sandy brown last time he'd seen her, and she had not worn so much makeup, particularly such dark makeup.

"I would've thought you'd have been the first at the bar," Mira said, and then walked out of the room. The light by the bed seemed harsh to him, and Frost reached up to switch it off, but then decided he might as well get up.

Frost glanced at his watch: It was almost seven fifteen. He'd been asleep for just over an hour. He felt anything but rested.

The bed creaked as he pushed himself up. He laughed at himself—he'd awakened with an erection, something that, as he was getting older, seemed more of a reminder of who he once was than of whom he'd become in the past few years. The voices had taken away his sex drive completely—this was another problem. He had tried a few times to get it back, that feeling of strength and manhood and power and pleasure, but in fact, it had always just remained flaccid. No amount of pornography, no glimpse of a woman's thighs, no touch of a woman's hair or skin had done anything to bring it back. He had nearly gotten an erection when he'd stayed at the Foundation in the city, but just as he was pressing his mind to conjure up images of naked redheads with titosauruses on their chests and snatches the size of small forests, just as his fingers began manipulating the tender skin, he'd been interrupted, and his little Frost had never woken up again.

In fact, the bitch had called him "Jack Frost" after that, like it was some kind of joke. She had said it to her friends—he'd overheard her. He knew she was a bitch, even if she pretended not to be.

Mira is nothing but a goddamn purple-headed bitch.

And now, here, in Harrow.

A hard-on. A nice big one, too.

Not bad for a forty-five year old. Not friggin' bad. Not bad for a guy who grew up with a warm father who caught him doing something pretty bad in the barn one day and took a pitchfork off the rack and pointed it right at the boy's peepee just to keep him from doing it anymore. Hey, hey, not bad, I say.

An extra ten minutes before he appeared in the parlor wouldn't be too awful. He reached down and felt the gabardine of his slacks, and the nice little lump that was there. He flicked the zipper up and brought it all the way down. *A little pride in ownership, sez I. Imagine all the women of the world blended into one suctioning woman with all of her soft parts being directed toward this magnificent lump of manflesh.*

Something both freezing and burning seemed to have taken over his loins. He could stroke right here, in this room, and they'd never know. He could play with himself, his hard-on, his MANHOOD HOT DAMN IT, and it was Harrow giving this to him, he was sure.

He would be powerful here.

Then he thought he heard that odd click again, just as he had when he'd drifted off to sleep.

He got up out of the bed, his fly down, the heat within him feeling like he would explode. He walked to the window and made sure the curtains were pulled tight. Then another click. He went over toward the door, and there, at one corner of the room:

A damn video camera.

It was a compact little camera, a red light above the lens, and it turned on a metal pivot. Drilled into the wall. *A mechanical eye.*

They're watching me.

They're not going to let me alone here at all. They're going to just film us and see everything we do and there'll be no privacy.

That bitch is probably laughing at me like she did before. She's probably somewhere watching this right now.

They're all bitches. They're nothing but a bunch of spying bitches, and this is not about Harrow at all, it's about finding out how to get the voices so they can do this, too. But they're not counting on Snapping Jaws and how it'll come and get them, how it will not let them treat me like this for long.

And then his erection died, as if it had slammed into a wall of ice: a fast and painful death.

His desire no longer interested him, and he felt a little sad as he went to put his shoes on and go downstairs to meet the others.

PART TWO

The First Night

Chapter Seventeen

1

"I see you've all found the liquor cabinet," Mira Fleetwood said, stepping into the parlor, feeling as if she wished she'd never promised her father to come and help out. This was a place full of those same freaky people as at the Foundation, and at least she didn't have to deal with them after six o'clock back in the city.

She felt fairly confident now; the caffeine had kicked in, and she had familiarized herself enough with the house and its rooms to feel as if she owned it, and not that crazy woman her dad wanted to get into bed. She had brushed her hair out and drawn it up in back, and put on a pure white shirt and oversized canvas pants—it was her version of dressing up.

She looked at each of them.

Losers. Complete and utter losers, but cool in some way she couldn't identify. Chet was a total babe but looked a bit trashy. His hair was too long, which was cool, but he looked lean in the way guys looked when they never got much to eat. She knew that he had been working at gas stations, probably making minimum wage. And the baseball cap on his head looked completely dorky; at nineteen he was too old for that. She hated boys who tried to still look like boys even when they should be men.

Cali, of course, looked hot and bizarre. She was leggy and steamy and dressed in the kind of clothes that Mira only dreamed about but would never wear in a million years. *When I grow up, I'm going to be Cali Nytbird*, Mira told herself. Then she saw the other one. The one she thought of as Mr. Wormy. He sat in the large high-backed, overstuffed chair and puffed on his stinky cigarette. Yuck. Mr. Wormy looked at her like she was some kind of . . . whore.

She hated him. He had leered at her the entire time he'd stayed at the Foundation, and now he was back. She was convinced he had even tried to get in bed with her one night, only she had raised such a ruckus, and kicked him right between the balls hard enough, that he had stopped, claiming he must be sleepwalking, because "I thought I was back at my old house, and getting into bed with Maria." Her father had bought the story, because it fit in with his theories about Mr. Wormy's voices from Beyond or some such bullshit, and the old lecher got away with it.

I'll kick you again where it counts if you don't watch out, Wormy Man.

He was, of course, drinking the Chivas. Hogging it, more like. She was a little shocked at the beer in Cali's hand—a can of Bud, which was Mira's father's favorite, but Mira thought Cali would be into White Russians, or maybe white wine, more than Bud. *She wears Kate Spades; why would she have a Budweiser? Miss Nytbird is just a mass of contradictions.*

Chet also had a Budweiser in his hand and from the look of the crunched-up can next to him, was already on his second or third.

"You look very . . ." Cali began, but no further words came out.

"I don't wear jeans all the time. I like these pants. I can store my cell phone in them," Mira said, drawing her small, sleek black phone from the third pocket down, near her knee. "My Palm

Pilot's in this one." She dropped the phone back down into the pocket and reached into the second pocket down, drawing up the handheld device. "And my Swiss Army Knife here." She reached into her left-hand lower pocket and brought out the knife her father had given her two years earlier. "Everything a millennium girl can use," Mira said, and then pointedly added, "except for a gun, of course."

"Heh," Frost Crane chortled.

She shot him an evil look. *I wish I had some kind of psychic powers to zap you, Mr. Wormy.* She walked over to the long, sleek dining table that had all the bottles and cans. She picked up a can of Coke, popped the tab, took a swig. *Lukewarm; lovely.* She grabbed one of the dining room chairs, swiveling it around so she sat in it backwards, facing the three of them. "Dad'll be down in a minute."

"Where's Conan?" Cali asked.

"I think he's so happy to be away from the city that it'll be about midnight before he comes in from the outside willingly. There are all kinds of holes waiting to be dug in the garden. And since the ground's practically frozen, it'll take Conan twice as long as normal."

"Conan?" Chet asked.

"My dog," Mira said. "He's a mutt from a very good neighborhood. Half border collie, and a little bit of Labrador retriever somewhere in there, too."

"Oh, yeah, I think I met him already." Chet nodded. "What about Ivy Martin?"

"She's around. It's a big property," Mira said. "I haven't seen much of her myself. Not since the night before last."

"She must be whacked to buy this old place," Frost said. "It looks like some of these walls could fall over at any minute."

"Structurally it's sound," Mira said, feeling smarter and more mature than the Worm. "She spent a lot of cash to get this place back into shape. When Dad bought the brownstone for PSI Vista, it took a year and a half to get the contractors to do their job. But Ivy, she got this done in less than five months. That seems like some kind of record to me. All this furniture, too. Reproductions from all over the country. Maybe even overseas, too. That sofa"—she pointed with her Coke can at the couch—"that piece of crap cost a fortune."

"So polite," Frost whispered under his breath.

"She must be a perfectionist," Cali said. "This stuff is beautiful. I'm not a huge furniture buyer, but those bookshelves must've cost a fortune."

"I guess some people have it and spend it," Mira said. "Someday, when I'm rich, I'll do better things than buy an old house."

"Money's the root of all evil," Chet said, his voice barely audible.

"Huh?" Mira asked.

"It's bad. The Bible says so," Chet said.

"And you believe that money is evil, but not the people who use the money?"

"Maybe it leads them to do evil things."

Mira glanced at Cali. *Christ, say something to this fundie dweeb. Please tell me we don't have a Born Again in here.*

Cali gave her a blank stare.

"I hear your talent is unusual," Cali said, looking over at Chet.

Okay, she's up to something now, Mira thought.

Chet shrugged. He nursed the beer. His left hand hung across his knee. He was uncomfortable. Even the chair seemed to intimidate him. "It's not even a talent. It's something bad. I can't control it."

"Maybe you've never tried. What is it?"

"Things happen. Around me. Sometimes. It's like lightning coming down. It doesn't always happen. But when it does, it's a lot. My foster mother told me I was a sinner. She may have been right."

"There were times," Cali said, sipping her beer, "when people like us might've been tortured and murdered just because of these kinds of things. Imagine that."

"Like witches," Mira said. "God, I love the idea of witchcraft. I'd like to put a few hexes on people I know." *Particularly in this room.*

"It's bad stuff," Chet said, looking down at his hands. "Although I guess it's not all bad. Once I saved a baby because of it."

"Whiny baby, I bet," Frost said, again under his breath, but just loud enough for Mira to hear.

"That doesn't sound like a sinner to me," Cali said.

"The baby still died, though. Later. I probably just made its pain last longer. Who knows?"

"And the butterflies," Mira said, her voice so sweet it felt like the onset of a toothache.

Chet glanced up, a harsh look.

"I work with Dad. I know this stuff. It's not a secret."

"That's private business," Chet said. "And it was a long time ago. Nothing's happened since. At all."

"Shit, then why're you here?" Frost asked, slurring his words a bit. *Ah,* Mira thought, *the Chivas is kicking in.*

Chet looked up at her, his eyes seeming like the saddest green eyes she had ever seen, and for a moment she wanted to actually mother the guy, hold him in her arms and just comfort him—

whereas a few minutes before, she'd thought he was cute in a Brad Pitt kind of way, he now seemed like a little four-year-old who has a splinter in his finger. He glanced over at Frost. "I guess the money. I'm broke. Most of the time, anyway. And I'd like to give some to this woman I know of."

Frost shook his head slightly. "The root of all evil."

"Well," Chet said, "I guess for me it is. I shouldn't really be here. You two have actual skills with your abilities. I've seen you on TV. I heard about your predictions," he said to Frost, his formerly somber mood brightening a bit. "You're famous. And you"—he turned to Cali—"you have a radio show and solve crimes and things. I've never really done anything . . . that worked."

Okay, now you're going from needy child to whiner, Mira thought. *You're getting paid a small fortune to sit in this house for a couple of days, and you're now going to become the crybaby. I guess everybody has their group dynamic, just like Dad says. Change the subject, Mira. Change it, before we all sink into Chet's clingy little world.* "Dad'll be back in another hour. He was down at the Foundation today for some presentation. Dinner arrives at seven, from the House of Hunan—yeah, I know, fancy for the first night, but there you have it. Dad's arranged with the restaurants in town for each of you to have a tab, and the Foundation will cover the expense. You just call them up, and they'll deliver. I don't cook or clean, so basically, it's a do-it-yourself kind of thing if you want to eat in. There's a woman who comes in the mornings for basic cleaning downstairs, and she'll also make breakfast and coffee. There are three big fridges in the kitchen, fully stocked. You can order from the local Safeway, and they'll deliver. Charge it to the Foundation, too."

"We can't just come and go?" Chet asked.

"What, you think they pay us ten thousand each to get out every day?" Frost said, doing a bad job of hiding his contempt.

"You only got ten thousand?" Cali asked archly. She winked at Mira, who laughed.

"Yeah, you do what you want. But part of the deal is, you stay here." Then Mira figured she'd have a little fun, particularly since Chet was looking at her with those soulful baby eyes. "No matter what. No matter what manifests itself, you remain on this property. No matter how frightening it becomes."

From behind her, her father said, "Oh, good grief, it's not going to get frightening at all. Ghosts are harmless. Ready for supper?"

2

They were well into the sesame noodles and spring rolls when Cali asked what she thought was an obvious question. "So, where is she?"

Jack Fleetwood leaned back in his chair, a bit of noodle in his chopstick. He seemed poised to say something, but instead got the noodle in his mouth.

"She?" Chet asked. "You mean Ms. Martin?"

Mira dropped her fork on her place and reached for one of the boxes of white rice. "That's the million-dollar question tonight. Everyone wants to know, Dad. Didn't you tell them?" She said it like it was the beginning of a punchline.

"Not yet," her father said. He quieted a bit as he said, "She's taken to staying up all night. She told me that since she's been here, she can't sleep. She manages to sleep during the day."

"She's a vampire," Mira said, arching her eyebrows.

Chet laughed. "I bet. I used to have trouble sleeping. She should try some melatonin. It always helps me."

It was Frost who finally said the obvious. "It's after eight. What time is she usually up?"

Mira and Fleetwood exchanged glances. Mira broke into a grin as she poured half the rice onto her plate. "She's around. She's sort of a ghost herself."

"What Mira means," Fleetwood said, "is that Ivy has been spending a lot of time down in the cellars. There are a lot of interesting things down there, not the least of which are rooms that haven't been opened since at least the 1920s, if not earlier."

"Cellars within cellars?" Cali asked.

"A house within a house, basically," Fleetwood said.

"Who has the moo shu pork?" Mira asked, glancing around at the plates and the boxes. "Someone must have it."

"That'd be me," Chet said, and lifted the box nearest him. He had to get out of his chair slightly and lean over the table to pass the box; his white shirt got some plum sauce on the sleeve as he did so, and he wiped it on his jeans after he sat back down.

"Who read up on Harrow?" Fleetwood asked.

"Me," Cali said, and then looked around the table at the others. She took a sip of her beer and then set the empty can down. "Oh, come on, no one else here looked up anything about this place?"

Frost Crane nodded. "I know something about it. Not very much. Just what you've written before."

"Good," Fleetwood said. To Chet: "You know nothing about it?"

Chet shrugged. "I looked it up on the Internet at the library. I only had about a half an hour online, but all I saw was stuff about the fire last year and the school."

"Well, on the one hand," Fleetwood began, "I wanted you to know very little about Harrow before you arrived here. I didn't want any preconceived knowledge of this house to influence you. On the other hand, it might not hurt to know a bit about its history."

"I heard it was the most haunted house in America," Cali said.

"No," Fleetwood said. "That's another house, I think. There are plenty of haunted houses in the world. Harrow has barely made a dent in recorded hauntings. However, it has had its share of disturbances over the years. Harrow has, in my opinion, a much more interesting focus than ghosts, Cali. I believe it is a portal of some sort, and I also believe it contains treasures that we have not yet found, but that are here in the house."

"So this is some big treasure hunt," Chet said, his mouth still full. "And we're like the metal detectors."

Mira snorted a laugh. "There ya go, Dad. Someone's smart enough to be on to you."

"In your book, you had a whole chapter about Harrow," Frost Crane said, his chin lightly speckled with food; Chet tried to point this out to him in some hand gestures, but Frost didn't get it. Cali had to smile as she watched the guy she considered the Pompous and Annoying Grand Poobah speak. "But I read another book in your library. It was called *Infinity.*"

"The Infinite Ones," Jack Fleetwood corrected him, a warm undertone to his voice. He looked over at Cali, briefly, and she felt embarrassed. For just a lightning flash of a second, she had detected some interest from him. Strange man. Then she grinned at her own thought. *Lots of strange men at this table.*

"That's it. By a woman who had lived here. Around 1900," Frost continued, although it looked as if Fleetwood wanted to jump in and say more about the book. "So, it seems that this house has had séances before."

"Are we going to have a séance?" Mira asked, sitting up in her chair, her face brightening. She shot a glance at Chet. "Séances can be fun, even if nothing happens."

"I've never been to one," Chet said. "I guess where I'm from it's considered 'of the Devil,' sort of." Then he quickly added: "Not that I believe that. I'm not the rube you all think I am. I mean, I was raised Christian and all, but it's not like I think there's Satan everywhere or anything."

"Do you believe the world was made in six actual twenty-four-hour periods?" Frost asked.

Chet squinted his eyes as if he didn't understand the question. "I don't believe everything everyone writes is literal. If that's what you're asking, anyway."

"I always say 'Keep an open mind,' " Cali said. "In my world, creation happened the day before I was born."

Fleetwood chuckled.

"Wait," Mira said. "I don't get it."

"I mean, the world couldn't have existed before I was born. Maybe I created it all. Maybe . . . you're a figment of my imagination," Cali said. "Now, can you quit hogging the shrimp and broccoli and pass some of it over?"

"Okay, but watch out, it's hot."

"Hot as Hell," Chet said, laughing, as he drew a small red pepper from his mouth and set it down on the edge of his plate. And then, "Sorry, I guess I take everything too seriously. I don't really know what I believe God-wise, mainly because where I come from was so screwed up. You hear about Hellfire enough as a kid, it's tough to shake it."

"Early training." Cali nodded. "Tell me about it. I'm still depressed because there's no Santa Claus."

"I don't believe in God," Mira said matter-of-factly. "I think this is all a big mess we've been thrown into, and we make up gods and devils and reasons for why we all do these things, and then we just die at some point like any other animal or plant." She bit down hard on a shrimp when she finished speaking.

"And yet your father works with the idea that there's something else out there," Frost said. "Perhaps you're just rebelling."

"Could be," Mira said. "Or perhaps . . . I'm just a bitch."

Her father laughed the hardest, although Cali was beginning to feel annoyed by Mira, as well as by Frost.

"Mira, you could never be a bitch," Fleetwood said.

"Oh, Jesus Christ," Frost said, wadding up his napkin and dropping it on his plate.

Cali glanced at Chet. *What's up with this?*

Silence reigned at the table for another few moments before Mira said, "I don't mind being called a bitch."

Frost glared at her and took a sip from his tumbler of whiskey. "I didn't mean to imply bitch. I don't like language like that. Not at the dinner table. I just meant you're your own person. A rebel. I didn't mean that word."

"That's right," Fleetwood said. He reached over and said, "Frost, she meant it in good humor."

"No, she didn't. She was dredging up muck, that's what she was doing." Frost's voice betrayed no real anger; he sounded as if he were a schoolmaster speaking of some naughty but adorable child.

Chet piped up. "Anybody want to fill me in on this?"

Mira obliged. "Frost stayed with us for a couple of months at the Foundation. One day I accidentally—"

"Accidentally," Frost said under his breath.

"Accidentally," Mira emphasized, "walked in on him in a, let's say, private moment, wink-wink, nudge-nudge—"

"Jesus Christ," Frost said. "Are you going to actually talk about it?"

Silence, again. Cali seized the opportunity to grab a fortune cookie from the small white plate at the center of the table. She cracked it up. "My fortune is perfect," she said. " 'You will go on a journey that will take you to happiness. Just do not step off the path, or you shall be lost in the forest of confusion.' Well, that's a bit of an elaborate fortune, but it fits with Harrow."

Chet grabbed his cookie and drew the slip of paper out. "Aw. Mine's kind of boring."

"What's it say?" Mira asked, reaching for her fortune cookie.

Chet held up the slip. " 'Fortune smiles.' "

"That sucks," Mira said. "Mine's better. 'Take one heart and add one other, and you will still have one perfect heart.' Now, that's sort of a Harlequin moment."

Frost Crane stared at nothing, and then closed his eyes. He took another sip of whiskey and said, "The book was called *The Infinite Ones*, and in it, this medium talked about how Harrow was a portal for another world. Here's the thing: I think she was right. That's the only reason why I'm here at all."

"A porthole?" Chet asked.

"A portal," Fleetwood said. "Anyone mind if I smoke my pipe?"

"I do," Mira said.

"Me, too," Cali added. "But go ahead. Maybe we can open a window."

"Too cold out there," Mira said.

"I have asthma," Chet volunteered weakly. "I mean, sometimes. When there's smoke around."

"Okay, okay," Jack Fleetwood said, setting his unlit pipe beside his plate. "Used to be," he added with some slight sadness, "a guy could smoke after dinner."

"Used to be," Mira said.

Before an uncomfortable silence ensued, Cali decided to get back on topic. "Portals," she said. "They're like doorways to something unseen, basically. At least that's what I've understood them to be."

3

"A portal is like that." Fleetwood nodded. "An opening from some other dimension. That probably sounds crazy to most people, but since each of you has had some event that might indicate there's another dimension, say, to our existence, an unseen one, I'd guess each of you understands that."

"I wrote about portals in my first book," Frost Crane said.

"Wow. You both have books?" Chet asked

"I have two," Frost said. Then he added, his mouth wrinkling into a half-smile, "Both of them best-sellers."

"Frost was on 'Jerry Springer,'" Mira said.

"I've heard of you," Chet said, although it sounded like a lie. Cali watched him for a moment. She had thought at first that he was a sweet if naïve All-American boy who was confused by whatever psi talent he'd received in life. Now she wasn't sure. He was cute enough, and seemed bright, if slightly backward. But there was something wrong there.

Something wrong. She could sense that.

"'Oprah,'" Frost said. "I was on 'Oprah.' Twice."

"I must've missed that one," Mira said. "I usually like Oprah books. I read Wally Lamb's book. The one about the twins."

"I Know This Much Is True," Cali said.

"Yep. That one. It was good." Mira nodded. "But I go more for John Irving. *A Prayer for Owen Meany* is one of my favorite novels." She turned and touched Chet's elbow. "What's your favorite novel?"

"Catcher in the Rye," he said. "It's funny, because I only got it from the library because I thought it would be about baseball. But I liked it a lot. I used to read a lot when I was in school. I really liked *Moby Dick,* too. I don't know why, because no one else in English class liked it. I think it was because something happened in it. In some books, nothing ever happens. But I probably watch too much TV." Then he pointed his fork at Frost, who looked as if he were about to be attacked. "But that's pretty amazing. A best-seller writer. That's cool."

"My dad has a book, too," Mira added.

"Mine," Jack Fleetwood said, "was a best-seller in my home, but that's about it."

"Four thousand three hundred and fifty two people bought it," Mira said, with some small spark of pride. "In hardcover, no less. Sometimes I think the better the book, the fewer people who read it."

"I read it," Cali said. "It was interesting."

"Thanks."

"It was good," Frost said grudgingly. "I really liked what you had to say about bending reality."

"Right," Cali said. "It applies to everything I've dealt with in my work."

Chet leaned back in his chair. "So a portal is a doorway? And this place is a portal."

"I think so," Jack said. "I'll play you the tapes tonight, if anyone wants to stay up a bit."

"Tapes?"

Jack nodded. "EVP—Electronic Voice Phenomena. There's been a lot of research done on recording haunted places—particularly portals—to see if anything will show up on the tape."

"Magnetic fields," Cali said. "I've interviewed some people about it. The ghosts—or whatever you'd call them—emit electromagnetic charges."

"That's right," Jack said. "We've got very basic motion detectors around the house, too."

"Yeah. I put most of them around. It felt like there were a hundred of them. And the thermal scanners," Mira said. "Plus, we've even got night goggles for everybody."

"Night goggles?" Chet laughed. "Cool."

Mira nodded. "You can get most of the stuff at Staples or Radio Shack—the taping is done with Panasonic voice-activated minirecorders, but the night goggles we got from a place in England. They're Gen III. All that really means is that they allow you to see farther in the dark than you can with the naked eye. They're cool."

"Outrageously expensive, but definitely cool. And EMF—that's an electromagnetic field meter," Jack Fleetwood said. "It's for keeping track of any fluctuations in the electrostatic charges. We've got one in each room. Digital thermal scanners, too. Just a couple of them, so that if we come upon any sudden changes in temperature, it can be measured."

"Sounds like a prison," Cali said. She didn't want to add: *And a colossal waste of money.*

"I brought a digital camera to take some pictures," Frost said.

Mira shook her head, "No, that won't work."

"Mira," her father said softly. "A little politeness goes a long way."

"Sorry," she said. Then, to Frost: "Sorry. It's not that digital is so bad, it's just that as evidence . . ."

"As evidence it won't hold water," Cali volunteered. "Digital imaging is too easy to manipulate."

"That's part of it," Jack said. "Plus, of course, there's the problem of an environment with insufficient light. In bad light, a digital camera might create the sign of a phenomenon when there is none. They're problematic. And we're after evidence here, not just an experience. I've experienced hauntings before. I know they exist. But to gather as much proof as possible seems to be the only way to convince anyone else. We have the video cameras around, too, as I've mentioned to a couple of you already, but even video is hard to use if you want to convince people of this kind of thing. Basically, anything on film or tape can become illusory and is very easy to tamper with. I'm just hoping to get enough down to bring a preponderance of evidence."

"Why not just hire some scientists? Why bring in . . . us?" Chet asked. "I mean, if you want proof, no one's going to believe a bunch of freaks of nature."

Cali's eyes widened, and she giggled.

"Speak for yourself," Frost said.

Yet another deadly silence overcame the table.

Mira broke it. "We use an Olympus camera, and sometimes Polaroid. Dad developed our first pictures this morning—the negatives go to the local photo shop to be developed as well, but they take forty-eight hours to get them back to us. But we have the first prints to see if there's anything worth looking at. We took some pictures last night, and got some orbs."

"Orbs," Frost said, a farting laugh in his voice. "That's . . . goofy. At best."

"Some people think so," Jack Fleetwood said good-naturedly. "But they're hard to explain away."

"Orbs like balls?" Chet asked. "Man, do I feel stupid here."

"It's not much," Mira said. "But sometimes in manifestations, there are these balls of light—not really balls. Sort of oblong. Like small balloons, sort of. And they're cool. I'll show you the pics later on."

"They're just tricks of light," Frost said. "Honestly, Jack, you can't go in for every bit of ghost-hunting bullshit if you expect to prove something here."

"I want every bit of evidence," Jack said. Then he stood up. "I need to go for a little walk and smoke my pipe. Anyone care to join me?"

Cali raised her hand, as if she were in grade school. "I'd love to see the grounds a little."

"You won't see much right now," Frost said.

"We've got lights out in the garden. That'll be a nice place for a smoke. And then, anyone who wants coffee, we'll make a big pot and have it in the library in ten minutes or so. Sound good?"

"Let me go get my coat," Cali said. "Should be fun hunting up some ghosts."

"I don't believe in ghosts," Chet said, leaning back in his chair and glancing up at the ceiling. Cali looked up also, and noticed the scorched area around what had once been a beautiful raised, circular surface. “I don’t think they exist. Not like everyone talks about.”

“You will,” Jack Fleetwood said. “Here, in Harrow, you will.”

CHAPTER EIGHTEEN

1

Cali tried to keep up with Fleetwood, but he was apparently in a hurry to get outside and light up his pipe. She had to take double steps to keep up with him. They went out the doors on what must've once been a conservatory—beautiful green glass all around—and she stepped out onto a flagstone walkway. The lights were harsh and nearly blinding as she closed the door behind her.

"They're usually used for making movies, those lights," Jack Fleetwood said, his pipe thrust into his mouth, a gentle curve of smoke coming from it. He spoke with his teeth clenched, and she nearly laughed at how boyish he looked, unlike the professorial air she'd detected inside. He had put a baseball cap on and a wool scarf, as well as a thick red sweater to keep out the chill. He looked like a deranged Little Leaguer of five foot eight or so.

She drew her jacket around her shoulders. "It's like a baseball stadium out here," she said, and as she walked beside him now, she noticed the older wall and the sprays of stone arches that grew like tentacles from the back of Harrow. "What's all this? An aqueduct?"

Jack laughed. "The ruins of an abbey. Nothing in Harrow is local. All of it was brought in from ruins in Europe and from

Central America. Very little of its wood was even from the U.S. Gravesend—"

"He's the architect?" Cali said, trying to keep up.

"No, he was the owner. I guess you could call him the creator of Harrow. It's his psychosis that planted this house here. Thank God. I truly believe that he was creating a haunted place. I truly believe that."

They spoke a bit about the others still inside, although Cali learned nothing she didn't already know: that Chet was a bit of an innocent, simple in some ways, but very much at the mercy of the phenomenon surrounding him; and that Frost Crane was a narcissist with a devilish lack of self-esteem that manifested itself in a big fat ego. "But I can't blame him. Or any of you," Fleetwood said. "I'm a bit jealous."

"Seems strange to be jealous of Frost."

"Not just Frost. All of you. You have Ability *X*."

"Ah. The infamous Ability *X*."

"Don't mock me," he said good-naturedly. "I have always been fascinated by the paranormal, but it hasn't really touched me, beyond my studies."

"Your life's work. That's getting touched a lot, you ask me."

"Ah," he said.

"Ah what?"

"The classic self-hatred of the talented."

She stopped and looked at him. "What's in that pipe anyway?"

"All kinds of wonderful things," he said. "All of them bad for me."

"Why self-hatred? I don't hate myself."

"No, I don't suppose you do, Cali. But you hate that you have the ability you've got."

"Well, I hate the fact that I spend too much on clothes, too," she said.

"Now who's mocking?" he asked. "Here, look at this."

A narrow path led through a hedge, and when she'd followed him through it, it opened up into a sunken garden that seemed as big as a football field. Patches of ivy and weeds covered much of it, but there were three statues standing there in the white, flat, artificial light. Each statue had a vaguely Greek or Roman cast to it; one was a winged Victory sort of woman—or possibly an angel?—and one was a satyr sitting on a large urn; and the third was a young, handsome man, laurel wreath on his head, grapes in his hands.

"Only one of them is original to Harrow," Fleetwood said, using his pipe as a pointer. "That one."

"The angel?"

"Yes. She's a Victorian sculpture that Ivy found in a shop in Toronto. The man who had given Harrow over to the school—named Alfred Barrow—had apparently gotten rid of this, but it was traceable, and Ivy managed to bring her back. She's a bit chipped, and her nose—see how it used to be?" He drew his pipe along the cracked nose of the angel. "The others aren't original. They're close approximations of a few of the other statues that were once here."

"One question?" Cali asked.

"Shoot."

"Why so few of us? And so few of you?"

"Six people are plenty," he said.

"But if you want some proof, something to take back . . ." she began.

"All right, here's the thing: Ivy is paying for everything. She is endowing this venture, and she didn't want ten paranormal investigators, all schooled in ways of approaching this. I'm interested in proof. She's interested in unlocking Harrow. And its secrets."

"And we're the keys."

"In some respects, yes. In others, no. But I agreed with her that we needed sensitives in this, and not just analysts and ghost hunters. The history of Harrow's hauntings is actually short, and limited to a few months at a time, and then—nothing, apparently. Why? Because when Harrow has exhibited haunting in the past, there has always been a psi talent nearby."

"But a girl died here last spring?"

"Yes, and she may have had some untapped psychic ability. Or not. But it was the first indication that something had not just burned out here with the fire. It was still smoldering."

"Did Harrow kill her?"

"No," Jack said, his voice a bit enraged. "And I don't think you need to worry about personal safety. The girl's heart gave out, and she'd had a condition for years. It happens. She could've been in an elevator that skipped a floor, or fallen down in the tub—her heart may have given out from those things at that moment, as well. She probably had a shock. She probably experienced her ability for the first time, and it probably was not good for her to be at Harrow when that happened."

"Oh," Cali said, understanding a bit. "Like the first time I experienced my . . . ability."

"That's right. Each of you probably had a big shock the first time. But after that, you began to understand it and get used to it. I doubt the girl who died here did. My guess is, she saw something, briefly, that frightened her, and then, given her heart condition, she died. Surely some of the things you encounter scare you."

Cali tried to suppress the mental image of Gloria Franco's body on the floor of the apartment, and the man with the knife over her. A brief flare of a thought came up with this image: *Why would he kill Gloria if he loved her? What would make Gloria beg to be killed like that?* They walked a bit in silence, Jack puffing on the pipe as if it were a lifeline, and Cali's mind elsewhere even as she looked across the well-lit autumn garden and admired the stonework and the urns that were set in rows behind some dried, twisted vines.

"That seems nuts," Cali said. She kept her voice down a bit. "Sorry if this offends you, but, Jack, Ivy Martin must be a lunatic."

"In some ways, she is. But she understands something about Harrow. Something that I might not have even understood."

"And what's that?"

"It's like a body," Fleetwood said. "It needs all its limbs and fingers and features if it's to come alive."

"And we're here to bring it to life."

Fleetwood turned to her, and his gaze met hers. For an instant she felt a spark—almost like a shock from touching something—and he said, "You're here because you are, in some ways, the flint."

"Yeah, I guess you're right," Cali said, but didn't feel so light and carefree on the inside. "Christ, it's cold out here."

"Yep, it may be the end of October, but winter's coming fast to Watch Point," Fleetwood said.

"It's beautiful," Cali said, turning to go back to the house. "But I want to get back to that fireplace and a nice cup of coffee."

Suddenly a blurred shape rushed out from between the statues, and Cali nearly screamed, but the blur slowed down and became Conan, the muttly border collie, again, and he came up to her and put his muddy front paws right on her thighs as he jumped up to bark a greeting. She practically collapsed with laughter, but Jack was a little less amused. He clapped his hands and came up and pulled the dog down. "Shoo!" he said. Then he said to Cali, "I'm so sorry about that. He's filthy. I told Mira not to bring him."

"It's okay, it's okay," Cali said, wiping at the mud, still giggling. "Dogs I can take. Ghosts are going to be a different story."

2

Cali carried the tray of coffee in and set it down on a side table. Conan followed her in, wagging his tail; but when Mira snapped her fingers he hunkered down and kept his muzzle to the floor, as if he'd been a bad dog.

"Decaf on the left, caf on the right. Very, very strong caf," Cali said. She poured herself a mugful and then mixed in some cream and sugar. She turned and got everyone's order: first Chet, who wanted regular with lots of cream, no sugar; then Mira, black. Jack Fleetwood came in the room and went to mix his own coffee, and then she turned to Frost. "You?"

"Me?"

"How do you like it?"

"Decaffeinated. Very blond," he said. "Very blond and very sweet."

"I bet." Mira laughed, and then covered her mouth.

Frost watched Cali carefully. She had something, he could tell. He wondered how far her ability went. He wondered if it had turned off once she had entered the house, just like it had with him. *All right, admit it: You want to fuck her.* His mouth went dry as he thought it. *You're a man. You can think it. You want to open her up. She's hot. She's steamy. Inside, she's probably like a moist suction.* Then it came to him: *What if she could read minds? Some people claimed they could. Damn. Anyone in this room might be able to, even the little bitch.* "Thank you," he said, his voice crackling slightly, as if he'd been filled with static. He took the pottery mug. For a second his fingers grazed hers, and it felt like a mild shock. *Can you hear what I'm thinking?*

"I put a ton of sugar in there," Cali said, and then turned and went to sit next to Mira.

"Here," Mira said, offering part of the comforter she'd dragged in. "It's too cold in here."

"It sure is," Cali said, and drew the comforter over her shoulders a bit. It became a tug of war between them, and Mira finished with a laugh that almost spilled her mug out all over the floor.

"Now for the ghost stories," Mira said.

"No stories," Jack said. "Just a video." He set his mug on the floor and went to switch on the small television that rested on the mantel. "Can you all see this okay?"

"If you'd move," Mira said.

"Fine," Chet said. "What's the movie of the week?"

"It's a ten-minute segment from a History Channel special," Jack said. "It covered Harrow's past quickly, and I figured before you got the tour and all head to your bedrooms, you might want a little preparation."

"It might influence us," Frost said. He glanced around. "I mean, if it tells too much."

"I don't know how much or how little any of you know about Harrow. You might've heard things. Frost, you've been through my library at the Foundation. Cali's read my book," Jack said. "This will give you a bit of background about the fire and the legend. I think it's good to know."

3

The TV monitor flickered on, and a shot of Harrow in daylight, parts of it still smoldering, appeared.

The voiceover of a narrator spoke as the camera moved around what looked like a bombed-out sector of some war-torn city. Still Harrow, the house, stood, even while the walls and rooftops near it had been burned and destroyed.

"A tragedy struck Harrow Academy a few months ago when part of the tower and upper rooms of the East Wing of the school burned during a candlelit fraternity hazing episode. Several boys died in the fire. A month later, with the school empty of students and faculty, another fire broke out, this one in what was once the caretaker's house on the property. That fire spread to other buildings on the school grounds. What was probably most mysterious about the fires, beside their origins, was how they seemed to destroy much of what was not original to the house, known at times as Nightmare House to the locals of this sleepy hamlet called Watch Point."

The camera had begun to move through the ruins, and the wavering lights of the camera crew flickered as they moved into the entryway to Harrow.

"In the spring, a local teenager was found dead here, apparently the victim of a heart attack at the age of sixteen. . . ." The camera moved to the walls, with the burned wallpaper. "Signs of some occult ritual were left here, and two other teens claimed that this was the site of a haunting."

A cut to: a dark-haired and pimply but handsome boy whose eyes seemed too large for his face. Someone held a microphone under his chin; behind him, the woods near Harrow. "We went there as a joke. I mean, everyone called it the haunted house. Even my grandpa said bad things happened there. So we were just kind of camping out, only something happened to Quincy." He turned his head slightly, looking off in the distance. "Something frightened her. That's what I think."

Cut to: a local policeman. Chunky and balding, with a nose like a ski slope and eyes that seemed to get smaller the more he spoke. "It was the strangest thing. She had drawings all over her body. Like crop circles almost, or tattoos, but it was drawn with charcoal or something. And stuff written on her. She was dead. But no one killed her. Her heart just went out. We thought the boys might've killed her, at first. But it wasn't that. I guess when your number's up, it's up. These kids—they get into all this ritual. This Satanic crap."

Cut to: a close up of the wall, with shredded wallpaper. Written in crayon on the wall, the word *Mercy.*

"But the history of Harrow goes farther back than this."

A series of still images came up, mixed with old documentary footage. A photo of a car stranded on a dirt road. A gatekeeper's house leading into a tree-lined lane. An early view of Harrow, while it was still being constructed: The towers were just going up. A view of the front door, with some unusual Mayan or Incan godhead above it. A minute or so of what looked like a séance from a silent movie—a young woman with beautiful locks of hair and luminescent skin touched hands with a large man who looked handsome and threatening at the same time. Another photo: Lizzie Borden, the alleged ax murderess. Over these images, the narrator told a history of the house that included visitations by the rich and notorious: Borden, Alistair Crowley, a Vanderbilt heiress, and several famous spiritualists. A still picture again: Isis Claviger. The beautiful woman from the silent movie portion; this was the author photo from her book. "The disappearance of the famed medium was only one of the mysteries of Harrow, including the madness of the grandson of Justin Gravesend, the creator of the house. In the mid-1920s, the man who was then known as Ethan Gravesend committed atrocities that shocked the conservative area, and sent ripples of terror up and down the Hudson River."

Another still picture: a wide-eyed, long-haired boy in a coat and tie: a school picture. "A boy committed suicide at the school that Harrow became. He left a note indicating that he'd found a door in a wall at Harrow and went through it and found that goblins were after him, although he did not elaborate further."

A final picture, this of a sweet-looking boy of fifteen or sixteen with neatly cut dark hair and some kind of deep sadness to his features. "Jim Hook was among the boys who dabbled in a secret fraternity at Harrow. But did they act alone, or was some supernatural agency involved?"

Then Jack Fleetwood came on screen.

Cali clapped, and Mira whistled.

The subtitle under his throat read: JOHN FLEETWOOD, FOUNDER AND PRESIDENT OF THE PSI VISTA FOUNDATION.

"Harrow has always fascinated me," Fleetwood said (Mira said these words as her father spoke them on the television). "Very little has been documented about the hauntings there, but I have no doubt that it lives up to the epithet given to it in 1926: Nightmare House. It was built by Gravesend to be haunted. And the recent events may be a senseless tragedy, or, in fact, may be one in a long line of aftereffects from the original haunting that was born there in the late 1800s by Justin Gravesend himself."

Cut to: a professorial-looking chap wearing a tweed overcoat and a bright red tie against his crisp white shirt. His eyes seemed owlish behind his round spectacles. A hint of hair crested his otherwise bald scalp. The subtitle read: PAYTON WINSLOW, PROFESSOR OF PARAPSYCHOLOGY. THE HUDSON INSTITUTE.

"If Harrow is haunted," Winslow said, "then I've never felt it. Yes, that horrible event occurred with the students. And a girl died there recently. So what? These events and tragedies occur daily, everywhere. But because there's some old story about a structure like Harrow, it's a haunting? I thought this kind of foolishness went out with table-rappings. A ghost is merely an electrical recording—a mirage of a previous life, if you will—that some human beings see now and then. Ghosts can't harm anyone. It's the living who are the problem, and I know the entire history of Harrow, and none of it leads me to believe it is anything other than a place where a few nasty incidents occurred over a hundred-year period. I would imagine the White House would be the site of more hauntings than that run-down place in Watch Point."

A still picture came up. A forensics picture? Subtitle: QUINCY ALLEN, 16 YEARS OLD, DEAD OF A HEART ATTACK AT HARROW.

Across her back, a charcoal drawing of what looked like an *H* with several lines through it, and a small circle within it.

The narrator said, "Still, it is hard to ignore the fact that something is terribly wrong at Harrow. Something is within its walls."

The video ended with a picture of static, and then a blue screen came up.

4

"That show still sucks," Mira said, talking as much to the television as to her father, who switched the TV off.

"I didn't know someone died here last spring," Chet said. "That's morbid."

"And I can see that the ghosts here are harmless," Cali said archly.

Mira nearly spilled the last of her coffee on the comforter but made a quick save. "That documentary was a piece of crap. Dad, I don't know why they needed to see it."

Her father stood at the mantel and glanced at the others. "Well, it's your first night. I don't want to make you think that this will be a vacation. The Foundation is paying you well, but for payment, there's a further price."

"Quincy Allen had a heart murmur, and her family knew about it for years. Plus, she was into some kind of bizarre made-up occult religion," Mira said. "She died because she had a very weak heart, she'd drunk too much cheap rum that night, there was some crystal meth found nearby, and she probably scared herself with her own rituals. A ghost didn't get her. And those boys." Mira was fuming, and Frost chuckled a little, watching her tirade. "Those preppies were high and had a ton of candles around and did their little frat hazing bullshit. They had nearly a hundred candles in the tower room, and they were drunk. It would've been more shocking if a fire hadn't started."

Frost grinned. He felt good. "So there are no ghosts here?"

Mira looked down at him. Then up to her father. "I didn't say that. I just think that documentary was like a . . . I don't know." She glanced down at her hand. "It was like a splinter from this place. It wasn't what it's about here. Dad—can we play them the tape?"

"I guess now's a good time," Jack said. He reached into his pocket and withdrew a small handheld device. "It's my favorite gadget—my pocket PC."

"His HP Jornada," Mira said. "He loves gadgets."

Jack's face erupted in a big, goofy grin. "True." He went and sat down next to Frost, folding his legs in front of him.

"Chet, come sit over here," Mira said, patting the edge of the sofa. "You'll hear better."

Chet rose from the chair near the door and loped over toward the sofa, sitting on the arm.

"I can do a lot of neat things with this little machine, but it also records. Not the best recorder, but unfortunately, I didn't have my Panasonic on me when this happened."

"You got something," Cali said.

"Play it, Dad."

"The thing with EVP is, sometimes it's soft as a whisper. If I'd had my usual tape machine, maybe I would've gotten more," Jack said. "Still, it's pretty clear."

Frost looked at the small handheld PC and watched as Jack flipped open its visor and pecked at it with a small plastic pointer. Jack looked at him and winked. They all leaned in toward the gadget.

A sound like whirring came up.

"Shit," Mira said after a few seconds. "You erased it."

"I didn't erase it. The file's right here."

"Oh, well," Mira said. "That was a lot of nothing."

"What's on it? I didn't hear anything."

Jack Fleetwood sighed and shut off the machine. "Well, it's gone. Damn."

Frost snickered. "I bet there wasn't anything there in the first place."

Jack glanced at him with the fatherly concern that drove Frost nuts. It was contempt; that's what Fleetwood had for him. Contempt. *He thinks I'm crazy just because I told him too much when I was at his place. Just because his daughter caught me doing that thing. If only the God of Snapping Jaws would come down and tear his face off.*

"There was," Fleetwood said, shaking his head slowly. He grinned, but it was not the grin of a happy man.

"You sure it was the right one?" Mira asked.

"What'd it say?" Cali asked.

Jack said, "They're playing with us already. I can tell."

Frost looked over at Chet. The farmboy looked skeptical. *Good. Don't believe in this stuff, kid.* Frost said, almost to Chet alone, "Maybe the ghosts don't like us."

"Look, Frost," Mira said, "I heard it."

Answering Cali's question, Jack said, "It was a girl's voice. She said a word over and over again. 'Mercy.'"

Chapter Nineteen

1

They sat in silence, and Cali felt as if she were around a campfire on the edge of some ancient savannah—as if Harrow were not a house after all, but some wilderness outpost. It was hard to believe there was a town just down the road from the house. They were beyond reach—that's what it felt like to Cali. As if they had isolated themselves from the entire world just by stepping into the house.

"These things happen," Jack said, weariness in his tone. "Crash course in recording a haunting: Ghosts are tricky. This is why it's hard to prove anything outside of direct experience." He brightened and then said, "Here's how we categorize manifestations: noise, movement of an object, physical contact, odor, and actual appearances. That's not something I made up—it's from one of the oldest investigative groups—England's Society for Psychical Research. Some of those things can be recorded; some can't. Be open, but keep your skepticism intact. No one wants anyone to see something that's not there. I will say that one of the blocks to a lot of ghost research—at least from my own understanding of it—is that the people looking for the phenomenon were not necessarily portals themselves."

"We're portals," Chet said. "Seriously?"

"I believe you are, Chet. Each of you has provided some opening of contact. Contact seems to me to be the key. None of you went seeking this. None of you has actually claimed to believe in ghosts as such. Frost, you believe your ability is from some shift in reality—the river theory, basically. You think that there's some continuum and you tap farther up the bend. And Cali, you've always stated, on your radio show, that it's purely a different level of intuition, and something of an inherited trait. Chet think's it's sort of spontaneous—it happens, and I'd guess that maybe he's not even sure what it's about. And then there's Ivy. Ivy, I have no doubt, is the catalyst for what will awaken Sleeping Beauty."

"Sleeping Beauty?"

"The house. It's dormant. It awoke last year with a student named Jim Hook, another catalyst. He had some ability to open the portal a bit. Perhaps not all the way, but he got it unlocked; and then it snapped shut again. In 1926, Esteben Palliser, then known as Ethan Gravesend, the grandson of Justin Gravesend, also opened the portal. And again, it closed, with only glimpses of it afterward. Now each of you are keys of sorts. Ivy, too."

"When do we get to meet our mysterious hostess?" Frost Crane asked in an overly solicitous tone.

"Sometime tonight, I'd guess. I try to give her every privacy. She has been more than generous with this project."

"It's nearly eleven," Chet said, a yawn in his voice. "I hope we meet her soon or I'll have to wait . . ."

" 'Til tomorrow night. She's a kook," Mira said. "But she's smart and she's pretty and she's rich, so she can get away with it. If it were me, I'd be in a straitjacket." Then she asked if she could be excused. As she pushed her chair in, she looked right at Chet and said, "I can show you where your room is, if you want. And it's really cool to wear the night goggles. Takes some getting used to, but you can see a lot in the dark with them."

"Now?" Chet responded suddenly, and then, "Yeah, sure."

"We've got to tour the house a bit before everyone goes to sleep," Jack said, a touch of paternal caution in his voice.

"Okay," Mira said. "Follow me." She went over to the doorway with a bit of a saunter in her stride.

Mira, you minx. You're after Chet. He's too old for you. Cali watched Mira transform fairly quickly into a fairly pretty young girl who was trying to show that she was mature for her new crush.

After the two of them had left the library, Chet with a bit of an apologetic look on his face, as if he was leaving too early, Frost returned to the topic of Ivy Martin.

"What's her ability?"

Jack Fleetwood said, "She is obsessed with Harrow. At the expense of all else. She wants something from Harrow, and I suspect that whatever fuels the hauntings of this property needs someone to want it. Badly. Unfortunately, in her time here, overseeing the renovation of Harrow, Ivy Martin has begun to believe that she was always meant to be mistress of the house."

2

Some feeble jokes were made, as if it was the only way to break the ice further than had already been done; Frost kept asking about Ivy, and Cali was getting bored with sitting on her butt so much. And then the cell phone began beeping.

"That's me," she said, reaching for her shoulder bag. She unzipped the top and dug down beneath the tissues and her purse, until, there, she grabbed the small phone. She lifted it up and pressed its ON button. "Hello?"

3

"It's me," Det said.

Cali glanced at the others in the room. Fleetwood and Frost had gone silent. She mouthed to them: "One second." Jack Fleetwood nodded; he understood.

"Det, what's up?"

"We caught him."

"Already? Wow. That was fast."

"It was easy. But, Cali," Det said, his voice a bit nervous, "this will sound crazy."

"Okay," she said.

"He told me that someone he calls Scotty left him. He said Scotty was the reason he killed Gloria. It was a ritual of some sort. She had paid him to kill her. She thought she was possessed by this kid. Her son."

"Oh," Cali said. She closed her eyes. She didn't want to imagine the boy she had felt had been there—the presence within Gloria Franco's apartment. "Can we talk about this later?"

"Sorry. Middle of something?"

"Sort of," she said.

"Okay. But you were right, babe. You knew—there was a kid, and Gloria apparently killed the kid, and then felt as if the kid's spirit wouldn't leave her. And this guy was haunted, too.

Sounds nuts, but knowing your take on all this, well, you were dead on."

"Yeah. Well. I have to go. I'll call you tomorrow," Cali said. "'Bye."

"I miss you," Det said, but she had just shut off the cell phone.

She shut the phone and put it in her lap.

"Bad news?" Jack asked.

"Not really. Work stuff, I guess," she said, pushing the thought out of her mind. The thought that had bothered her like a mosquito would bother her, buzzing around her head.

Like a gnat.

Like a fly.

Poor old lady she swallowed a fly.

4

"I should've emphasized this, but I don't really want cell phones here," Jack said.

"You have your computers," she said, and then laughed a little. "I sound like a third-grader."

"And the reason I don't want cell phones is not because of some electromagnetic goof. It's simply because I'd like each of you"— and here Jack glanced at Frost as well— "to concentrate on Harrow and what's here. I don't want outside influences on your time here. One thing that the Foundation is paying for is your focus. On the other hand, you're not required to do anything I ask. But I think you'll find your time is better spent here without contact with the world beyond these walls."

"Spooky," Frost said cheerily.

“No prob,” Cali said. “I’ll lock it up in my car in the morning. I don’t really want calls anyway.”

“Great.”

“Now, can we get some kind of tour?” Cali asked, rising from the chair.

Chapter Twenty

1

"God," Chet said, laughing. "It's huge."

He stood in the doorway of the bedroom and glanced at the antique furniture. The bed was a medium-sized one, but it seemed ancient.

"That's a sixteenth-century–style bed, but it's a reproduction done in the early twentieth century," Mira said. "This is supposed to have been the bedroom that Esteban Gravesend slept in, but I think it was just yet another little classroom for the school a year ago. That writing desk is Chippendale." She pointed to what looked to Chet like a dresser with an extra slat of wood jutting out from it. "And that," Mira said, pointing to the large mirror with curved edges and a plain iron frame, "is original to Harrow. I don't know much about the rest of it, but I would guess there's even a chamber pot in here somewhere."

"Wow." Chet shook his head. "Ivy Martin is something."

"She's really over the top," Mira said. She stood behind him, and Chet wanted to turn and ask her not to stand so close—it made him slightly uncomfortable, but he didn't want to offend her. She was just a kid, after all—a few years younger than he was, but a world away from him. He detected her crush right away. He always did when girls had crushes on him—which they had—but he'd done his best to discourage them. Now, Mira, whom he had just met, had already given off signals of her interest, and he'd played dumb, hoping it would go away.

"She must have a fortune," Chet said, stepping into the bedroom. He turned to face her.

"I think she's throwing it away on this house," Mira said. She leaned into the door frame and watched him. She pointed to a writing desk near the long window, covered with a large forest-green curtain. "Dad says that desk cost at least six thousand. At least. She found some of the photos of the house from the 1920s. She wants the rooms to look the same. And that chair"—she pointed to a chair that was pressed against a closed door on the other side of the bed. "That's a Louis the Sixteenth something or other. I had to help inventory a lot of this stuff. That's probably only worth a little over a thousand."

"That's a lot of cash," Chet said.

"You smoke?"

"No," he said. "I thought you didn't either."

"I mean, *smoke* smoke," Mira said, putting her fingers to her lips, miming a joint.

"No," he said quickly. "That's illegal."

Mira grinned. "Yeah," she said snappily. The gleam of interest remained in her eye. "I bet you're just an All-American boy. Baseball, apple pie, and Mom."

Chet closed his eyes for a second. His head hurt. *You're tired,* he thought. *Tired and confused by this whole thing.* Opened his eyes. Mira was funky and cute—her face was a little pear-shaped, and her lips glistened with blood-red lipstick and gloss; her mascara was heavy, and her purple-black hair actually made him notice her eyes more. She had deep-sea blue eyes. If he had been a couple of years younger, he probably would've hung out with her, but he felt old even at nineteen, and she looked like a child to him. "Yeah, I like all those things."

"Something wrong?" she asked.

"Just dizzy for a second," he said. "It's sort of stuffy in here."

"It is," Mira said. She walked past him to the window and drew the curtain back. "Look at that," she said. "Not all windows have it."

There was a stained-glass picture in the window of sloping green hills and a castle.

Mira unlocked the window and cracked it slightly. A cool rush of air came in. "God, it feels like it's gonna snow already. Brrr," she said, and leaned over to close it again.

"No," Chet said, taking a step. "I like a little fresh air at night."

"Okay."

"I'm fine, Mira. Thanks. I probably should just get ready for bed. Thanks for showing me those paintings and stuff."

"Okay," Mira said, her voice getting meek.

"We'll do the night goggles tomorrow night, I promise. I'm just exhausted."

"Sure," Mira said. "Tomorrow. Hey, and you know the baño is down the hall, right?"

"The what?"

"The can. The john. It's two doors down on the left. There's a tub with claws for feet and you can shower in it if I want. I mean, if you want. It works fine. It's connected to Dad's room, so be sure and close both doors when you go in there," she said, and then nearly backed out of the bedroom. "Fresh towels in the wardrobe"—she pointed to the far right— "and even a bathrobe if you want one. But they're not mandatory."

And then she was gone.

2

A quick shower sounded good, so he went and grabbed a towel and headed down the dimly lit corridor. The floorboards looked as if they needed sanding—he had taken his shoes off in the room, and it felt a bit rough. The lights in the hall were small overhead ones that reminded him of school, so he assumed they were leftovers from the house's previous identity. Two doors down, the bathroom was open. It was a fairly small room, with green-and-gold-mosaic tile running along it, and the mirror above the bowl-like sink was small and cracked on one side. The bathtub was also small, but Chet was fascinated by the claw feet that held it up. They looked like eagle talons wrapped around small globes. There was no shower curtain, and he saw, instead, a red rubber hose that ran from the faucet down into the tub.

He figured out quickly that the only way to shower in this tub was to sit in it as if taking a bath and then use the rubber hose to pour water over himself. He turned the hot and cold water on simultaneously, and then went to close the door leading to the bedroom. There was no way to lock it, and it had an enormous keyhole; he suddenly had a vision of Mira sitting on the other side of the door, watching him bathe.

The keyhole, in fact, was in a direct line from the edge of the tub. He smirked, thinking that he had a dirty mind. *Only men think of things like that. Only guys would be that perverted as to watch someone through a keyhole.*

When the water temperature seemed about right, Chet stripped off his clothes, leaving them in a pile on the floor, and stepped into the tub.

It felt good after the long day and all the new people and this whole house thing that he had committed himself to seeing through. He let the warmth of the water loosen up his back muscles a little, and for a second or two he closed his eyes.

3

Mira watched him through the keyhole, feeling silly and wicked for doing it. But she had loved watching the way he let his jeans drop to the floor, and the hard curve of his calves and thighs; and then his shirt had come off, and for a moment, in her mind, she imagined licking his washboard abs; and a goofy and girlish moment of spying began to give her a feeling of heat, as well as an inability to look away from the keyhole; she felt tingling sensations along her skin as she watched him drop his shirt and then reach under the elastic of his snow-white briefs and slowly draw them down.

It was an amazing show, and just as he was turning toward her—toward the tub, to turn off the water before getting into his bath—a feeling of dreadfulness overcame her. She was doing something irrational, something that weirdoes did; she felt it, she shouldn't be doing this. He needed his privacy; this was wrong.

She closed her eyes and stood up. She looked at the closed door, and then, tears of embarrassment and longing in her eyes, she turned away.

4

Mira went down the corridor, feeling alone and ugly and miserable. *No boy is going to want you. Not like this. Not spying on boys when they take off their clothes. Not watching for some perverted payoff when the underwear comes off. It's funny if you're with your friends, but not like this. Not like this. He'll never like me. He doesn't even think I'm pretty.*

Her room was just around the corner—almost at the edge of the staircase. It had been, according to Ivy Martin, the nursery, where Gravesend's son and daughter had been taken care of when they were born; Mira felt like a big baby as it was, so it seemed appropriate that this was her room, with its small bed and miniature dressing table. She reached for the light switch, but her hand didn't find it immediately.

In her mind the images of Chet's naked body, his sinewy musculature, his round ass, even the Adam's apple at his throat, all was in her brain, but along with this was an undercurrent of heat and guilt, as if she was both fascinated and disgusted by her own interest in him.

Where's the damn light switch. Mira reached into the darkness.

Finally, she switched it on.

She was in her room again.

She felt safe.

Her dog, Conan, lay asleep on his back in the middle of the

bed, his paws moving slightly as he chased rabbits in his dreams.

She went over to the dressing table to write in her spiral-bound notebook that doubled as both her history notes and her diary.

5

Dear Fucked-up Diary,

Bite me, and I don't mean that literally. He hates me. I'm a perv. Nicki would call me kinky, but that's because she likes to talk like that. I hate myself for this. I can't believe I sat there and watched him take off his clothes. I can't believe I've sunk that low. I'm so gross, nobody is ever going to want me, especially not an older guy like Chet, who is perfect and nice and innocent and even unaware. I wish I were back home. I wish I could call Mom. But of course she's still in London, and that would mean that I'd wake her or whatshisname up, and over nothing. I wish I could've made Dad leave me back in the city so I could just have my normal life instead of this. Ever since we got here, I've wanted to go home. I know this is important to him, and I know I practically volunteered to get out of school for a week and a half, but I wish I were back there instead of here. This feels wrong. And Chet. If I had never met him today, maybe I wouldn't build up these expectations. I don't care about boys that much; I'm not one of those stupid girls who chases boys and thinks of boys all the time. But I feel like that here. I feel like an idiot. I'm horny and stupid, and I shouldn't even be here. Christ. I wish I had brought at least one joint to get through this.

And on top of it all, thank you thank you, I think I'm getting cramps. Oh, joy. How fun and attractive and happy I will be over the next few days.

What's going on with me? I don't get it. I just finished having my period a week ago. And that weirdo Frost is here and looking at me funny of course, although I think he's just scared of me now. Ivy with her weirdness. It's all weirdoland here, and I'm the biggest weirdo of them all. I usually like feeling like a freak, but something's wrong with this place. Something's wrong here.

I want him to love me. I just know he will. I know he will. And there's nothing I can think about. I just saw his face and I knew he was the one.

The one for me.

The one who I must have.

Chapter Twenty-one

1

"There are twelve rooms open at Harrow," Jack said. "Originally, there were seventy or so, but you'll notice that some are off-limits from either construction work or fire or water damage."

"Water?" Cali asked.

Jack nodded. "The water damage was at least as severe as what the fire did. When the fire spread, it made some major openings in the roof, basically, and then, of course, you had every fire truck for miles around hosing the place down. A lot of rain came down last year, too, and most of it seemed to seep down the walls of rooms."

"Why is it so dark?" Frost asked. He stayed just to the left and a step behind Cali, which annoyed her. It was a bit like having someone breathing over her shoulder.

"Ivy wanted to induce a mood," Jack said. "I can't say that I agree with her. I'm not sure, if there's a haunting here, that the ghosts would care if the lights were bright or dim."

"Or whether it was night or day," Cali said.

"It's always dark in the hallways during the day, at least here in the west wing of the house. The east wing is shut for now—the renovations aren't complete there," Jack said.

"That's nice." Cali reached up to touch the edge of one of the wall lamps. "It's like a gas lamp."

"It's authentic. Ivy's a stickler for authenticity. Gravesend originally would allow no electricity in the house. Ivy was unwilling to go that far, but she managed to keep the look of the era here. The school had destroyed much of this in its years." Jack pointed to the floor, although all Cali could see was darkness. "They'd covered over it with a cheap parquet, but it's beautiful oak, these floors."

"I bet she spent three million on this," Cali said. "It's like walking through a museum."

"Here we go," Jack said, opening a door. "After you."

2

Cali caught a light scent of lavender in the room—it was a long, spacious bedroom, and on the ceiling was an intricate plaster pattern of leaves and birds. The bed was almost a Stickley style—very spare, flat boards made up the head and footboards, and the wood had not been touched with the intricate carvings found elsewhere in the house. "This was Genevieve Gravesend's room. She liked more modern furnishings than did her husband," Jack said. "She slept here only a short while before moving to the New England coast, without her husband. She wasn't fond of Harrow."

"Did she hang herself by that?" Frost pointed to the single-tier chandelier that hung from the ceiling.

"Not at all," Jack said. "She died of natural causes."

"Oh," Frost said. "I thought perhaps everyone who had ever lived here had gone mad."

"Perhaps we'll all go mad," Cali said with a grin. She felt a bit light-headed and sleepy, despite the surging of caffeine in her veins. "And then we'll throw ourselves from the tower. How romantic."

Jack gave her a bemused look. "I hardly need tell either of you that not everyone who has set foot in Harrow has died a horrible death. Thousands of boys and their teachers have come through these hall and lived perfectly normal lives."

"Perfectly normal," Cali said wistfully. "Not like us." She shot Frost a wicked glance. "We're freaks. We're meant for houses like this."

"Speak for yourself," he said. No humor in that one, Cali thought.

"The bed is a reproduction, of course," Jack said, "but the mirror near the chiffonier—that was an original to Harrow. Ivy felt it should go in the mistress's room."

"Is this where she sleeps?" Cali asked.

"Not on your life. When Ivy sleeps, it's usually down in the cellar."

"Good God," Frost said. "She owns this place and she sleeps down there?"

Jack shrugged. "It seems eccentric, but it's her decision."

"This should be my room then," Cali said. She went and sat on the edge of the bed. "Please tell me I can sleep on this beautiful bed. Please."

"Your wish is my command," Jack said. "Want to see the rest of the place?"

They walked from room to room, oohing and ahhing over the antique furnishings, some of it reproduction, some original pieces. Because both Mira's and Chet's rooms were locked, they decided to bypass them, although Cali had to stop in at the bathroom off Jack's room to admire the claw-footed tub. When they arrived at the room that Frost had claimed, Frost flicked the light up in the room and said, "Something's changed."

Jack Fleetwood glanced around the bedroom and then looked skeptically at him.

"Someone's been in my room."

3

"What's different?" Jack asked.

Frost looked at him, and then at Cali. "I guess nothing. I guess it's nothing," he said. "I thought the curtains were closed before. Now they're open."

"Well," Jack said, "if it's a spirit moment, it'll be captured on camera. Let's hope it is. If not, then probably Ivy has been in here."

"That's probably all it is," Frost said, mild irritation in his voice.

"Yes, she wanders. I don't want to unnerve any of you, but she goes where she pleases here, and as much as I'd like to limit her, she is the money here, and none of us would be here without her." Then, more mildly, Jack added, "We'd prefer that all the rooms remained unlocked, but if a door is closed, rest assured someone will knock before entering."

"Good to know," Cali said. She turned and went back out into the hallway. The corridor was a long one. At the end of it were double doors that no doubt led to other parts of the house. She went down to the end of the hall and pulled back the left door. It was completely dark on the other side, but she saw wisps of plastic sheets and plywood boards leaning. An icy breeze came through, and she stood there, wondering why she felt as if someone might be there, in the darkness, waiting for her to step into the other side.

Jack called down to her, "That's the off-limits area. Nothing exciting there—just the mess the contractor left in late September."

Cali glanced back at him. Jack had begun walking toward her. "This the east wing?"

She noticed that Frost had not reemerged from his bedroom. When Jack reached her, he shook his head, chuckling. "That Frost. He's a character."

"What's up with him? He's acting all nervous and guilty."

"It's his basic nature," Jack said. "We had him over as a guest for several months a while back, and he has a strong streak of paranoia running through him. I know for a fact that the curtains of that room were open—I think he's trying to draw attention to himself by pretending that something supernatural has already happened to him. He's a bit of a showman."

"Lovely," Cali said.

"He's not a bad guy," Jack said. Then he turned to the left and reached for the knob of a narrow door. Cali had assumed it was a closet or a bathroom. "Let's go up now that we're here."

"What's this one?"

"It's the stairs up to the turret room in back. The one you can see from out in the statue garden. It was completely closed off from students by Alfred Barrow, the founder of the school. It's a special place."

"How so?"

"It's where Justin Gravesend bricked his daughter up alive," Jack said.

Chapter Twenty-two

1

The stairway was winding and narrow, and Cali had to keep putting her hand against the wall to steady herself. There was very little light on the stairs themselves, so Jack's flashlight came in handy. Above, a dim but warm glow of light descended as they rose, and by the time they reached the landing of the tower, the room was well lit with several floor lamps all connected to one socket with an extension cord. The room was chilly, and there was nothing terribly interesting about it—it was curved as a tower room would be—and the stones were not covered over with plaster or wood, so it felt more like being in a medieval castle than did the rest of the house. Cali noticed the ever-present video camera above one of the lamps; an EMF meter sat in a corner of the room, also.

The room was bisected by a wall and a doorway through the wall—but there was no door.

"She died here," Jack said, motioning with his flashlight into the other half of the turret. Cali glanced in the room. The light shone across the far wall. Scratches and unusual symbols covered the stones. "She had lived most of her life within Harrow itself. It was a terrible monstrosity, but in those days insanity was little understood."

"Oh my God," Cali said. "She was insane and this is what he did to her?"

"The story goes," Jack said, "that she was just a child when her psi talent began showing, and manifesting itself in presumably dangerous ways. Nobody has the details, but from what I understand, there was even an exorcism to remove the demons from her—when she was barely eight years old."

"Jesus." Cali shook her head.

"And then she died."

"In here? At eight?"

"No, she was much older. Supposedly she died of some childhood ailment and was interred in the family crypt, but that must've just been the word that got out. She had not died at all, but, in fact, was alive and living in the house into middle age. Her father, in his madness, built a house within Harrow—walls behind walls—and it became her asylum. She lived within the house without ever entering the house proper again. We don't know much about her, but we have found some of the passages through the house. The fire last year exposed them," Jack added.

"That's awful. Just . . . terrible," Cali said.

"Maybe. But bear in mind the state of mental institutions in the late 1800s. They were nightmarish places. What father would've been able to bear to put a young daughter in one of them? Particularly Gravesend, who had watched his mother go insane in her thirties and spend the next thirty years of her life in the dungeon of an institution farther up the river—a place that would mildly be called a torture chamber by today's standards? I would guess, sadly, that Gravesend was doing the best he knew how, given the difficulties he had in the world."

"Why not just keep her in the house? Why build another world for her?"

Jack shrugged. "Could be she was violent. Could be that the shame of her insanity was too much. But I suspect something more, because you see, Gravesend belonged to an occult society. It was called the Chymera Magick, and it has been claimed that they committed atrocities and were devil-worshippers, among other wonderful but probably misguided notions. They were a secret group that may have been around since at least the thirteenth century, although it may have gone even farther back in history. Gravesend, in his youth, watching his mother's insanity, had sought them out and performed feats for them—presumably of a magical nature—that impressed them enough to induct him at the age of twenty-three, which made him their youngest member. He amassed great wealth in his life, too—and this was something the Chymera Magick sorely needed, because some members had squandered what treasures they'd built up.

"Gravesend began an international trade—on a small but significant scale—of antiquities and religious artifacts, and, in effect, raided the Chymera's storehouse by buying sacred objects from its membership and their heirs. Ancient books, objets d'art, even an abbey from a then-isolated part of France. And he built this house as a museum, and he built the house within the house to hide his museum of the sacred and the profane. Relics of saints; dinosaur bones that were then thought to be the bones of ancient dragons; demonic vessels—it was rumored that Gravesend owned some of the most legendary objects of the holy and unholy world. Why? My guess is, he wanted to help his daughter. I think he believed in these objects. He believed they would cure his daughter's soul of the madness and release the demons within her, and protect her from the evil that surrounded her. He didn't understand that she had Ability *X*. She also very well may have had multiple personality disorder, as well as violent mood swings, all of which would've contributed to the effect of terror. And worst of all," Jack said, almost sadly, "Gravesend had some tremendous guilt for the early acts of his life—and his guilt fed into the darkness to which he consigned his only daughter."

All Cali could think to say to this was: "Holy shit."

It was as much for the story as it was for the darkness within the other room. She thought she saw something moving—a shadow at the edge of the beam of light. A large shadow.

A woman's shadow.

2

Stepping into the flashlight's beam: a woman who looked only slightly older than Cali, tall and slender, with hair barely brushed, nearly strawlike. The woman's eyes were encircled with purple smudges of what could only be sleeplessness, and her face seemed quite drawn. "It's terrible what he did," the woman said. "But probably worse than that, what he created here."

Cali nearly jumped, and felt goose bumps along her arms and neck. Her heart pounded, and she quickly glanced at Jack, who observed her expression.

He had a twinkle in his eye. "Cali Nytbird, meet Ivy Martin."

3

Ivy Martin was a vision of failed beauty, and Cali could not help but feel sorry for her in some way, although she wasn't quite sure why. She was young, probably in her early thirties, which surprised Cali, who had thought Ivy would be much older, given her wealth. She seemed entirely self-possessed, and that must have been the money and drive, because Cali knew few people who seemed this together. And still, an air of sorrow and dust accompanied her, as if she, herself, were a ghost.

"Holy shit," Cali repeated, feeling a whoosh of air escape her lungs. "Holy, holy shit."

"Hello," Ivy said, extending her hand in greeting. Cali took it and gave it a brief but firm shake.

"Hi. Christ, you scared me."

"Oops," Ivy said. "I didn't mean to." Then she glared at Jack. "You could've told them all I was around."

"I did," Jack said sheepishly. "Honest."

Back to Cali, Ivy offered a weary grin. "Sorry about that. I've been exploring, and I lost my flashlight down the stairs somewhere." She indicated the other room with a wave of her hand. "It's filthy down there, and I think there are rats."

"Down there?"

"It's one of the entrances to the inside part of the house," Ivy said. "Jack? Have you told her nothing?"

"No, he told me. I just didn't know this was a way in," Cali said.

"Well, I'd give you a tour, but it's a little rickety down there. And look." She held a hand up to Jack, who took it in his. "I cut myself. I think I need a booster shot now. Damn it."

Cali noticed that Jack held her hand a bit tenderly, and then felt right away their connection. Jack was in love with her. It was right there in his eyes when he watched her, in the way he became a little boy, a boy in love.

"Damn it," Ivy said. Then, "So, you're the psychometric one, right?"

Cali nodded.

"Good," Ivy said in a businesslike manner. "Here, try this." She reached into her pocket with her free hand and brought out what looked like a small shiny rock. "It's from a piece of jewely. I think it's alexandrite."

Cali went over and put her hand out; Ivy set the stone into her hand; Cali closed her fingers around it and then closed her eyes.

This is why they pay me the big bucks, she thought, as she tried to clear her mind.

But in the night of her mind, nothing came to her. She stood there for several minutes; Ivy and Jack were silent; *they're watching me; clear your mind; clear your mind; think: nothing.*

Finally, she opened her eyes. "I'm sorry," Cali said.

"You're exhausted," Jack said. "Maybe tomorrow, after you've had some rest."

"Not even a spark of something," Cali said. "Maybe you're right. Sleep might be good."

Ivy looked skeptical. "Interesting," was all she said. Then, "Well, get some sleep. Tomorrow we'll see how it goes."

Part Three

The Second Day

Chapter Twenty-Three

1

Morning was pissing with rain; that was how Mira felt about it as she got out of bed and already knew a cold was coming on within her—she sneezed twice on the way to the bathroom. Her back hurt *(this better not be my period)*, and the bottoms of her feet were freezing from the icy floor as she went to get her bathrobe; she felt chilly from just seeing the rain coming down outside her window. She glanced out across the yard and saw some vaguely human form running around in what looked like shorts and a sweatshirt and a dumbass baseball cap turned around backward so he looked like a genuine goofball.

He's out there. In the rain. Freezing his ass off.

It was Chet.

Behind him, Conan also ran, barking at his heels like he was Chet's own dog.

2

By the time Mira had made it out to the kitchen door, she was already well into her baggy jeans and the only clean T-shirt she could find, which, unfortunately, was purple and too large and made her look boxy. She had slipped into a pair of Nikes and managed to quickly brush the stickies of night out of her hair so that she felt fairly presentable.

"Hey!" she called, as Chet was jogging by again. It was a nearly frosty morning; a few more degrees and it would've been sleet.

"Hey!" Chet called out, his hand shooting up in a wave as he jogged by.

She whistled, and Chet glanced back with a confused look.

"Just calling my dog!" she shouted. Then she clapped her hands for Conan, who pretended not to hear her and ran alongside Chet as he tried to avoid stumbling through a stubble of rocks and a tree stump that was low to the ground. He glanced back again at her, and she pretended to be looking off in the distance. Then she looked back at him, but he and Conan both were just rounding the bend by the stone arches.

"Shit," Mira said, and went back into the kitchen. *He's a dumb jock and you're in lust. This is just plain dumb.*

3

Cali had gone through three volumes in the library by nine A.M.—mainly skimming. The books, mostly from the PSI Vista collection, were reproductions of older books that Jack had told her were locked away in safe places. "They're worth thousands, at the very least," he told her.

She had skimmed *The Aegyptian Book of Darkness,* which was mainly ramblings of some disturbed writer sandwiched between hieroglyphs, the main content of which seemed to be incantations and exhortations to Horus and Isis for passage to the underworld;

another book was called *The Grand Grimoire of Judas Magnus,* which purported to have been held in safekeeping by the Knights Templar (all of this Cali got a good chuckle over, since she very much doubted the Knights Templar possessed heretical grimoires); but the third book held her interest completely. It was called *The Infinite Ones* by Isis Claviger.

The book had a picture of the oddly named Claviger (and the name reminded Cali of something—some word she had once heard somewhere, perhaps in school)—the author was beautiful and mysterious all at once, and the first thing that struck Cali was that she reminded her a bit of Ivy Martin herself. No, she didn't look like a beautiful Thoroughbred (which the exhausted Ivy had seemed to Cali the previous midnight), but there was something in the in the mysterious pools of those eyes that was the same in both women, and something about—*I know what it is. They're both mesmerized by something. They have a look of hunger. Fair-haired, obsessed Nordic goddesses, that's what they are.*

And although there were chapter headings that looked fascinating, dealing with spiritualism, hauntings, and even "ectoplasmic manifestations," Cali flipped to the various Post-It Notes that Jack had placed around the book.

The first one had to do with Harrow itself.

CHAPTER TWENTY-FOUR

1

From The Infinite Ones *by Isis Claviger*

. . . I had been at Harrow six nights when I knew that it had become more than merely a house. Justin had, through his interests and intrigues, created a locus for hauntings. Not just the haunting that would no doubt befall all of us who stayed there, the creature we only saw fleetingly when looking in the mirror or the shadow at dusk that moved away from us as we moved toward it. The meaning of the house became clear when Justin began to show me the artifacts he'd been collecting his whole life, and then I asked to see the original design of the house, and he drew papers from his study and tossed them on the floor. The house was built as a gate into another world. It was built to break the barrier to the Other Side, and this aroused my curiosity to no end.

How could I leave such a place? I still had appointments in other parts of the country, including an evening in Boston with Mrs. Grace, the famous Widow of Commonwealth Avenue, who wanted to contact her late husband again and again. And I was asked to go to Washington, D.C., by my friend Verena Standish to experience something of the place she believed to be infested with spirits. But I had to turn down these invitations, for I began an inquiry into the spirit world at Harrow, and only my dear friend in London could draw me from this unlikely palace of night along the muddy Hudson River, at the edge of one of the most dreadful little villages in existence.

For, the night of my first séance at Harrow, I felt the presence of elementals. These are spirits, if you will, in the form of energies, and the salamander of fire was present, I felt, as were the goblins of the earth and the water sylphs. I do not mean fairy folk at all, but the energies of the elements were there, within that house, and something even more frightening to me existed there, as well:

A magus of such power, which he would not even recognize. Yes, Mr. Gravesend has power beyond dream, the kind of psychic energy that few in any generation possess. But it is ineffective in Harrow. It may take several of us who possess psychic talents to sweep Harrow of its shadows and dark recesses, for it is even more powerful than the two of us together. Nothing was meant to flourish in this house. Yet, I have found it seductive and entrancing, and I believe that my greatest understanding of the Other Side will come within the sacred walls of that house.

Dear Reader, allow me to describe this place. Upon arrival in a carriage, one is first struck by the desolation of the landscape. The estate is far from the village of Watch Point, and the road through the woods is narrow and grows dark even at midday. Yet the woods are sparse, and the hedges grow wild along the outer stone wall. It is a romantic feel, as the novels of the Brontë sisters would have the world. It is indeed its own *Wuthering Heights,* for there is great beauty and a stark grandeur about the place, and nothing invites and everything invites. There is a stone guard house before a clutch of trees. The birdsong here at twilight is endless, and in the summer the locusts make sounds like shh-shh-shh, and I have seen, in the spring, flocks of white doves that roost high in the towers of Harrow. Deer feed along the sedge by the outer ponds. As one passes through the gates of Harrow, the desolation comes at one swiftly. It is like a breath of still air, while a storm rages beyond the treetops. The trees as one goes up the path to the house are few and far between, and the sloping hillside to the back of Harrow and to the right of the carriage gives an almost romantic and old-world feeling to the place. For, even in its separation from the world, and the bent trees along its drive, Harrow is magnificent. It is a European chateau, but with the stern American touches of arrow-sharp gables that give it a puritanical atmosphere. Its towers are long and tall, and one half expects soldiers wearing mail and armor to walk the battlements. The front door is crowned with a carving from a foreign land to the south. It looks like a creature's head with flared nostrils and an empty gaze in its eyes. The door itself is exquisitely carved oak, with arcane symbols of some secret society, Masonic perhaps? I do not know to this day, but they are beautiful and intricate.

The hallway that greets you is vast, full of statuary and paintings, and before you rises a grand staircase and, going up the stairs, more paintings, more beauty, and it is only the feeling one gets as one enters that causes a panic within. For something is wrong here. One can sense it, particularly if one is sensitive to such things.

One knows upon entering that Harrow is the mouth of some great beast.

2

Cali flipped to another one of the Post-It Notes in the book.

3

From The Infinite Ones *by Isis Claviger*

. . . Aleister Crowley had Rose Kelly on his arm, although Victor always remained nearby—we called him Aleister's Shadow, and he truly was like a shade, following the proceedings. Crowley had a room at the Memnotoch Hotel; it was one of those lavish places that had gone to ruin, just on the outskirts of Cairo. It was beautifully tiled with a deep red clay and images of papyrus and ibis all along it; a courtyard defined the hotel, with colorful birds flying about at midday, and an enormous fountain at its center. Rose and I often spent languid afternoons with sips of what I was later to learn was laudanum, but at the time, Crowley told us it was anise. The dreams we had on those golden afternoons! Rose never imbibed, but I had no problem filling my thimble-sized cup several times from Crowley's bottle of what he had told me was a liqueur called Love-in-Idleness, amial-sur-colloundria in the language of the C.M., a language I was sure that Crowley himself had made up from bits and pieces of other tongues.

I spoke with Victor about coming out of the background; it was obvious that he was attached to Crowley, but he told me it was unseemly to be so obsessed with the man known to the psychical societies as the Great Beast. Crowley was anything but beastly; he was a delight, and he was bad in all the ways that you'd want a very refined gentleman to be bad. Soon I grew tired of waiting and demanded to go with Crowley to the club he frequented each evening.

"It is some diabolical mass?" I asked, straight out.

He chuckled at this. He was very much old school, and could be condescending to women, but I found him enchanting.

"Hardly," he snorted. "Isis, if you were to come with me, do you know what they would say? They would say I was betraying them."

"And just who are they?"

"If you're clairvoyant, you know," he said.

But I did not. It was the laudanum, you see. I didn't know it at the time, but Crowley was purposefully having me take it. It dulled my sense of the Otherworld, and did not allow me to see much beyond the horizon of my senses. Had I known that I was taking a tincture of an opiate each day, I would have been furious, but I was not aware. Let me say, I do not approve of this powerful stuff. It is the lotus for the idle and wicked and wretched, and I was none of these.

So I could not go within myself and appeal to my higher consciousness. The drug that I unwittingly took blocked my ability.

But finally I set a plan to follow Crowley down the narrow streets beyond the hotel. It was Candlemas Eve, and the heat was bitter, with dust storms abounding. Rose was fiercely sick of Egypt and longed to return to England, or at least France. I was more determined than ever to find out why Crowley no longer discussed the Anubis Invocations, and was furious with myself for the exhaustion I felt each evening. I overcame it with tea and an ice bath, a rarity there, but I had managed to bribe a young man in the kitchen to fetch me ice from a not-too-distant icehouse along the river.

At midnight I saw Crowley leave, and I wrapped myself in as much of a robe as was afforded by the sheet on my bed and followed him.

It was that night that I was to see the first of the Mysteries, and to hear the Sacred Words of Power.

But all along I yearned for Harrow, for what I had left behind for the cause of my beliefs, for my search, what I had sacrificed so recently to my journey into the Otherworld.

I longed for him. I prayed he was well. I wanted to return more than anything in the world.

But still I ventured into the subterranean tunnels beneath Cairo, into the very heart of the Mystery. . . .

And I lost Crowley. He had somehow evaded me, but I found something that night that opened an entire world to me, something that I knew even Justin Gravesend would desire, but more importantly, what I would need to overcome my great sorrow that had never left my heart nor my mind in all those intervening years. . . .

I began to see how life and death had no barrier, and I allowed myself to undergo initiation in a cult as ancient as the world itself.

And through the burning of my soul, I knew that I must return to my Osiris, that I must stop what was evil in that house, that I must close the door to the Infinite in that house.

For during one of the rituals, I was no longer in the ancient tomb of a Queen of Egypt, but in Harrow again, and I saw—as if I were a ghost—what Justin Gravesend had done, and how I must be the undoing, for even the house of spirits needed cleansing, and I now knew how it must be done. . . .

I had entered the Dimension of the Forbidden.

And I had discovered the secret there. . . .

4

"Good reading?" Jack asked. Cali glanced up, her eyes refocusing.

Jack stood over here, a boyish look on his face, as if he'd just fallen in love for the first time. He wore an oversized plaid flannel shirt, the shirttails sticking out, over a pair of brown slacks. He hadn't shaved, and something about him made Cali think that he hadn't slept the night before. It might've been the dark circles under his eyes.

"Yeah, old Isis Claviger was pretty spooky."

"That wasn't her real name, of course. Nobody knows who she was, really. 'Claviger' generally means *caretaker*, or something to that effect. Which is interesting, because in some ways, she took care of Harrow while she lived here."

"Oh," Cali said suddenly. "Now I know. I was thinking *clavier*. From French class. Keys."

"I think Claviger is a play on that word. A caretaker is basically the keeper of the keys, no?" Jack said.

Cali set the book down. "You been up all night?"

"I couldn't sleep much," he said. "I got something on tape."

Cali counted to three before she asked. "Um . . . can I see it?"

5

"My office," Jack said, opening the door to a room that was just larger than the furniture inside it. Two computers sat side by side on a low table that filled up most of the space. Each monitor's screen was divided into eight separate windows, and different rooms of the house were pictured in each one. "Look at this," he said, as excited as a kid on his birthday. He sat down in front of one of the keyboards and tapped in a few commands. Suddenly a new window came up on the screen, blocking out the others.

"Watch," he said.

Cali saw an image come up on the screen.

The room within the image was very dark, with only slight ambient light coming from beyond a slightly closed door. It was enough to make out that someone lay in the bed, tangled in a sheet. Who was it? She moved closer.

He films us in our sleep. Jesus, I wonder if we have any privacy.

The word that had been used the previous night, *guinea pigs,* came to her. *He's paying us to be guinea pigs.*

Finally, she made out who it was, purely by his size. It was Frost, lying asleep in bed. The camera slowly zoomed in and out. Jack clicked the computer mouse several times, and there, just beside the bed, there was a streak of light.

Like lightning almost, but it remained there.

"That's a ghost?" she asked.

"Well, that I can't say," Jack said. "It'll take some more analysis. But it's something, isn't it?"

She stepped back. "Well."

"Cali?" Jack asked, turning.

"We're just here to be watched, I guess."

"You understood that," Jack said, and then added, "I hope."

"Of course I did. Of course. It just seems different now. Watching Frost," Cali said, trying to shrug it off as nothing important. "It seems different, that's all. Knowing that it could be any one of us."

Chapter Twenty-five

1

She felt less invaded by the way the cameras were set up several minutes later, and she mulled over the whole situation of staying at Harrow at all in her mind. It was an experiment. They were all well paid. And if she were running this, with this kind of money invested, she'd feel that she owned the subjects for the period of time specified, as well. *So, you either leave and give him half the money back, or you stay. And find things out.*

They returned to the library, because Jack had yet another book to show her. This was not a duplicate or reproduction of an older tome—this was the book itself. A leatherbound diary.

"Esteban Palliser kept it," Jack said. "From the 1920s right up until a year ago. When he died."

"You and your Post-It Notes," Cali smirked.

"I'll get you some tea and toast and you just settle in and do some reading," Jack said. Then he left the room.

2

From the diary of Esteban Palliser:

I am in my room. I am ancient—I feel ancient, anyway. The body is a vehicle for consciousness, one supposes. My brain still has its daily fevers. My hands curl in pain at times, but I will keep writing for whoever comes after. I still smoke unfiltered cigarettes, rolled for me daily. I defy Mr. Death to come take me, although I know Mr. Death will arrive soon enough.

Still, another smoke, a sip of thick coffee, spattered with cinnamon and nutmeg, and I will write more in my journal of that early time at Harrow.

I am now looking back on what I considered the prime of my life, although I was probably just around the curve of it at twenty-nine—for I would soon grow serious with the shadows that emerged from Harrow. I have lived through wars and peace and technological furies the likes of which I could not imagine in my youth; I am over one hundred years old. Can you imagine what I saw then? The wonders in the sky—for we had begun what was then a miracle, called Air-Mail, by which an airplane could transport packages and letters from one end of the country to another in a few days, whereas it would take weeks for letters to travel before this marvelous change. And the radio—I was completely mesmerized by it, and would even close the newspaper with my beloved Krazy Kat and the funny pages to listen to the news of the world or the broadcast of a boxing match. And the movies! I was in Harrow one night only and already wished that I could rush out to one of the great movie palaces in Manhattan to catch the latest Charlie Chaplin.

Certainly we had terrors in the world then, we had the fears and paranoia of menaces and foreign evils, we had serial killers the likes of which would curl your hair, we had all the good and bad that is forgotten and years later sifted through for moments to be relished as quaint and sentimental. There never has been an innocent time in human history—I suppose Harrow, in many ways, stood for that idea alone. There was no innocence in the world, and to pretend so is to bring a veil across one's face and never look beyond it. The 1920s was no golden age; it was no calm before the storm. We even had boredom and craziness. It was a different time; it was another world; it was beyond anything you can probably imagine, you who are alive and reading this now, and yet, I tell you, it resembled this world, now, near enough to the birth of yet another century.

These were the years I felt most alive. They were imperfect years; they were years of absolute confusion for me, between the end of my marriage, the losses of both my parents, and the loss of my distant but beloved grandfather. But they were my years, and I won't give them up without a struggle.

These were the years I often return to in order to feel that breath on my face again, that tender kiss of all that life takes from us as we grow beyond what life is meant to allow us.

Yes, I have been accused of clinging to life—but why shouldn't I?

Yes, I return in my mind to my discovery of Harrow, my ownership of it, my legacy.

But in those days I was young in that way in which the last year of one's twenties is still young. I was nearly as young as the century itself.

Do you know the Hudson River and its beauty? Have you been there?

I imagine the beginnings of Watch Point and Harrow—not when it was owned by a Dutch-English family—but in those eras going further into prehistory. The glacial movement creating the wormholes that became the river nearly twelve thousand years ago; the primeval forest, the strange creatures as they appeared . . . then something happened—nothing cataclysmic, but something happened, and the land where the house would be built acquired a sense of being unclean.

There is even a story—though no doubt created by some local wit—that Henry Hudson paused somewhere on his exploration of the river that would later bear his name, and mentioned, "This is a very bad land to fall with, and an unpleasant land to see." He was, according to local wags of Watch Point—none of whom are to be believed in this—referring to the property that would become Harrow.

In the 1620s, the Dutch West India company sent families to settle the river, but Watch Point was largely overlooked, owing, it was suggested, to the way it jutted into the water and the menace of the natives of the specific area.

When the land that became Watch Point was first known, it was settled by natives who called themselves Mahanowacks, a variant spelling of what we know as Mohican, but nonetheless, this group was distinct and more closely related to the nearby tribe known as the Wapping and somewhat related to the Schaghticokes. They were distinct from the other tribes of natives in that they were not welcoming to the invader.

Warlike and unwilling to transact business with the Dutch, the Mahanowacks along the river by Watch Point ended up being massacred in an event that was all but erased from the history books.

Some of the survivors, no doubt, went up the river to join with the tribes of Mohicans, some went east to share space with the Pequots and the Mohegans (again, a separate but similar group), others west across the river. Many were killed and one can only suppose this killing took place near Harrow.

This is purely my own conjecture, from what I know now about the property, and from my grandfather's collection of artifacts.

But I won't get ahead of myself.

It was 1926 when I arrived, and it was October, and my body was still strong and invulnerable, and my hair was thick and dark and my skin was perhaps too pale, except where it was ruddy around my face, and I didn't know that the feeling of being young would ever end. My first full day at Harrow, I woke up late in the morning surrounded by such luxury as I had never before imagined.

3

Cali skipped several pages to the next yellow sticky note that Jack had left. This part of the diary seemed to be about Palliser's childhood at Harrow.

4

From the diary of Esteban Palliser:

That night, I lay back in that treasure box of a bed and began creating imaginary playmates for myself, out of thin air. First I thought of a giraffe with two heads who spoke a quaint version of French—what little I knew of the language—and then I imagined a jaguar from South American jungles speaking perfect English to me.

I grew thirsty, and was about to call out to Hildy, my nurse, but she snored so loudly and had worked so hard to force feed me her awful cabbage and broth, that I let her rest. My fever was not burning quite so strongly. I marshaled what energy I could.

I fumbled with my nightshirt, drawing my shivery, scrawny legs over to the floor.

Catching my balance, I grabbed one of the bedposts and nearly crawled over to the big pitcher and bowl.

Once I reached the chiffonier, I lifted the pitcher up to my face to drink directly from it. As I did so, I caught a glimpse of my own reflection in the mirror.

I was parched and burning up again. I had half a mind to pour the entire pitcher over my head in order to cool my blood. The candles in the wall sconces lent a hazy glow to the shadowy room (and my even more shadowy vision), like streetlights through heavy fog.

I saw my face, waxy and yellow in the candlelight.

My eyes were sunken, my hair greasy and pressed flat against my face, although some of it stuck out at the top of my scalp. My face was puffy from the bites, and my left eye still looked swollen shut, although I could see fairly well through it.

I could neither laugh nor shudder at this vision of myself. I felt sorry for it and at the same time, I felt that I looked like someone other than myself: This wasn't me, after all. It was some other boy who had stepped into a nest of flying monsters, and he looked funny and pathetic.

Then I noticed a movement back by the lamp near my bed. Just a blur. My vision followed the movement in the mirror.

What was it? I found that I could not take my eyes away from the mirror. It was the old sort, with an oval and beveled glass, which distorted the edges of what it reflected.

Was it a sparrow trapped in the room? What moved so frantically at my bed?

I could see Hildy in the chair, her head lolling back a bit against the blanket she'd propped as a pillow. I told myself that I was just imagining things. I was fine. There was no one and nothing else in the room.

Then I saw the blurred thing again, only this time it was in the bed, and I realized, suddenly, that there were two indentations in the bed—

mine, that I had just left—and this blurred thing, this smudge of something, next to where I'd been sleeping off my fever. I quickly glanced back, nearly toppling over in the process, to see what was on the bed, but the bed was empty. Then I checked the mirror.

A little girl sat in the bed. A little girl with a round face and long dark curls, and eyes that seemed impossibly small. I watched her in the mirror, to see if I really saw her. I kept repeating something to myself—perhaps even aloud—something about the girl not being real, that she was imaginary, just like the jaguar and the two-headed giraffe. But she sat there, her head resting on one of the pillows. Not watching me. Not watching anyone. It was as if it was her bed, and she lived in the mirror all the time.

When I turned around she was right behind me. Her hollow eyes. The look of yearning and pain within her flesh.

In the blink of an eye, it was not a little girl at all.

Now, after the memory returned to me, I can look back on what I saw and know that it was probably induced by the venom of those insects within me. But then all I knew was fear, and the heat beneath my skin that seemed to steam as I saw it.

It was, very simply, a wisp of smoke hanging in the air. Smoke and a voice, which said in a man's voice, "Esteban, you belong to us."

I dropped the pitcher to the floor. It shattered at my feet, and the smoke dissipated. I felt the full force of fever hit. Hildy jumped from the rocking chair and grabbed me up in her heavy arms. She brought me back to the bed, scolding me for getting out of it.

I spent the rest of the night huddled in a corner of the bed, staring at the pillow, my teeth chattering from fear and fever.

A slight indentation remained along one of the pillows in my bed, as if the little girl still lay there, beside me. I even imagined that I could hear her breathing.

My fever burned, and what—of my body—was not swollen was on fire. Every ounce of my being ached and felt as if the bones wanted to tear from my flesh.

Yet, after an hour or two of this, I became very detached from my body, and felt as if I were watching this little boy toss and turn in yellowjacket-inspired fever. I saw the nurse, with her round fish eyes and her cold Watch Point manner, as she hesitated to put the cool, damp hand towel on the boy's forehead. I watched myself—the boy—open his eyes briefly, looking as if he was fighting to wake from a dream.

And knowing that, somewhere in the room, the little girl waited for me. I didn't know why, or what she wanted, or who she was.

All I knew was that I didn't want her to come near me again.

5

Cali glanced up from the diary. Jack had been sitting in the settee across from her chair, tea tray balanced precariously on his lap, as he watched her with a look of such expectation that it was like having to tell a little boy on Christmas Eve that there was no Santa Claus. But she said it anyway: "The diary is interesting, but I get a sense that Esteban Palliser is mad, mad as in crazy. And he was a hundred years old when he wrote this all down?"

Jack nodded. "Most of it."

"What a great document to have," she said, and then added, "but I don't see the point. Is there the ghost of Matilde Gravesend here? And if that's what we're after, why even worry about portals?"

Jack seemed to be listening as he poured a cup of tea out into one of the small china cups, but Cali had a vague sense that he was already somewhere else. "I don't think Matilde Gravesend is lurking nearby. I think this house is an energy. I think, as a portal, it lets in all kinds of . . ."

"Energies?" Cali set down the book on the elegant walnut table beside her chair and rose. She walked over to Jack and took a cup and a spoon. "Mmm . . . English Breakfast. My favorite."

"We're the only caffeine addicts here, apparently, you, me, and Mira," Jack said. When he looked at her again, he had some sadness etched along his sleepy eyes.

"It's funny," Cali said, blowing lightly over the surface of the cup to cool the tea. "I've always wanted to believe that there was a place like this. A place where things happened. Sort of a crossroads. But I'm not convinced this house is it." She went back to the chair, but instead of sitting back down, she looked around at the books that were stacked rather messily on the beautifully carved bookshelves. "It's too perfect for a haunting."

"And that makes it bad?"

"No," she said. "It's just that it has been my experience that whatever residue the living leave behind—after they've died—is more likely to be in the cities, on street corners, in the subway. You know"—she turned around—"places with the most life."

"Harrow has held a lot of life," Jack said. He leaned over, setting the tea tray on the floor with a bit of a clatter. "And then there's the rooms off the cellar."

"Rooms?"

"Sure. That's the rest of the tour. I figured I'd gather everybody just before lunch and we'd see the artifacts. Or at least what's left. I think they indicate state of mind."

"State of mind of Justin Gravesend," Cali said.

"No." Jack grinned. Damn, he was always grinning like a Cheshire cat. "State of mind of Harrow."

The dog began barking, practically howling, out in the yard, and Cali and Jack looked at each other. Cali broke up laughing.

"The howling of the hellhound," Jack said, amusement in his voice. "Must be an omen."

CHAPTER TWENTY-SIX

1

The gray sky spat rain. Spiderwebs up in the frame of the large front door had pearls of water along their edges. Mira stood on the front stoop, her hair stuffed up in her sweatshirt's hood, a look of fury on her face. "Look what the fucking cat dragged in," she said to her father when he came running out to see what the barking was about.

Behind Mira, Conan barked and ran around, his tail going a mile a minute, a snarl on his face that was nearly comical.

Nearby, the antlered head of a deer lay on the driveway.

2

"It's in the shed now," Jack said, coming into the kitchen from the pouring rain, his dark hair slick and thin against his scalp. He shook off the rain from his leather jacket with a shiver. "I guess I'll what—bury it tomorrow? Or something? What do you do with a deer head?"

"Mount it, I guess," Cali said. Then she added, "That was a joke, by the way." Then, "There's a woodshed?"

"Just a shed. No wood to be had. Just out back here." Jack pointed beyond the small window with the blurry glass that went from the kitchen out to the backyard. As an afterthought, he opened the window slightly. An icy breeze swept through the hot kitchen—it was a bit of a relief to Cali.

The kitchen was long and wide and held far too much empty space. Jack had already pointed out where an enormous floor-to-ceiling fireplace had once been in it. It had been converted to more of an industrial kitchen when the school had opened, and all the long rows of metal shelfing and sinks had been torn out and taken by the school just after Ivy Martin had bought the place. It was not the gorgeous place that Jack had described of its heyday; instead it was just long and wide, and now had a fairly normal-sized range near the kitchen door, a large double-doored Amana refrigerator, and a full-sized freezer next to it. A wooden butcher's block table served as the breakfast area, and this was covered with cheap blue placemats that looked like they'd been bought secondhand from a local diner.

Cali had just finished off an English muffin and a poached egg—cooked superbly by Jack—and was ready for something else. She eyed the pot of marmalade as if it were gold. "Another muffin?" she asked.

"Coming right up," Jack said. He reached over to the package of muffins, wrestling with it a bit before getting another muffin out and popping it into the toaster.

"That's just sick," Mira said. She went to check the water boiling on the stove. "Sick sick sick."

"It's the locals," Jack said. "It's still hunting season or thereabouts, and I guess Frost's taxi driver felt the trophy should go to him."

"Glad they didn't leave the venison," Cali said.

"Sick sick sick," Mira said. "Cutting off a deer's head and leaving it out there."

"Some people collect antlers," Chet said. "I used to know men who went and picked up the carcasses out on the roadside just to get the antlers and say they'd shot the deer." He had just come down from his morning shower, looking shaved and handsome and sparkling, and Cali watched as Mira pretended not to notice him.

He was gorgeous, and it made Cali wish she were a few years younger just so she could've caught his attention. He was definitely eye candy.

She thought of Det: Det was not eye candy, but he did care for her. He probably genuinely loved her, but it was a misplaced love, and there really was no trust between them. She needed to think of him more—she knew this. She should love Det, but something within her resisted. *Love should be more logical.*

Mira looked over at Cali. "Don't you think it's sick?" Mira seemed to have some kind of excitement in her face, as if the deer head itself was not what was getting to her.

Cali shrugged. "I'm not fond of hunting, anyway. Bunch of men get drunk, go in the woods, and shoot animals who can't shoot back. Not much sport there."

"I would've thought you'd love it," Mira said, quasi innocently. Cali cocked her head to the side slightly, trying to figure that comment out. Mira hastily added, "Because of your gun."

"You've got a gun?" Chet asked.

Cali nodded. "Guilty. It's something I carry purely because of my part-time job. It can get dangerous out there. In the world. When you get press for helping cops solve homicide cases."

Mira laughed. "Sorry. The way you said it sounded funny."

Jack came over to the table with a big bowl of cornflakes and a glass of milk. He drew a chair back and sat down. His rangy frame seemed ill-suited to the small wooden chair. "New York seems safer than ever to me these days."

"It is," Cali said. "I got pulled into an alley once and nearly beaten up by the relative of someone I suppose I helped put behind bars. Nothing really happened. But it shook me up. And then a friend"—she didn't want to talk about Det to them, and some little warning bell within her knew that it was because she wanted Chet not to think of her as being attached to anyone—"got me a gun. It's just a Sig Sauer. I've never used it, except in target practice."

"Wow," Chet said, his eyes lighting up. "I hope nobody decides to go psycho and steal your gun and shoot all of us in our sleep."

Jack held his spoon midair, milk and limp cornflakes dripping from it. "Thank you for that thought, Chet."

"Maybe it'll be the ghost of that deer," Mira said. "Coming back for revenge on Frost and his cabdriver."

"I used to hunt," Frost said, coming into the kitchen behind Chet. He had a neatly pressed yellow shirt and a silky blue tie and looked as if he was heading to either an office or to church. "It isn't much sport. My father used to drag me and my brothers off the farm when we were too young to hold a rifle very steady and put up a salt lick out in the woods for deer. Always made me feel bad. And I hate gamey meat. Some years were bad for the farm. To save on groceries we ate venison and wild duck all the time, and I got skinny because I just wouldn't eat either one. Wild game has a taste I don't like."

"It's yours, you know," Jack Fleetwood said. "The head. Should you want a trophy to hang up in your den."

Frost ignored him. Then, "God, I slept well last night."

"Me, too," Chet said. "Better than in a long time. It was so . . ."

"Quiet," Cali added for him. "I'm so used to city sounds and sirens that I don't think I realized how quiet it was."

"Any ghosts on film, Jack?" Frost asked as he walked over to the fridge and opened the door, peering in.

"No," Jack said. "No ghosts anywhere."

3

They all went through the various videotapes that Jack had recorded and checked in the night; Chet went around and took notes on the EMF meters but found nothing beyond what might be considered ordinary fluctuations; Frost insisted that Cali explore more of the house with him, and when they opened one of the bedroom doors, there was Ivy Martin, curled up, snoring lightly, her bedcovers thrown from the bed, her flannel nightgown around her neck. She shivered in her sleep. Cali went to the windows and secured each of them, and then took one of the covers from the floor and laid it across Ivy's form. She seemed so small and vulnerable, as opposed to the lanky ice queen she had seemed the previous night. Frost remained in the doorway of the room, as if afraid to enter. Once they were back in the corridor, he whispered to Cali, "Mira told me she's in love with a ghost," but then would not elaborate on it.

The day proceeded from gray to grayer; Cali read some more of the tomes Jack had laid out for each of them in the library and Mira shouted at some point that it had stopped raining—"Finally!" she said. "I hate this weather!"

4

The rain subsided by three, and the sun came out for the few hours left of daylight. The afternoon even warmed slightly, and Chet discovered something mainly because he wanted to see the deer head in the shed. The shed was about the size of one of the house's bathrooms, and Chet had a strange feeling that it had perhaps once served as an outhouse, although it did not seem that old. But it did stink—*maybe it's the deer,* he thought. Behind the head, which had been unceremoniously dumped into a pile of newspapers that lay atop a wooden crate, Chet saw what seemed like a real treasure. It was some gym equipment left over from the school; he managed to coerce Mira and Cali into playing a light game of softball—they each got gloves and Chet used his bare hands with the ball. They played around the driveway because it was too muddy anywhere else.

"You like baseball?" he asked Mira, who had a funny look on her face the entire time they played. Her lips were scrunched up a little, and her hair kept falling over her face when she got up to bat.

"Sure," she said, swinging the bat perfectly. "Keith Hernandez. He's one of my faves."

"I've always been partial to Cal Ripkin, Junior," Chet said. "Since I was a kid. I just want to be him so bad, but I know I'm not. But in my dreams I am."

"In my dreams, I'm Angela Bassett," Cali said. She stood out as far from the little scratch of chalk that served as first base as possible. "Angela Bassett crossed with Sigourney Weaver, crossed with maybe . . ." She let the thought fade as she tried to think up who else she wanted to be in her fantasy life. Then, "Ever play love child?"

Chet laughed. "No. What's that?"

"It's great. My sister and I play this all the time. Mainly on the subway. It can be a very rude game, but it's always fun. It's where you look at people and identify who they might be the secret love child of. Like, someone might look like the love child of Michael Jackson and Madonna."

"A two-headed monster!" Chet said. "So, okay. You're the love child of Angela Bassett and Sandra Bullock."

"Ah," Cali said. "A same-sex tryst. Too complementary. You've got to put a little sulfuric acid in it. Okay, and you, Chet, look like the love child of . . . this is tough . . ."

"Brad Pitt and Matt Damon," Mira said, too quickly, and then looked down at her catcher's mitt. "Maybe."

"That's good, but you're going to make his head get so big, he won't fit through the front door. And I don't want to have to imagine Brad and Matt conceiving," Cali said. She looked at Chet, squinting as if trying to reconfigure him. She swung the bat, preparing for Chet's pitch to her. "I'll go with . . . Jamie Lee Curtis and the Lion King. Sure."

"Ah, beast lust," Chet said.

"I'm the love child of . . ." Mira began, but Chet interrupted.

"Wait, that ain't fair. I don't think you get to choose for yourself in this game," Chet said. Mira pouted a bit. Then he pitched the ball, and Cali took a good, strong swing. The ball went up straight into the air.

Mira caught the ball and thumbed Cali out, her third time at bat, only her first time in which she actually hit the ball. ("I was always more of a field hockey kind of girl," Cali said.)

The game played out a bit like charades, because there was more exaggerated movement than there was actual play. Cali was awful at catching the ball, and her pitching was worse. Mira was a bit sharper with her pitch, and she nearly hit the ball through one of the front leaded-glass windows, but it missed it and bounced off the wall of the house. Chet seemed in fine form: He moved with the grace of a young lion, and for purely entertainment purposes, he spat and scratched his butt until both Cali and Mira started imitating him. Chet managed to crack the bat when he hit what should've been a homer. The ball flew up into the trees somewhere and was lost.

Eventually, Conan, after much scrambling and rolling in the mud, found the ball and retrieved it but would not return it to them, but that was after Cali and Chet had searched for it, and Cali had fallen in the mud. Chet had lifted her up, and something had happened between them without either one of them being sure what it was. To Cali, it felt like an uncomfortable reminder of something missing from her life; to Chet, it felt like the warmth he longed for.

Mira seemed happy to be out in the brief sunshine of a chilly day, until she walked to the edge of what seemed to be endless bramble bushes and there, on the other side, she thought she saw Chet holding Cali, holding her the way he was supposed to hold Mira herself, at least in her fantasies, and Cali, that witch, loved it; Mira could tell.

Mira turned away, whistling to her dog to come to her, and went off to brood.

5

Cali pushed her way out of Chet's arms, gently, with words meant to excuse the closeness they'd had, to deny the feeling she had as he held her in his arms for brief seconds. She didn't look back to him as she returned to the driveway, to the house, but she was sure that he was watching her.

She almost wanted him to run after her, but she knew that was wrong. They weren't right for each other; Det, back in New York, loved her, and despite the fact that that relationship had led nowhere so far, this man—*no,* she thought, *this boy*—needed a girl his own age, another nineteen- or twenty-year-old, or perhaps someone as old as twenty-two or twenty-three. Not her, not a twenty-eight-year-old whose life was messed up, who was not fit to have the kind of innocent and pure affection that Chet would no doubt offer a girl closer to his age.

When she headed for the house she thought she saw someone's face up near one of the gothic-arched stained-glass windows. She couldn't tell who it was, but she knew it most likely was Frost Crane.

6

Frost went to meet Ivy, who was just waking up at four in the afternoon after having been up until six that morning. She surprised him with her sullenness and lack of interest in his books and his ability. He didn't like the way she seemed to be watching him from the corner of her eye; and Jack, meanwhile, had returned to his work of checking the meters and the cameras and seeing if any phenomenon had yet presented itself.

He showed Cali and Chet how to use the night goggles, and how they had to get used to them first, because it was a bit disorienting to see in the dark with them. The goggles looked alien to them, and attached with a kind of headgear; Cali complained a bit, saying she had to keep her head balanced better, which felt impossible. To try them out, Cali and Chet and Jack went into one of the rooms that had no windows and shut the door, sealing cracks of light from under the door with a towel. "Ambient light is helpful but unnecessary with these," Jack told them. "Most night-vision goggles are very limited, but Ivy spared no expense. We have enough of these for everyone. All I ask is that you be gentle with them when taking them on and off because . . . well, they're expensive."

In total darkness, Cali felt a slight headache. A sickly green light came up, as if from the edges and corners of the room. She saw what looked like a shimmering green-yellow version of the person she assumed to be Chet, and off in another part of the room, Jack, who leaned against a wall as if he was just watching them.

"How's it feel?"

"Weird," Chet said. "Cool!"

"You don't need to shout. We're both right here."

"Oh, yeah," Chet said. "And you both look like you're from outer space."

"What I don't understand," Cali began, "is why we really need these. I mean, lights are all over the house."

"The cellars," Jack said. "There's no light to speak of in some parts. There are these passages down there with zero light. We can take flashlights down, but not much else. If someone gets separated . . . well, it's good to see in the dark, that's all I can say."

7

After setting the goggles carefully on a table, Jack took the two of them to see yet other rooms in the house, a few of which seemed to be nothing more than glorified closets. Mira caught up with them and tagged along, staying close to Chet, who virtually ignored her. They went out near the statue garden, and Jack pointed out how the abbey had existed on the grounds up until the 1950s, at which point it had to be taken down because it was falling apart. "These stone arches are all that's left," he said, pointing to what seemed like cathedral arch ribs that sprouted from the earth, surrounded by dead grass and large stones that were laid out haphazardly in piles. An icy wind came up that sent Cali into a coughing fit, and it was at that point that Chet said, "I just realized, I haven't had a problem since coming here."

"Chet?" Mira asked, touching his arm.

"Well, like asthma. I haven't had it. I mean, my breathing is better than it has ever been. In my entire life."

8

"Here's the Gravesend crypt," Jack said. They'd hiked up through the woods, to an area that Jack called "Bald Hill." A small graveyard was there, with no more than a dozen or so markers, as well as the miniature stone house that was the crypt. "It's locked up now, but it holds the graves of Justin Gravesend and his wife. Once, it can be assumed, there was an entry from it to the house. At least, according to Esteban Palliser's diary, but again, it was closed off with concrete and brick well before the school opened, and the tunnels flooded from an underground stream. In fact"—he pointed around the dusky woods—"there were various streams here at the end of the nineteenth century, but Gravesend had them either filled in or diverted farther away, but they still exist to some extent. They cut the first tunnels that served as Matilde Gravesend's underground home."

"And some people believe that underground water is sometimes responsible for disturbances in electromagnetic fields," Cali said.

"Yes," Jack said. "Exactly. But all of this only shows me again and again that Harrow was built by Gravesend to become a haunted house. He had the artifacts and the rituals and the design. I think he wanted to make a place for the dead. He wanted an underworld at Harrow."

CHAPTER TWENTY-SEVEN

1

Mira sat on her bed, Conan curved against her, impossibly furry and comfortable. She wrote furiously in her diary.

2

From Mira's diary:

I fucking hate her now. She is too old for him, and it's disgusting and ridiculous. I thought I liked her at first, but she's some bizarre freakazoid who is probably afraid that no one is ever going to love her, so she wants him, and he doesn't even care for her. She really is a witch. I can't believe someone as pure as Chet would walk into my life like this, and now I just sit by and watch that witch take him away or seduce him or whatever she does.

I saw the way she touched him. I saw the way he pushed her back to get away from her, but she clung on. She is ruining my life and I don't get it at all. I don't get why he hasn't come to me yet. When we were playing baseball, I knew he and I were meant to be. It felt right, and he even made me feel happy, but then that witch was there the whole time, trying to get him to herself. It was laughable. It was ridiculous. God, I wish I had never come here, but it was worth it to meet him. He's three years older than me. She's probably as old as thirty and still trying to hang on to him. It's completely unnatural. I usually see old men doing that, but Cali is obviously just as warped as a dirty old man.

And he was meant for me.

HE WAS NOT MEANT FOR SOME OLD BITCH WHO ONLY WANTS TO USE HIM.

I HATE HER MORE THAN ANYTHING OR ANYONE, AND I HATE HER BECAUSE SHE IS TRYING TO RUIN IT FOR ME.

3

After writing in her diary, Mira felt a hundred percent better, and actually seemed lighter on her feet as she walked down the corridor to Chet's bedroom. She glanced up and down the hall to make sure no one was around, and then she went into the room. She stood near the door so that the video camera wouldn't film her. She looked at the dresser and the desk and the straight-backed chair, and the bed with the sheets all hanging down, and even his underwear on the floor, and she began to feel a surge of some delicious energy flow through her, despite the fact that she'd had cramps earlier in the day.

It was almost like a feeling of fire deep in her belly, a glorious little fire that made her want Chet even more. She closed her eyes and imagined his fingers touching her warmly, and his mouth burning against her neck.

But something about it frightened her a little; she opened her eyes. It was just the room again. Nothing more. It had begun to seem real for a second. It had been unpleasant, that thought.

For it was not Chet that had been there in her imagination. It had been some other man. Some other horrible man with wolflike features.

4

It was nearly suppertime when Chet followed Jack Fleetwood out back along the stone arches. Jack had Conan on a leash and wore boots and a long jacket. Chet had pulled a down jacket over his sweater and wished he had boots—his sneakers kept getting sucked into the mud.

"You think anything's going to happen?" Chet asked when he caught up to Jack. Jack's pipe was lit, and the smoke from it hung in the air beneath the bright lights of the statue garden. Conan peed on one of the urns.

"I don't know," Jack said.

"Well, I'm sorry."

"For what?"

"All this money she spent. You spent. Getting each of us here. And nothing."

"It's only been two days. We have a couple more to go."

"Yeah, but seriously, I'm not feeling anything. Cali isn't either. It's not like, you know, the weird talent I have ever happened much, but even when it wasn't happening, I felt like it might. But up here, it's like I never had anything."

Jack sighed, tugging Conan away from peeing on the angel statue. "Well, not every haunting will show itself when you want it to."

"Sure," Chet said. "You seen a lot of ghosts and stuf?"

Jack remained silent for a few minutes, walking along with Conan pulling at the leash so the dog could get to some better sniffs along the thin trail between the ivy beds. Then he said, "Want the truth, Chet? I've never seen a ghost. I've observed phenomenon, but I don't really know if what I've seen is a ghost or just some perfectly explainable thing. I believe in psychic ability. I've spent my life studying it. But the dead? The residue of the living? No. I'm not sure I even believe it."

Chet looked at him incredulously. "Then . . . I don't get it."

"I'm in love," Jack Fleetwood said. "I didn't think I was, but I am. I have been since I met her."

"Oh," Chet said. "Cali?"

Jack glanced sidelong at him, his eyebrows arching. Then he let out a big belly laugh. "No, not her. Good Lord, Ivy. I've known Ivy Martin ever since the boy she loved died. He had a connection to Harrow, Chet. That's why she's obsessed with this place. And that," he added, "is why I'm here and hoping we find something for her. Anything."

5

Supper consisted of pizza, ordered from the Pizza Hut out by the highway in Watch Point; the man delivering it said that he was the manager of the carryout, and he had wanted to have an excuse to visit Harrow since the fire. Chet offered to show him around, but the man looked around the foyer and shrugged. "It looks about the same, I guess."

The four pizzas were too much, and after Cali had stuffed herself with pizza topped with broccoli and pepperoni, and Conan had managed to steal the crust that Chet left on the edge of his plate, Ivy came into the dining room and turned her chair around. She watched the others eat, but mainly nibbled at a slice of plain pizza. She drank a few glasses of wine but didn't seem drunk at all. Cali had felt nearly under the table with just a glass and a half of the Vouvray, and Frost was slurring his words by his third glass of beer. Mira skipped supper but sent a message through her father that she'd be down later for all the festivities.

"Festivities?" Frost asked, chomping on a cheesy slice. He had eaten almost an entire pizza.

"Sure," Jack said, and then frowned a bit at the pizza that had been left to him. "Looks like someone mowed their lawn for this."

"It's spinach and broccoli. With pepperoni," Cali said. "And it's absolutely delicious."

"We having fireworks or something?" Frost asked.

"Well," Ivy said, sipping from her wineglass, "we're living inside a ghost story, aren't we?"

"A ghost story without ghosts," Cali said.

"Right," Ivy said, somewhat dismissively. "I'm going to take you down to the cellars tonight. They're more catacombs than cellars, but I wanted to wait to see what influence the house would have on each of you." She looked at her wineglass as if it contained some secret. She looked at Chet. Then Cali. Then Frost. Each with what might've been contempt. "I don't understand why nothing has happened yet."

"I'm sorry," Chet said.

"Don't be sorry," Cali said. She raised her glass as a pointer toward Ivy. "It's not like we're doing stupid pet tricks. Maybe there's nothing here for us."

Jack began to say something, but Ivy stepped across his words with her own. "Look, I know this place has spirits. And I know that you three can unlock it. You three can make it come back."

Neither Cali nor Chet nor Frost said anything in reply, but Cali wondered if they were each thinking what she was:

Ivy Martin is insane. She has fixated on Harrow and she is insane and should be diagnosed. She looks like she hasn't slept in weeks. She looks like the last place she should be is in the cellars of some gothic manor looking for the dead.

6

Frost was not thinking any such thing as he sat there, his belly full of pizza and his thirst a bit sated with Sam Adams' Lager.

Ivy looked to him like a blond kitten who needed petting.

Frost wanted to rip Ivy's silky shirt off her. He wanted to press his lips to her nipples and taste her and feel her. The voices were still AWOL, and he didn't give a damn. He felt more like a man in Harrow than he ever had when he'd been married to that bitch Maria. And Ivy was milky and silky and sulky and sultry, and the words just flowed through his mind when he thought of her body, of her hips that were just wide enough for thoughts of lust and narrow enough that he could get a good handle on them. Her eyes were pools of crystal blue water. Her lips were wet and ripe.

It was happening again. He felt it. His manhood was growing, and he hadn't really expected it to, not after that brief moment the other night. He was hard, as he sat there in the cushy chair; he was erect beneath his jeans, and he wanted to let the animal inside him out to race across the room and leap onto her and just taste every part of her.

She spoke as if she wanted him, as well.

She wanted everything about him.

She wanted all of him.

In his head, Frost thought he heard a voice, and he didn't know if it was the Voices coming back, or who it was, but he listened to it.

Are you the consciousness or the carrier of consciousness? If you are the carrier, than your life is no different from a cat's or a mouse's. But if you are the consciousness, then you must admit to being part of what is bad in all consciousness as well as what is good. There is no good or bad consciousness. There is only consciousness, and it is part of what we all are who are the consciousness.

Who are you? Frost asked within his mind.

Snapping Jaws, the voice said. *I am your god.*

7

"Where's Mira?" Ivy asked as she led the others into the parlor.

She glanced over to Jack as if he'd know, but he just shrugged. "She told me she wasn't feeling well. She said she'd have leftovers. She's probably just resting."

"The goggles, oh, fun," Cali said, walking over to the coffee table to grab a set.

"Those look like cameras," Frost said.

"They're slightly heavy," Jack warned him as he picked up a set for himself. "But these are featherweights compared to the kind I've used in the past."

8

Chet stayed close to Fleetwood, mainly because the lights flickered in the basement area. It was a long, flat room, with doorways and archways that seemed to go on at some length beneath the house.

"This was the school's boiler room and maintenance area, pretty much destroyed in the fire, but"—Fleetwood pointed to the new paint job—"Ivy wanted to make sure it was close to the original design. It was a bit of a wine cellar at one time in its history, and this was one of the entrances to the underworld."

Cali giggled nervously. "Hell?"

"Well, not exactly. You see, Justin Gravesend had a certain mania. You know of the Winchester House in California?"

Cali nodded. "The widow of the riflemaker felt that men who had died by the gun were coming for her. So she built addition after addition onto the house."

"Right. Staircases going nowhere, doors to empty space. She had the house built up her entire life. Justin Gravesend had a similar but different mania. His grandson left a written record that was found after he died. The grandson lived until he was just about a hundred years old, and apparently he was sharp up until the end. He described how—and, more interestingly, why—Justin Gravesend built Harrow the way he did.

"Essentially, he built a house within a house. His grandson called the other house a 'Looking-Glass House.' Gravesend had a daughter who had shown evidence of being insane, at least to Gravesend and his specialists. He somehow felt that something he had done had made her crazy. Not abuse, necessarily, but some occult work that Gravesend had been part of before the child was born. By the age of four, I would guess, she was showing signs of multiple personality disorder—which at the time was severely misunderstood, to the point of brutality. She also seemed to have a bit of a dangerous streak to her. I can guess from what I've read that she also exhibited paranormal abilities, which, in the late 1800s would be considered embarrassing and shameful to someone of Gravesend's class. His grandson even claims he called in a priest to perform rites of exorcism on the poor girl.

"Gravesend kept her hidden from the world, even hidden from his wife, the girl's mother. He created a separate house within the house, a home asylum for her, and he used all his knowledge of arcane ritual and occult artifact to keep her there, to hold back whatever evil he felt she contained. But as you can guess, this kind of imprisonment therapy only made the girl worse, and as Matilde grew older, her personalities seem to have manifested themselves in terms of an unusual kind of haunting. In my opinion she had a very definite paranormal ability, and perhaps each of her distinct personalities had one, as well. One of them was psychokinesis. One was astral projection. Another was sort of a reverse psychometry."

"Reverse?" Cali asked.

Jack nodded. "She could bring the histories of certain sacred objects to some form of ectoplasmic life. Well, that's what was claimed, anyway. And then she died when she was in her forties, still living in a prison that her father had created for her, still not knowing that she had created several distinct personalities, all of whom had an astral reality."

"This all sounds made up." Chet shook his head. "This is like hearing a fairy tale. Maybe someone believed this, but if a guy is a hundred years old and writing this stuff down, well, all I can say is, I bet he wasn't as sharp as you think."

Fleetwood shot him a glance. It was businesslike, and Cali noticed that the entire group had somehow lost its sense of humor down there, beneath the house. It was as if this was beginning to seem real. Not the house, not the haunting, but the job.

We're here as bait, she thought, and wanted to say it aloud but was almost afraid to do it.

"Goggles on," Fleetwood said.

Chapter Twenty-eight

1

"It's a green world," Cali said as she glanced over at Chet, who looked like a shimmering yellow-green fog. "You're the green man, Chet."

"You callin' me Kermit the frog?" Chet asked, chuckling. "And you're green with envy."

"And I'm just green with nausea," Frost said, behind them.

Ivy turned about and seemed about to say something, but then turned back around and led them down what seemed like a long flight of rickety stairs. Frost mumbled something about "Doesn't anyone believe in electricity down here?" The stairs led to what seemed like a sloping room—the floor had been damaged, not in the fire, but in a later flooding—and here, Jack explained about the floor and the walls and the water and the fire and everything, until Cali was about to tell him enough already. As she thought about how tired she was of the waiting game, and how she wished she could get away from the house for just one night (one night, and maybe a coffeehouse or a movie or something other than this house), she realized that she had a sense from the others:

The level of frustration was rising.

The house may not contain anything other than a somewhat colorful history, Callie thought.

2

They went through room after room, some small and narrow, a few large and deep—and Chet whispered aloud, "We're going down farther," and Ivy moved ahead of them in the green glow of all that Chet could see—for all he could follow were the flashlight beams and the wispy green of the outlines of things. The rooms seemed unreal with the goggles on; at first Frost giggled too much; the rooms were damp, and what felt like a stone floor was slightly sticky.

"What's so funny?" someone asked, and Chet wasn't sure whose voice it was. Wearing the goggles brought on a sensation of disorientation—they went through a green darkness and only the yellow-green forms of the others kept Chet aware that he wasn't alone. Because there was something about these tunnels and rooms that seemed desolate, that made him imagine that they were all marching, singly, to their own graves.

3

"Here," Ivy said, in the next room. Jack held up his hand at the doorway—which was stooped and narrow, so they had to duck their heads to go through it. Ivy shone the flashlight up at the ceiling.

It was vast, this room. It was as if they'd gone through a small series of hallways and closets to come out in an enormous ballroom. The ceiling was shiny and black.

"This was the entrance from the crypt," Ivy said.

"You mean—?" Cali gasped.

"Jesus," Chet said. "We've walked beyond the house?"

"The entire hillside, basically," Jack said.

And then Ivy brought them over to a far wall.

There, scratched into the surface, glyphs and symbols.

"It's a mix of ancient Egyptian hieroglyphs and what I'd generously call black magic mumbo-jumbo," Ivy said. "Well, it may all be mumbo-jumbo. None of it really makes sense and none of us are archaeologists. I'd place this room as the main temple. The Egyptian period of Harrow, if you will. I will take a not-so-wild guess and say that those"—she pointed specifically to a line of hieroglyphs that showed an ibis, a jackal, and what might've been a crocodile— "are from the *Aegyptian Book of the Dead*, or perhaps one of the books upstairs. And this"—she waved her hand around another part of the wall—"this is some ritual about Harrow itself. See the *H* within the design? It's repeated in the front gate of the house, and if you look at two of the stained-glass windows in the front, it's there as well. And that"—she pointed off toward what might've been a series of squiggles and lines that reminded Chet of forks and *S*-shapes and backward *3*'s—"is occult language, basically. It's the Chymera Magick ritual he developed, I have no doubt. Gravesend kept his daughter in these tunnels, but he also had his worship."

"He worshipped the Devil?" Chet joked, and swiftly wished he hadn't said it.

"Well, whatever he worshipped," Ivy said, "it remained behind, didn't it?"

"What's that?" Chet asked.

"What?" Cali said, turning toward him again.

Chet pointed to something in midair. "That thing. That . . ."

There, slightly above and in front of Ivy, was what looked like a light mist—as if someone had just taken a puff of a cigarette and it floated there in the still air.

Then it was gone.

Jack held up his EMF, but when he read it he said, "Nothing."

Frost snickered a bit, and when Cali asked him what was so funny he said, "Nothing is so funny."

4

Frost saw her, of course. The girl with the hot body standing there, watching them.

Picking out which one of them. Who would be her dance partner?

But Frost knew on the inside that he would be the one chosen because he was the most special of all of them. No one else saw her.

She's revealing herself only to me.

She wants only me.

He knew about Snapping Jaws and Voices and why one man sees smoke in the air while the other sees the truth in the form of a pretty girl who looks like she's sixteen and is only revealing herself to her one, true, snapping love.

5

It was hours before they returned to the aboveground house. Cali was growing weary of the goggles and took them off at one point and nearly tripped over herself in the absolute darkness. Instead of putting the headgear over her scalp, she carried it in front of her for the rest of the trip, which ended as they went up a series of narrow stone staircases. When they finished they were in the tower room, the one in which Cali had first met Ivy. The story of little Matilde and her life in the darkness and bowels of the house as she grew to middle age, her personalities getting loose in some kind of astral projection nightmare, her ghost opening the way for other ghosts to enter the house—it had all been told and retold, and at one point, Chet gave Cali's hand a squeeze, which made her feel better.

Back in the hall near their bedrooms, Ivy stopped in her tracks and turned to face them. "Nothing?"

Cali shook her head. "I still haven't felt anything—nothing in terms of psychometry or even a slight sense or intuition, since I got here. It's like it's gone."

"Me neither," Frost admitted. "It's like I never had it now. Sometimes I guess it goes away."

Ivy rubbed at a spot just above her wrist as if she itched there.

Cali nodded. "I've tried concentrating . . . but this has never happened before. Not since I knew I had the ability."

Ivy glared at Cali as if she was ready to spit. Cali wished she could say something, or do something, that would help ease the frustration, but she just stood there with the others in the hallway. "I have spent the past year withdrawing every fund I have for this house, for what I think may be here. I know this is a psychic place. I know it is." Even her anger had grown anemic by the time she finished speaking, and she seemed on the verge of collapse.

Jack grasped her elbow, nearly holding her up from collapse. "You're tired. You haven't slept well for days. Look, I've got some

Ambien, and you can take it and get at least one good night's sleep while you're here."

"I don't want to," Ivy said, but something in her voice lacked resistance. "Jack, I don't want to, I really really don't want to."

6

Cali felt comfortable enough, alone in the parlor, that she decided it would be all right to fall asleep near the hearth, like a cat curled up on the rug. She stared into the flames, hoping they'd help her block out other thoughts, but it was too much—Det's face seemed to be there in the yellow fire, and Chet's, also. *Chet and Det. They rhyme. There's some symmetry there: Chet and Det. Both are "et" words. What if I et Chet and Det. Debt. Chebt. Dead. Chead. Threat. Met. Fret. Set. Pet. Let. Wet. Bet. Net.* The words that were born from her playing with the names seemed to lull her to sleep, and then, as if she had invoked him with her thoughts, Chet came to her and sat beside her.

After that, she could not sleep at all.

7

So he had returned, just as she was afraid he would, hoped he would, and they'd begun talking and revealing themselves: She talked about Det and how she didn't love him the way she knew he needed to be loved; about the stresses of her work; and Chet told her about St. Chris and the Big Woman and the legend within his own mind of who his mother was. "If your mother's such a . . . well, not much of a mother, why would you look for her?" Cali asked.

"Here's the thing," Chet told her. "Ever since I was little, I've had this feeling. I mean, I lived with people who were not exactly loving. I saw some bad things, too. Some awful things. A lot of human ugliness."

Cali took a sip of cognac. It burned on her tongue but felt like a sweet, delicious warmth as it went down her throat. She felt a luxuriousness that she hadn't been sensing before; Harrow seemed as much a retreat as it was an investigation. This was a rich place. This was a treasure, and the cognac and the warmth that went from her throat down into her body added to the wealth of this moment. The rest of life was distant and not particularly appealing. Finally, nearly smiling, she said, "Human ugliness. That's the world for you."

"No, there's more than that. There's human beauty and strength and kindness. There were times when I saw beautiful things, too. When even another person, maybe a kid, maybe even the mother of a friend, did some small thing. Not for anyone. Not for someone to see or notice. But some really beautiful thing. And then I figured: That's what my mother did for me. She gave me up because she was probably worse than the places I ended up in. She was probably more miserable than even my foster mother. But she gave me up because she loved me enough. Now, I don't think I'd ever let go of my kid if I had one. Ever. But I'm different. That's one thing Rustic Acres and St. Chris taught me. I'm different, and part of me being different is me understanding that human ugliness and misery are what gets put in most peoples' paths. And they embrace it. And maybe I'm different, so I see that, and instead I know that whoever or whatever gets put in my path, I'm going to hug it to me like there's no tomorrow. Misery isn't in my path. I don't know why. It never has been, no matter what else goes on around me. But I really believe, for better or worse, when life—or God—or whatever runs this universe, even fate, puts someone in your path, to avoid it is some kind of death. I think my mother did that. I was put in her path, and she avoided me. That was probably best when she had me. But now I'm going to find her again, and she's going to be in my path this time, and I am going to make sure I love her and I let her know it, and that I'd rather have her crazy and hard to deal with in my life than on some other path."

Cali watched the fire crackle and sputter; outside, the first rays of dawn were coming up. She felt like weeping, from hearing this and from sleepiness, but no tears came. She thought of her own mother and father, and all the difficult years. She wondered about the paths of life, and how they twisted and grew wild. "Damn it," she said.

Chet chuckled. "I pour my heart out and that's all you have to say?"

"No, I mean, damn it, because you're making me think about my dad and mom and how I love them anyway. They were always there for me, even after they divorced. My nosy sister, Bev. And my brother . . ."

"Where's he?"

"Dead," Cali said, and realized it was actually the first time in her life she had said that aloud about him. Usually, she avoided the subject, or used words like *gone* or *passed on.* "His name was Ned. He was my twin."

"I'm sorry," Chet said. "I don't want you to think about sad things. Not now."

Cali shrugged. "It happened a long time ago. We both had it.

The famous Ability X. His was a little different, I guess. His drove him . . . to do things . . . bad things, to himself and others. He had to be put in a special home, because his mind went haywire . . . and . . . well, he killed himself, finally."

They were silent. The fire crackled in the fireplace.

"It's funny," Cali said after the long quiet. "I've felt guilty all this time because I feel like I shouldn't have outlived him. Not if I had this ability to see things, to connect with objects and their histories, just like him. Why didn't I become insane, too? Why? I had the same visions he had. I got scared, too. I didn't understand it. Why did I stay sane? That's what I've always been thinking. Inside."

"Maybe it's—"

"If you say 'God's will,' I will slap you," she said, and it sounded as if she meant it.

"No. Maybe it's because your sanity and his state of mind had nothing to do with the ability," Chet said. It sounded so simple, but Cali had never considered it.

"Could be," she said softly. "You know, Chet? You're a sharp cookie."

They talked some more, vented a little about Ivy and her strange mania, Frost and his google eyes, Jack Fleetwood with his pipe and little techno-gadgets . . . Cali felt lazily sleepy and didn't even notice how much she had fallen in love with Chet, from a foolish lust to a genuine sense of love, and all within a couple of days. The subject of Death, once introduced by Cali, seemed to weave in and out of the conversation, and not evaporate as Cali had hoped it would.

"I think about dying sometimes," Chet said. "Sometimes I wonder if after we die, we'll miss just breathing. We'll thank anyone for bringing us into the world to have the adventure we were meant to have. And we'll even miss suffering in the afterlife—we'll get jealous of people who are still alive, and think: What a blast, what a screwed-up and wonderful trip it was, to be able to hurt over something, to cry and feel a little pain. And then experience joy, too."

"How'd you get to be so wise, kiddo? You don't even talk like most teenagers I know."

"I'm almost twenty," he said with mock-indignity. "Mira told me I'm an old soul." Chet grinned, winking. "Just this morning. She said I probably had several incarnations, and she told me she didn't really believe in it, but she thought if it was true, then I was an ancient soul."

"Oh, that little vixen." Cali wagged her finger at him. "She's after you. She's got a crush."

Chet scratched at his side and said, "Yeah, I know. Crushes are nice. My first one was when I was eight. This girl who sometimes baby-sat for the Big Woman took me to the local grill. She was fourteen or fifteen, and she had guys crawling all over her, but when she put her song on the jukebox, all she wanted to do was dance with me. I had the biggest crush."

"I once had a crush on my gym teacher."

"Oh," Chet said, his eyes brightening. "One of those crushes."

"It was a man." Cali blushed. "My lesbian crushes came later. No, I was eleven, and in the little school I went to you had your English teacher for gym. He was smart and handsome and probably only twenty-three, but he seemed so mature and . . . well . . . well-developed. Bulging muscles. Great smile." She sighed. "It's sweet to have crushes. I guess when I think of Mira that way, it's cute."

"Don't worry, I'm not into fourteen-year-olds," Chet said.

"Sixteen," Mira said.

Cali glanced up from the fire.

Mira stood in the doorway. *God, how long had she been listening?* Cali felt terrible. *What kind of game am I playing? I'm too old for Chet, he's a baby, and Mira's a child, and I'm a moron.*

"Aw," Chet said. "Damn." He rose, fumbling a little with his balance. "Mira!" he called out, and went after her.

8

Chet found her out among the statues, with Conan whimpering at her side as if he, too, was crying for his mistress. Mira was crumpled into a bench, her hands covering her face.

"Mira," Chet said. He sat beside her and touched her shoulder. She shrugged him off.

Between sobs, she said, "Get away from me. Just leave me alone. Leave me alone."

"We didn't mean—I didn't mean it like it sounded."

"That's a lie. You did. Just leave me alone," she wept. "Just leave me alone."

"Just come inside. It's freezing out here," Chet said, and took his jacket off, wrapping it across her shoulders. "Please. Just come inside."

"I will," she said, her heaves subsiding a bit. "Just go away. Leave me alone. I'll go in. But after you leave."

9

When Mira was alone, a light snow began to fall. It was early in the year for snow, and the flakes were small and fine. *It's almost*

November first, she thought. *Halloween. All the parties back in the city. I'm missing everything. Just because I have to be here with Dad. Just because of Dad I'm stuck in this hellhole, and then he has to be here, the one that I know should want me, but that witch is after him, and I'm so ugly. I'm ugly and disgusting and no one will ever love me. No one will ever love me. I will die a virgin.* She reached down and hugged her dog to her, raising him up on the bench, like a large child in her arms. She buried her face against the thick ruff of fur along Conan's neck.

In her left hand, a pair of night goggles.

"You love me, don't you, Conan? At least you love me, at least somebody does," she wept as she cuddled her pet. He pressed his icy nose against her throat and made noises that sounded like sweet comfort. "Let's not go back to that house again. I don't want to see any of them ever again. I hate all of them. I wish I hadn't come. I wish we could just go someplace safe. Just you and me. Just somewhere small and safe where no one can find us."

10

It was four o'clock in the morning when Frost awoke and saw the girl standing by his window in the dark. He glanced up at the camera in the doorway. Would the camera capture this?

All he could make out was her small form. He reached beside his bed for the night goggles. He slipped them on, and then could see her more clearly.

Yes, it was her, the little one, the pretty girl from the cellar. She was a teenager, from the look of her torn clothes, from the look of wildness and innocence on her face; and it excited him that she was there. With the night goggles on he saw her clearly, saw her half-smile, her long blond hair, and as she moved closer to him, he could see the markings on her skin, the symbols that had been etched upon her, all glowing in the greenness of the goggles.

He knew that she was Quincy Allen, the teen who had died the previous year. It was her spirit, lingering like residue here. Within his mind, her voice spoke to him.

She would become one of his voices, he was sure.

She would come into him, inside his flesh, and dwell there, and make the voices speak again.

And he knew that he was the most important one in the world to her.

He wanted to love the dead girl very, very badly.

"Take me out to the ball game . . ."

—traditional

"Everyone has a devil in him that is capable of any crime in the long run."

—Henry David Thoreau,
"Wednesday," A Week on the Concord and Merrimack Rivers, *1849*

"Here comes the God of Snapping Jaws!
He'll take you up between his claws!
He'll chew your face and scrape your innards,
Oh, Snapping Jaws just wants his dinnards!"

—a song, by Frost Crane

When Bluebeard's wife opened the door, she brought her lamp fully into the room so that she could clearly see what sort of treasure her husband kept here. He was a wealthy and important man, and might have hidden any number of jewels and gold from her, but what she saw within the room made her blood run cold, for it was a charnel house.

—from a retelling of the classic fairy tale "Bluebeard"

BOOK THREE

Empire of the Mind

PART EIGHT

The Third Day

Chapter Twenty-nine

1

Frost spent the early morning hours feeling the Voices come back inside him. It was like an earth-shattering orgasm to feel them go through him again. It was Snapping Jaws coming back! It was a tickling in his throat, a fiddling within his mind, and he felt stiff and firm and erect and whole as he heard them speak within him.

"She's going to die, you have to know that, she needs to—"

"Look, in a few more minutes you're going to want to stop all of them, because they're out to destroy you. You know that, don't you? Frost? Can you hear me?"

"Of course he can hear you, look at him, he's excited again. It's been a long time since he's been this aroused."

"Do you want to see true beauty, Frost? We can show you our treasures, we can show you the other side of everything, you know."

"The inside out of it."

"The turnabout of flesh."

"Yes," one of them whispered softly, a sweet woman's voice within him. "The other side of things. The infinite."

"It has great beauty."

"Great beauty is no accident," said another. "Frost, do you understand? We will give you power, if you like. We have made you potent. You are more than you've ever been. Here, here with us, in Harrow."

Frost closed his eyes. He asked them: "What are you? Are you the dead? Can you show yourselves to me?"

"Would you like to see us?" one of them asked.

"Yes. Oh, yes. Oh, please, yes," Frost said, feeling something in his mouth that was like licorice and a memory.

"Open your eyes. We are here with you," the sweet-voiced woman said.

Frost went from darkness to light and saw, for the briefest moment, what seemed like a brilliant star going out into an absolute darkness.

And yet, in the dark, his goggles on, he saw them as they crawled toward him. Some of them moved as if they had no legs, crawling with their arms; others came on all fours like animals, their stringy hair hanging down.

They're an army. A fucking army. An army of nightcrawlers. Coming to me, coming to me. The thoughts spun through him a mile a minute. Soon their arms writhed around him, and he saw the green glow of their faces, and there were children with teeth like knives, and there was a man with a spike in his hand, and there were even soldiers in dented armor, and the stories that Ivy Martin had told in the cellar came to him again: Gilles de Rais and the children he killed, the Knights Templar, and all of them wanted him, and there she was, the most beautiful woman of all, an angel in human flesh, Isis Claviger, with her mouth open for him, her lips drawn back across her teeth.

They covered him and held him and pressed themselves deep into his body, and he trembled and shook and wept and rejoiced until morning's light. He drew the curtains back on the dawn, letting the sunlight flood his room. Then he went to look at his new, shining self in the mirror. He saw them, all of them, within his own eyes; he felt a delicate shiver run through his being. They were no longer voices alone. They were actual creatures within him. They shared his thoughts and tasted his love, and it was as if everything Frost Crane had ever wished for had come true.

It was only after he'd come down from the incredible high of this that he went over to his battered American Tourister suitcase and opened it. There, in his shaving kit: fingernail clippers.

Frost Crane sat on the edge of his bed and began carving the symbols into his skin. He had watched them the previous night as they'd come alive before his eyes, just for him, showing him the words and the phrases and the pictures that were necessary. They had it all wrong! Ivy and Jack and their crude companions! Words on a wall were meaningless! It was the flesh of humans that needed the words and the images to open the door wide and let in the divinity of Harrow. His skin felt ripe and tingly, his fingers moving the sharp edge of the clipper over his belly and thighs with an artist's precision but a factory worker's speed. The holes of his body expanded so as to allow more of them to enter him, to be within his flesh.

And as he drew the ritual symbols that they showed him, he felt something like a door within him open up; not a metaphorical door that opened his mind or heart but a literal door, creaking open, a door of bones and organ meat and pumping blood, opening, and his skin began turning outward, but he did not scream.

He did not scream.

There was great pleasure to be had as his flesh became the doorway of Snapping Jaws. He began seeing how the light changed, and how what had seemed painful was in fact like an exquisite tickling, a kind of loving, a meeting of the inner with the outer, of the spiritual with the material, and he was, in fact, he himself, Frost Crane, was the suit that Snapping Jaws wore as it came through him.

And then Snapping Jaws told Frost where to find the pitchfork of his dreams.

2

"Mira's gone," Jack Fleetwood said. He stood in the doorway to Cali's room; she had just opened her eyes and was shocked to see him standing there.

"Gone?" she asked, rubbing sleep from her eyes and the last fragments of dreams from her memory. "What . . . what do you mean?"

"Gone as in gone," Jack said. Worry was in his features, in his eyes. For the first time he looked concerned about his daughter. "She didn't sleep in her bed, and I can't find her."

"Maybe she went to the village?" Cali offered.

Jack shook his head. "I don't know. It's not like her. Chet's already going through rooms, trying to see if she's hiding, but I know her. She doesn't hide. I'm sure she's all right, wherever she is. I'm sure she is. But I just wish I knew where she was. I just wish she was here. I'm going to keep looking around. In about an hour we'll have coffee in the library, all right?"

3

Chet carried one of the large boxes into the library; two of them already sat in the middle of the floor on the Persian rug. Frost came in, walking as if he had been drinking all morning, and Cali came downstairs a few minutes later, fresh from her morning bath. Jack had already laid out some buttered toast, coffee, and tea on the black-lacquered table near one of the overstuffed chairs.

"You cold?" Cali asked, noticing that Frost had his shirt buttoned up to his collar, which was turned up, and a long jacket wrapped around him as if it were twenty below.

"A little," Frost said. "Yes."

Cali raised her eyebrows in a silent question for Chet, who noticed. He went over to her; all she said was, "Jack can't find Mira."

Ivy strode into the library, wearing what looked like muddy work boots, her jeans tucked into them, her black sweater looking filthy, and that tired look about her, as if she'd carried an enormous burden for years and would not let it go.

4

"I got some sleep, thanks to some pills," Ivy said matter-of-factly, after she'd settled into one of the chairs by the fireplace. "Look, I don't think this experiment is going to work. At least not the way it was planned." She shot a glance over to Jack, then scanned the rest of them. "I know you've only been here a couple of days. I've been here for months, and I'm beginning to think . . . well, I want to inspire you here. Now. I wasn't going to show you any of this, partly because of its possible value, and partly because Jack and I didn't want to influence any of you in any way. We wanted the purity of Harrow to filter through each of you. Each of your abilities. But now I think we need a nudge."

"Both Ivy and I think what's in these boxes is what makes Harrow most unique. Particularly among haunted houses," Jack added, and then quickly shut up again, like a boy who was about to get a scolding.

"Justin Gravesend was not just a member of a secret society in the late 1800s. He was a bit of a grandmaster for them, and as such, he collected quite a bit—objects both sacred and profane. These are some of them. We don't yet know how valuable they truly are, but they are, at the very least, intriguing. And perhaps something within them will help each of you." She looked directly at Cali. "Particularly you, Cali. I would think that if you could focus on any one of these objects . . ."

"I haven't felt it," Cali said. "Not since coming here. I feel like it's gone."

"We all do," Chet said softly.

Frost said nothing, but watched the cardboard boxes as if they contained gold. He kept pulling his collar up around his neck.

"Well, let's try, anyway," Ivy said. And for the first time since Cali had seen her, it seemed as if a spell had been broken. Ivy did not appear to be intimidating or unusual or driven or even beautiful. She was a woman, an ordinary woman, who had somehow gotten trapped inside an idea of a house that might hold something important for her.

"Jack, would you do the honors?" Ivy asked.

Jack Fleetwood stood up and went over to the box farthest from Ivy.

"No," she said. "This one. By me."

Dutifully—an obedient lover, Cali thought, and then wasn't sure why she had thought it—Jack stepped over the box he'd approached and then knelt down in front of Ivy, opening the box nearest her.

"Gravesend created a museum within the house, and most of the artifacts have been lost over time. There were stories of mummies and great underground tombs, rebuilt from Mayan and Egyptian temples, and even a story that there was a torture chamber—a medieval torture chamber, at that—somewhere within the walls, but all we've uncovered are empty rooms. But some items were either found in the rubble from the fire, or Jack and I found them in the cellars. I want you to see these. I want each of you to handle them to see if you have any reaction or insight into them, beyond what we know."

Jack drew out what Cali thought was at first a broken bowl. It was crude pottery but had curious figures drawn along it, and she thought it might be some ancient Grecian art. Jack took it over to Cali and put it in her hands; Chet leaned forward to look at it.

"A man who worked at the school named Gus Trask found this, after the fire. It came into the possession—at least temporarily—of the PSI Vista Foundation. I bought it as part of what I hope will be a valuable collection from Harrow."

"What's it for?"

"It may be an ordinary drinking bowl," Ivy said. "We suspect that it is two thousand or more years old. The fact that it is only part of the bowl adds, for me, to its authenticity. We don't know what it was used for ritually, but we do know what Justin Gravesend believed it to be; it was rumored that he owned such a bowl, and in the bowl the future could be divined."

"My God," Cali said. "Someone thinks this might be the holy grail?" She was joking, of course, but Ivy barely blinked.

Frost let out a little laugh that was more like a shriek, and Chet squinted as he looked up at Cali and then back to the bowl and its white and black markings.

"Gravesend thought so," Jack said. "This probably isn't the real thing. But the Chymera Magick believed it was."

Cali held the bowl in her hand. She tried to let the darkness within her mind's eye take over and emptied her thoughts, but she could not stop thinking about what the bowl might truly be. Or how crazy it was to even imagine that a grail actually existed, a cup that was used at the Last Supper or that caught the blood of Christ on the cross—an ancient, mystical idea that had always seemed more poetic to her than anything.

She could not concentrate. She was hyperaware of the others around her, and in some respects it was as if she'd donned the night goggles again and could see their green outlines in the dark of her mind.

She opened her eyes.

Ivy watched her with such an intense need in her eyes, it almost hurt to have to tell her. "Nothing," Cali said.

Jack drew out another object. It caught the light from the chandelier above and glistened darkly.

"One obsidian dagger. Possibly sacrificial, definitely from an Aztec grave or holy site. Perhaps a Toltec relic, perhaps a more modern creation," Jack said as he held it up for them to see. "How he got it, no one knows." Other items came from each of the boxes, a catalog of unusual items: a warrior's leather helmet, a long spike that Jack claimed was supposedly the object that the rather notorious Gilles de Rais, both the right-hand man to Joan of Arc and a notorious child-killer, used to disembowel the children he murdered in the fifteenth century ("It was alleged that de Rais himself had been a member of the Chymera Magick, assuming that group went back that far in history," Jack added as he passed the spike to Cali); wrapped in paper, out came what looked like a stone head of a dog. "Head of a jackal sculpture. Probably not so old, but definitely part of what was probably once a recreation of an Egyptian pharoah's tomb, for the Chymera Magick's ceremonies," Jack said. Smaller pieces, sculptures, what Jack called "Venuses and goddess figures," as well as one bit of shiny bronze that was in the shape of a large phallus. They passed the pieces around, although Frost seemed to have no interest in touching them, until the phallus reached him, and then he rubbed it a bit. Cali noticed that Frost's hands seemed to be peeling. Psoriasis? She hadn't noticed it before.

"And now," Ivy said, "I've kept away from you somewhat for these past two days because I wanted you to pick up whatever vibes you could. I'm not a terribly secretive person, but I wanted to explore the house and find out what I could from it. Other than these artifacts, there hasn't been much. Those symbols drawn down in the tunnel that you saw last night." She shrugged. "It's like a puzzle, and I was hoping you three could understand what pieces were missing."

"I just don't get it," Chet said, frustration rising in his voice. "We're brought here to hunt for ghosts, but you want something. You don't want us to just find out things or, I don't know, see ghosts."

Ivy smiled, nearly sweetly, but there was something terrible in her smile nonetheless. "I want something that no one is supposed to get, I suppose."

CHAPTER THIRTY

1

Ivy's story

"Several years ago, I fell in love. That's not all that unusual, but the guy I was in love with was—well, roughly your age, Chet. Perhaps a year younger, and I was . . . older. Just a few years, but enough to make a difference. At first he lied and told me that he was my age, but I found out the truth. I felt our relationship was wrong and was going to break it off but discovered that I was pregnant with our child. I wasn't sure what to do. The young man came from a good family, and he loved me, and he wanted to marry me. As much as I loved him, I felt he should not get married yet. He should get through college and then later, if we still loved each other, we could raise our child together and do the legal thing. One night his father came down with him to the city, to talk with me about how we were all going to handle this. Although I have been independently wealthy from a young age, I suspect his father felt I was after money in all this.

"Let me just move this along. It went badly, the meeting

between the three of us, and I lost my temper, as did his father. It was a stormy winter night, and they left together, and I was furious at the man I loved, so I put my coat on and followed them to his father's car, and the arguments continued. I wasn't sure if I would ever love again, and I had the baby growing inside me, and I wasn't sure how any of it would turn out, but I had a rage that needed to be quenched. They drove off, and I looked at Stephen—that was his name, dear Stephen—as he glanced back at me, and I remember thinking: This is not the way it is meant to turn out. This is not the way it is meant to turn out.

"So I got in my car and I followed them, and at some point on a dark road off the main highway the snow came down faster, and the whole world seemed to be a white blur, as if the snow just erased everything around it.

"And there was a crash.

"Afterward, when I remembered anything, I could not even recall the last moment. I could not even imagine that I had crashed into them, and they into me, spinning on an icy, snowy road, but the two of them were dead.

"And my child, within me, died, also."

2

Ivy paused, closing her eyes. When she opened them, she wiped at the tears.

The others watched her in silence.

3

Ivy's tale, continued

"I had lost Stephen, lost my child. I was told that I could not conceive again. And I was close to . . . well, the extremes of life, I'd guess. Stephen had gone to Harrow Academy, and I had met him when he was eighteen—a senior—and I was just finishing college. But four years' later, Stephen's younger brother, whom I had not met, arrived at my home, and we spoke about Stephen, that night, and I felt a strong connection to his brother. In fact, I would even consider it a psychic connection, if I believed that I had any psychic ability, because that teenage boy had some power within him. It was almost like a shock, when he hugged me before he left.

"He was part of what happened at Harrow last year. I'm not sure how much of it he knew or didn't know. I know that he was there when the fire occurred, and I know . . ." She wiped at the tears. "You don't need to know any of that, other than the reason I'm here. I believe that there is an opening here at Harrow. I believe that Justin Gravesend had discovered a key to a doorway to another . . ." She glanced at Jack Fleetwood, as if he could help, but his eyes were downcast. "And then, of course, I found out that I had yet another connection to this house. One I had never known. One that had been hidden from me by the purest of coincidences. And I now think that I met Stephen and his brother purely because Harrow wanted me to come to it.

"My great-grandmother's sister was the medium who vanished sometime after leaving Harrow. Isis Claviger was her stage name. Her real name was Isobel Saul. I have no doubt she was murdered within these walls. Certainly, Esteban Palliser says so in his diary.

Stephen is still here. Isis is still here. I have no doubt that she was truly psychic.

"And now I have no doubt that there is something here at Harrow for me. That I will see him again. I will see Stephen. And I will know what my great-great-aunt knew. I believe I was meant to buy this house, and I was meant to master it and its spirits in some way."

4

Chet was the first to stand. "It's . . . we're . . . not here for what . . . for what I thought."

Jack Fleetwood leaned back on the palms of his hands, like an overgrown child splayed out on the rug. "You're here to find the location of the haunt. Your abilities—"

"Our abilities don't seem to work here," Cali said, feeling defensive of Chet.

"No," Chet said. "We're here to help find something that can't be found."

"Someone else's past," Cali said, staring at Ivy. Sensations of both compassion and confusion stirred within her.

Ivy Martin pushed herself up from her chair, her eyes still glazed with tears. "You live your lives with this gift that God gave you, or some freak of nature endowed each of you with—and you have been paid good money to come here, and if you think you're just entertaining some vain woman's whim . . ." Her eyes took on a steely aspect. Her complexion seemed to change, from pallor to fiery red. Then she whispered something, as if to herself, and slumped back down in the chair.

"You all right?" Jack asked softly. He reached over from where he sat and placed a hand on her knee. "Ivy?"

Cali glanced at Frost, who seemed to be humming to himself.

"Fine," Ivy said. Then she leaned forward in the chair and looked Cali directly in the eye. "If you don't have your Ability *X* anymore, then something in Harrow took it from you. Have you considered that possibility?"

Cali might have been the only one aware of it, but Frost Crane giggled next to her. Annoyingly. He had been giggling to himself, and humming, and making sly faces when he thought no one was looking. She turned to give him a cold stare, and at the same time he turned toward her and whispered nearly under his breath, "Poor old lady, she swallowed a fly. I don't know why she swallowed a fly. Perhaps she'll die."

And then Jack Fleetwood let out a yelp; they all looked at him; he was touching something in the air, as if sculpting from the invisible.

He didn't look at anyone, but kept his eyes midair in front of him, and curved his hands around something.

"Where's the fucking EMF meter when you need it?" he said.

CHAPTER THIRTY-ONE

1

Frost excused himself, leaving the room as if he had an appointment to keep; Ivy got down on the floor next to Jack; Cali watched Frost leave, stunned by his words. Had she imagined it? Or had he known what the little boy in the dark closet had said? The little rhyme? And had he known that other little boy? The little boy who had once said the rhyme over and over again, knowing every word, every single word, all the way to the last part. *Poor old lady, she swallowed a fly . . .*

2

"It's a cold spot," Jack Fleetwood said, his eyes wide and his expression broad and exaggerated in its happiness. "My God, we finally have something."

Ivy just stared into the empty space he defined with his hands.

Then she reached near it, touching it. She quickly drew her fingers back. "Icy."

"Yeah, damn icy," Jack said.

Chet went over and pressed his fingers against the air and felt nothing. Then, as he moved his hand around the general area, he said, "Tingly."

"Not cold?" Cali asked. She stood up and stepped around an empty box. She stayed back a bit, watching the others.

"No," Chet said. He swiftly moved his hands in and out of what Cali had come to think of as an invisible perimeter of about three feet high and a foot wide. "Like little electrical charges. I guess maybe it's a little cold."

"A lot cold," Jack said. "I've never experienced this quite . . . quite like this."

"It's a child," Chet said.

Jack laughed. "An icy kid, I guess."

"No, it's a child. I can feel him."

"Him?" Cali asked.

Chet nodded. "I don't know why, but it is. It's a little boy. He's . . . he's zapping all over the place. Like a ball of energy. Almost." Chet grinned as if it were Christmas morning. "He's playing here."

"This I have to try," Cali said. "I've always heard about cold spots, but I thought they were just basic energy farts or something." She took another step forward and reached her arm out and felt what at first seemed like a burning sensation, and then a brief chill in her fingertips. She drew her hand back at first, instinctively, but then thrust it in. "Wow," was all she could muster. She found that as she pressed her hand farther into what seemed like a series of curves, each one getting colder, she had the sensation of pins-and-needles in her fingers, her hand, her wrist, and, finally, her forearm. It was like the cold spot was moving up here. And suddenly she was stricken with panic. It was *moving* up her arm. Irrational thoughts came into her mind—

What would it do? Would it take her over? Would it take all her strength? Her life?

And then something exploded for her—as if the windows had just been blown out. She stood there near the others, and a little boy stood in the center of their group. Her hand was on the boy's shoulder, and he was the little boy from the dark closet, and he looked up at her and opened his mouth as if to scream, as if seeing her there was as terrifying to him as it was to her, and then, she was no longer in the room with the others but in her twin brother's room back home, back years ago, and he had written it on the walls in his own feces, her brother had, he had painted the walls of his bedroom with the words:

POOR OLD LADY SHE SWALLOWED A FLY PERHAPS SHE'LL DIE.

Blood and feces both, smeared across the wall, the rhyme went on and on, and somewhere another little boy was laughing, laughing at her, and Cali told herself that she was in a moment, within a psychometric moment, somehow taken into it, pushed into it by the cold spot, but part of her felt that she had encountered the Devil himself.

Her brother, as she remembered him with his beautiful dark skin and almond eyes, just like hers, and his unkempt look, and the secret and silent understanding they had about their ability, all the love she had for her twin brother—it all was there. Flies had begun circling the room, great black and green flies, as the shit on the walls began to run, and she knew then—back when she was twelve—that her brother was insane, and that there would be no going back for either of them. He had the greater ability.

And he had never left her. He was within her and always had been. Just as the boy Gloria Franco in Manhattan had murdered—he still existed in some form, as well, and he, too, was with Cali.

But they were in Harrow now.

All of them.

Cali felt the flies buzzing around her arms. She looked down at her left arm. It was covered with the sticky brownness of the room, and the houseflies and greenflies lit upon her arm and moved like erupting sores up her arm; maggots began dropping from her flesh; and soon the flesh itself was being eaten away at by the devouring white worms and the flies. Puncture holes went into her skin—human teeth? Unseen mouths seemed to bite at her, while the flies moved in a jiggling mass around the flesh of her arm.

It's an hallucination. Don't let it take you. Don't believe it. Don't give it power.

Then she realized the significance. Poor old lady, she swallowed a fly. Her brother, found with his mouth open, flies around him, he had been dead for two days when the institution found him, finally, where he had lain as he died.

The flies. And they were here, in this cold spot.

Coming to her. Coming to cover her.

To get into her mouth.

So she would be the poor old lady who swallowed a fly.

It had been a warning. It had been a portent that she had seen.

And then it was over.

The flies were gone; the chilly energy dissipated.

3

Cali nearly crumpled to the floor, feeling nauseated. It was as if the air had been knocked out of her, and she felt both light-headed and retchingly sick. She managed to steady herself with the help of Chet, whose hands were under her elbows.

"You okay?" he asked.

"I think so. I guess my abilities aren't quite gone."

"Well, the cold spot's gone, anyway," Jack said. "Damn." Then, barely missing a beat, to Cali: "What was it? What did you see?"

Chet gave him an angry glare. "She's not feeling well. Can't you see that?"

Cali opened her mouth to speak but then shut it again. Then, softly, she said, "It was wrong to bring us here, Jack. It was wrong."

4

"I think I need to go lie down for a little while," Cali said once she was out of the room and heading up the stairs. She felt better, slightly stronger, but a devastating exhaustion coursed through her now.

"You saw something in there." Chet touched her shoulder lightly. "You okay?" They went up the stairs, with Cali practically clinging to the banister for balance.

"We're the wrong people to be at Harrow," Cali said. "People with psi talent should not be in this house." She didn't need to add her next thought: *We should all three of us leave. As soon as possible.* But she couldn't quite get it out.

Once they got to her bedroom, Cali lay down, not letting go of Chet's hand. "Stay here, Chet. Just until I fall asleep. I shouldn't be tired. I just woke up, practically. But I feel . . . drained. Like . . . well . . . and I don't want to sleep long. Not long."

"It's the house. It's getting to us."

"Give me a few minutes. Don't let me sleep for even an hour," she whispered. "Just stay here."

"All right," he said. "All right."

5

But when Cali woke up several hours later, she was alone.

6

It was a sound that woke her up more than anything. It sounded like laughter, but also a scraping sound, like someone was raking leaves on pavement. She took a quick shower, dressed in slacks and a clean shirt, and then went to find Chet again.

7

She found him in the hall outside her room.

"You still want to leave?" Chet asked.

"Yes," she said. "But . . . I feel stronger, which is weird. I mean, really stronger. Like I actually got something from that . . . cold spot. I thought it took something from me. But it's almost like a gift, to have that kind of vision. As frightening as it seemed at the time."

He touched her arm lightly. "We'll get going in a bit, then," Chet said. "I don't mind giving the money back."

"Greed is hard to resist, but I feel the same."

"Okay. But we're still looking for Mira right now. Once we find her—"

Cali had completely forgotten about Mira. "Oh, God. Mira."

"Jack says he's calling the police in another hour if we don't find her," Chet said. "He's only a little less worried because the dog's gone, too."

"He must be worried sick. I'm sure she's fine," Cali said, but the truth was, she wasn't sure at all. Not after what she had seen crawl up her arm. Not after the feeling that she had been psychically sucked by a big vacuum from hell. "If Conan is with her, she's probably just pissed off. She probably is in town somewhere. Or she went back home. Has he tried calling his house?"

Chet looked at her blankly. "Frost is acting screwy, and Ivy is down in those . . . tunnels . . . trying to see if Mira's hiding below somewhere."

"Have you looked down there?" She pointed down the long corridor to the other wing of the house. The part she had considered the forbidden area, with its interior skeletal structure of the house, its gaping empty windows covered over with plastic sheets. The west wing. Jack's words were in her head: *Don't go over there. Not for evil house reasons, but because it's got cracks and holes and rotted wood and practically zero insulation. And it looks like shit.* "She might be there. She had to chase Conan through there the other night."

8

She craved a cup of coffee, but the truth was, she'd had a curiosity about the other wing, the crumbling, run-down part of the house that was virtually off-limits to them. Even in their tours of the house, they'd just been shown beyond some plastic sheets that hung down as insulation to the rooms that seemed to have been destroyed, not by fire or water, but by some idiotic contractor who had torn the floors up mistakenly, and then had, no doubt, been fired by Ivy Martin herself for destroying the integrity of the house. She and Chet went through the double doors and carefully walked on the more solid planks, avoiding the boards with upturned nails. It was icy here—there were fist-sized holes in the roof—they could look up through what seemed a cathedral ceiling to the late afternoon sky above, clouded over but with still enough light to guide them. Cali called out for Mira, and Chet ran about—giving Cali minor heart attacks as she watched him barely miss putting his foot through a stairway or step off the edge of a floor into a room below. Bricks were piled up in corners, and the remnants of the school still existed in these broken rooms—student desks were piled up in a room that had an acoustic-tile ceiling and floors with torn-up linoleum.

Finally, when she'd caught up to Chet, he grabbed her around the waist and said, "You can stop me from doing this if you want," but she hadn't wanted him to stop, and they kissed, and she felt guilty for the kiss, but she let it continue for a long while. *What the fuck are we doing?* she thought. *Why am I letting him kiss me when everything in my gut is telling me to get out of the house?* But part of her had begun to suspect that the cold spot was just a hallucination—completely—a trick of a haywire consciousness. A trick from within herself. Just like the tricks her brother Ned had experienced, the tricks that drove him crazy, perhaps. It was crossed wires of psi and maybe one of the others—Frost or Chet, too—had overloaded her circuits in some way. She could explain it all in her head, and then she felt less awful about kissing Chet and feeling what she let come through her bloodstream.

They only stopped when he looked up and noticed a light snow—just a few small flakes—drift down through the gaping hole in the roof and rafters above them.

"Look," he said. "It's already snowing. Not even officially winter yet, and we got snow."

Chapter Thirty-two

1

"I felt so alone. I mean, even with people around. You understand that, don't you?" Chet asked, arms entwined around her. They lay on what should've been a group of planks, but it felt fine to both of them. It had not gone further than kissing and embracing, and it felt slow and easy to Cali.

"Sure. You mean the psi talent," she said sweetly, feeling as if love were taking her over for the first time in her life.

"It's like I know it's in me, and I have to be real careful. It gets out when I lose control. So I can't lose control. I can't get mad, not at other people. It might get awful if I do. And if I'm happy—I mean really happy—well, something strange happens. You don't know about the time with the butterflies, do you?"

"Butterflies?"

"At least Dr. Fleetwood doesn't tell everybody everything. Nice to know. When I was making love for the first time in my life, all these butterflies showed up—they just flew out of nowhere, and they covered me. They just covered me like they wanted to take me with them. Out into the sky or something. It sounds crazy now, but it happened. And people thought I was a freak. The girl I loved back then, she thought it was freaky. A year ago, I got married, but you know, I never had . . . well, I never had relations with her. I couldn't. I was afraid of what might happen. I was afraid she'd see what a freak I was."

"I understand that," Cali said, remembering the night with Det when something else took over—some residue from the homicide scene. "Completely. I guess we're abnormalities in this world. But somewhere, we're probably perfectly normal. Who knows? Maybe a thousand years from now, there'll be more of us."

"Naw," Chet said sadly. "There won't be. I think people like us lived centuries ago and died out. We're mutants now, that's all. We're . . ."

He leaned over and looked at her face, as if seeing it for the first time.

Oh, God, Cali thought. *My heart's racing. He's going to kiss me again and it's going to go further. This nineteen-year-old is going to kiss me. Please don't, Chet. Please don't kiss me. If you do, I may . . . I may want to kiss you back. I may want to take this all the way to sex, and then that'll screw everything up for us. Let's keep it on low flame, please. Let's both keep it warm but not hot.*

The next kiss arrived, and it was sweet and filled with its own kind of juice, fire burned in it; and she tasted his sadness and his happiness in equal measure; she kissed him and her mind went into a kind of blankness; their kisses became stronger and blotted out their surroundings—they were no longer in the construction area with the rafters and the holes in the roof and the wet snow coming down in a shaft of hazy light. They were joining in some way that felt warm and homelike, as if Cali had known that Chet would be the one who would fit her right, would taste right as she pressed her lips to his, as their bodies moved together. Their clothes were minor obstacles; their wills bent; their sense of right and wrong seemed to melt as they drew their flesh together in a perfect rhythm, a genuine union.

Then the sound began.

2

It started as a whirring kind of noise, followed by a gentle cooing—Cali opened her eyes—in the light from the ragged hole in the roof, doves were flying—flying together as if they'd been nesting in the rafters and had just been disturbed; Chet's eyes remained closed as his passion grew, and she kissed his forehead as he pressed his lips to her throat, as their bodies moved together in a final press, but she could not take her eyes off the white birds as they flew, flapping against each other in the same lazy circles that the snow made as it fell.

Finally, she whispered, "Chet, my God," and she drew back from him.

In his eyes there was nothing but love and innocence, and the doves flew maddeningly close, until they were around his shoulders, cooing and flying, their feathers drifting with the snow.

"It's happening," she whispered, with more shock than tenderness in her voice, and Chet craned his neck around and a small yelp came from him, and when he turned to face her there were tears in his eyes. "Love me," he said. "Please. Someone has to love me. You understand me." Tears flowed down his face. "Please. We're both freaks, but right now, I want you and I want you to want me. I don't want to live my life afraid that . . . things will happen."

"I know," Cali whispered, and then closed her eyes to the doves that circled the air, the white doves that had come from nowhere except the snow-filled sky, and she felt his tears burn against her cheek as she allowed herself to love for the moment, and to love for a reason.

And it was the greatest heat she had ever had in her life, and she didn't want to let go of the man who held her.

3

And then Cali felt it inside her.

After she and Chet had spent their hour together, with the doves circling among the snowflakes, the doves becoming snow, and the snow becoming a kind of whiteness that took over the shadows of this part of Harrow, as it seemed to fall apart around her.

Cali whispered to Chet, "Oh my God, Chet, dear God, it's not the house. It's us."

"Huh?" he asked sleepily.

"The house. The haunting. It's not about us waking it up. We came in here and our abilities were gone."

"True," he said, his lips against her neck.

"It took them. It's using our talent." She pulled away from him and looked up among the lazily flapping plastic sheet, the exposed woodwork, the hole in the roof. "This is where she died."

"Who?"

"Quincy Allen. Oh my God, I can feel it. She was here. She was here in this place. The girl who died. She had an ability. Jack told me he was sure. She had an ability and she became part of a ritual. This is where she died. This is where she saw it."

"It?"

"Look." Cali pointed to something that seemed impossibly blurry, and it wasn't quite snow and it wasn't quite doves flying in lazy circles. It was a whirlwind of whiteness—no, not whiteness, but emptiness, as if part of the world were being erased right before her eyes, leaving a dead white background, a nothing. The streak of emptiness began moving like liquid dripping from the sky, moving toward the two of them as they lay there. "We haven't been waking the house up. Dear God," she said. "We've been feeding it."

The doves seemed to not be beautiful birds anymore, but a terrible whiteness, a fury that came from the descending chill, with talons of lightning, toward the two of them.

"My God," Cali said.

"It's inside me," Chet gasped.

"What?"

"The house," he whispered. "It's happening."

Part Nine

The Infinite

Chapter Thirty-Three

1

Chet screamed as if he were burning from what looked like a white, drippy wax as it sprayed across his left shoulder.

Cali felt it. Something had shifted within the house, just as if there had been a minor earthquake. Something had changed.

There, in the whiteness that the world was becoming, she saw the word:

Mercy.

And then what seemed to be figures of emptiness, carved from the flesh of whiteness, drew forward, ambling toward them, and she didn't want to let go of Chet for fear, but she felt a pulse of terror in her heart—and she tried to think of words to calm herself, ways of keeping the fear back, but it engulfed her.

The little boy named Scotty, the boy she had envisioned in the dark closet of an apartment on the Upper West Side of New York, stepped out from the whiteness, his hand reaching for her. He opened his mouth to speak, and a dove emerged bloody from his throat and flew toward her, but as it came to her, she knew that she couldn't let it touch her, and it sailed down into her hair and began pecking and scratching at her; somewhere, perhaps miles away, Chet screamed; Cali was no longer where she had been, but in a dark closet with a little boy who told her the most terrible truths about herself and about her brother and about how life really was.

The buzzing began, and at first it sounded like Frost humming as he had downstairs, just humming, but soon it was a full-volume buzz, and she knew that it was flies, and she herself began whispering in the darkness, "Poor old lady, she swallowed a fly, I don't know why she swallowed a fly."

2

Chet could not help himself—they were in his hair, they were on his back, these things, these white demons, these—birds, that's all they were, birds, but they had talons that felt like razors and his skin burned from their touch. Had they pecked out his eyes? He wasn't sure—he was blind from blood that dripped from his forehead, and his mind raced against his own confusion. "Cali!" he cried out, "Oh my God! Make them stop! Please!" he shouted. They were like maggots on him more than birds, and they felt squishy and dead but still wriggling; they were warm and moved around his thighs like snakes and up his spine they clawed their way to the small of his back, where he tried to reach back and pull them off him.

He didn't even know where he ran—he just moved where he could, with a sense of desperation and fear, and it was only when they seemed to be shredding his skin that he fell and knew that this must be the end of his life.

3

It was as if a spark had ignited the human fire within Harrow.

4

"Ivy," Frost said.

Ivy Martin in the darkness of the tunnel below, her night vision goggles on, turned and saw nothing but the green shadows of the walls and doorway behind her.

And then she saw him.

Frost Crane, not green with the goggled light, but clearly, as if he stood in a halo of daylight.

He was naked, his flesh covered with hieroglyphs and symbols that were like the ones in the tunnel beneath the house.

In his hand, a pitchfork.

And then, she felt them—touching her—and the glow of their forms became apparent. It was like a dream she'd once had about Harrow, a dream of brambles and knives in the air, shining, and bites along her arms—for they had begun nibbling at her as if they meant to tear her flesh with their hungry mouths—

And the pitchfork gleamed brightly in the dark room as Frost brought it down, and into her flesh, and the dream seemed to take her over as she felt the puncture wounds within her flesh. Her goggles flew from her head—pulled with force from her. But still she could see them, in the darkness, they were like angels of green fire, not just a few of them, but a city of the dead surrounding her, boys and women and old men and children, and there, before them, their henchman:

Frost.

"Mercy," she whispered, as if the word itself would save her, as if it would be understood by Frost. And by the people who appeared around her, the little girl and the woman who might or might not have been her own great-great-aunt, the beautiful woman who looked something like Ivy herself, as she formed, as Isis Claviger formed, and then Ivy knew that she had sought what she should not seek at Harrow. But she had no word for it, for these were not ghosts, nor were they hallucinations from the pain in her body where the thick tines of the pitchfork went in—these were energies and she, herself, would soon leave hers behind.

She remembered her dream of knives in the air, and of going to the house, and of feeling the bites on her skin, and knew that she had dreamed her own final moments but had dressed them up in beauty and metaphor, when, in reality, it was a cold, damp basement she would die in, and the love she would feel, the want, was from a pitchfork as it slammed into her again and again.

And then, as she fell, and as the man stood over her in the dark, she saw the only man she had ever loved, Stephen Hook, standing there, reaching for her. She made a feeble attempt to reach for him, but the pitchfork came down again and again, and her dream took her over as life bled from her.

Frost whispered, with each pitch of the fork into the dung of the woman's body, "The Infinite is coming! Prepare the way!"

5

Mira awoke in the shed. She kicked the door back so that it creaked open. The brilliant lights from the garden poured into the darkness of the shed. What she could remember was that she'd crawled inside and had fallen asleep. An hour? Two? How long had it been?

She glanced at her watch with its neon digital numbers.

Jesus. Asleep all day. Almost six P.M. No wonder I feel like shit.

She sat up, shivering.

Christ, it's fucking freezing.

Conan, the ever-faithful border collie mutt, was curled up near the door of the shed, just inside it. He glanced up at her, and she reached over to pet him. The dog growled, and, instinctively, she withdrew her hand.

"Conan? Baby?"

Conan rose up and stretched. Mira felt a little crazy for thinking her dog would growl at her.

"Hey, boy, you been sleeping with me all this time?" She snapped her fingers and let out a brief whistle.

The dog came over into the spear of light of the shed's doorway.

Something's wrong. Something's up with Conan. He looks . . . like he's been in a fight or something.

And then her dog began whispering, or at least that's what it seemed like. Mira giggled, the aches in her back and along her stomach subsiding. *Yeah, right. Conan's whispering to me.*

"That's right," the dog said.

6

"You fucking bitch," Conan said, his muzzle moving in impossible shapes to form the words. "You're a self-centered little bitch who thinks that everyone has to do what you want, like what you like; well, nobody is gonna play that game anymore, Miranda Fleetwood, and you better just get used to it. I know what you really need, bitch, and you're gonna love every fucking minute of it. We've had this date since the moment you brought me home, since all those times when you cried into me, when you used me like a chump, but I'm gonna put it to you now, bitch, I'm gonna show you what the fuck it's all about, what the Infinite can do to a little bitch like you."

He approached her, a snarl still on his lips. His breath was foul, and there was a sourness to the smell of his hackled fur. His growls continued, growls and obscenities. For a moment she was sure he had a look in his eyes that was nearly human. Human and burning with an angry lust. And even worse, these were not Conan's eyes at all, but someone else's, someone's she had seen before, someone's she knew.

Frost. She was sure it was Frost.

Inside her dog. His eyes, there. His awful eyes. Watching her. Wanting her.

I'm hallucinating. I know I am.

The dog's spittle dribbled across her arm.

She moved farther back into the shed, feeling the spiny tips of the antlers press against her back, and in front of her, her pet dog began to whisper awful, obscene things, things that only an animal would desire.

She moved as far back in the shed as she possibly could and grabbed the antlers for some sense of protection.

Behind her dog, the shed door closed and left her in total darkness.

Goggles. Get the goggles. They're here, somewhere. They're here. I dropped them. They must be.

Mira slipped her goggles on, but instead of seeing the green outline of her dog, she saw several outlines.

Men, standing around her within the darkness. The green-yellow glow of their bodies pulsed as they moved toward her.

She held her breath and wished the world away.

And then someone tore the night goggles from her face.

CHAPTER THIRTY-FOUR

1

Chet was inside a baseball game, and he took the cheers of the crowd well, even if the crowd seemed to have pointy teeth. The stadium seemed enormous and filled to capacity, so, of course, he went to get his bat because they'd been shouting "Batter up! Batter up!"

2

Frost emerged from the cellar, his naked body covered with blood, and all the running sores and words on him bubbling and wriggling like delicious little parasites, and he went to find the others, to tell them that Paradise was opening that day, that the Flowering of the Infinite was going to take place, and that he, Frost Crane, the Avatar of Snapping Jaws, was the one who had begun it, and his Voices told him that it was just like the time they had helped him kill the woman in the woods, that it was neither bad nor good, but just part of his infinite consciousness, part of what he had plugged into here in Harrow, the socket for his bulb.

3

After several minutes in the darkness, Mira Fleetwood emerged from the shed with what looked like a headdress of antlers upon her forehead, and what might have been the skin of some black-and-white furry animal thrown over her shoulders. Around her mouth, a generous smear of blood.

Within her mind, a wilderness of dogs, all telling her that she was their queen.

4

Jack Fleetwood had postponed calling the local police long enough—he had become worried sick about Mira and had spent the past hour going over the videotape of the rooms, when he noticed Frost, in a tape that had registered as 4 A.M., and all Frost did was go to his dresser and take out some small object. A penknife? Jack wasn't sure. It was dark in the room, and the way the camera recorded in darkness was not as clear as the goggles would've been had Jack been there watching, but it appeared that Frost was taking his clothes off and beginning to touch his skin all over.

And then the film had shut off.

The camera had malfunctioned.

Jack rewound the tape a few times, concerned, but he figured he'd ask Frost in a bit what that was all about. Had Frost been sleepwalking?

Then he heard what sounded like a big cracking sound out in the corridor and went out to investigate.

5

In the dim, wavering light of the corridor, a man stood there that Jack Fleetwood did not at first recognize.

But it was Chet.

In his hand, a baseball bat.

His eyes were red with blood.

6

"Chet, what's going on?"

"It finally happened, Jack. It finally fuckin' happened," Chet said. "We are in the stadium of the Infinite! We are at the portal, opened wide, and ready for some sacrifices, Jack! This ain't just any ordinary game, this is the fuckin' World Series of games, Jack! It ain't just a portal, this place, Jack! It's the place itself! It seats millions and it costs a lot to get in, but man, the show is a good one, Jack!" Chet raised the bat, and Jack knew he had seconds to get out of the way.

Jack turned and ran down the other way, hoping to make it to the stairs; but when he reached his bedroom, he thought he saw Mira there, standing near the bed, or someone who looked like Mira. He had to get her out of there. He couldn't just save himself.

"Mira! Get out! Come on! Hurry!" Jack shouted, and ran into his room, but Mira was not there at all.

Chet stepped into the bedroom, shutting the door behind him. Jack went for the door to the bathroom, but it was locked.

"Harrow doesn't want anyone leaving. Not now. Not when we're only in the first inning," Chet said.

7

Chet raised the bat against Fleetwood. "TAKE ME OUT TO THE BALL GAME!" he shouted.

Jack raised his hands, "No, Chet, come back, don't give in, don't let it have you!" He turned and went for the door, but Chet, sprang for the door and closed it, locking it behind him. He took the key and raised it up, grinning. "Woof," he said. Then he put the key between his lips and swallowed it. "Ha ha," he said. "Ha fuckin' ha."

"Please, Chet. It's me. It's Jack. Listen to me. Please. Try to think. Think about what you're doing."

"I am thinking," Chet said, his teeth clenched, his bat raised. "I'm thinking, well, shit, if I can just hit one out of the stadium, I can run for home and then I'm safe. That's the way the game goes, Mr. Umpire, right? That's the way it goes!" He swung the bat through the air, nearly hitting Jack's chin. Jack fell backward, landing on his back.

"TAKE ME OUT TO THE BALL GAME! TAKE ME OUT TO THE CROWD!" Chet cried out, swinging the bat downward, across the bridge of Jack Fleetwood's nose. "BUY ME SOME PEANUTS AND CRACK"—and here another swing and hit—"ER JACKS! I DON'T CARE IF I NEVER GET BACK!"

And Chet Dillinger kept swinging that bat, and as he did, he imagined the homer he must be hitting because everybody was cheering.

Everybody was cheering, and somewhere, nearby, the Wolf came out to finish the game.

8

The bat smashed down. It had a life of its own as he brought it up and down and up and down against Jack Fleetwood's skull. The Wolf—for that's what he was now, a bonafide Wolf—was loose, and he felt fucking good and full of life and the need to spatter some more blood. He needed to take a leak badly, but he didn't want to stop. Something surged through him—the energy, God, it was more than energy, it was a fire in his belly, and all those years it had been waiting to come out and he'd never let it go.

Up! Down! The bat went crunch-crunch-crunch, and the Wolf let out a big old howl as the rich red blood spewed upward and covered his chest and mitts. Damn good! Tasty red gobs of liquid, all hot and sweet. Oh, good God almighty, didn't he want to pull out the bones and suck out the marrow of that pile of meat.

The hunt is on, sons of bitches, the Wolf said, and he kept beating the bat down on the body until there wasn't much left there except for a river of blood and flesh and eye and bone and other soft, gooey things that just kind of slipped around in all the squishiness.

"Woo hoo!" he cried out and dropped the bat. It rolled across the rubbery flattened feet of the dead man, and as it rolled, it turned completely red with blood.

And then he saw himself in the mirror by the bed, and what he saw was not a wolf but a man, barely a man, a scared and shivering boy of nineteen with his naked body covered with blood, and his sandy hair matted down with the dark redness, and his eyes like pinholes from the smudges on his face.

His muscles were taut, and his penis had grown long with excitement, and his face twitched near the mouth.

Chet recognized himself. There was no wolf. There was no animal inside him.

He stood there for what felt like hours as an immense sorrow flooded his insides and hosed down the heat that had been burning there.

No. No, please, let this be the house's dream. Don't let this be real.

"The Wolf's at the door," the dream-memory of his mother whispered to him.

But it wasn't at the door, not in Harrow, Chet thought. *Not outside the door, anyway. The Wolf was inside the door, the Wolf had him, and it was already inside the house. The Wolf was not outside in the wilderness because the fucking wilderness was within this place.*

"Don't let this be real," he whispered to his blood-soaked reflection.

But, of course, it was real, for this was not a house of dreams or a place of visions.

Harrow was reality, and the reflection in the mirror felt more real to him than he himself felt.

He could not bring himself to look down at the mutilated body of Jack Fleetwood.

Chet's shoulders slumped. He sat down at the edge of the bed. "Oh, Jesus Christ," he prayed, his hands locking together. "Please help me. Please don't leave me to this. Please let this not have happened."

He felt a terrible hunger in his stomach, followed by nausea. He scrambled for the door, but the lock held. He angled backward and then gave the door a huge kick—the lock and knob broke, the wood cracked, and the door came open.

Chet ran down the corridor to the bathroom. When he got

there he threw up in the sink, although not much of anything came up except for some blood and the key to the room.

Then he sat on the edge of the bathtub and ran the hot water.

9

In the tub, he let himself sink down beneath the water's surface. It was so hot that it was nearly scalding, but he didn't care. He wanted to burn the Wolf out of him for good.

As he lay there, eyes closed, beneath the water, he thought he would just let himself drown like that. *Just let it go. Don't live. You can't live with yourself anymore. You don't want to come back from this. You don't want to face this. Drown now and go to Hell and let eternal Hellfire take you, but don't face this, don't let the Wolf out again, don't let it . . .*

But in less than a minute he had pushed his face above the steamy surface again, gasping for air.

And everything around him had changed.

You've sacrificed to us, someone said. *You're in our world now.*

10

Mira felt as if she was the most beautiful woman on earth, and she admired her form in the mirror, with the crown of nature on her head and the robe of purity around her shoulders. She had torn the robe with her own bare hands, and with the help of the others, the people she had seen in the dark, all of them helping her, bathing her in blood, baptizing her. Her mind had short-circuited briefly, but now she knew that she was a goddess and, as such, she demanded a sacrifice.

She knew who would be her first human sacrifice.

Her handmaiden to do with as she wished.

To torture as she wished.

And the lucky person was: Cali Nytbird.

11

The hunt began using her new heightened abilities. She had learned from those in the shed that when one makes a sacrifice and drinks the blood, one takes on the skills and talents of the victim. Mira had noticed immediately her heightened sense of smell from her first victim, and she used it to track Cali. It led her to a bathroom, and then to a bedroom, but neither held the victim. Then she saw the open door leading to the other end of the house, a part of the house she had known well.

When she entered it darkness was everywhere, but she followed the scent in the dark until she found her victim cowering in a corner, hands over her mouth as if trying to keep something from getting inside her.

"Bitch!" Mira screamed, bringing her fists down on Cali's face. "I will skin you and wear you for my pleasure!"

12

Break through this, Cali told herself. She felt invisible fists coming down, smashing at the flies that covered her, blinding her, the flies that were crawling into her ears, into the small holes at the edge of her eyes, into her other places, trying to find entry into her body, but she had to stop them. She had to keep them from getting inside her, because she knew if they did, it would be over, over for her just as it must have been for her brother.

My brother.

My Neddy.

My twin.

Please help me, Ned. You never died within me. I never stopped caring for you or loving you. I'm sorry I wasn't there to help you, the way we helped each other when we were younger. I'm sorry we weren't the team we should've been.

Someone seemed to be clawing at her now, and the flies were biting.

And then Cali felt it.

Ned. He had died, but he was still with her. Somehow he was with her. Somehow he was not just a painful memory. His strength must be there, too. *Must be.*

It must be within me. The source of this. If Harrow is opening, it's because of me, Frost, and Chet. It's not because of Harrow itself. We are the keys. We are the keys.

With all her might, she focused on the flies. She focused no matter how hard they bit or tried.

Fighting them, I give them power.

Fight, and I lose.

It's within me.

Then Cali opened her eyes and her mouth to the flies that swarmed across her.

She whispered, her throat nearly choking, "Poor old lady, she swallowed a fly."

At first she felt as if she was going to vomit and then choke on the wriggling mass that invaded her.

And then she thought of Ned, and her love for him, and her love for that little boy that Gloria Franco had murdered, and she knew that the power of love, the power of perfect love was her own strength and always had been.

It was not in the objects she held.

It was in her. She was the vehicle for the power, and its source was even greater than she.

Doves or devils, she thought, remembering the white birds as they had descended from the rafters.

And then the flies were gone.

But a girl of sixteen clawed at her, and Cali found that she could not use whatever inner strength she had to get the girl off her.

So she went for outer strength.

13

This is where her brief police training had come in handy. She fought against Mira, and Mira seemed as powerful as a bull, but Cali felt that she was not going to die in this house, she was not going to give Harrow her power and the power that her brother had left within her, not today, not now, not ever.

When Cali had managed to knock Mira away from her, she crawled and then stood and loped—for her left leg was covered with scratches, her slacks torn up—in the darkness, avoiding putting her foot down on torn floor, hoping that a plank full of nails would not be in her way, and as she went, something about the walls seemed to shimmer.

And when she reached the other side of the house it had all changed.

It seemed to have flesh covering its walls, flesh stretched as tight as a drum over it.

And it was breathing.

Harrow was alive.

Get your gun, you stupid idiot, she thought, and then laughed at herself in a way that felt as if she *were* insane now, as if she were seeing and feeling what Ned must have felt, what had brought him to write on the walls with his own shit, as she stepped down onto a floor that was smooth and wet like just-flayed human skin.

In front of her, Frost Crane, only not quite Frost Crane. He held a pitchfork in his hands, and his body was soaked red, with blood gushing from his own wounds.

"Snapping jaws!" he sang.

14

"Here comes the God of Snapping Jaws!" Frost sang as loud as he could, his voice so beautiful as it joined the chorus of Voices within him. "He'll take you up between his claws! He'll chew your face and scrape your innards, Oh, Snapping Jaws just wants his dinnards!" It was the most beautiful song he had ever heard and it was completely off the top of his head, but its loveliness echoed down through the flesh of Harrow. "We are one in the Body and Spirit of Harrow. "We are the dove from Hell and Heaven's sparrow!" It was the BEST SONG EVER WRITTEN as far as he was concerned, and he composed the soundtrack to it at the same time, and all the instruments were playing like the London Philharmonic.

He raised the pitchfork like a conductor's baton, and he led them all in another chorus of the Snapping Jaws hymn, and the fleshy floor rippled, and the veins along the ceiling pulsed as blood flowed through the house. There was Snapping Jaws's next meal: scrumptious Cali Nytbird, and behind her, delectable little Mira Fleetwood, and how Snapping Jaws wanted them both for his dinnard (hardy-har-har, it's dinnard time, boys and ghouls! Come and get it!).

15

Cali glanced back for a second: Mira stood there, blocking her way. She looked like some pagan goddess—the deer antlers on her scalp, the war paint of blood around her face—and some kind of cloak of animal fur. *Dear God, she killed Conan,* Cali thought. *Dear God, there is no escape from this, is there? Please. Please. Someone.*

God. Anyone. Help me.

16

"Wanna know what happened to Ivy?" Frost asked. "I devoured her! I DEEE-VOURED her! I et her and she was good!" he shouted, his voice echoing. He glanced to the others—there was the large soldier with the great and bloody beard, little sad-faced boys surrounding him, all of them torn and ragged; and the beautiful woman with the golden hair who smiled just for him and had told him exactly which parts of Ivy would taste the best, and now she gave him the recipe for devouring Cali, as well; he was sure he even saw someone who looked like a saint standing there, blessing him in his feasting.

It's the damn Feast of All Saints! That's what this is! The body and blood sanctifies me into the Church of Snapping Jaws!

The Voices whispered and sang his praises, and Frost plucked a last bit of Ivy that had gotten stuck on the pitchfork tine and dropped it into one of the pulsing wounds along his stomach.

Then he went running at Cali with his dinner fork.

17

Cali made an attempt to run past him, but the pitchfork grazed her arm and hurt like hell. She dropped to the floor and felt what might've been some kind of fatty tissue—*this has got to be an illusion. The house could not have changed. It has to be us. Giving it a psychic charge. It has to be.*

Ned? Are you here? Are you inside me? Can you give me your strength? Can you let me have it? I don't care if I go insane, Ned, I need you—is this what happened to you? Did the world go haywire and you saw things like houses that were covered in human skin? Please help me.

And then the door to her room opened.

Mira was nearly upon her, and Frost had turned about, with his pitchfork.

Cali crawled quickly through the doorway, into her bedroom.

The door slammed shut behind her. She raised herself up and touched the knob. A brief electric shock went through her.

The doorknob turned, but the door did not open.

They're out there.

Waiting for me.

Oh, Christ. They're waiting for me. The bed itself seemed to have changed, for it was bowed and rippling slightly, as if something heavy and alive lay beneath its covers. She had a terrible feeling in the pit of her stomach and went to get her gun, wondering if it would be effective on Frost or Mira at all, or if she would have to use her Sig Sauer on herself.

And then a sound like ripping flesh came up from beyond the door, and the door crumpled in on itself, and the wall tore apart, and the flesh of the house opened itself to her, to them, and that terrible whiteness streaked across it, the whiteness of bone.

Cali turned, the gun shaking in her hands, and pointed it at Frost as he came to her with the pitchfork raised. Tears flowed down her face and she felt as if she was burning up from fever. "Please, Frost, please don't make me do this. Don't make me do it. I don't want to. Just stay where you are. Just don't move."

But even this did not stop him.

18

Mira leaped into the room like a panther and crouched at Frost's feet.

Frost grinned and said, "You can't stop the Infinite once it's inside you, Cali. I guess it got in me a long time ago, but just a little bit of broken glass from it, just like you have, and just like Chet has, and maybe just like Mira has, too, although maybe she didn't know it because sometimes you don't know you have it in you until you get a little older. And maybe Harrow is the doorway of the

Infinite and we were all meant to be here and to be part of it, using our flesh to open it, to let it loose here, to let it breathe in the human realm. Let it into you, too. It loves us, Cali. It loves what we can do."

And then Cali looked down at Mira. "I know you, Mira. You don't want to be part of this. You don't have to be. I fought it. I fought it and it didn't get me. It tried to get inside me, but I overcame it."

Mira looked up at her and licked her lips lasciviously, as if she didn't comprehend.

"Somewhere inside you," Cali said. "Somewhere, you have the strength."

Frost stepped forward with the pitchfork and jabbed it at Cali, who took a step back but tripped and fell. The floor was soft and inviting, and Frost stood over her with the tines of the fork pointed at her neck.

"I'm sorry, Frost," Cali said, and then pressed her gun against his heart and shot twice until he dropped the pitchfork and fell on top of her.

Perhaps dead, perhaps not.

She didn't intend to stick around to find out.

19

In Frost Crane's last moment of consciousness, he didn't see Snapping Jaws or the beautiful woman with golden hair, but instead he saw the farm he'd grown up on, and he was being called with his pitchfork to come clean out the stables, and then come home to supper.

20

Cali pushed Frost off her and let the anger and fury take her over. She pointed the gun at Mira, "You move, I shoot," Cali said. "Look at Frost, Mira. The house didn't save him. Whatever the house did to you, fight it. Fight it now. You can't be weak. You can't give in to it. Whatever thing the house did to you—whatever it made you do—we have the power within us to fight it. I know we do. I know it," Cali said, but she wondered if she was just spouting bullshit or if it was true.

Ned, help me. Be here. Give me strength. Let me get through this.

"Fuck you, bitch," Mira spat and rose to her full height. A white-hot aura surrounded her. "I am goddess here and you are meant to give your life and blood for my worship."

"You are a little girl," Cali said. "You are sixteen and you killed your dog and you are somehow locked inside your mind, but I am going to let you out, and you know how I'm going to do it?"

Mira seemed about ready to pounce, and Cali felt she only had seconds before she would have to shoot Mira—and she did not want to do that at all—so she let the girl pounce on her, and it was like a beast of prey coming down on her, but Cali held her ground.

And closed her eyes.

And embraced Mira as if she were one of the objects she had to read.

And she let her mind—her ability—take her down into the terrible and twisted tunnels of Mira's inner world.

21

Cali saw Mira shivering in the shed as her own pet dog came at her, teeth bared, a lustful power within the animal, and she saw how things in the dark scraped at the animal as it mounted Mira's body, and how she fought and tried to cry out, and Cali saw the spirit of evil that had entered the dog, and that entered Mira as she clawed at her own pet to save herself.

And then Mira had gone into another shed—a shed within her mind, and she was locked there.

Like the boy in the closet.

Like Cali's brother. None of them could fight, so they allowed something awful to use them and their ability.

Not this time, Cali said.

And within the night of the mind, Cali gave up some of her own strength to Mira and led her out of her own trapped mind.

22

"My father's dead," Mira said, but there were no tears in her eyes. It was as if she was in a trance, and not completely on the surface of her being yet.

"Let's go," Cali said, "Let's get out now."

23

In the hall the doors were slamming open and shut and the walls were melting and there were people, as if at a great party, but just standing there, watching them—Cali saw soldiers holding the head of some bearded man—

And boys, dressed in dark robes, with faces partially burned—

A little girl of six or seven in a smock, holding the hand of a woman with blond hair and a dress from—perhaps—the early twentieth century; and Ivy was there, as well, Ivy, blood pouring from her—

And others, too, people who seemed real and insubstantial at the same time.

It's all illusion. It's all us making it happen. It's just the portal. It's not the people themselves.

It's the energy.

She tugged Mira by the hand as they slowly walked through the crowd of spirits, to the staircase that seemed to be made entirely of human bones; the wallpaper dripped blood; the skin of the house breathed in and out.

And there, in the foyer, stood Chet—

But it was not Chet anymore. It could not be.

He looked as if he had transformed, as if his face had melted across itself and turned his features downward.

Without wanting to, Cali was sucked into his dream, into the world he saw, into his mind. It had taken over all of them. It had won.

Chapter Thirty-Five

1

The Wolf was gone. It had left him as if it had other urgent business to take care of.

Chet was alone, and his bat had been taken, and he knew that he had done something terrible—but it had been like a dream, a dream of a World Series game, a dream of Cal Ripkin, Jr., batting a ball out of the stadium. And he was alone, but the house had changed—it had grown into a medieval castle, and the night sky above was lit by a perfect moon that emerged through wispy clouds. It was freezing, and he could not remember why he was here. Chet wasn't sure if it was Harrow at all, for the walls seemed to stretch up all the way to the sky, and the ground was flooded with shiny black water. He stood on the third step up from the water (although, when he thought about it, he wondered just how many steps down there might be beneath its blackness).

He glanced forward and up—there looked like a thousand steps more going up to the top. He thought he saw a woman waving to him from the other side of what he now knew was a river *(river of night, river of night)*. She wore a long white dress and her hair, though soaked to her scalp and shoulders, was long and honey-blond. She called to him, although her voice echoed a bellowing nothingness, as if she could not form words.

This is the empire of my mind, Chet thought and took another step up. The water rushed by, nearly touching his toes. His feet were bare, and a bit of water slushed along his toes—it was freezing. He went up another step.

"Whose kingdom is this?" he shouted to the woman, who continued waving, as if for help.

The Kingdom of Dreams, someone whispered, but it was not a woman's voice. It was an old man's feeble words. *The Kingdom of the Infinite. The human underworld beneath the world of life.*

The woman on the far wall bellowed, and yet no words accompanied the noise. She sounded something like an ox—it made him smile to think of it, for he had never really seen or heard an ox before, except when he thought of the Bible and the parts where oxen were mentioned, or where Jesus was born and the ox and lamb lay down before the Savior. He shrugged off that thought. The woman was something bad—that was what she must be, he thought. *She's some kind of protection from me. She's not from Harrow, I can feel that. She's from inside me.* He tried to think of women he'd known, but his mind was blank, and the icy water came up to his feet again, so he had to advance one more step up.

The smells came to him again—this time it was a slimy stink, like rotting algae. Could be the walls—the stones were wet and slick. He reached out to touch the stone, and his hand felt as if it were touching a slug. He drew it back instinctively, and then noticed what seemed like tiny gray buds along the walls. He touched them, and they felt more like warts. They were fleshy. Nearly vulnerable. The stones themselves were soft to the touch, and he pushed at one of them.

His hand went through, and something grasped his wrist on the other side of the wall.

The water below splashed against his ankle, and he looked down. The dark water was nearly touching his toes. He tugged his arm, to pull free of the spongy wall, but something on the other side—or within the wall itself?—held him fast. Tugging some more, it began to feel like razor blades were slicing his wrist each time he tried to draw his hand back. He felt an overwhelming weakness, and he glanced across to the woman with her arms raised.

It was no longer a woman, and he could see her from the distance as if she was near him—as if his eyes had become telephoto lenses and she stood before him, but a mile away.

It was Isis Claviger, he thought. At least she looked like Isis Claviger from the picture that had been in the book that Ivy had shown them. But she had transformed in this vision *(vision of the house's? Can a sleeping house envision something and plant it inside me?).* She had a thin, aquiline nose and eyes that were translucent blue. Her golden hair (no longer honey blond, but golden like gold, like shining gold in plaits along her shoulders, now untouched by the rain), her white dress that was like a wedding gown. Wedding gown, he thought. Wedding. Wetting. Wetting gown; Chet began giggling. Was he saying any of this aloud? He wasn't sure—there were no voices in this realm. He thought he heard the distant cry of something. A baby?

No, a sheep. A bleating sheep.

"Bleeding sheep," he said, or thought he said.

Isis watched him as if she were a calm within the storm, a private place for him to go within the raging of the wind and water.

It's up to my ankles and freezing now. The river's rising.

The bleeding sheep began crying out again, and he saw that Isis carried the sheep as a shepherdess would. *(No, I don't know any shepherdesses, it's the little porcelain figure, from my bedroom. She's here. She's Isis.)* Isis tried to say something to him, but her voice was filled with oxen's laments, and then a bray like an ass came from her, and the water had risen within a few moments until he could feel it at his calves.

He looked down into the water and saw what could only be snakes drizzling like rain around his ankles, just beneath the surface of the river. Dozens of long, thin, wormlike snakes—perhaps they were worms. He tried to focus on them, but the rain kept coming down and the wriggling things encircled his knees now as the water rose.

He gave his hand one last tug, but it was stuck, and he could no longer see Isis and her bleeding sheep on the far wall. *I am alone with this place. I am within it; it is within me. I can't go anywhere. Why struggle?*

He had the sense that the water continued to rise, but the feeling was gone from his legs completely, and he wasn't aware that there was anything beneath his torso. *My balls are gone? Are they?* He reached down with his free hand; there was nothing. The water and the drizzling snakes were causing him to vanish as they rose.

If it gets to my arm, I'll be free of the wall, he thought. A memory came to him, like a breath of chilly air sucked back into his lungs: strong and clear. He was five, and his hand was caught in a mousetrap. It had come down hard on his knuckles and he was crying. He had just begun living at Rustic Acres with the Dillingers, and this was one of the first pranks that one of the Big Boys played on him. His fingers were bruised from the mousetrap, and he tried to get it off him before the Big Woman came and got mad at him for playing with the traps. *All right, this is my mousetrap,* Chet considered. The water had covered his stomach, and he felt as if he truly did not exist down there. The snakes encircled him with their thin bodies, and he wondered if they were eels after all—

In his mind, he saw a man with a wriggling eel thrust down his throat.

My God.

He saw the man in the water, not in his mind. It was beneath the dark waves that were becoming more translucent. It was Fleetwood, and he lay there, floating, staring up at Chet, a big fat eel thrusting and squirming in Fleetwood's wide-open mouth. And then small eels began to come from Fleetwood's eyes, and even thinner ones from out of his nose.

"Nest of eels," someone said, and Chet felt his hand come free of the wall, only he was completely submerged under water now, and the water was neither cold nor warm. It was almost like air, although it became murky, and soon he saw others there, shapes and forms of people within the water, all turning gently in the current. He didn't recognize them, although there were boys of about fifteen or so, and a little girl (or so he thought), and then more, an army of those who floated in this strange underwater world in which Chet found he could breathe perfectly well.

And then someone said, "Chet."

It was annoying, this voice. He turned to find its source, but all he saw were the lifeless bodies turning in the water.

"Chet," someone said. Was it the woman in white? "Chet," she said. It was an achingly familiar voice. "Chet, the Wolf's at the door."

2

"No!" Cali cried out, reaching as far as she could across the chasm. "No! Chet, don't!"

"I have to!" Chet shouted. "The Wolf's at the door! I can't let it out! Someone has to shut the door to the Infinite!"

And then he stretched his left leg across into the milky whiteness, the light that was brighter than daylight, with the white birds floating in it as if they were trapped underwater.

The faces, too, not human at all, but like curdled skin surrounded eyes and maw, and the eyes like—the Devil, the thought came to her, but it wasn't the Devil, and it wasn't anything wonderful either, Cali knew now—it was the Mystery beyond knowing. Brilliant wings like a dragon's rose up, slapping at the air, and Chet began floating upward into the whiteness, into the absolute whiteness of the Infinite. Hands and arms grasped at him, tugging at his face and arms and stomach, tearing off his shirt and then clawing at his skin until it was red with scratches of blood.

The birds swooped down—small snow-white doves—pecking at his face and eyes—

Through it all, a tornadolike wind swept through the milk of the Infinite, turning it, splashing it—

Chet cried out once, and then again, but Cali could not make out the words. They sounded ancient and foreign, and she wondered if these were the very words of creation that Justin Gravesend had learned once upon a time, and that the gods themselves had inspired in priests and mages in a world dead thousands of years—the words of ritual.

The words of closing.

Cali clung to the edge of the large stone and only looked down once into the depths beneath her; the wind began tearing at her, shredding her shirt, and her hair felt as if it would be ripped from her scalp.

And then, through the storm that lived at the heart of this

place, she saw Chet, his eye sockets empty, his mouth open impossibly wide, hanging as if his jaw had been broken, his arms and legs twisted at unnatural angles.

One last cry came from him. This sounded like "Ay-alar-yii—"

And then a howl came from somewhere within Chet's body, not merely from his lips, but from somewhere within his blood and flesh, a howl that was painful to hear and that echoed against the distant stones.

Cali felt something hard slap against her—some invisible thing—and she began weeping uncontrollably, weeping and laughing both, and it was as the shadow of a great beast had bounded into the milky fog. Where Chet's body had been were a thousand multicolored objects, like tiny shards of painted glass, as if a cathedral window had burst and yet still hung in the shape of a man.

And the colored glass became winged and flew—butterflies? Were they butterflies?

And then they were gone.

A sucking sound arose, as of an enormous vacuum cleaner turned on full blast.

And then the whiteness grew smaller—it was being pulled back into something.

The portal's closing. It's closing. He did it. Oh, God, he did it. Chet, you did it.

And they were again in the foyer of the house and Chet lay on the moist floor that was no longer flesh but oak.

"You're still here," she said, happiness surging within her. "You did it, Chet. You did it."

He looked up at her—the irises in his eyes were gone. They were completely white. His skin was shiny and pale, and she could see through his skin to the bone and meat of him—he was translucent. His lips were sewn shut. He grabbed her hand in his and held her tight. In her mind, he said, *It's inside me. The Infinite is inside me. You have to kill me now. It's the only way.*

"I can't," Cali whimpered. "I can't. No, not now. I just—"

You must. If I live, it will open itself using my flesh. If I live, it will all come back. I am the portal now. I am the way. It has to be closed. This is the only way.

And she knew it was true, and it destroyed her, then, what she must do. It burned away her love for life in a single moment.

Kill me. It will bless me and send me home to where I need to go. Please. As long as I live, it will open again.

He let go of her hand.

Cali glanced at Mira, who stood, in some catatonic state, behind her. She looked down at the gun in her hand. *If only I had not brought it. There has got to be another way. There has got to be . . .*

Cali closed her eyes as she knelt beside him again, praying to God that this did not have to happen, that she did not have to kill this boy who had barely been allowed to live. When she opened her eyes he was still there. He touched the edge of her face.

It is growing stronger inside me, Cali. Please. I won't be going anywhere horrible. It's not evil, not where it's supposed to be. It's Creation itself, I think. The Infinite breaks through here, but it's not evil. It's how human souls twist it, how it was brought to this house, that did that. Let me go, kill me, and I'll be there. But there's one thing I want you to do for me.

"Anything," she whispered, her tears blinding her to the way his body was shimmering. "Anything."

I want you to look in my knapsack. After I'm gone. Something for my mother. I want you to find her. I think you can do it. There's something of hers there. A letter for her. Hold it. Find her. And give her what I want her to have. Remember our talk?

"Yes, my love. I do." She could barely see for the tears in her eyes.

Thank you. Now, please. In my heart. Then it will be over. Cali, I love you. You are the soul I love. If the Infinite is there for the dead, then I'll see you there and we'll laugh about this. I'll wait and you won't feel bad about this, then. I promise.

"I can't," she wept.

Now, Cali. Now. It's starting to burn inside me. It's starting to take me over. Don't let it. Don't let it.

Cali, feeling as if the world was hell itself, raised her gun, her little Sig Sauer, and then lowered it, pressing it against his chest. She shut her eyes. *One last prayer,* she thought. *Dear God, forgive me for this.*

She opened her eyes and kissed him on the edge of the cheek. Then she fired the gun into him.

3

Cali rested beside his body, not caring if the others had gone to Hell. She felt as if she lived in Hell now, and there was nothing but hatred within her.

She had been forced to kill the boy who loved her, loved her despite the impossibility of his love. And she had killed a boy who had never really lived beyond a misery and a pain. She had killed Frost. She had killed Chet. To the world, she was now just a killer.

She lay down on the floor. She felt as if a freeze were setting in, within her. Even Ned was gone from her now.

After an hour she got up, and went and put her arms around Mira, who simply stared off into space.

4

Mira was all that was left; Jack lay upstairs, his body smashed, and Ivy Martin and Frost were dead. Chet . . . gone . . . and now the energy of the house had been stopped.

Harrow felt safe, but Cali did not trust it, not by a long shot.

5

The first thing she did, before taking Mira to the emergency room at the hospital in Parham, was to make a call on her cell phone.

"Det," she said.

"God, it's good to hear from you," he said.

"Don't talk. I have something to tell you."

"I'm listening."

"You won't believe this, but I want you to. I want you to, because no one else will, and I'm going to need someone on my side. People are dead here, and I have a sixteen-year-old girl who is in shock, I think. I'll be at the ER at St. Francis Hospital in Parham. It's a long story. But I need you first to make sure this is handled right. It's going to be exhausting. It's going to be unbelievable. I took a gun and I shot two of these people myself. But I want you to believe me: It was the house. And everything that it held. And it's over now. But I need your help. And I need your understanding. And I need your belief."

Det said, "All right. I'll drive up right now."

"Thank you," she said, and closed the cell phone.

6

It would be six weeks before Cali would wake up in the morning and feel that the worst was over. It would be four months before the police investigation was complete. It would be six months before Mira Fleetwood would begin speaking again, and recognizing people, and understanding that her father and the others had died at Harrow.

The first person she asked for was Cali Nytbird.

7

"Did I kill him?" Mira asked.

"Your father? No."

"Anyone?"

"I'm sorry, Mira. You killed your pet. Mira, you have to understand: Harrow used you. Of all of us, you had the greatest ability. You had Ability *X*, and the house fed on that, and it fed on us."

"Do you think I was just insane?"

"What do you think?"

"I guess I believe it wasn't me. I don't remember it clearly. I remember bits and pieces." Then, "I miss my dad. He's all I had."

"Well, you have me now. I've made legal arrangements. If you want, you can live with me and go back to school next year and move on with your life. You'll come into some money, so you don't have to feel you owe me anything, and if you can't stand me, it can probably be arranged that you live on your own."

"Moving on." Mira shook her head. "How do you move on from this?" She looked up at Cali with tears in her eyes, but Cali saw the bravery in the girl, the sorrow and bravery all at once.

"Your dad would've wanted you to move on. It's what we have to do because it's the only way life works."

"An unnatural disaster," Mira said. "That's what I read in the paper. They finally let me read about it. Some of the nurses here think I'm some kind of freak for having been there. They're a little scared of me."

Then Mira began weeping; Cali sat on the edge of her bed and pulled her into her arms and held her the way that Cali's older sister, Bev, used to do with her when she was upset as a girl. "I can't tell you that it'll ever be all right," Cali said. "But I can tell you that life is still worth living. And I'll never forget them."

"I know," Mira said. "I know."

Cali wanted to add: *and it's gone. The Ability* X *I've had since childhood. The psychic spark that led my brother into a darkness from which he never escaped alive. Harrow took it from me.*

"Frost called it the Infinite," Mira whispered. "God, I hope that house gets destroyed."

EPILOGUE

Chet's Last Wish

1

They met again, the following week, and then, within a few months, after Mira had been released into Cali's care, Cali solved a special mystery. Mira still had her purple hair, and now a new set of nose rings and four piercings in her left ear and even a tattoo of a dragon on her shoulder, and all the things that made her beautiful and wonderful in Cali's eyes. Mira had even gotten used to seeing Det now and then, although Cali told her that they were just friends now, nothing more.

They went into the city and got a cab up to Grand Central Station. "For Chet," Cali said, feeling a bit nervous at what they were about to do.

2

"I'll never forget him," Mira said. "I hope I never do, anyway. He saved my life."

"He saved a lot more than our lives. You ready for this?"

Mira nodded. "I would've done it a week later if I could've."

"All right. The Oyster Bar at two P.M. What do you expect?"

"Someone crazy. In all the right ways. Just like Chet."

"I haven't been up here in a while," Cali said. "Man, they jazzed this place up."

Mira nodded, pointing at all the shops inside Grand Central Station. "It's like an old lady getting a face lift. Looks great, doesn't it? I love the shops here."

They got to the Oyster Bar, which was a long restaurant that occupied more than one dining room.

"We're waiting for a friend," Cali told the restaurant host. Impulsively, she grabbed Mira's hand and gave it a squeeze. "You as nervous as I am?"

"Not nervous, exactly. Maybe excited and a little sad because of what we have to tell her."

"One thing I learned in doing psychic readings, Mira: Tell it all, but save the best for last."

Mira smiled. Cali felt it was like seeing the sun come out from behind gray clouds when she showed all her teeth and her lips curled up in an almost embarrassed way. "I guess the best is who he was."

"Yep. So we'll start with the good. And we'll go to the best."

"She may hate us."

"I doubt that," Cali said. "My guess is that despite everything, she loved her baby."

3

A woman dressed in a beige camel's-hair jacket that looked as if it had been passed down from someone in the 1950s walked over from the bar to where they stood, feeling like a couple of spies. Her hair was a tawny brown color, right out of a bottle, and her eyes were small and squinty. She had a sexy air about her, and Cali identified her immediately.

"Roselle?" she asked.

"Rose," the woman said. She looked from Cali to Mira. "You're Cal?"

"Cali," Mira said. "And that's her." She reached out and tugged at Cali's elbow. "I'm Mira Fleetwood." She reached out, offering her hand, but the woman named Rose just glanced at it.

Rose's confidence faded fast; she looked at them suspiciously. "You said you had some information about my boy."

"We do, Rose," Cali said. "Let's get some coffee and dessert and have a chat, shall we?"

"You buying?" Rose asked.

"Absolutely," Cali said. "You can have a late lunch if you want."

"So tell me," Rose said. "Is he okay?"

Mira glanced at Cali, whose gaze remained steadily on Rose. "He's dead, Rose. Chet died in October."

"I knew it. I felt it," Rose said, and Cali saw tears rise up in her eyes.

"I'm sorry," Mira said, and reached her arms out in some vain attempt to give the woman some human comfort, but Rose just stared at her.

"He was a good kid, I knew that," Rose said. "I had a dream when he was born that he would grow up and do something with his life. Become something."

"Let's get some coffee," Cali insisted. "I have a letter for you that he wrote."

4

After the coffee had been served, and Mira was already halfway through her cheesecake, Rose put both her hands on the table. "I've had a hard life."

Cali tried to remain sympathetic, but it was getting difficult. Rose seemed sad about her son's death, but she kept going on about her life and how difficult it had been. Finally, Cali said, "Here's the letter."

She drew the crumpled piece of paper from the envelope she'd kept it in for the past several weeks and passed it to Rose.

The woman took it up and looked at it. "He wrote a lot."

"Would you like me to read it?" Mira asked. Before Rose could reply, Mira snatched it from her hands. Then she began,

"Dear Mom,

"It's strange even calling you that. I know your name is Roselle Goodfellow. I know you loved me even though we don't really know each other, except maybe when I see you in dreams. In dreams, you're always telling me things, good things usually, but sometimes bad things, too. But all of it helpful. I can't help but feeling I've made you up in some way, and if I could meet you face to face, we might not even get along. But I know I love you for bringing me into this wonderful and wacky world, for letting me go when you probably couldn't take care of me or even make sure I got to school or went to church. The people I lived with growing up had their problems. You probably knew the Dillingers, I guess. They drove me nuts, but I moved on, and I created my own life.

"If you're reading this, and I'm there, then we'll probably laugh or cry over this and knock back a beer or two. If you're read-

ing this and I'm not there . . . well, maybe there's a chance I'm dead. Maybe I got run over in traffic. Maybe I died of a brain disease. Maybe an early heart attack. Hell, I don't even know if we have hereditary diseases or stuff in the family, so I'm not sure what could get me.

"But, if I'm not there, here's the thing: I forgive you. That's all I can say about the past. There's no point in digging it all up. I forgive you and I love you the way a son is supposed to love his mother, and I don't care what your life is like. You could be living in a mansion or in a trailer. You could be working some great job and have four kids of your own and married to a great guy in Brooklyn, and that's fine by me. Or you could be homeless and having difficulty getting by. It doesn't matter to me, because I know who you are. You're my mother, and there's nothing you could've done in your life that I wouldn't understand, because we're blood, and I know you because I know myself and where I'm from, too.

"If I'm not there to give it to you, someone should be there who can. I have several thousand dollars set aside just for you. I figure I can always earn my fortune in the world still, but you might need a little money to help out. I hope you'll accept it. It's not to buy your love or to buy your happiness, because I don't believe money can do that. I want you to have it so that you can know that I want the best for you, and your happiness will mean more to me than anything. If you have a dream, use the money to help you reach it. If you have someone you love, use the money to help build a life together. If you want to give it to charity, then that's good, too!

"And that's it, I guess. How many times can a son tell his mother that he loves her just for being his mother? I'll try.

"Assuming I'm sitting across from you right now, laughing my head off because you're probably bawling or else making fun of my

sentimentality, either way, I love ya, Roselle Goodfellow! And they were wrong about you back in St. Chris. They were plain wrong. You're some kind of angel because you made sure my life went the way it was supposed to.

"All my affection and as much love as you can bear from your kid,"

"Chet"

5

Cali could barely see when Mira ended the letter, because tears had begun blurring her vision from the fourth sentence in. She finally felt some peace, now. She had done what Chet asked of her. Cali reached in her handbag and withdrew a packet of tissues. She passed one to Rose, who took it and slowly dabbed at her eyes.

"He steal it?"

"Steal what?" Cali asked.

"All that money," Rose said, pressing the tissue against her nose and blowing. "That's a lot of cash."

"I can't believe this," Mira muttered under her breath. She shot a glance at Cali, who shook her head slightly.

"It was his savings," Cali said. "Rose, he died. Do you understand that? He wrote this letter for you, and then he died."

"Like his father," Rose said. "Just like his father."

"His father? Is he dead?"

"Maybe. Who knows? He was a dreamer. He played some baseball, in the minor leagues," Rose added, as if this meant something completely unimportant. "I never loved the man."

"Do you want to know about how your son died?" Mira asked, dumbfounded.

Rose gave her a blank stare. "A lot of people get killed in this world. I never saw my son much. I had a few other kids. I'm not really the mother type." She sipped from her beer. "Thanks for this." She held up the check.

"You don't want to know more about him? What he did?" Mira asked, her eyes practically spitting venom.

"I'm sure he was like his father," Rose said, and got up from the table. She glanced at Cali. "It was nice of him to give me this."

Rose turned and walked off across the now-crowded dining room. Cali thought it was something of a wonder that she had ever tracked her down, and then a miracle that she'd shown up.

6

"I can't believe it," Mira spat after Rose had gone. "She couldn't really be his mother. Not that woman. Damn. We probably just gave the check to the wrong Rose Goodfellow."

Cali half-grinned. She had a bittersweet feeling in the back of her throat. "He knew she was like that. He told me, late one night when we were telling each other a lot. He knew that she would never match his expectations. I tried to tell him that he was wrong, but you know what? Chet was right. She's a mess, and yet she gave birth to one wonderful human being. You can't point to heredity for everything, can you? There's a mystery to existence, to who we are. Chet was a man among men, and what he did, and maybe where he went, is probably better because he's there. His mother is caught up in her own small world, and in it, I'd guess, misery rules. Chet was never part of that, even when he was surrounded by the miserable and the mean. Even when that thing had gotten loose inside him—the way Harrow made his body do things that his spirit didn't want to. Even then, he could make it right. Let her have the money. It was his wish. You don't go against one of those last-wish type things. It's only money, anyway."

"Only money? That was some serious pocket change," Mira said.

"For Chet, it wasn't. For him, it was something to give to his mother, and let her have a chance to get beyond her everyday problems. That's all. For Chet, it was just part of the burden of life. Maybe we can start some kind of search for his dad. Maybe his dad, if he's alive, will want to know about Chet. Maybe his dad didn't even know he had a son. There's some important inner work we can do with this. I have this instinct. It's like karma. Or some greater will than mine."

"You're beginning to sound suspiciously spiritual," Mira said, a scoff in her voice.

"I guess I am. I guess I've always been, but I never really understood what spirituality was before," Cali said, and raised her coffee mug. "Here's to a spiritual life for even Rose Goodfellow."

"I can't drink to that," Mira said. "No way in hell. I'm sorry, Cali, but he was willing to take on all of that, and die, and she's just some . . . some . . ."

"All right," Cali said, her mug still aloft. "How about: to the guy we both loved who did something to stop the Infinite?"

"You ask me," Mira nodded, lifting her cup, a trace of sadness in her voice but also a bit of cheer, "that's something."

7

Up the Hudson River, in a town called Watch Point, the house is locked; and what isn't locked is boarded up; and what isn't boarded up is sealed with concrete, including the many cellars beneath the house. Chains hang across the gate; windows are filled with bricks; and someday, perhaps, someone will open it again, but it will not be within the lifetime of the young woman who now owns it, left to her father in Ivy Martin's will, and now, belonging to Mira Fleetwood, an heiress at sixteen, a teenager who has no intention of ever opening Harrow up again, as long as she lives.

Perhaps it is dark now, like a candle that has been snuffed.

Perhaps the sacrifices appeased the shadows.

Or perhaps some sentience remains within the house.

Some kindling, piled in a corner, overlooked, full of possibilities.

Waiting for a spark from some new human fire.